# Ghosts of the Past

## Mark Downer

OLD STONE PRESS

*Ghosts of the Past*
By Mark Downer

First Edition—2012
Second Edition—2021

© 2021, Mark H. Downer
All rights reserved.

For information about special discounts for bulk purchases or autographed copies of this book, please contact John H. Clark, publisher, Old Stone Press at john@oldstonepress.com or the author, Mark H. Downer at mark.downer@landstarmail.com

This is a work of fiction. Names, characters, businesses, places, events and incidents are either the products of the author's imagination or used in a fictitious manner. Any resemblance to actual persons, living or dead, or actual events is purely coincidental.

Library of Congress Control Number: 2020922810

ISBN: 978-1-938462-50-4 (print)
ISBN: 978-1-938462-51-1 (eBook)

Published by Old Stone Press
an imprint of J. H. Clark & Associates, Inc.
Louisville, Kentucky 40207 USA
www.oldstonepress.com

Published in the United States

*To my mother who always believed I could, and*

*to my father who passed on the skills to make it a reality.*

# Prologue

The sound inside was deafening as the whine of the sputtering engine gave way to the rush of air against the metallic body tilting earthward. The smell of burning oil was overwhelming in the dense, white smoke, which choked off not only the oxygen, but the visibility outside.

The altimeter spiraled counterclockwise, increasing in speed to the point that it looked like an additional propeller, but offered none of the benefits. Another volley of fifty caliber bullets strafed the fuselage of the helpless craft, a rapid succession of dull thuds into the lifeless body.

His hands fumbled blindly inside the cockpit, searching desperately for the release handle to the sliding canopy. His goggles were caked with black residue from the oily smoke and he reached up and ripped them from his face. Sweat dripped out from under his flight hat and into his eyes, and he tore at the leather gloves, removing them from his trembling hands. He reached the handle and pulled at it, only to have it break off in his hand.

He was growing disoriented and delirious, and he could sense the charge of oncoming ground. Banging at the canopy overhead, desperately trying to unseat the seal, the specter of death crept inside the airplane with him. He had envisioned dying many times, almost welcoming and inviting its finality, but not this way…not now…not yet. He still had to tell someone.

He needed to reveal the whereabouts of the crash. It could all be returned, given back to the original owners, absolving him of his responsibility, all sins forgiven. It was time to tell someone, but now there was no time.

He cried out, "It's in the rock! The treasure's behind the rock."

He patted his flight jacket, reassuring himself that the letter was there. He couldn't feel it; he couldn't feel anything, his hand passing through his body as if it were air.

"Look in my jacket. Tell him to start with my flight jacket," he mumbled aloud.

The rush of air had grown quiet and a cool breeze flowed through the cockpit. Bright light replaced the smoke, and a sense of euphoria overtook him. He was floating next to the plane and then it disappeared. Soft, pleasing music tickled his ears and he heard his mother calling to him through the veiled illumination.

The monotone hum of the heart monitor registered a flat line and the nurse reached over to switch it off. She looked back at the elderly man and stroked his hand softly. "Goodbye, Mr. Hignite. May the peace of God passeth all understanding."

# Chapter 1

*March 22, 1945. Kelheim, Germany*

It was cold. Not the bitter, biting cold of mid-winter, but the wet, bone chilling cold of an early Bavarian spring night. Major Max Hignite, all six feet and two inches of him, was hunched into a knot under the gray wool blanket, the rock-hard bench barely noticeable through his overwhelming fatigue. He had been falling in and out of sleep waiting for some explanation as to why he had been summoned from the warm confines of his squadron's barracks earlier in the evening.

He and the young lieutenant, lying on the opposite bench in the back of the Mercedes M-366 half-ton truck, had been driving for almost two hours. Mercifully, they had come to a halt in the woods just outside of Kelheim, about 20 kilometers southwest of Regensburg. Another identical truck, filled with a rag-tag collection of enlisted men, idled behind them. A kubelwagon with two officers and a driver angled around the parked vehicles and moved forward another few meters into the clearing, just off the dirt road they had navigated. The flurry of activity and noise from the disembarking soldiers was still not enough to keep him from slipping out of consciousness.

"Max, you're not trying to sleep in there, are you?"

The voice was a deep sleep nightmare, until the canvas drop flap was thrown open and a cold blast of air rifled through the back of the truck, immediately returning Hignite to his senses.

"Come on Herr Major, you'd think this was a holiday compliments of the Führer!" bellowed the voice of the intruder as the narrow beam of a flashlight probed the dark interior of the truck.

"I should have known you'd be responsible for this intrusion on my peaceful duty to the Fatherland, Dieter," Hignite muttered as he rolled over to face the old acquaintance.

Max Hignite was tired. Over four years of war had sapped his energy. The once sharp, rugged features appeared to sag under the weight of stress and strain, and with the two-day old stubble, he looked ten years older than his twenty-six years of life. His only saving grace were the sharp, penetrating green eyes inherited from his mother that still flickered with life.

Born and raised in Munich, Hignite's mother was an elementary school teacher and his father a university professor. His younger brother and sister, along with himself, were all born and raised with a distinct eye towards education and cultural pursuits. However, outside of school Hignite had developed a passion for flying. Fueled by his Uncle Wilhelm, himself a World War I ace, Hignite spent many weekends at his Uncle's farm, just outside of Augsberg, mastering the old Fokker D-7 that Uncle Wilhelm had meticulously restored.

As Hignite grew to adulthood, the political climate was shifting dramatically. The family was very cognizant of the birth and ascent of the *Nationalsozialistiche Deutsche Arbeiterpartei*, and the injustice and evils that were inherent with the Nazis' rise to power. Nevertheless, the allure of the emerging military air force, known as the Luftwaffe, was too great for Hignite to pass up, and he enlisted in 1937.

Hignite, however, never believed in National Socialism and never trusted the actions of the Nazi party. Therefore, armed with the knowledge of the impending invasion of Poland, certain to take place sometime in the fall of 1939, Hignite had warned his father, who packed up the entire family and snuck out of Germany into Switzerland. Hignite's father, mother, baby brother, and sister all found their way to the United States less than two months later.

Hignite remained behind, and distinguished himself as one of the finest fighter pilots in the Luftwaffe. With 46 kills to his credit, he had been shot down once, wounded in action twice, and decorated with every medal available. However, the winds of war had shifted dramatically, and the heady days when he and his comrades had ruled the skies were long gone. The war was winding down and Germany was being decimated with each passing day. Moreover, with no forewarning, he had been summoned to this remote wooded area, and instructed to wait for orders.

Oberst Dieter Heinrich hoisted himself into the back of the truck and was busy slapping at Oberleutnant Wilhelm Gernert with his riding crop. Gernert was fumbling his way to his feet in anticipation of saluting the superior officer who had so rudely awakened him also.

"Stay seated young man," Heinrich interrupted him. "Just scoot yourself over and allow me some room to sit."

"To what do we owe this pleasure, Dieter?" Hignite inquired.

"Business before pleasure Max. I have volunteered you and young Gernert here for a very important mission. And you start tonight!"

"Thanks for the advance warning," Hignite scoffed. He leaned over to shake hands with Gernert. "Major Max Hignite. I apologize for not introducing myself earlier, but I didn't see the need in waking you when they picked me up in this luxury mode of transportation."

"No apologies necessary Major," Gernert replied, meeting Hignite's hand halfway. "Rudi Gernert."

Heinrich leaned back toward the rear of the truck and again applied his riding crop to lifting the drop flap, his aristocratic Prussian background evident in his handling of the equine instrument. Yelling down at the milling soldiers outside, he said "Unteroffizier, bring us a lantern in here, *bitte*."

The young corporal standing outside clicked his heels and retreated into the night.

"So, we've been volunteered," Hignite shivered as he returned everyone's attention to the conversation. "I have never liked the sound of that."

"You may like the sound of this one," replied Heinrich. "It will allow you to exit this war before the final outcome is determined."

"This war is over, Dieter, you know that as well as I do. It was over months ago. Hell, for that matter it's been over for more than a year. Why that maniac in Berlin can't see it is beyond any reasonable comprehension."

"Careful Max," interrupted Heinrich. "Keep your voice down and your thoughts to yourself, at least until you're on your way with this mission. If it's any consolation, I agree with you, but I have managed to hold my tongue this long, at least until I can find a way out of this mess as well."

"Sorry Dieter, I'm a little tired, cold and irritable."

"No need to apologize to me, old friend." Heinrich smiled.

The flap once again pulled back, and the winded corporal stuck his arm in holding a hissing lantern that cast a greenish white glow on the inside of the dreary truck.

"I'll get that sir," said Gernert, as he reached out and grabbed the lantern handle, and nodded to the corporal, "*danke*." Looking up he found several rusting hooks wired to the metal supports holding the camouflaged canvas cover over the back of the truck. He selected one toward the front and hung the lantern at the far end away from their eyes.

Gernert returned to the bench and he and Hignite both cast their gaze to Heinrich, who shuffled his body on the bench in a futile attempt to make himself more comfortable.

Dieter Heinrich was tall and muscular, with sharp features carved by generations of his heritage. His once piercing blue eyes were fading to gray, overcome by the weight of too many sleepless hours. He was thirty-one years old, but as with most soldiers at this point in the war, he appeared several years older.

He and Max had met at flight training school in Hamburg and had immediately developed a strong friendship. That bond was made even stronger when Heinrich discovered he was colorblind and was unable to continue flying. Max had spent many long hours consoling his despondent friend, a majority of those accompanied by binges of heavy drinking and womanizing.

Heinrich's influential family managed to keep him in the Luftwaffe, and to their delight, he was commissioned an officer on Hermann Goering's personal staff. Heinrich was not as pleased. All he ever wanted to do is fly fighter planes. Moreover, to add insult to injury, he had no great interest in the Nazi party, but found himself smack dab in the middle of it.

Turning to face Hignite and Gernert, Heinrich began, "You're both flying tonight." Holding the palm of his hand face up to Hignite, "Before you interrupt me, let me finish. You're going up in a Ju-52."

Hignite's reaction was subdued. He reached up with his left hand and massaged his neck, but managed not to interject.

"This flight was authorized by Goering himself and there will be no record of it ever having transpired. I was given the freedom to choose the best pilot I could find, so here you are Max. No disrespect to you Oberleutnant, but they wrestled you up because you were available."

"No disrespect taken," said Gernert.

Hignite could not wait any further. "I don't like the sound of this, Dieter. This has the makings of something covert, and I am not about to start being a spy now. Or it has the nasty smell of being illegal, and I'm not interested in pissing off the enemy any more than we already have."

Before Heinrich could reply, the rumble of an approaching car engine, and the authoritative shouts of officers, captured the attention of all three men. It was Gernert's turn to crouch forward and lift the flap to observe the disturbance.

Two large, black Mercedes sedans accompanied by four BMW motorcycle sidecars and two half-ton Mercedes trucks were all vying for parking rights in the clearing where the other assemblage of vehicles had congregated. They all seemed to come to a halt in unison, as if this show of force had been choreographed many times before. Jumping out from the passenger door of one of the sedans was a leather-coated Luftwaffe captain, who never broke stride as he approached a young lieutenant snapping to attention and offering up the Hitler salute.

"Heil Hitler, Herr Leutnant!" barked the captain as he returned the salute.

"Heil Hitler, Herr Hauptmann, what can I do for you sir?"

"Where can I find Major Heinrich?"

"Right over here Hauptmann." Heinrich stepped to the back of the truck and hopped down to the soft, moist ground. As he made his way closer to the captain, he mimicked the young lieutenant's curiosity, "What can I do for you captain?"

Again, the captain raised his arm at the required forty-five-degree angle. "Heil Hitler Herr Major!" Heinrich returned the salute with a casual flip of his hand. "Sir, the Reichsmarschall would like to have a word with you." And as if on cue, out struggled Reichsmarschall Hermann Goering from the back of the second sedan, while an obedient sergeant held the door for him.

He was immaculately dressed in his medal-studded Luftwaffe uniform and full-length wool topcoat, and as usual, carried with him his trademark baton. He was a large man, who seemed to grow larger every day, not only in physical stature, but also in what he perceived was left of the disintegrating Nazi regime. He walked powerfully over to where Heinrich was standing and before Heinrich could muster a salute, Goering placed his hand to the brim of his hat in a traditional salute, which Heinrich duplicated immediately.

"Good to see you again Dieter, and *danke shoen* for dealing with this delicate matter." Goering laid his hand upon Heinrich's shoulder.

"Nice to see you too, Herr Reichsmarschall. I've secured everything according to your orders," replied Heinrich.

"Who did you select to fly?" Goering inquired.

"Major Hignite. I believe you're familiar with him?"

"Quite. I believe I gave him the Knight's Cross last year. But I didn't know he was flying transports?"

"He hasn't been, but he has flown them before. He is also familiar with the terrain, having actually flown into the Swiss Alps on numerous occasions before the war. In addition, I thought he was the best pilot available in this area, under such short notice. His squadron just returned from combat yesterday afternoon, and there were not many aircraft left. In fact, there were more pilots than planes, so I took him and a newly assigned leutnant, who would not have been much use in combat anyway."

Goering nodded "Very well. Does he know the nature of the cargo?"

"No Herr Reichsmarschall, I haven't mentioned any of the specifics of the mission. In fact, I was just briefing Hignite and Gernert when you pulled up."

Goering turned away from Heinrich and observed the congregation of men milling around waiting for the orders to proceed. With a flip of Goering's hand gestured toward him, the captain barked several orders at the drivers still seated in their trucks. Everyone began to move toward the clearing, where four waiting soldiers were already drawing back the camouflaged netting that had been covering the Junkers Ju-52.

"There will be no need to get specific with Herr Hignite and his co-pilot regarding the cargo, is that understood, Heinrich?" Goering returned his focus back to Heinrich, locking his eyes in a cold stare.

Heinrich snapped to attention. "*Jawohl*, Herr Reichsmarschall."

"Good to see you again, Dieter." With that, Goering turned and walked over to the clearing and spoke briefly with the captain. Once their one-sided conversation was complete, he strutted back to the waiting staff cars, returned to the backseat from the one in which he came, and sped away.

Heinrich watched as the captain retrieved a Kriegsmarine metal briefcase that had been delivered to him from one of the cars. He placed it on the top of one of the wooden crates being unloaded from the first truck in line and removed a single sheet of paper. Walking over to the back of that same truck, he began to check off the crates one by one, as they were carefully moved from the truck to the waiting plane.

"That's my plane, I assume," Hignite said as he and Gernert walked up to Heinrich from behind. He leaned his head forward to observe the Reichsmarschall's entourage, "Even in the grip of defeat, he is one pompous asshole!"

Heinrich glared at Hignite and then relaxed looking away, "He represents everything I detest about the Nazi party. Him, Hitler, Himmler, Goebels, Bormann...they have brought Germany to the brink of destruction, and now he wants me to be a part of making sure his ass will prosper from the spoils of war. You're too kind with your description Max."

Hignite and Gernert followed Heinrich's lead as he turned and they all began to walk toward the plane.

The night was peaceful, except for the occasional bark of an order, and the constant cadence of soldiers' feet moving to and from the parked trucks and the awaiting plane. The cold, damp air was invigorating to Hignite's face. He consciously ignored the noise and stared out into the darkness of the surrounding countryside.

This area had been principally spared from the Allied bombing, and the ground war had not yet punctured the pristine beauty of the land. The ground was lit up dramatically from a three-quarters waning moon, with every star visible in a pitch black, cloudless sky. The gently rolling landscape was spotted with patches of unmelted snow, and way off on the northwest horizon, highlighting the far western range of the Black Mountains was the ominous, yellowish glow of Nuremberg ablaze from an aerial bombardment earlier that day.

With total control of the skies, the British and American bombers were pounding the major cities and industrial centers just north and south of here with devastating accuracy. The beautiful cities, the history, the architecture, the memories of his childhood...all disappearing at an alarming rate. *The end was near. Please, let it come soon*, thought Hignite.

"Do you smoke?" Gernert's question returning Hignite to reality.

"I'd love one, *danke*," replied Hignite, as he slid the protruding cigarette out from the pack in Gernert's extended hand.

"There are no markings, Major," Gernert said nonchalantly.

Hignite hesitated in confusion, and then realized what Gernert was referring to. He glanced over to the Ju-52 and noticed the lack of any insignias. The entire body and wings painted one dull, gray color. Nothing to note its origins or owners.

"It must be a secret," chuckled Hignite sarcastically. He leaned over into Gernert's cupped hands, igniting the cigarette on the dwindling match Gernert had struck up for the both of them.

Hignite wasn't sure which was better, the long inhale of the smoke, or the crisp, fresh air he sucked in on top of it. The enjoyment was brief however; as an acknowledgment from one of the soldiers to Goering's captain-in-charge indicated the plane was being loaded with the last of the cargo.

Heinrich moved toward the captain, who was motioning for the last crate, upon which lay the briefcase and his checklist, to be loaded onto the plane.

"Herr Captain, may we borrow the crate for a few moments, *bitte*? I need to review the flight plan." Heinrich cocked his head toward the approaching Hignite and Gernert.

"Gladly Major. Unterfeldwebel, please load this onto the plane as soon as these gentlemen are finished."

"*Jawohl*, Herr Captain." The young sergeant saluted and backed away toward the plane to wait.

Heinrich pulled out a rolled-up sheet of paper from the breast pocket of his coat and spread it out on the crate. He reached down to his belt and released the buttoned flap to the holster, and removing the Luger pistol he placed it on the map to keep it from rolling back up. He looked for his own flashlight, but realized immediately he had left it in the truck. He beckoned to one of the soldiers who had just sat down to relax. "Bring me a flashlight, *bitte*."

Hignite and Gernert arrived the same time as the flashlight.

Hignite spoke first. "We're going south I presume."

"Very perceptive Max." Heinrich looked up from the map in front of them. "Now shut up and listen. You're going into Switzerland, and you're not coming back."

***

Heinrich's briefing took less than ten minutes. The flight plan was simple and the discreet destination clear-cut. At this point, neither Hignite nor Gernert had any illusions as to why they were going and what they were transporting. It was even clearer when Heinrich lifted his map, and the captain's checklist, still lying on top of the crate next to the closed briefcase, was exposed for all of them to see.

Hignite picked it up and studied it briefly, "I'm not much of an art expert, but I'd say we've got enough masterpieces here to rival some of the best museums in the world."

"I'd always heard he was quite the collector," Gernert observed.

"Yeah, of art that belongs to everybody else," interrupted Heinrich. "I've been told that he's amassed an incredible collection by stealing, blackmail, and in most cases, murdering off anyone connected to the goods you're about ready to fly off with. His own private assemblage of wealth, while the rest of Germany and our people are destined to suffer for years to come. Max, you had better get moving, before I lose control of my senses and blow up that plane right here and now."

"Dieter, I can make that plane disappear once I lift off!"

"I realize that Max, and the thought has crossed my mind, but I value the lives of my family, and my life, too. There is no doubt we would perish immediately if that plane does not make it safely to Glarus."

"I understand Dieter. Myself and Gernert here will check out of this war and deliver the Reichsmarschall's precious cargo intact, so I can come back to visit you after this hell is over."

At that moment two privates, slapping their hands together to stay warm, accompanied by the lieutenant, stepped in between them. Apologetically the lieutenant spoke to Heinrich, "Excuse me Herr Oberst, but we need to load the last of the cargo, *bitte.*"

With an acknowledging nod from Heinrich, the two soldiers slid the briefcase to the middle of the crate, lifted them up, and made their way waddling toward the plane. Hignite turned slightly as if to look away, discreetly folded up the checklist, and slipped it into the pocket of his flight jacket.

"It's time Max." Heinrich said with a sigh. "Here, you might need this." He handed the flashlight to Hignite.

Hignite looked back, took the flashlight and tucked it into his flight jacket, nodded in agreement, and then turned to Gernert. "Are you ready Oberleutnant?"

"As I'll ever be, sir," replied Gernert.

"Please call me Max."

"Only if you call me Rudi."

"That I can do."

The three of them turned and followed the trampled, wet grass to the waiting aircraft.

"Rudi if you want to get on board, I'll give her a quick once over," Hignite shouted as he walked to the front of the Ju-52, beginning a cursory inspection of what had been the workhorse and backbone of the Luftwaffe's transport fleet.

With a wing span of just under 96 feet (29.25m) and a length of 62 feet (18.9m), her three BMW 132T engines were capable of handling a fully loaded weight of up to 24,000 pounds (11,030kg), and Hignite figured they were going to test that capacity tonight. He noted that this one had seen plenty of hours, but because there were no armaments, she had probably seen very little, if any, of the combat zones.

Satisfied with her external condition, Hignite waved up at Gernert, who had settled himself into the cockpit, ducked under the front engine, and walked up to Heinrich. He looked over to see the caravan of trucks, re-loaded with their human cargo, pulling away under the direction of Goering's captain. Disappearing from whence they came as if this evening never happened.

"Well, I guess this is goodbye Dieter."

"Good luck Max. Stay in Switzerland until this is over...it won't be long. And be careful when you meet this Hauptmann Brewer, I don't trust anyone affiliated with the Reichsmarschall, particularly when it comes to something as clandestine as this."

"*Danke*. You would have made a great pilot and even better wingman Dieter. I'll watch my backside. And I'll look forward to hoisting a beer with you very soon."

With that, the two men shook hands, hesitated, and embraced each other as if they would never see each other again.

Hignite backed away as the first of the wing engines coughed, sputtered and them came to life. He saluted Heinrich, turned, and climbed aboard as the roar of the second and third engines drowned out the peaceful sounds of the night.

By the time Hignite had crawled into the cockpit, strapped himself in, and pulled on his headgear, Gernert had the plane ready for take-off. Hignite took the wheel and Gernert applied the throttle as they made a slow one hundred and eighty degree turn away from the wood line out onto the open field. At that moment the captain came running up to Heinrich, as the prop wash threw a chilling blast of air against the both of them.

"Herr Oberst," the captain yelled over the noise. "My list, the briefcase, do you have them?"

"*Nein.* If I'm not mistaken, they went on board with everything else."

"*Verdammen*," muttered the captain.

Without any hesitation, Gernert drove the throttles forward and the Junker bumped its way down the field and lifted off into the bright moonlit sky.

***

First Lieutenant Bruce Miller, USAAF, was having a hard time enjoying the beautiful moonlit evening. The majestic, snow covered mountains and valleys were all around him, bathed in a heavenly blue-white spotlight, as he navigated over them in his P-51B Mustang fighter. The object of his concern was just off his port wing. Second lieutenant Charlie Hathaway was struggling to keep himself conscious, and his chewed-up P-51 in the air.

The bright moonlight highlighted the olive and black camouflage finish of his aircraft, revealing a starboard wing badly riddled with .50 caliber holes from a close encounter with a Messerschmitt Me-109 earlier in the evening. However, most obvious was the canopy on the same side that was halfway disintegrated, and the inside of the cockpit littered with Plexiglas, oil and the blood from Mr. Hathaway.

He was still in radio contact with Miller, who was doing everything in his power to keep Hathaway on target and awake. The two of them had become separated from the rest of the squadron while they had gone into action as bomber escorts over Nuremberg earlier in the evening. After Hathaway had been hit, they had drifted considerably further south than Miller wanted, but Hathaway was still flying and appeared to be alert. Miller knew they had plenty of fuel to return to base, and because of the terrain they had deviated over, and the banged-up condition his wingman was in, he knew that they had to try to make it home. Trying to ditch here or parachute out was probably suicide. Hathaway still had enough of his senses to realize that as well.

"Where are we now, Brew?" Hathaway's voice came through the radio.

"You be comin' 'round the mountains buddy! Try to bring her to port a couple degrees, and hold steady on the altitude."

Hathaway had been flying half blind for the last twenty minutes and he was losing track of time. His goggles were fogging up and they were caked in blood that had splattered from the serious damage inflicted on the right side of his body.

He had taken two rounds. One had sliced through the bottom of the right thigh, exited above his knee and lodged in the instrument panel. The second entered at the right shoulder blade and stayed at home. On top of that were the multitude of Plexiglas shards from the exploding cockpit that had embedded themselves from the right elbow, up the shoulder, into the neck and side of his face.

The loss of blood was starting to take its toll, along with the limited oxygen and the icy cold air that was rushing through the gaping hole in the cockpit. Ironically, the freezing temperature had done a very good job of cauterizing the wounds and slowing the blood flow.

"It's a beautiful night out Charlie. Stay alert and don't you nod off on me. We're both gonna make it back, do ya hear me?" Miller yelled into his microphone with his unmistakable, south Alabama drawl.

"If it wasn't for the wind whistling through my ears and all the holes in my body, I'd hear you loud and clear." Hathaway could still make out the picture of his wife and three-month-old son taped to the inside of the front windscreen. "But I copy. Just keep me straight and true."

***

Hignite was also having a hard time enjoying the brilliant scenery unfolding beneath them. His concern was the night was so clear. He was flying an unarmed transport in hostile skies that belonged to the allies, and there wasn't a lick of cover if he was spotted. The movement of Gernert's head as it searched up and down the sky through his window belied his nervousness too. They had been in the air about ten minutes and were about ready to cross the Swiss border, where they both, without acknowledging it, knew they could probably afford to relax slightly and enjoy the flight. There had been little conversation between the two other than confirmation of instrument data and heading.

"Do you have anybody back home that's going to miss you?" Hignite broke the tense silence. "Any family or loved ones I mean."

"My parents are dead, they were both killed in a raid on Augsberg, and my brother has been a P.O.W. for over a year. Not to mention, you would have to be crazy to try to marry a girl in the middle of a war. Hell, that's if I could find one," sighed Gernert.

"I'm sorry about your parents. But since we're about to go missing in action, it's a good thing nobody's going to lose any sleep over us."

"That sounds like you're without family as well," Gernert inquired.

"My family wised up and got out of Germany in '39. They immigrated to America shortly thereafter. How's that for coincidences. I'm fighting against the very country my parents now call home."

"Do they know you're alive?"

"As of last November. That was the last time I got mail out. We were...uh oh we've got company, four o'clock low."

As Gernert leaned over and stretched his neck to look out the right-hand window, the silhouettes of two American-made P-51 Mustangs against the snow-covered mountains were clearly visible roughly 500 feet below. They had just come through an adjoining pass and they were flying into the oncoming valley at a forty-five-degree angle toward the Ju-52.

*** 

The faint reflection of the aircraft caught Miller's eye almost immediately as it emerged from the adjacent valley. He had not had an opportunity to engage one, but he was quite familiar with the three-engine outline of the German Ju-52 Junkers aircraft. This was very much an unwelcome surprise. Nevertheless, it presented a sitting duck at exactly the moment that revenge was in Miller's heart.

"Damn Charlie, we got a bogie at two o'clock high. Looks like a Junker out for a midnight spin." Miller yelled into the radio, scanning the sky all around the enemy intruder. Doesn't look like he has company either."

"Do what you have to do Brew, just point me in the right direction and go," came the reply.

Miller hesitated as he looked down the valley and considered the consequences of leaving Hathaway on his own to go hunting.

Hignite was already pulling up and away as he started to formulate a strategy to avoid the two American fighters. *There are no clouds, the damn Mustang has twice the speed of this clunker, there are two of them and one of us, and we don't have a single ounce of armament on board.*

"We're in big trouble, Rudi. I had hoped we would not run into anybody this far south, much less this low. Any thoughts?"

The Junker was elevating quickly as Hignite was making for the top of the first mountain ridge to the south.

"You're headed south, that's a good start! We can't outrun them and we definitely can't engage them. Gernert hesitated and then quickly added, "I would suggest we head for the deck."

"I concur! We're better off getting low enough to make their speed a liability in these valley walls. If I can turn in and out of these ruts, maybe we can cut down on their straight-line advantage. Hang on!" Hignite had reached the peak and immediately dove hard down the slope into the next valley.

Miller didn't have much time to ponder the situation. The Junker was starting evasive action, with what looked to be an attempt to jump to the next valley.

"Charlie, I need ya to elevate a couple hundred feet and stay on your line. The valley is widenin' out. I'm gonna go visit our friend. I'll be back in a jiffy. Stay in contact and holler if you can't see what you're doin'."

"I'm okay! Good hunting Brew."

Miller's P-51 was in a hard-left turn climbing up and over the same southern ridge at full throttle. At roughly 380 miles per hour she was diving down the valley hard overtaking quickly the weighted down Junker who was also rattling under a maximum speed that was just over half of the American predator.

The pilot was good thought Miller. He was as low as he could get and he was seesawing back and forth as best he could in that boat. It looked heavy. Miller gained ground from behind, he thumbed the trigger to his weapons, and the four wing-mounted .50 caliber Browning machine guns exploded shells toward the weaving Junker.

The lumbering transport pulled hard left and snaked into a contiguous ravine as the last of the Mustang's burst slammed harmlessly into a rocky outcropping. Miller could not make the same turn at his speed, so he pulled up and made an ascending left-hand turn until he was over the same ravine. The Junker was running straight down the line of a large stream below, and Miller plunged into the narrow gorge at a thirty-degree angle from above.

"Charlie, are you still with us?" Miller barked into his radio.

"I'm still here. But I'm not real confident. I can't make out my instruments anymore."

"Hang in there, I'm on my way."

\*\*\*

Hignite was throwing the airborne hulk all over the place. He had just managed to make the left-hand turn into the narrow ravine, having to keep the wings tipped at an angle for several hundred yards to prevent the ninety-six feet of wingspan from burrowing into the rocky bluff that guarded the exit of the stream into the valley below. It was some nifty flying, and he knew it, but he expected the P-51 to be right on top of him again any second.

"He's coming down on us from behind, six o'clock high." Gernert confirmed his fears.

Hignite pulled back hard on the wheel and started to climb above the steep walls, searching frantically for the next narrow depression or hollow to dive into. The subsequent sound of tearing and pinging metal alerted him that his adversary had him in his sights and they were taking hits. He banked hard right as the speedier Mustang buzzed by his left ear.

"I'll be right with ya buddy." Miller radioed to Hathaway as he figured one more good pass at the German would do it.

There was no answer.

"Charlie! Do you read me?" It was more a cry of anguish than a question.

"I'm still here." Hathaway replied lethargically. "I need your help Brew. I can't see for shit."

"Damnit!" Miller yelled aloud. "You're a lucky bastard tonight!" A very good, lucky bastard he thought to himself as he broke off the attack.

"I got ya in my sight, pal." Miller sighed, as he soared over the snow-capped mountain peak and visually picked up Hathaway just below and in front of him. "You're doin' good, right on line. Let's get ya home."

\*\*\*

"He's gone."

"What do you mean he's gone?" Hignite asked incredulously.

"I mean he disengaged and took off." Gernert gave him a bewildered look.

"Where's the other one, I never did see him enter in?"

"I never did spot him. I don't believe he joined the fun."

Neither one of them considered it was over, and they were intensely scanning the sky for the return of one, or both of the fighters. They stayed low to the ground, flying into more open ground, the two of them staring silently out into the night in a state of befuddlement.

After a few minutes, the tension and nervousness subsided and Gernert leaned back into his seat.

He broke the quiet. "I don't believe it! They had us easy."

"I think the other one was in trouble," Hignite pondered. "Why would only one of them hit us, when two could have downed us in a heartbeat? That explains why they were so low and off course."

"Yeah, that makes sense. He left us, because he couldn't leave his friend that long. God is watching over us tonight, Major."

"Yes, we're very fortunate indeed." Hignite scanned the instruments for any signs of trouble from the damage they took. "Rudi, you may want to go back and check on the cargo and look for any problems. We took a good number of hits on that last strafing, but so far everything looks good on the panel."

"I'm on it," Gernert replied, while he was un-strapping from the co-pilot seat.

Hignite now had time to get his bearings and get back on course. They would be no more than an hour away, if there were no more surprises.

***

It had taken roughly thirty seconds for Hignite to put the Ju-52 through some maneuvers that would identify any structural damage that might interfere with the overall control of the plane, and for him to analyze the gauges and dials on the cockpit flight panel for any warning signs. Everything appeared to respond normally or be within optimum parameters.

He couldn't hear Gernert in the back, who was trying to crawl over and around the largest flying museum in history, in the hope of spotting anything out of the ordinary. So far, nothing sounded or appeared out of sync. He would give it a few more minutes, sitting in the back and listening for any telltale sign of concern. The crated artwork had shifted dramatically during the confrontation and was sprawled all over the back of the plane, several crates wedged up against the outside door and two others that had catapulted themselves all the way back to the tail.

As he stretched out on top of a handful of the crates, he looked out the window on the left side studying the wing and port engine for any damage or smoke. Satisfied with his visual inspection, he rolled over and glanced out at the right wing and engine. There was definitely some damage, but nothing obvious that indicated trouble. What he could not see, was the nicked oil line that was starting to show signs of a weakening wall under the pressure of the lubricant.

Up front, Hignite was really starting to wind down. The stress and strain of years living on the edge all seemed to be vacating his body at once. The realization that it was truly over was starting to sink in. If they could manage to land this hulk on the remote valley strip near Glarus, stay out of trouble with the party they were to meet, and disappear into Switzerland until the inevitable outcome was concluded, he was going to survive this war.

"Everything appears okay, Major," Gernert announced as he bent down to enter the cockpit again.

"Yeah, the bird seems to be holding up."

"I did notice some pretty significant damage on this side, up in the wing and around the engine, but nothing was smoking." Gernert added as he strapped himself back into his seat.

Hignite glanced over at the oil pressure gauge for the starboard engine and noticed a slight dip, but nothing noteworthy. Gernert followed his reaction and came up with the same conclusion.

"Keep an eye on that," Hignite nodded toward the instruments.

The next fifteen minutes were uneventful. They had managed a visual of the southeastern tip of Lake Zurich off in the distance and altered their heading to the southeast, making the turn over the town of Uznach. It was the first time in a long time Hignite had seen the lights of any town at night from the air. Blackouts had been the norm for most of the cities on both sides of the war.

Gernert noticed the problem first, "Major we've got a problem with my engine over here."

The smoke started billowing out almost immediately, followed by a spontaneous drop in the oil pressure gauge. The injured line had burst and was now throwing oil all over the engine.

Hignite leaned forward and eyed the damage. "The bastard did get us!" He sat back, reached for the throttle on the right-side engine, and eased back on the power. "I'm not real confident we can stay afloat without it."

The two of them started looking groundward simultaneously. Almost in unison, they somberly looked back at each other with identical concern.

Gernert peeked back at the engine, which was now starting to pop bursts of flame. "She may be getting ready to burn Major."

"Shut her down!" Hignite barked.

Gernert reached for the ignition switch and flipped it off, watching the propeller slowly wind down, and stubbornly come to a complete stop. Hignite could feel the precipitous drop in power and the heavy load was self-evident as the weighted down Junker began a gradual uncontrolled descent.

"We're going to have to dump some of the loot," Hignite reasoned.

"I hate to be the bearer of bad news Major, but our little rendezvous with that Mustang moved things around back there. The stuff has been slammed back into the door so hard, it would take a miracle to get it open."

"You better head back there and start praying for a miracle, because if we don't shed some weight, we're going to have to put her down in the next few minutes. I assume you noticed, as I did, our choice of landing strips appear to be more vertical than horizontal."

Gernert did not bother to reply, he was already making his way back to the belly to see what he could do. As he crawled his way over the wood encased treasures, his worst fear was realized...the door was blocked completely. He stripped off his flying gloves and tried desperately to jam his hand down to where the door handle was located, but the small crease allowed only four fingers and half his palm to wiggle their way in. He rolled over on his back and repeatedly started kicking at the door with the heel of his right foot, to no avail.

"Max, I'm not having any luck back here, how much time have we got?" he yelled as loud as he could.

Hignite was trying to hold her up as best he could, without success. He was looking frantically down on the terrain below for any semblance of lights that would indicate a village and a flat spot that would function as a landing area. He was headed over a valley wall when he spotted the long, irregular, virgin patch of snow that meandered around the valley they were dropping into fast.

As he banked left to get a better look at what might be their only opportunity, he heard Gernert yelling in the back.

"We're out of time, get yourself strapped in back there," Hignite screamed, knowing Gernert probably stood a better chance in the back than up front with him.

As he held the Junker in a thirty-degree turn he could see much better the untouched, pure white blanket below that he undoubtedly knew covered a frozen lake beneath. It appeared to be long enough, as he leveled the wings and started to line up an approach, but it hooked slightly to the left as it tracked around the steep mountain slope. To the right and at the top of the bend was a steep, long, overhanging face of rock and ice that seemed to disappear down into the bleached abyss. The cliffs presented a problem if he didn't take the proper angle across the curve of the lake. Fortunately, the leading edge and ground leading up to the cliffs looked pretty close to water level.

Hignite veered to the right just enough to get in position, and then he gradually put the struggling aircraft into a wide, left-hand, descending turn to take them in. Tilting his head back over his right shoulder, he yelled as loud as he could over the intensifying noise of the dive. "Hang on Rudi, I've got an opening, but it's gonna be tight."

Gernert needed no warning. The sudden drop was enough to let him know they were going down, but without an opportunity to know where. His choices were limited to where he could seek shelter, but he had managed to rig up a couple of the loose shoulder harnesses, just a few meters behind the cockpit, that had not been covered up by the mess of tangled crates scattered about.

Hignite had never landed on ice of any kind, so he really had no idea how the plane was going to react. His biggest fear, as he measured his final approach, was the depth of the snow over the ice. He also began to realize the closer he got, the once big swath of flat, washed-out landscape started to take on some definition nearer the ground. There were emerging mounds and outcroppings on what probably were the irregularities of the shoreline.

*This ought to be very interesting.*

Hignite leveled out and set the trim to keep more of the weight back on the tail. He knew the minute he hit the snow, it was going to be like slamming on the brakes, and the plane was going to pitch forward if it didn't have the proper balance. He could not have been any more correct.

As the wheels on the landing gear plowed into the foot-deep snow, the resistance was too much. What little angle he managed to achieve without slamming the tail down first, was instantaneously negated and the plane balanced out for the first fifty meters and then progressively tilted forward. Hignite compensated by throwing the flaps up and throttling up the remaining two engines to try and keep her from going nose down and into a flip. The maneuver gained them a few more precious seconds of time, but cost them dearly in the end.

The power boost, minus the starboard engine, pushed the plane and the flight path significantly to the right. Thirty meters later the right wing cruelly slammed into one of the nearly invisible, snow covered rocky protrusions jutting out from shore.

"*Sheist!*" were the last words muttered in unison by Hignite and Gernert as the impact tore off the right wing and slingshot the rest of the plane forward and to the right, head first into the face of one of the magnificent cliffs that stood guard over the frozen lake.

# Chapter 2

## *May 14, 2001. Louisville, Kentucky*

Matt Ferguson sat straight up in bed, the mind and body going from deep sleep, to wide awake in a matter of seconds. He reacted immediately to the sound that had awoken him by reaching over to hit the snooze button, but the second ring of the telephone shook him into complete reality. Bypassing the clock radio, Ferguson snatched the telephone up on the third ring. "Hello!"

"Mr. Ferguson?" the voice on the other end inquired.

"Speaking."

"Mr. Ferguson, this is Nurse Tackett at Jefferson Manor."

"Yep, Uncle Max?"

"I'm afraid so. He took a turn for the worse about a half hour ago."

"I'll be there in about thirty minutes."

"Please hurry!" The line went dead before his feet hit the floor.

The mental and physical jolt of being improperly awakened was enough to propel him immediately out of bed and toward the closet. He glanced at the clock resting comfortably on the nightstand, undisturbed by the noise of the phone. It read 2:08 AM. *Damn! I've only been asleep for a couple of hours.*

Ferguson stopped in front of the vanity mirror in the bathroom and rubbed his eyes with the tips of his fingers. He opened them slowly to the soft, dim glow of the nightlight and examined his reflection. He was two months removed from his twenty-sixth birthday and in the best shape of his life. A little sore from his weekly basketball game the night before, and a little hung over from the five pints of brown ale he had consumed afterward. Still, his six-foot three-inch frame was lean and muscular. The full head of dark brown hair accented the sharp, rugged facial features and brown eyes. He pondered whether to jump in the shower, but the urgency in the nurse's voice convinced him to get dressed immediately.

After brushing his teeth, he pulled on the jeans that had been hanging from the bathroom door hook and ripped off a sweatshirt from a hanger in the closet. The Kentucky Wildcats hat went on the head to mask the two hours of sleep damage to the hair. Slipping on a pair of Cole Haan loafers that were waiting by the door to the garage, he was out of the house in just under ten minutes from the time he hung up the phone.

He would have roughly another ten-minute drive from his house off Elmwood Lane in the St. Matthews area to the Jefferson Manor nursing home about eight miles east on Herr Lane. Ferguson punched the overhead garage door button as he exited the house, climbed in and started up the Eddie Bauer Explorer, backed out into the street and drove away in the quiet darkness of the morning.

Ferguson turned on the radio, and inserted the CD protruding from the slot. Otis Redding's *Sittin' on the Dock of the Bay* came on soothingly, allowing him to relax and think about how he was going to handle the inevitable.

Taking care of his great Uncle Max Hignite had been pretty much Ferguson's responsibility since Max had been sent to the nursing home late last year. However, that was fine with Matthew Hignite

Ferguson. Sharing his great uncle's name had always provided Ferguson with a kindred bond with Uncle Max, and when he had finished graduate school at the University of Kentucky, and moved to Louisville to enter the working world, Ferguson found it easy and rewarding to spend time with the old man.

Ferguson's mother, Uncle Max's niece, had died several years prior from a short and intense battle with cancer, and his father had moved to San Diego to try to pick up the pieces. He had since remarried, retired, and spent most of his time never leaving the golf course and southern California. Ferguson's older brother was still trying to step into reality, moving from Aspen ski instructor during the winter months to building houses in the Denver area as warmer weather set in. Neither had time for Uncle Max, and neither did any of his other nieces and nephews scattered around the states. Uncle Max had never married, and Virginia, his live-in significant other for the last fifteen years, died two years ago, prompting his move into the nursing home.

Eight weeks ago, Uncle Max had suffered a stroke, and the lingering effects coupled with the inescapable reality of old age placed the end in sight. It was a finality that both Uncle Max and Ferguson had accepted, although it was still a bitter pill for Ferguson, since he had truly come to love Uncle Max.

Ferguson pulled into the parking lot at 2:27 on the dashboard clock, parked and quickly hustled inside, waving at the night duty receptionist on his way down the west hallway. Nurse Tackett was waiting at the nurse's station as he made the right-hand turn into the last corridor. He knew in an instant that he was too late.

"I'm so sorry Matt!" She reached out to give him a hug.

The tears welled up in Ferguson's eyes, but the huge deep breath kept the emotions from exploding. After an almost never-ending exhale, he regained his composure. He certainly did not realize his reaction would be so intense. He had told himself on the ride over that Uncle Max had had a long and very fruitful life, and that it had come to an end peacefully. Moreover, as Uncle Max had said repeatedly, 'Don't shed a tear for me, for my time on this earth has been long and my life has been full.' Nevertheless, the tears were destined and they came naturally.

"Thank you, Judy!" Ferguson gratefully accepted the hug. "I know he meant a lot to you, too! He cared about you very much, even though he tried very hard to be a pain in the ass."

Nurse Tackett nodded her head appreciatively and then cocked it with a pained expression. "He was talking about the treasure again...right before he passed away. He had been harping on it for the last couple of days. I couldn't tell if he was delirious or not."

"Yeah, he'd been talking to me a lot about it lately, too. He had all sorts of names for it. 'Antiquities in the Alps', 'the treasure of the lost souls'... buried in a wall of rock. As senile as he was getting, there still appeared to be some serious truth in what he was saying."

Ferguson averted his eyes from nurse Tackett's and stared off blankly down the hall toward Uncle Max's room. "He was always ashamed to talk about it, kind of embarrassed and always talking about being responsible. He told me over and over that he could never go back for it. He could never have it. It did not belong to him. 'Too many ghosts of the past' he'd say."

Tackett broke his reflection, "He kept repeating that you have to start with the flight jacket. The treasure...you have to look in the flight jacket. Does that make sense?"

Ferguson turned back around to face her, his eyes squinting from the strain of deliberating the instructions. "I don't know," he said almost apologetically.

He spent the next ten minutes reciting what he knew from conversations with Max and his mother and father, about Max's last flight. How he had crashed in the Swiss Alps toward the end of the war. The manner in which he was discovered by a pair of farmers, severely injured, half frozen, and not far from death; his lengthy recovery at a hospital in Zurich, and subsequent transfer to another hospital in the United States for additional rehab. There he was reunited with his family, who helped nurse him back to health.

Uncle Max's memory of the events always remained fragmented. He would struggle mightily to remember the details, but it would never come in total. The crazy story of a plane buried inside a cave behind a mountain cliff, full of treasure, full of original artwork. However, the one thing he always recalled was the other pilot. The one he tried to save and didn't.

Ferguson left the nursing home thirty minutes later after spending a last few moments with Uncle Max alone.

***

The funeral was two days later. Very few people attended. There was one old card playing buddy from the Pendennis Club, another lone survivor of the golf group from Harmony Landing Country Club, several elderly friends from St. Francis in the Fields church, and two of Ferguson's cousins that he didn't recognize, but claimed to be related to Uncle Max in some far-reaching capacity. Ferguson assumed they were there to advance the possibilities of laying claim to some inheritance. After it became obvious all his worldly possessions had been left to Ferguson, they could have cared less about sticking around to reminisce.

The Reverend Robin Jennings was dutiful and kind in his remarks, and Ferguson left the church accompanied by Uncle Max's remains, which had been neatly reduced to several pounds of ash stored in a simple sterling silver urn. His wish of having his ashes spread over the Oldham County countryside from an airplane would have to be settled at a later date. Ferguson's curiosity over the dying remarks of the treasure and flight jacket had provided for two nights of fitful sleep, and he was determined to investigate the pronouncement to unravel the enigma once and for all.

***

Uncle Max's home, soon to belong to Ferguson, was a quaint three-bedroom, two-bath, one-story log home located just off Rose Island Road in Oldham County. It was just minutes away from the church, and Ferguson had no problems arriving there shortly after the service.

The inside was in disarray from the abandoned labor of remodelers who had postponed their efforts after the news of Hignite's death. They had kindly informed Ferguson they would not return until they had been paid for work already completed, and would be happy to finish the job if the money continued to flow. He made a mental note to contact them on Monday.

Ferguson loved 'the cabin', as Max had referred to it. He was very grateful that Uncle Max had noticed his affection for the place, and decided not to sell it when he had to move into the nursing home. Max had made it clear it was to be his when he passed away.

It sat on almost two acres of land that had been meticulously cared for by the adjoining neighbor. Uncle Max had seen to it that he was more than adequately compensated for keeping the grounds nice.

Everything should be in order and safely stored away Ferguson thought, so his main goal was to track down the flight jacket and start with it. However, what was he supposed to be looking for?

It took less than twenty minutes to track down the jacket, neatly stowed away in a zippered plastic hanger bag tucked into a remote corner of the master bedroom walk-in closet. Ferguson removed it from the hanging rod, walked it out of the closet, and laid it across the king-size sleigh bed.

He meticulously scanned the outside of the old, worn, World War II vintage, Luftwaffe flight jacket, and then began warily reaching into the pockets. All of them were empty except for the left inside pocket, which produced an unsealed envelope folded in half. He removed the single sheet of paper inside, and began reading the hand-written contents while sitting down on the edge of the bed.

Matt,
This letter will guide you to a safe, built into the wall behind the antique mirror, found in the master bedroom.
*The combination to the safe is 18-35-7.*

*May God Bless You,*

*Max*


Ferguson glanced up at the massive, gold-framed mirror occupying the far corner of the room. He stepped over to it, ran his hand down the right-hand side and discovered the hidden latch halfway down. A quick flip of a switch and the eight-foot tall mirror easily swung back on left-hand hinges to reveal a safe half the height.

Following a couple of botched efforts at dialing in the listed combination, the third effort yielded an open door exposing a leather handle attached to the end of a small gray trunk. Deeper inside were two wood crates, each about the size of a seat cushion, stacked on top.

He pulled all three pieces out via the trunk handle. He felt intimidated by the sense of history he was about to open up.

While on his knees, the latches on the trunk opened easily and the top lifted up with a slight creak. Lying on top inside was an old piece of paper, discolored with age. Ferguson was in awe as he lifted it out of the case and gingerly laid it on a lamp table to the side. His mouth dropped and the chills ran down his spine as he slowly started to lift up one-by-one the rest of the military life of Major Max Hignite.

The uniforms, the boots, hats, the albums of old black and white photos, and the shoe boxes containing various pieces of jewelry, insignias, patches, and a myriad of other assorted trinkets. Lastly, at the bottom was a leather case, that once opened, revealed the iron cross with clusters and a handful of other various medals. Ferguson knew he could spend hours wading through the memorabilia, but he returned his focus to the single sheet of paper.

It appeared to be a letter and a list. Unfortunately, it was all in German, and Ferguson did not have a clue as to how to speak, much less read German. He scanned it briefly, noting how legible the typed portion and even the hand written checkmarks next to each of the numbered items in the list were. At last, he glanced at the letterhead insignia at the top and was able to read the embossed name of Reichsmarschall Hermann Goering.

Ferguson held the paper gently between his fingers, intrigued by the discovery. He flipped it over, and it got even more interesting. All over the back were hand written notes and some crude drawings. The handwriting was unmistakably Uncle Max's. *This is it. This has to be it. This is the link to the so-called 'treasure'. But what the hell is it. I can't read it!*

He re-packed the trunk exactly as he had found it. However, the letter stayed with him. He found a freezer size, zip lock bag in one of the kitchen drawers and the letter went in it for safekeeping.

He returned to the bedroom and decided to see what was in the wood crates. The wood was very old and grayed in color. He carried one of the crates into the kitchen and found a hammer and large screwdriver in a junk drawer. He spent the next five minutes removing the nails holding the wood shell together, eventually releasing one of the flat horizontal planes on one of the sides. He lifted it away and peeled back the canvas cover protecting the contents. His hands started to tremble as he exposed a beautiful gold leaf frame surrounding a magnificent oil painting of a young girl sitting on top of a wood fence in an open meadow. Ferguson was no expert, but he recognized the impressionist style from the broken brushstrokes of bright, mixed colors and lack of detail. *Holy mackerel!*

Fighting the urge to open the other crate, Ferguson knew immediately he was holding in his hands a very valuable piece of art and an incredible piece of history, and undoubtedly, the other was more of the same. The next step was to find someone who could read German. He had to get someone to translate the letter, front, and back, as soon as possible. He would deal with the art later. *The University of Louisville was certain to have someone who could read German.*

***

Pence Hall was abandoned, the last of the classes having finished two hours earlier. The sound of Ferguson's shoes on the waxed floor eerily reverberated off the walls of the stairwell on his climb up, and then off the walls of the long empty hallway of the second floor. Dr. Karl's office was supposed to be halfway down the corridor on the right, adjacent to room 216.

The phone call three hours earlier to the U of L information services had gone from the operator, to the Foreign Languages

Department, where a secretary had answered and directed him on to the Dean of the department.

After leaving a message on his initial attempt, Ferguson had called repeatedly, every fifteen minutes for the last two hours. On the third ring of his ninth attempt, Dr. Johann Karl picked up. The conversation was brief and to the point, resulting in an appointment in Dr. Karl's office for a translation of the letter and the accompanying notes. He would be available at 5:00 p.m.

At 4:53, according to the round, black clock located directly above his head, Ferguson knocked on the frosted glass door in front of him. Stenciled in bold, black type on the glass was the name of the man he was looking for. "Please come in," came the accented reply from within.

"Dr. Karl?" Ferguson inquired as he opened the door and peeked around the edge.

"*Kome in, bitte.*"

Dr. Johann Karl was seated behind a large, antique mahogany desk, congested with a morass of papers and books. His full head of white hair and pale, wrinkled complexion made him and the desk complementary collector's items. He stood up, slightly bent at the waist as he welcomed Ferguson into his office with a gesture of the hand to the seat in front of the desk.

"You must be Herr Ferguson, *Ja?*" The German accent still heavy in the delivery.

"Yes sir," Ferguson moved toward the chair. "Thanks for seeing me on such short notice."

"My pleasure young man. What is it I can help you with? Your phone call seemed to be most urgent."

"Well...I have a letter that I recently inherited from a close relative, and before he died, he was rather emphatic that its contents were... important," Ferguson reached into the manila file folder he had brought with him and removed the letter encased in the zip lock bag. "My dilemma is that everything in it is in German, and I'm afraid I can't read a lick of what it says."

Dr. Karl reached an open palmed hand through a crevice in the quagmire that was the top of his desk. "May I have a look at it, *bitte*?"

Ferguson, with a considerable amount of trepidation, leaned toward the desk and handed it over. "Please be very careful, I haven't made any copies, and it's very old."

Dr. Karl nodded and gently lifted the letter over to him. He carefully unlocked the plastic zipper and slid the contents out in front of him on the only remaining portion of his blotter not engulfed by the chaos. He raised the reading glasses that had been resting on his chest, held there by the chain around his neck, placed them on his crooked nose, and proceeded to study the letter intently. Ferguson leaned forward some more, keeping a cautious eye on the precious piece of paper.

After flipping it back and forth several times, and showing no outward signs of any emotional interest, the old man set the letter down with a grunt.

"Most interesting. I am not an art expert, but it appears you have a manifest or bill of lading in the form of a letter, and the goods listed suggest a significant assembly of artwork. I recognize several of the artists, but I'm sorry, I don't recognize the titles."

Ferguson straightened up, and then fell backward into the soft burgundy leather back of the chair. "What about the notes and stuff on the other side?"

"Those are a little more difficult. They're legible enough, but I'm not sure I understand their meaning."

"What exactly does it say?" Ferguson queried.

Dr. Karl referred back to the letter. "It's a series of notes that provide several descriptions of a lake, a boathouse, and cliffs that are in the shape of a 'W'. It mentions a plane. It says where it crashed and entered the cliffs. It is specific about the plane being intact, the fuselage of the plane being intact, and it is inside a cave that is behind the cliffs. There is a crude drawing of a map, with an arrow pointing to an "X" that has 'Ju52' next to it. There is also, what I would assume, a series of directions, they seem to be map coordinates, from 'Glarus', and the 'Swiss border'. Does that make any sense?"

"It's starting to," Ferguson stared at the framed map of Germany hanging behind Dr. Karl's left shoulder. "It's definitely starting to."

"I have someone that I'm currently tutoring that may be of some help with identifying the list of works on the front side of this letter. She is an assistant curator at the Speed Art Museum, and has been going through a fairly intensive one-on-one program studying several languages through our department. Ironically, I am scheduled for a session with her in about an hour. If you would like to come back, I am sure she would be very happy to try to help you identify these artists and their work. I recognize several of them...quite famous."

"That would be excellent! Are you sure I wouldn't be imposing?"

"Not at all Herr Ferguson." The old man stood up again, still possessing the crook in his body. "We will study for an hour, you can join us afterward...say two hours from now."

Ferguson got a better look at him as he circled his desk and extended his hand. He was very old, that was obvious, but not frail by any means. He found it remarkable that this man was still teaching, not to mention being Dean of the department. Obviously, senility had passed over this relic allowing him to do what he loved to do...teach.

"Thank you very much Dr. Karl," Ferguson reached for the extended hand and was surprised with a very firm shake. "I'm very grateful for your help."

"*Bitte* Herr Ferguson, I'll see you in a couple of hours," Dr. Karl handed back the letter, having returned it to the bag, and gestured toward the door.

Ferguson turned, opened the door, and exited the office trying to think of how to kill two hours with the excitement of the discovery barreling through his body.

***

One hour and forty-nine minutes later, Ferguson was standing in front of the same office door, his pulse still well above normal. He knocked and the same voice responded, "*Kome in, bitte.*"

Ferguson opened the door, nodded at Dr. Karl, and approached the desk. "Sorry, I know I'm a little early, but I'm pretty excited about what we discovered."

"I understand. Miss Lewis will be back in just a few minutes, she went to her car for something and then to the restroom. Please sit, make yourself comfortable until she returns."

Ferguson returned to the same chair and pretended to study the office furnishings as Dr. Karl returned his attention to the pile on his desk.

Mercifully, the brief silence was interrupted by a knock on the door and a self-invited entrance by Courtney Lewis. "Hello, sorry I took so long!" She held out her hand.

Ferguson rose and turned to face her as she came through the door, and was immediately struck by how beautiful she was. Tall, at least 5' 10", an incredible pair of slender legs that finally ended in a curvaceous upper torso, everything accentuated by a pair of tight-fitting Gap jeans and sleeveless, white cotton blouse. Her long, wavy brown hair was pulled back in a ponytail, revealing a long face illuminated by a soft, healthy, tanned complexion. Her bright green eyes met his as he reached to shake the extended hand.

"Hello, I'm Matt Ferguson."

"Hi, Courtney Lewis." She was also beset by a sudden awareness of how attractive Ferguson was, shaking his hand and then turning to Dr. Karl. "So, this is our treasure hunter."

"This is the young man I spoke to you earlier about who appears to have stumbled across a letter that lists a significant amount, of what we think, may be works of art. Whether they are fictional or real is what we hoped you could shed some light on."

"I appreciate your coming back to take a look at this," Ferguson retrieved the letter once again from inside the folder and removed it from the plastic bag. "I assume Dr. Karl has filled you in on what little we know?"

"He gave me a brief overview of how you got the letter and the gist of what was in it."

"The list in question is on the front, numbered as you can see. If you need me to translate, please point out anything in question," said Dr. Karl.

Courtney gingerly received the letter and leaned back against the wall as she scanned the contents. Her reaction was much more animated. A series of raised eyebrows, a twist at the corner of the mouth, finished off by a whistle.

"This is artwork alright, and there's nothing fictional about what I'm seeing. In fact, I recognize a few of these pieces and they are quite famous. Some of the others I don't know, but I'm very aware of the artists, and they are a who's who of the art world. Where exactly did you get this?"

"I inherited it. Why?"

"Some of these works that I recognize have been missing for years. My guess is they are presumed lost or destroyed. Two in particular were known to have perished in World War II."

"Take a look at the top Miss Lewis," interjected Dr. Karl, "the letterhead."

Courtney took in the embossed Nazi eagle's wings and the name of Reichsmarschall Hermann Goering at the top of the letter. "Wow! He was a huge collector of art. Most, if not all was stolen and looted during the war. You're not going to tell me you know where this stuff is?"

"No, we don't know, but there is a chance it might still exist. Finding it might be a different matter," Ferguson said.

Dr. Karl stood up from his desk and began to walk over to Courtney. "There are some notes and other musings on the other side that indicate a geographical location. Whether there is any relevance to that description, and if these goods could be there, together and intact, is not entirely clear."

At this point, it dawned on Ferguson that maybe this whole process had gone too far. There was an awful lot of information and knowledge being accessed by two total strangers, who unfortunately seemed to know more about his letter than he did. Now might be the time to take possession of the letter, return home for a clearer review of his situation, and how to proceed from here. He reached out at Courtney, physically asking for the letter back. She handed it back to him with great care.

"Do you really have any idea if these works are still around?" inquired Courtney. She was beginning to feel the excitement of the potential existence of an incredibly significant find of lost masterpieces. The implications to the art community would be incredible.

"I don't have a clue," Ferguson said, packing the letter away again.

"But the clue might be on the back of the letter Herr Ferguson. Should we not try to analyze it further?"

Ferguson was looking to stall, and it was time he made an exit. "Dr. Karl, let me go back and look through some of the other stuff that was with this letter to see if there's anything else that might be able to help."

"Miss Lewis and I would be glad to help in any way we can."

"Yes, definitely. Here is my card. You can reach me at the Speed Art Museum during the day, and here's my home number," Courtney scribbled down her number on the back of the card and handed it over to Ferguson. She was beginning to understand that this was starting to become overwhelming for him, and that he was looking for some time to think.

Nevertheless, Dr. Karl was still pressing to get some answers. "If you would like to stay late this evening, I'll be happy to phone in something to eat, and we can work until we flesh out some details."

"Not tonight, thanks. I think I'm going home to examine the other things and think this out. I'll contact you soon."

"*Ja*, quite. If I were you, I wouldn't let too many other people in on your discovery. Information like this has a tendency to take on a life of its own if it were to become public."

"I couldn't agree with you more, Dr. Karl. Would you please keep this between us Miss Lewis?"

"Courtney, please. And yes, this goes no further than this room."

"Thank you, Courtney. And thank you Dr. Karl for all your help."

With that, Ferguson walked out of the office with Courtney trailing him.

She accompanied him to the parking lot and grabbed him by the forearm as they reached his car.

"Mr. Ferguson, I didn't want to pry in front of Dr. Karl, but do you have anything, any tangible evidence that this whole thing is real?"

Matt looked at her skeptically, but thought that with her background and connections she could help him determine if what he found was real. He decided to let her in on his artistic discovery, and he opened the rear passenger-side car door, retrieved a portfolio case, and laid it on the front hood.

"I have two paintings." He held his hands about a foot apart. "Small, but I'm assuming very valuable. They were in a safe at my great uncle's house. Here's one of them."

As he unzipped the case and lifted the bubble wrap encasing, Courtney leaned in to look at the gold leaf framed oil painting of a young girl perched upon a split rail fence. As her heart nearly skipped a beat, she searched the bottom corners, and found the Morisot signature in the lower right.

"Oh my God," she mumbled aloud.

"That was my first reaction," said Ferguson. "My second reaction was is it real."

Courtney touched it gingerly. "No way to know unless you have it authenticated and appraised."

"Can you do that?"

"I can't, and I'm not confident of any talent here in Louisville for something of this magnitude, but if you don't mind taking a trip to Chicago, I know someone we can trust to get it done."

# Chapter 3

*May 17, 2001. Louisville, Kentucky*

Courtney Lewis was beautiful. She had recognized it when she was young, and so had several others. Her zest for enjoying life, and the persuasion of one very influential modeling agent, had led Courtney to drop out of college her freshman year and pursue a career as a model.

The jobs were plentiful, as well as the money, and the travel was fabulous. The majority of her time was spent in New York and Paris, the latter affording her the luxury of traveling all over Europe. She developed an intense interest in art and architecture, and found herself increasingly involved with the art community. It was an interest that came as no surprise, since her father had been an artist in his younger days, and was now curator of the Chicago Art Institute. His connections also accelerated her association with some of the who's who of the art world.

After three years, her interest in modeling dwindling, she decided to go back to school and pursue a degree in the field of her newfound passion. Four years after that decision, she had a degree in art history. Through the help of her dad, she landed in Louisville at the Speed Art

Museum, functioning more as an intern than the glorified title of "assistant curator".

Sitting in her office at the museum, she had just finished her second cup of tea when she glanced up at the clock on her computer screen and knew it was okay to call Chicago, which was an hour behind. She picked up the phone and dialed her father's office. Grayson Lewis picked it up on the fourth ring.

"Hi daddy, it's me."

Hello sweetheart, how are you doing?"

"Life's good Pops."

"How's your love life, still stuck in neutral?"

"Stop it. Listen up. I've stumbled across something that is very interesting. It involves some stolen artwork from the World War II era that has been missing for over fifty years, but may be intact and discoverable. The list I've seen is unbelievable...Renoir, Degas, Cezanne, Seurat, Monet, and many others. The *Peach Orchard, Steps of Clay, Tulips in Water,* just to name a few of the works I had heard of, but were presumed lost. There are two pieces I know that do exist, and I've seen one of them. It's a Berthe Morisot...*Girl by a Fence.*"

"What do you mean by discoverable?" Mr. Lewis inquired.

"Well, I traced this piece and several of the other pieces I recognized to a collection from Franz Tolberg, who was killed in one of the Nazi concentration camps in 1943. His collection was missing, suspected to have been stolen, and never recovered. "Well, I may have found somebody that has information that could possibly lead us to their whereabouts," Courtney responded excitedly.

"Who is this somebody?"

"A young man I met recently. He inherited information from a deceased family member who catalogued the works and actually details where they were lost in a plane crash in 1945, but that they survived the crash and may still be undamaged, if sixty years of weather hasn't destroyed what was left of them. Dr. Karl, the professor at the University of Louisville I told you about…the one I'm taking language classes from, he was able to translate a letter and shipping manifest that confirms everything I'm telling you about. Dad this could be huge and I need your help. I promised the person who discovered this that I would keep it as hush-hush as possible. You know as well as I do that if this leaks out, it will stir up the art world like proverbial flies on you-know-what."

"I understand," acknowledged Mr. Lewis. "You've got an incredible discovery little lady, if it's truly intact and the works are genuine. I know a little about the Torberg collection. He was up there with the Rothschilds, Schlosses, Kahns and other well-known Jewish collectors. The Commission for Art Recovery has been looking for a sizable balance of his collection for years with no luck. In particular, he held a large collection of impressionist works rumored to have been stolen and funneled to Maria Dietrich, an infamous German art dealer in Paris during World War II. The looting of art in France was particularly obscene, and her dealings with Hitler, Goering, Goebels, von Ribbentrop, and others was well known.

"Most of the Nazis were interested in the old masters and German romantics and thought the 20th century and impressionist works degenerate and lacking in worth. However, it was rumored that late in the war Goering secretly was hoarding anything he could get his hands on, including impressionist works that he publicly disdained. Ironically, their stupidity did not foresee the incredible value of impressionist works today. There is no question that what you have described tells me that you might be dealing with one of the greatest missing treasures from World War II. If they were packed and stored carefully, and the elements, particularly moisture, have not gotten to them, there's a chance they could be restorable."

"So, you think it's worth pursuing? It's not a wild goose chase?" Courtney was beginning to think there was no way this collection could have survived.

"I would tell you to have this gentleman take his two pieces to get them authenticated, and if they're authentic, immediately have them appraised and insured. There's no question that what he has is worth millions. His only concern will be rightful ownership, but as we all know possession is nine-tenths of the law. If I had to make a guess, I would say it's unlikely that something like the other pieces in the crash could have survived unless they were stored correctly and protected. But anything's possible."

"You read my mind Dad! You have the contacts. I want to bring him, by the way his name is Matt Ferguson, and the two paintings to Chicago, and was hoping you could have some of your experts there that could authenticate, appraise and insure them on the spot."

"I'm sure I can arrange that."

"Great, how about tomorrow?"

Mr. Lewis tried to suppress the chuckle. "Tomorrow?"

"Tomorrow…or the next day would be okay."

"I'll see what I can do. Can I reach you in your office?"

"I'll be here 'til lunch. After that, I'm headed to Keeneland to watch the horses. Try me on my cell phone."

"Fine. Let me get on the phone and you'll hear back from me by the end of the day."

\*\*\*

Ferguson was in the middle of a "don't-interrupt-me" strategy session with the creative director and copywriter on the Papa Johns Pizza account, when his secretary tapped on the conference room's glass wall, held an imaginary phone to her ear, and shrugged her shoulders apologetically. He swore under his breath as he excused himself and walked out on the meeting to answer the phone in his office.

"Mr. Ferguson, Courtney Lewis. I hope I'm not interrupting you."

"No, not at all," lied Ferguson.

"I told your secretary it was urgent, because I have arranged to have your new art collection authenticated and appraised. If it is genuine, you will want to get it certified and insured immediately, particularly if you care to sell it. You may also want to speak to people that may be able to help you find the original owners."

"Sounds good. Where and when?"

"Well, I told you it would probably be Chicago, and it is. Unfortunately, I have set it up for tomorrow afternoon."

"Damn lady, you don't waste any time."

"Sorry, about the timing, but what you have Mr. Ferguson is explosive. The sooner you can determine if we're talking the real thing, the sooner you can determine the disposition of the two pieces you have, and for making plans to determine the crash site and investigate the remains. I am not sure you understand the significance of what you are sitting on. This is huge, and believe me when I say; it won't take long for the rest of the art world to catch on. Things in our business can sometimes get seedy and the sooner you can head off those eventualities, the better."

"It's beginning to soak in. The thought of millions of dollars usually has that effect on me. By the way, please call me Matt."

"Matt, I have already taken the liberty of purchasing you a ticket on an eight o'clock Southwest flight, and if you're available, I can pick you up in the morning at 7:00."

"Like I said, you don't waste any time. Fortunately, we are slow right now, so I'll be ready to go at 7:00. Let me give you directions to my home."

"Already done. Matt Ferguson on Elmwood?"

"One and the same."

"I'll see you in the morning."

# Chapter 4

*May 18, 2001. Chicago, Illinois*

Grayson Lewis hugged his daughter as she emerged from the limousine onto the sun-drenched steps in front of the Chicago Art Institute. He greeted and shook hands with Ferguson as he climbed out after her. The chauffeur met the three of them with two hard case portfolios, one in each hand, and passed off one to Ferguson and Mr. Lewis.

The walk to the second-floor offices was filled with idle small talk as Lewis showed them down a marbled hallway into a wood paneled conference room.

As they entered, Mr. Lewis offered up introductions to the three gentlemen that were standing in unison around the antique cherry conference table.

"This is my daughter, Courtney Lewis, and Matt Ferguson," Lewis turned and gestured across the table from left to right. "Mr. Ron Keeney, Vice President of Fine Arts Department of Sotheby's Chicago office. This is Jason Allen. He is an art consultant, authenticator, appraiser and broker and is assisting with the evaluation. And lastly, Clark Hancock is the Midwest Regional Director for AXA Insurance out of New York, one of the premier art insurers in the world."

Everyone immediately began exchanging handshakes from across the table, while Ferguson and Lewis laid the portfolios on the table next to a laptop, an elaborate microscope, and a hi-tech tabletop video camera platform.

Ferguson was immediately uncomfortable with the additional number of people that were involved in this process and he eyed Courtney with an apprehensive look.

She caught his stare and understood. She too, was a little concerned with her father's inclusions.

Mr. Lewis restored order to the meeting, and turned over the room to Courtney.

"First off, thank you to everyone for coming, particularly on such short notice. Mr. Ferguson, excuse me, Matt, has recently inherited what I believe are two beautiful Pisarro and Monisot impressionist works and is anxious to have them evaluated and determine their authenticity, and based on their worth put an insurance policy in force. Matt, I'll let you do the honors."

Ferguson opened up both cases and carefully removed the wax paper and padded bubble wrap, and placed the two paintings in the center of the table.

With nodded approvals and a low whistle, Jason Allen and Paul Keeney reached out simultaneously and selected one each, gently sliding both compositions in front of them. After several quiet minutes of close inspection of the pair, they jointly pushed aside the Morisot, slid the Pissaro in front of the microspectroscopy and reflectography equipment, and began their technical evaluation.

Grayson Lewis looked at Courtney, Ferguson, and Hancock. "This might take a while. Can I offer you some coffee or soda?"

In unanimous agreement, the four of them left the conference room and walked down the hall to a small break room, where they selected soft drinks and accepted Lewis' additional offer to a private viewing of the upcoming Van Gogh and Gauguin-The Studio of the South exhibition.

\*\*\*

The ink had barely dried on the appraisal certification, letter of authentication, and insurance policy, and Ferguson, in a much more relaxed state, was now in possession of nearly four million dollars' worth of art. The whole process was eye popping, and had now opened up more questions than it had answered. Grayson Lewis surprisingly asked the biggest question while they all sat around the conference table.

"So Matt, Courtney tells me you have some additional information on the potential whereabouts of several more pieces similar to what we've seen today."

"Have you had any opportunities to determine if the others are salvageable?" asked Jason Allen selfishly. "A find like that would be incredible. I'd love to help in any way I can."

"I'm fluent in German," chimed Hancock. "I would be happy to help you translate the information if Professor Karl was unable to help."

Courtney nearly passed out as the blood flushed to her extremities, and Ferguson was caught completely off guard. It was as if everyone in the room could smell the money, and they all had a chance at jumping on the gravy train. They were both thinking the same thought, hoping her father's lack of discretion had not gone any further than this room.

"Dad, I believe that's private information that Matt would care not to share with anyone at this time."

"I'm sorry honey; I thought Matt might like to ask any questions of these experts, while they are assembled together. No one else besides these folks knows anything about what we discussed. I can certainly vouch for everyone in this room and their ability to keep a secret."

Ferguson thought it time to speak for himself.

"Thanks for the offer Mr. Lewis, but I believe I have everyone's business cards, so if you all don't mind, I'll call you if I have any questions. I appreciate that all of us here will not discuss this information outside this room."

Affirmative replies came from everyone.

Mr. Lewis recognized Ferguson's message, stood and signaled an end to the meeting. "I'll have the limo pull around. Are you sure you won't stay the evening Courtney, I would love to treat you and Matt to dinner? Matt, we have a suite reserved across the street at the Hilton, and you're more than welcome to stay the night."

"Thanks for the offer Dad, but I need to get back." Courtney glanced at Ferguson, who gave a discreet nod in agreement. "I know Matt has to be back as well."

With that, everyone shook hands for the last time and the meeting adjourned. Allen and Keeney left first together, while Grayson Lewis and Clark Hancock waited another ten minutes and escorted Courtney and Ferguson down to the waiting limo. Hancock hailed a cab and said his goodbyes, as Ferguson's newfound wealth was loaded into the back seat.

Before the limo had pulled away from the curb, Jason Allen sat down in a cushioned Starbuck's lounge chair just down Michigan Avenue and placed a very important long-distance call to the Caribbean. At that same moment, Clark Hancock passed by in a cab and punched in the number to a coded cell phone just outside the city of Munich.

# Chapter 5

## *May 19, 2001. Louisville, Kentucky*

The call by Clark Hancock to the secure phone in Munich had produced instantaneous results. Armed with what little knowledge he had to go on, Mr. Jones had called and scheduled a meeting with Herr Karl, armed with a proposition that he was certain the good professor could not refuse.

Dr. Karl walked into the Bristol Bar and Grille just before the lunchtime rush. He gave his name to the ample-breasted, young hostess standing inside the door, and headed up the handful of steps to the bar. He was twenty minutes early for his appointment, but it gave him time to order a Dortmunder Union from the bartender and reflect on the phone conversation that had brought him here.

From the minute he had first read the letter that Mr. Ferguson had brought to him, he realized the financial implications, and that once people learned of the existence of the crash, it would bring out the thieves and treasure hunters. Still, it amazed him that the wheels had turned as fast as they had, and that he had received the call from a "Mr. Jones" this morning.

The restaurant was busy, and he had no idea who to look for, but he was pretty confident Mr. Jones would find him. The beer tasted good! He was preparing to order another, when the tap on his shoulder interrupted him. He turned to find a small, white-haired man, in his late fifties or early sixties, dressed in a gray, three-piece suit.

"Dr. Karl, my name is Irwin Jones. Please follow me and we'll have some lunch."

"My pleasure," replied Karl, as he followed the hostess and Jones to a table discreetly isolated in the front corner of the restaurant by the large window overlooking Bardstown Road. Menus were left with them as they took their seats.

There was an eerie silence between the two as they surveyed the menus, while the bus boy brought water and the waiter introduced himself and the daily specials. They both ordered immediately and allowed the waiter to leave before Jones initiated the conversation.

"Well, it appears Doctor that you have stumbled on quite a find. We had assumed that the flight containing this precious cargo had been destroyed in 1945. We were aware there was a survivor, but since he never made any attempt to return to the crash site, we felt there was no need to pursue it. Our mistake."

"So, there is some validity to Ferguson's letter," inquired Karl.

"Completely!" affirmed Jones

"You seem to know a lot about this whole affair already, do you mind if I ask who you are and what you do?"

"Certainly. My name is Irwin Jones, and I represent an antiquities dealer who in turn represents several interested parties that would like to purchase the recovered artwork from Mr. Ferguson…should he have any luck finding the missing pieces, and they're in restorable shape of course."

"Of course," mimicked Karl.

"This is very big Herr Karl. Very, very big."

"Oh, I can only imagine how much this could be worth. What do you need from me?"

"I need a translation of the letter. I intend to talk to Mr. Ferguson and persuade him that we would like to pay him an advance, and we will take the risk of the salvage operation. If we are successful, and the art is restorable, he will get a sizable percentage. You will also be compensated handsomely Doctor. I will pay you half up front and the other half upon completion, but from here on out I would like for you to take receipt of the letter and verify its authenticity, translate it and then transfer the letter to me. After that we will never speak again, is that clear?"

"Very! Nevertheless, how will I get the letter, and I am assuming that I will not be involved with the negotiations with Mr. Ferguson?"

"Absolutely not! I will arrange for all of it. As I said, you will receive the letter, verify and translate it, and then you will get the letter to me. One week from today, same time, we will meet back here. You will bring the letter and the translation then."

Mr. Jones slid a business size envelope across the table. "In there is $25,000 dollars. I will bring the same amount with me next week upon the conclusion of our transfer. If you have any problems or questions in the meantime you may reach me at this number." He handed him a blank business-size card with a single phone number printed on it.

The waiter appeared with two of the lunch specials and two glasses of white wine as ordered. After he disappeared, Jones picked up where he left off.

"Do you have any questions Doctor?"

"*Nein.*"

"Very well then, enjoy your lunch!"

\*\*\*

The morning at his office had been very unproductive for Ferguson. He was having a hard time concentrating on anything work related. The previous day's events were strange, but Courtney was right when she had indicated on the flight home that wrapping up the details of the two paintings should have been a relief. They were back in Max's safe, and he could now think about determining ownership, and what he might realize from their sale or return.

The new problem was the bigger prize. He had visited the copier and made a copy of the letter and list, and was now staring blankly at the sheet with the sketched map. Out to the side of Max's scribble, he had written down a few of the translated specifics he could remember from the visit with Dr. Karl, but he realized there were several words on the map that he could not translate without additional help. He would also need help identifying the map coordinates that were indicated.

He closed his eyes, and his mind started to wander. He visualized a peaceful lake in Switzerland surrounded by lush green mountains, or were they covered in several feet of snow.

He opened his eyes and popped out of his chair. He was losing his mind thinking about what might be. He had to get some fresh air. He called his secretary and stepped out of the office for a bite to eat.

For lunch, he stopped into Mancinos for a 'Grinder' sandwich, and afterward went next door to Hawley Cooke booksellers to purchase a German-English translator book. While he sat in his idling car the urge overwhelmed him, and he drove up the street to the AAA office and picked up a map and tour book of Switzerland.

He wasn't back in his office an hour before he came to the realization that the urge was a once-in-a-lifetime opportunity. Not just for the potential financial reward, but also for the sheer adventure of trying to track down a piece of history and a piece of his great uncle's past.

Ferguson picked up the phone and dialed the three-digit extension. "Jerry, it's Matt. Listen, I've got to take some time off. Max's death has left a whole bunch of loose ends that I'm going to need to get cleaned up, and to tell you the truth my head is just not into work."

He waited for the reply, fully expecting to have to argue the necessity further, but was pleasantly surprised when the president of the agency encouraged him to take as much time as he felt necessary.

"Thanks Jerry. I'll brief Sheri on everything I have in the hopper, and I'm sure she can handle anything that comes up. There's really nothing urgent right now." Another endorsement came over the phone and the line went dead.

Ferguson turned to his computer, summoned the internet home page, typed in the 'Travelocity' site and began searching for airfares to Switzerland.

***

By 4:15, everything at the office had been secured and Ferguson was on his way home to pack. It was all happening so fast and the adrenaline rush was incredible. He would be on a plane to Zurich in two days, and whether there was anything to be made of the whole quest remained to be seen, but he was determined to have fun in the process. He laughed to himself and realized he'd never even been to Europe.

As he pulled onto his street and turned into his driveway, he never even noticed the black, Pontiac Trans Am parked fifty yards down and diagonally across the street.

Jimmy Syron followed the Ford Explorer in the binoculars as it entered the subdivision, turned down the street and into the driveway of the address written on the paper lying in his lap.

"That's him," he said to the man behind the wheel, without ever moving his eyes away from the lenses.

"He's alone?" Jay Nieron asked as he sat up in the seat to peer over the steering wheel.

"By his lonesome," snickered Syron.

Jimmy Syron and Jay Nieron were both big-time losers in the game of life. Inseparable, they had dropped out of high school together at the age of 17, convinced that the money they were making moving drugs was enough to make them big shots in the small bedroom community on the south end of town.

They hadn't counted on being nabbed in a Federal cocaine sting a year and a half later. Both copped a plea on lesser charges, but managed to do some hard time in Eddyville Penitentiary. Between the young Asian public defender, the Jewish judge who sentenced them, and the black inmates who had their way with them inside, they were ripe for the recruiting when they were paroled two years later.

The leader of the local Aryan Nation cell met them at a rally in western Kentucky one week after they set foot outside the prison, and with very little effort convinced them of the cause. Their devotion to the organization and their beliefs led to connections with other white supremacy and anti-Semitic groups across the country. They matured from drug pushers to thieves and hit men.

"I'll give him a few minutes to get comfortable, and then I'll go in. I'll make it look like he walked into a robbery and got whacked in the process," Jimmy said proudly.

*\*\*\**

Without even a thought of getting comfortable, Ferguson had entered through the garage door and made a beeline to the bedroom, where he was busy changing out of the suit and tie into a pair of khakis and golf shirt. A little freshening up over the vanity and he was ready to head back out for a cocktail and some dinner.

He had decided on the ride home from work that he would need something to help take the edge off of the turmoil his mind had been in all day. That something was going to be a couple of manhattans and a nice meal on the patio of Azalea's restaurant. That would also allow him the opportunity to look over the map and notes some more, attempt to identify the approximate location in Switzerland he would need to start with, and do a complete translation of every word scrawled on the paper. He was in and out of the house in less than ten minutes as he switched off the lights inside and flipped on the outside porch light.

\*\*\*

Syron had waited uneasily for eight minutes, but the anticipation of the kill was too much. He looked at Nieron, produced a long stiletto switchblade from the back pocket of his pants, and opened and closed it to make sure the action was correct. He placed it back in his pants, and with a sinister grin, gave a wink as he exited the car.

Casually, as if out for an early evening stroll he started down the street and meandered up the adjacent driveway to Ferguson's house and ducked into the bushes that would conceal him while he climbed the fence into the backyard. As he was rounding the deck, he nearly jumped out of his skin as the garage door started up and the engine of Ferguson's Explorer turned over. Crouched under a large honeysuckle, he watched as Ferguson pulled out and drove away.

*That stupid asshole, where the hell is he going?*

His cell phone went off almost the instant the engine noise had disappeared.

"Jimmy, are you alright?" Jay's voice asked over the line.

"Yeah! The son-of-a-bitch just bugged out on me. Fuck it. I'm goin' in anyway. I'll wait for the fucker to come home and do him then."

"Don't forget the paper, they told us that's the most important thing," Nieron reminded him.

"Yeah, Yeah, I'll look for that right now. Buzz me again, when he's coming back."

Syron broke through the backdoor window, and entered easily through the door. He spent the next fifteen minutes ransacking the house, pocketing whatever valuables he could find. On the dresser in the bedroom, he found what he was looking for. It was a photocopy, but it had the personalized Nazi letterhead of Hermann Goering, and the list in the body of the paper, just as they told him it would. He folded it once and stuck it in the back pocket of his pants removing the stiletto as he did so.

He walked into the den, sat down in the big leather chair, and turned on the television with the remote control. He was perfectly willing to relax until his prey returned.

***

Pulling down the driveway two hours later, Ferguson noticed through the den window the flickering images of light coming from the television. *That's not right, I never turned the TV on.*

He steered the Explorer into the garage, killed the engine, and got out. For some reason the question of the television being left on had heightened his senses, as he climbed the three steps to the landing and slowly opened the door to the den. He leaned his head in first and noticed the television was now off.

His heart was beginning to beat faster as he stepped carefully over the threshold and into the room. Simultaneously, the movement behind the door reflected off the darkened television screen and he picked it up instantly. Without hesitation, he leaned into the door as hard as he could and slammed it into the intruder.

There was a muffled groan and then the door came forcefully back into Ferguson knocking him backward onto the landing and then tumbling head over heels down the steps. As he got to his feet, Syron was coming into the garage in pursuit, blood pouring from his broken nose.

Ferguson recovered onto his feet quickly and picked up the softball bat lying on the shelf to his right. Just as Syron had reached the bottom step, the stiletto still firmly in his grip, Ferguson swung the bat backhanded and landed it squarely in Syron's right rib cage. The force produced an exhale of breath followed by a spontaneous scream of agony, the knife and Syron both dropping to the ground.

Ferguson, however, was not about to wait around to assess the damage. Holding on to the bat, he turned from his attacker and ran out of the garage, down the driveway, and headed for the nearest neighbor with the lights on, which happened to be the Saunders. He didn't bother to knock as he disappeared through their front door.

***

Jimmy Syron was on the verge of suffocating. The blood and swollen tissue from what once was his nose, and the stifling pain coming from the right side of his torso, was making it almost impossible to breathe. He was virtually crawling down the driveway while dialing Nieron on the cell phone.

"You finished?" Nieron inquired as he punched the 'Talk' button.

"I'm fucked up man, get the car down here to..." Syron stopped to spit out a mouthful of blood, "get down to the end of the driveway...NOW!"

Nieron raced down the street and skidded to a halt. He opened the door and dragged Syron in over himself and onto the passenger seat. The piercing cry of anguish from Syron's injuries could be heard through the window of the Saunders' house, as the black Trans Am sped away.

***

Officer Gil Brucker and his partner were wrapping up their report at the dining room table inside Ferguson's house. Ferguson had been picking up the destruction for the better part of half an hour, while Brucker had been asking him all the pertinent questions as to the evening's events. Additionally, he was keeping a tally of all the items that appeared to be missing.

There had been a couple of watches, an envelope containing $350 in cash from his winnings in a recent golf tournament, everything that was a precious metal or jewel from his jewelry case, and his jade and ivory pen set Max had given him at graduation. However, nothing of any size. No electronics, his golf clubs were still there, and his Browning 12 gauge had not been discovered in the top shelf of his closet.

"Looks to me like you caught him in the act before he had time to pick you clean of the big stuff. Although, getting away in a car...they were not going to haul away anything too big. You got insurance don't ya?"

"Yeah, I'm covered," Ferguson replied.

"Well, I think we're about wrapped up here." Brucker picked up the plastic zip lock bag lying on the table and examined the contents.

"We'll run this for prints, and if we score someone, we'll have somebody get back to you. Thanks for your patience Mr. Ferguson."

"No, thank you officer, I appreciate your help."

"You gonna be alright here by yourself tonight? You got any relatives or friends you could stay with?"

"No, I'll be fine. I do think I'll bring my shotgun to bed with me though."

"You do have a permit for that?" Brucker cocked his head in mock concern.

"Yes sir officer, I'm fully compliant," Ferguson laughed in reply.

"Good! My guess is that whoever was here has no interest in coming back. That's if he's capable of even walking around. Goodnight Mr. Ferguson. We'll be in touch."

***

For the better part of the remaining evening, Ferguson tried to put everything that wasn't broken back in its place, and everything that was, he put in a pile by the same back door that had helped him save his life earlier. The biggest problem he was having, however, was the half-angry, half-disgusted feeling of having been violated by some 'shithead' stranger that had just stolen his property... his stuff.

Dragging himself off to bed, he undressed and emptied his pockets and laid his wallet on the dresser. He retrieved his cell phone, the translation book and the copy of the map he had stacked by the phone in the kitchen. He set them down next to his wallet, right where he had left behind the other photocopy of the front of the letter...but it wasn't there.

He didn't notice it before. He had accounted for a lot of missing things, but not the letter, at least half of the letter. The other half, containing the map had been with him at dinner.

He scoured the floor, behind the dresser, in the garbage can, under the bed, and then stopped dead in his tracks. He stared blankly at the wall, while a small chill made its way up his spine. *He was here for the letter.*

# Chapter 6

*May 19, 2001. Chicago, Illinois*

Jason Allen had been perched on one of the bar stools that fronted the long mahogany and brass bar at Kitty O'Sheas on Michigan Avenue. His average height and build, along with indistinguishable features, made him a very ordinary man at the age 46. He had never stood out physically among the crowd, and he had never separated himself from his peers with his talents as an artist. His short and unremarkable career had led him early on into administrative work in the fine arts to help pay the bills, and he leveraged the contacts and connections he had made into a lucrative appraisal, authentication and brokerage business with an impeccable reputation. He had worked with Grayson Lewis for years and had never done anything to cause Lewis to question his intentions. However, alcohol, gambling, and several risky investments gone bad had taken their toll as of late and he had recently begun secretly associating with some rather unscrupulous characters, even resorting to capitalizing on several questionable opportunities that had presented themselves, in most cases at the expense of others.

He had visualized a golden opportunity when he heard from Lewis, and naturally had sworn the secrecy Lewis demanded. He had just the person in mind, when he was able to recover from the significance of the artwork that Grayson Lewis had discussed with his daughter.

The black stretch limousine pulled up to the curb, just in front of the Hilton's cab line, outside the bar's front door. Allen had been periodically eyeing the street and needed no prompting, immediately standing down, knocking back the remaining portion of his half-and-half, and depositing a ten-dollar bill next to the empty glass. He hurried outside into the cool, overcast evening, walked over to the chauffeur holding the rear door open, nodded and climbed in.

Guillermo Rocca was comfortably squeezed between two incredibly beautiful and scantily clad ladies of the evening. A half empty bottle of Perrier Jouet Champagne lay in an ice bucket, while all three had arms and legs entwined, and were sipping from one another's glasses. Rocca peeled away from the emerging orgy and slipped into the seat next to Allen, holding his hand up in a gesture of patience to the two young girls.

"Jason, good to see you again."

"Thank you, Mr. Rocca, it's always a pleasure to see you. You look as if you're in good hands."

"Yes, these are my friends Ginger and Sabrina. They come highly recommended," Rocca looked at the two and winked, and quickly returned his attention to Allen. "You have some good news for me?"

"Well, good news and bad news I'm afraid," said Allen somewhat nervously.

Rocca's seemingly happy demeanor disappeared and he focused intently on Allen, his coal black eyes cutting into Allen's soul. He sat back slowly in his seat and again held up his hand at the two giggling ladies, this time asking for quiet.

Guillermo Rocca was a physically intimidating man. Tall, muscular, dark-skinned with jet-black hair and mustache, and at 57 years old, he was probably the wealthiest man in all of Ecuador. He had grown up dirt poor in an orphanage outside of Zamora. However, as a young teen, through an incredibly fortunate set of circumstances, he obtained information that implicated some very influential people in the local government. He successfully blackmailed his way into ownership of some presumably worthless land that ironically turned out to provide one of the wealthiest gold strikes in Ecuador's history.

His amassed fortune now included numerous commercial properties and developments around the world, three mining operations, and agricultural plantations throughout South America. However, well-hidden and intensely protected in a Caribbean island mansion just south of Barbados, was one of the greatest accumulations of artwork the world never knew existed. It was Rocca's greatest passion in life, and he had stopped at nothing to build and add to his impressive collection over the years.

Allen was aware of his reputation as a collector, and he was also aware of the unsubstantiated rumors that people's lives had been ruined and lost when they got in the way of his obsession. He also had heard of the astonishingly generous compensation Rocca lavished on those that had helped him acquire the art he pursued.

"The works I mentioned to you may or may not still be in existence." Allen continued.

"I don't follow you Mr. Allen."

"Let me try and explain," Allen gave him as much of the story as he knew, which was lacking details and specifics, but in general was quite accurate.

"So, this collection of Goering's might have been destroyed in the initial crash. Or, if it survived, could have been ruined if it was never found. Or if it was found, may be in the possession of another owner. Or, might still be intact, even in relatively good or restorable condition, if it had been packaged properly before it was to be transported," said Rocca, as he tried to digest the facts presented to him.

"Correct!" Allen was beginning to relax since Rocca's well-known short temper had not exploded.

Rocca reached over the two pair of long, gorgeous legs stretched out in front of the television cabinet and picked up the cell phone lying in an open tray. He punched through several menu options, and finally selected a stored entry.

"Juan? Yes, it's me. I need you to be on the plane in thirty minutes. I need you in Louisville, Kentucky. I want you to keep an eye on a young lady there by the name of Courtney Lewis," Rocca looked at Allen, as if to confirm the accuracy of the name. "Yes. Hang on," Rocca lowered the phone and spoke to Allen. "I need a physical description, work and home addresses, make of automobile, and anything else that will help." He raised the phone back to his ear. "I'll contact you again in flight with everything you need. Please be very discreet! No contact unless I say so. We just want to keep tabs on her whereabouts at all times. Understood? Thanks, I'll phone you shortly."

Allen had already pulled out his business cards and was busy writing down the details Rocca wanted on the backs of four cards. While he was completing the information, Rocca had repositioned himself back between his amorous companions and was giving instructions to the driver through the slight crack in the privacy windows.

Fifteen minutes later, they were back in front of Kitty O'Sheas and the rear door on the limo once again had been opened. Rocca whispered into the ear of the blonder of the two blonds and she shifted her gaze from the floor to Allen. After an exchange of kisses, Ginger smiled deviously at Allen and moved from her position in the back seat, to the side of Allen's arm.

"Thank you for the information Mr. Allen, I am very grateful to you for having thought of me. Ginger is your reward for the evening. Let us call it a good faith gesture on my part. If anything comes of this enterprise, I can assure you that you will have enough money to buy thousands of Gingers. I will be in touch."

"Thank you, Mr. Rocca!" Allen could hardly contain his enthusiasm. "Your generosity is much appreciated. I look forward to working with you!"

Ginger escorted Allen from the car, and the two of them headed north on the sidewalk and disappeared into the front door of the Hilton as Rocca's limousine pulled into traffic on Michigan Avenue and headed north into the city.

# Chapter 7

## *May 20, 2001. Louisville, Kentucky*

The doorbell startled Dr. Karl. He had just sat down at his kitchen table to consume a toasted bagel with cream cheese, and relax with a nice cup of coffee and the morning paper. He certainly wasn't expecting any visitors at 8:28 a.m., looking up at the clock on the microwave. The bell rang again impatiently.

He reached the front door as the bell rang for the third time, and opened it up with a jerk. "Would you mind not ringing the doorbell again please!"

Standing side-by-side on the front porch were Jimmy Syron and Jay Nieron. Syron's face had a crisscross bandage around the nose, leaving the purple tip exposed, and he leaned at an angle on a cane in his right hand. Nieron appeared to be supporting him as well.

"Are you John Karl?" Syron said with a snarl.

"Johann Karl," Karl replied

"Close enough!" Nieron chimed in as he helped lead Syron through the door and into the small foyer.

"Excuse me, but who in the hell do you think you are barging into my home?"

"We have a package for you, special delivery. I believe it's a letter you're looking for," Syron continued.

"Ah, yes! Yes, please come in." This was sooner than Karl had expected the letter to surface, and the messengers left a lot to be desired. Nevertheless, this was a welcome intrusion.

Nieron offered the envelope and Karl took it. He pointed to the tapestry couch in the adjacent living room, "Please have a seat," while he sat in the striped wingback chair across from the coffee table separating them. He tore open the envelope and removed the single sheet of paper.

After turning it back and forth twice and then checking the envelope again, he looked up at the pair. "This is a photocopy, and where's the rest?"

The two wretches looked at each other and then back at Karl. "What do you mean the rest?"

"This is only the front of the letter. There is a back that contains the map. The map is what I need," Karl was growing uneasy and irritated. What have you done with the map?"

"Fuck you old man!" Syron jumped to his feet, his face twisted in pain. "That's all there was!"

"Calm down Jimmy," Nieron stood and grabbed him.

"No, you don't understand there was more than just this!" Karl shook the paper at him.

"No, you don't understand you old fart!" Syron exploded. He came over the coffee table, disregarding any pain, and slammed the end of the cane into the nose of Karl, sending him back into the chair as both flipped backward into the wall.

"Take it easy Jimmy!" Nieron stepped in between the two. "This ain't gonna get us our money."

Karl crawled out from behind the chair, stood up, and slowly backed away toward the dining room entryway. He was starting to realize the seriousness of the situation. These two miserable boys were big trouble and he wondered why Irwin Jones was associated with them. He tried to think of a way out. He would try Jones on the number he had given him, since these two most certainly had to answer to him. He was bound to have some control over their actions.

"Please! Please, calm down!" Karl implored. "Let me get in touch with your boss. I have his number...right here," Karl stumbled through the dining room into the kitchen, picked up his briefcase off the kitchen table knocking the cold bagel to the floor, and retrieved the card with the phone number from his Daytimer.

Syron drug himself to his feet, staggered through the foyer, and entered the kitchen from the other door, "If that's anybody else, you're a dead man!" He produced another stiletto knife similar to the one he had lost at Ferguson's, and flicked open the blade.

Karl had already entered the number into the phone and Jones answered on the second ring. "Mr. Jones, Dr. Karl here. We have a problem."

Syron reached over and snatched the phone out of Karl's hand. "Who is this?"

"I'm sorry, who is this?" Jones retorted.

"This is Jimmy Syron you stupid fucker! Now who's this?"

"Mr. Syron, this is Walter Smith, what seems to be the problem?"

"The problem is we got the letter like you wanted. We didn't get Ferguson, but we will. This old turd here in front of me tells me we didn't get the entire letter. No one told me there was more than one page. You said, 'The letter with the Reichsmarschall Goering head on it'. Shit, I don't care. All I know is we got what you wanted us to get, now we want to make sure we get paid."

"You will be paid, Mr. Syron, please calm down. I'm on my way now, and we can discuss payment when I get there. Let me speak to Dr. Karl please."

Syron turned the phone back to Karl. "Yes?"

"Dr. Karl, I'm in route to your house, I'm only a few minutes away. Please remain calm and review whatever they brought you and tell them it should be sufficient. I will deal with those two punks when I get there."

"Thank you," Karl hung up the phone and turned to Nieron who was holding the crumpled-up letter. "Let me see that again. It may be enough."

\*\*\*

Mr. Jones entered through the front door of the house unannounced.

"We're in the kitchen," Syron called to him.

Jones entered the kitchen to find Karl seated at the kitchen table with Syron seated in a chair next to him. Nieron was standing behind them, leaning against the counter next to the refrigerator.

"We're having a party I see."

"This ain't no fuckin' party Mr. Smith, Jones, whatever your name is. You asked us to do a job and we did it. Now we want to get paid."

"I told you that you would be paid when you got the letter and took care of Mr. Ferguson. You completed the first order of business; however, we have some problems that still remain. The second item has yet to be fulfilled. You will be paid in full, through the account as we agreed, when the job is completed."

"Well, that's where we have a difference of opinion." With that, Syron pulled his hand out from under the table and plunged the stiletto into the side of Karl's throat. Karl's mouth opened and his eyes bulged in shock, his hands clutched at his chest for a brief instant and then he fell forward. Syron slid the knife out while Karl's life bled away onto the table. "We'd like our money...Now!"

"That was a very stupid thing to do Mr. Syron." The whole sequence had caught Jones off guard. He thought he was prepared, having tucked the silenced Walther PPK into the waistband behind his back before entering, but he did not anticipate them to act irrationally and kill Karl. He had made a grave mistake picking these two to handle this particular job. He thought they were ready, but he was wrong. They were nothing but insignificant, second-rate losers, and always would be. He had screwed up, now it was time to correct the mistake.

Syron stood shakily, while Nieron leaned over to help him to his feet. That was all the time Jones needed. He reached expertly behind his back, retrieving the Walther and bringing it up immediately. He clicked off one round that landed just over the right eye of Nieron sending the majority of the back of his head splattering against the white refrigerator door. Nieron wobbled slightly, and then hit the floor with a thud. Syron froze in shock, panic stretching across his face.

"Very stupid Jimmy," Jones was slowly shaking his head back and forth.

The last sound Syron heard was the 'cough' of another round discharging into his forehead.

***

Soft, filtered rays of early morning sunshine radiated through the half-open blinds. Ferguson wasn't sure if he had been to sleep at all, except for the faint remembrance of it having been dark the last time he had looked over at his sleeping companion. The Browning 12 gauge was clearly visible lying on the top of the sheets, and the LED readout on the alarm clock confirmed that he had been asleep for the last two and a half hours.

He struggled mightily with his eyelids until there was enough lubrication to his contacts to bring things into respectable focus. Lying on his back in the big king-size bed, his head propped up on two down-feather pillows, he was sure he hadn't moved during the brief period of sleep. Unfortunately, it didn't take long for all the events of the last 48 hours to come rushing back into his consciousness.

*God Almighty, what have I gotten myself into?*

He looked around the room and felt again the wave of disgust over someone having encroached upon his personal space and property. He was proud and protective of his home. Even as a bachelor, he had taken great pains to have a designer's flair to his house and accessorize it accordingly. There were also distinct signs of a woman's touch, the result of having lived with Whitney for over two years.

The time with her had been fun and exciting, but unfortunately, it had been self-evident to both of them that they were not compatible for the long haul. They arrived at the decision to go their separate ways almost simultaneously, and she moved back to Tampa shortly thereafter to resume her career in broadcast television.

That was five months ago, and now, the only beautiful woman he had met in that time was probably responsible for the destruction his house endured last night. He had wracked his brain late into the morning hours, searching for someone to fix the blame on. He was determined to confront Courtney Lewis and find out what her, or her father and his friend's involvement might be, just as soon as his mind and body had two Advil, a hot shower, cup of coffee, and breakfast...in that order.

He also couldn't discount Dr. Karl as maybe having been involved, but why would an old college professor have an interest in a potential art discovery. No, with the Lewis' background, Ferguson reasoned the art connection lay with one or both of them. He rolled out of bed and stripped off his boxers as he headed to the medicine cabinet and the shower.

***

The combination of Ibuprofen, steaming water, liquid caffeine, and food had worked wonders mentally, physically and emotionally. Ferguson had rummaged through his briefcase and found the business card to Courtney Lewis he had saved from their meeting at Dr. Karl's office. He went to the other bedroom that functioned as his office, picked up the phone, and suppressing his anger dialed the number on the card.

"Speed Art Museum, Miss Lewis' office," came a very pleasant voice.

"Is she in please?"

"No, I'm afraid she's out of the office until about two o'clock. Can I take a message please?"

"Yes please. Tell her that Matt Ferguson will be in her office at 2:01 to discuss the results of our meeting yesterday," Ferguson was short, but cordial.

"Mr. Ferguson, she has some other meetings this afternoon that may prevent her from being available, I doubt she'll be able to fit you in today." The smooth voice was doing her best to cover for Courtney, having sensed the tension in Ferguson's voice, and not recognizing his name at all. "Why don't you leave a number and I'll..."

Ferguson cut her off, "She'll see me! Thanks!" He hung up before another word was uttered.

***

1400 Willows Tower was one of Louisville's premier addresses. Located in the heart of Cherokee Park, it was one of the oldest and most affluent residential towers, in one of the oldest and most dynamic areas in town. Courtney loved living in the Willows, which offered her the cosmopolitan setting she had become accustomed to in her years of travel, and placed her conveniently close to the city's most prolific restaurant and bar scene that lined nearby Bardstown Road for several blocks.

Courtney's ninth floor apartment was decorated remarkably like a contemporary art museum. Other than the two bedrooms and baths, there were no walls to speak of. It was one large open floor plan with whitewashed walls, and light-colored hardwood floors. The walls were dotted with a wide variety of paintings, each highlighted spectacularly by various cannoned lights that were controlled by a large panel next to the front door. The furniture was sparse and contemporary, and was broken into spaces, defined by rugs and structural columns with ornate Romanesque moldings. Interspersed, in no particular pattern, were a half dozen incredible sculptures, including one bronze nude that was at least two times scale and had to be assembled at its present location.

Courtney stood in her robe behind a large granite counter that separated the kitchen from the rest of the open space, finishing her espresso and listening to Joan Bullock on the speakerphone explain the strange phone call she had just received from a 'Matt Ferguson'.

"...if you don't want to come in today, I'll make up some excuse for you," Courtney's secretary finished up.

"No, no. I do want to meet with him. It's okay, really! I'm sorry, I should have told you before, but that's the fellow I flew to Chicago with yesterday. I'll be in there a little before 2:00 in case he shows up early."

"He was really short, he sounded upset or angry. I'd be very careful."

"Thanks Joan. Really, he's fine. I'm not sure why he would come across that way with you. He's been very polite. He's actually very cute."

"Well, not on the phone he isn't!" There was a slight pause for effect. "I'll see you this afternoon then."

"Yep! Thanks again Joan for watching out for me, I appreciate it. I'll be fine. See you after lunch."

Courtney could barely control her exuberance as she hung up the phone. *What additional help does he need? Does he need my help? This could be the find of a lifetime! I'd love to discuss it further over dinner. He is quite attractive.*

She picked up her cup of espresso and headed to the shower, her head pounding from yesterday's marathon day in Chicago, followed by an evening of dinner, drinks and dancing with Sheikh Mahmoud and his entourage.

\*\*\*

The shower and espresso had provided their magic and Courtney felt like a new woman. She had pranced around the bathroom naked while she administered her make-up and dried her hair, periodically examining her reflection in the mirror over the sink and analyzing the small flaws in her body that didn't seem to be there a few short years ago. She slipped on a silk robe and went out to the nook in the living room that served as her office. She sat down at the glass-topped table and turned on the laptop computer, determined to finish up some work and answer e-mails before heading to the museum.

Two hours later, she entered her walk-in closet and went right to the outfit she had decided upon in the shower. She pulled from the hanger an Escada two-piece suit, sophisticated, but tailored and low cut enough to accentuate her feminine assets. She slipped on a pair of

Gucci pumps, teased at her hair for some body, and re-examined herself in the full-length mirror. That ought to get his attention, she thought to herself.

She returned to the kitchen, called her office, punched in the appropriate numbers, and listened to the four voicemail messages. Nothing of any consequence. She headed out the front door and took the elevator to the parking garage. She climbed in, turned over the black Porsche 911 and headed out of the garage into traffic toward what she believed was going to be a very interesting afternoon, and hopefully evening.

*** 

Julio Bolivar closed the detective mystery book he had been reading to kill time while he waited for Courtney Lewis to emerge from her residence. When the black Porsche appeared out from under the Tower, a single beep on the one-way phone alerted Carlos Garagua in the white *Taurus* rental car parked thirty feet away in front of one of the park's multitude of children's playgrounds.

Bolivar stood up from the park bench, tucked his book under his arm, and signaled to Garagua as he pulled away from the curb and settled in comfortably behind Courtney as she sped away. Bolivar slipped his suit coat onto his broad-shoulder frame, straightened up his hand-made silk tie, and ran his fingers straight back through his thick black hair. He had been sitting on the bench, in the shade for the better part of two hours. He had been in town less than twelve hours.

Bolivar had dropped what he was doing, as he always did, when Guillermo Rocca called from Chicago, and flown in early that morning with Garagua on Rocca's personal Gulfstream 300 jet. He had been Rocca's right-hand man, and at 31, more like a son to Rocca. He was eternally grateful to Mr. Rocca for having sought and recognized his technological expertise and intelligence gathering savvy, plucking him out of the Ecuadorian military intelligence service, and offering him a lifestyle that he could never have achieved elsewhere. In return he was totally committed to Mr. Rocca, was willing to do anything for him, and had proved it several times. Armed with a few tidbits of information, he had developed all the background knowledge he needed to create and maintain a tight surveillance of Miss Courtney Lewis.

As he crossed the side street, he opened the door to another rental, a silver Chrysler Concorde, tossed in his book and retrieved a logo'd retail bag. Walking into the lobby of the tower, he handed the security guard a *Verizon Wireless* business card that identified him as a local sales representative.

"I have a new phone I'm delivering to Courtney Lewis in 901," Bolivar said confidently as he opened up the plastic bag with a phone and several other accessories inside.

"Go on up," responded the guard, without a trace of hesitation or concern. He sat back down behind the desk and picked up his own novel, the latest best seller from Tom Clancy.

"Thank you," said Bolivar, as he walked down the corridor and into an open elevator. He punched in the seventh floor, a sigh of relief that the guard must not have seen Courtney leave several minutes before.

It took only seconds for Bolivar to pick the deadbolt lock to Courtney's front door, and he slipped inside unobserved. He went straight to the telephone behind the kitchen counter, removed the back cover and inserted a small bug inside. He replaced the phone and crossed over to open living space, nodding his head in appreciation. He spotted the large sculpture and ran his hands over the entwined pair of naked female bodies. It was a perfect spot for another bug, well hidden under the cupped hand of one of the groping participants.

He repeated the same process on a lamp in the bedroom and then beeped again for Garagua on the one-way.

"Yeah boss?"

"You still have the girl?"

"Yeah, I think she's headed for her office."

"Good, don't lose her. Also, switch on the receiver. We're live, I need a reading."

Garagua leaned over to the passenger seat and flipped on the switches to the equipment stacked in the seat. "Go boss."

"Test, test, test," Bolivar walked from the bedroom into the living room. "Test, test."

"Loud and clear boss."

"Good, let's try the phone," Bolivar picked up the phone, and waited for the dial tone.

"That one's good, too," came the reply over the one-way.

"Excellent, I'm heading for some lunch. Call me when she gets to where she's going and I'll drive over to you and pick up the equipment. You can stay on the girl."

"You got it boss."

Bolivar walked out of the tower into the warm sunshine, took a left toward the park and decided to walk toward Bardstown Road and lunch.

\*\*\*

The pasta special at The Comeback Inn was incredible as usual, coupled with the glass of merlot, it had taken some of the edge off Ferguson's anger. He was still mad, but he decided on a long lunch to determine his line of thought and how he would proceed in the conversation he was about to undertake with Courtney Lewis. He wanted to make certain that she was aware of the danger that she put him in, the damage to his personal property, and that she was no longer to involve herself in any way, shape, or form. If there was even a hint of somebody or something that had the remotest connection to the letter, he was going to the police.

He checked his watch. It was 1:28. He signaled the waitress for the check, paid, and headed for the car.

***

The administrative offices for the Speed Museum are on the third floor of the main gallery building located on South Third Street adjacent to the University of Louisville's Belknap campus. Ferguson had to pass through a security gate at the front entrance, receiving instructions on where the offices were and where to park. He wound his way around the large, pillared structure to an adjoining parking garage, and entered.

He followed the ramps up three levels and found a spot on the exterior next to a beautiful, black Porsche 911 convertible. He exited the Explorer, thumbed the lock button on his keyless entry remote, the locking mechanism responding with a chirp, and stole an admiring glance at the Porsche as he headed for the door leading into the museum. Inside, on the third floor, he had to take one last pass at a security guard seated behind an unassuming desk, and then he made a right turn at the end of a short hall into the well-appointed waiting room.

"May I help you?" The petite, blond receptionist looked at Ferguson as he approached her desk.

Yes, I have an appointment with Courtney Lewis," said Ferguson cordially.

"Your name?"

"Matt Ferguson."

"Thank you!"

She dialed in an extension on the phone console and announced Ferguson to Courtney when she answered.

"She'll be with you in just a minute. You may have a seat if you like," motioning to the chairs and loveseats behind him.

Before he could find the time to locate a seat, Courtney Lewis emerged from the only hallway that led from the reception area.

"Good to see you again Matt!" Courtney smiled affectionately.

"Miss Lewis."

"Please, come on back to my office."

"Thank you," Ferguson dropped the magazine he had picked up on the coffee table in the waiting area and accompanied Courtney as she pivoted and retreated down the hall.

"Please hold my calls Joan."

They walked in silence past three offices and a conference room and entered the second to last door on the left. Courtney could feel the tension, and tried to break it as she offered him one of the two brown leather chairs that faced each other in front of the modest Queen Anne's desk. "Please, have a seat."

"May I shut the door?" Ferguson asked. "What I have to say should be in private," he reached for the door, while Courtney moved to seat herself in the other available chair.

"Absolutely. Should we sit?"

"If you'd like. What I have to say won't take long."

Courtney could feel the agitation in his voice. This meeting was not heading in the direction she was expecting. "Would you like something to drink...coffee, a soft drink?" She was grasping at anything to cut the tension that had settled in the air.

"Miss Lewis, up until twenty-four hours ago, there were only eight people that knew about the letter outlining the possible whereabouts, of what could potentially be one of the art world's find of a lifetime. One was my uncle, and he's dead. The second would be me. The third is an old professor, with no apparent knowledge of the artwork under consideration. The other five are you, your father, and his three associates, all with an accomplished understanding of art, and the impact that a discovery of this magnitude might generate.

"I mentioned twenty-four hours, because since then there is at least one other person who knows, and was willing to try and kill me to recover that letter."

Courtney's eyebrows rose, and a slight tinge of disbelief ran through her body. Before she could even respond, Ferguson pushed on.

"He was successful in obtaining a copy of one side of the letter, detailing the list of works, but not the map indicating the crash site. In the process of destroying quite a bit of my home and personal property, he damn near cut me in half," Ferguson's voice was beginning to rise with the anger that was returning, as he was reliving the previous night's episode.

"There are only six people that could have been responsible for leaking the contents of the letter, or deliberately orchestrating the theft of the letter itself. And I've come to the conclusion it wasn't Dr. Karl."

Courtney's jaw dropped, hung for an instant, and then returned to meet her top teeth in a clench, as she started to flush with anger.

"Wait just a damn minute. Are you accusing me of trying to arrange for someone to steal the letter from you, and have you knocked off in the process? You've lost your mind!"

Ferguson was slightly taken aback at the outburst. "Well explain to me then how a complete stranger breaks into my house and is after one thing and one thing only. How does he have any idea what to look for? And I'm having a real hard time pinning this one to the good professor."

"So, without a shred of evidence, you put the finger on me!" Courtney was livid. "I think it's time for you to leave!"

"Not until I find out if anyone else knows about the letter. I am not going anywhere until I get some answers from you as to whom you and your father spoke to. I would like to know more about Allen, Hancock and the other one's name. Who the hell were those folks, and why am I to believe your Dad when he says he trusts them? I want some answers, otherwise I'm going back to the police, tell them everything, and implicate you and your father."

"Paul Keeney is the other, and I haven't spoken to anyone!" However, before she could get the last word out, she realized that she did not know much about the other three. She also had taken her father at his word. Her wandering eyes gave her away.

"Who's the no one that you just remembered."

"It can't be…my dad wouldn't do anything like that."

"Your father?"

"He's an art expert, he knows history, and I can trust him to keep his mouth shut. He can't be responsible!" Courtney's anger was turning to anguish.

"Well if you're not responsible, and you believe your dad can keep the secret that narrows it down to his trusted friends."

Courtney knew her dad was not capable of something like this, and if she swore him to secrecy, he was certain to have abided by it. It has to be one of the others.

"Look, Matt you may not believe me, but I swear to you that I had nothing to do with the things you're accusing me of. I promise you that I spoke to no one else other than my father. And I know my father. There is no way in hell that he could be involved with this at all."

Ferguson was skeptical, but recognized the sincerity in Courtney's voice. "What do you know about the others?"

"Not enough. I have met Jason Allen before, several times as a matter of fact, and I know my Dad thinks highly of him. Paul Keeney and Sotheby's reputations are impeccable, and he's been there for years. AXA is well known and respected for their art insurance products. As for Mr. Hancock, I have never met or heard of him before. Listen, are you so damn certain that Dr. Karl may not have mentioned it to anyone else."

Ferguson was not certain. He just couldn't believe that Karl could be involved. However, he didn't contemplate the possibility of Karl inadvertently letting the information slip. Maybe Courtney was right. Either that, or she was a superb liar. There was only one way to find out. "Let's go see him!"

"Who, Dr. Karl?"

"Yeah. Both of us, you and me together. We'll find out from him what he knows. Somebody's responsible, and I want to find out who."

"That's fine with me. I have nothing to hide. I had nothing to do with this. What are you going to do even if you do find out who's responsible?"

"I'm going to threaten them with the police. I've already written a synopsis of the events that have transpired and I've indicated that the focus of attention be directed at all of you," Ferguson lied. He had no such written document at all. "And I can easily add Dr. Karl's name as well. I've placed it with my will in case anything happens," Ferguson lied again.

"Well, once again you have nothing to be afraid of from me. I swear to you that my father and I have nothing to do with your troubles. I'll be the first to admit, I'm very interested in the letter and the possible recovery of the art, but certainly not at the expense of stealing anything, much less trying to have you hurt. I don't know what I must have been thinking, but I was hoping your visit here today might lead to something more along the lines of an invitation to dinner, not an accusation of attempted murder."

For the first time, Ferguson felt that he might possibly have made a mistake. Maybe he had falsely accused her without analyzing all the facts and everyone else involved. Nevertheless, the fact remained that she was still one of only two original people he confided in, and she could still be lying through her teeth. The dinner comment was intriguing, he thought.

"Do you have time right now to visit Dr. Karl?" The mellowing of Ferguson's tone did not go unnoticed by both of them.

"I do. In fact, I'd welcome a visit to the professor," Courtney picked up her phone, punched in a three-digit extension and told the receptionist that she and Ferguson were going to step out for an hour or two.

With that, both of them rose, and without saying a word exited the museum and began the one-mile walk through campus to the Language Arts building.

# Chapter 8

*May 20, 2001. Louisville, Kentucky*

The Ford Crown Victoria slowed as it approached the cluster of emergency vehicles crowded into the driveway and front yard of the modest one-story ranch house on Grandview Avenue. Detective Toby Shutt maneuvered through the opening of gathered neighbors and bystanders, created by two uniformed Jefferson County police officers.

He parked behind one of the three police cruisers on the scene, killed the engine, and stepped out to greet one of several officers on the scene.

"Hello David. Looks like we got ourselves a mess here," Shutt addressed officer David Laise, who was shaking his head back and forth, as he flipped open a small steno pad in his left hand.

"I think you could say that, Lieutenant. This is a real cluster fuck," Laise replied.

"Lay it on me. Start with the victims."

"We've got three males, all Caucasian, all deceased by the time we arrived an hour ago. Two appear to be in their early twenties, the other is an older chap, in his late seventies. The house belongs to the older one."

Shutt turned and started to walk toward the front door, waving his hand at Laise to follow. "Keep talkin'."

"The old one appears to have been killed from a knife wound to the neck. The other two took single rounds each to the head, I'm guessing a mid-caliber handgun. They're all in the kitchen."

"What do you mean you're guessing?" The two of them entered the house.

"We can't find the gun. We have the knife. The positioning of the bodies," Laise paused, "it just doesn't look right."

"Somebody else?"

"That'd be my guess."

Toby Shutt had been on the Jefferson County police force for 22 years, the last six in homicide. This afternoon he was tired. He had not slept well again for the third night in a row and his partner had taken a personal day, which left him working his ass off at the station. He was starting to feel the effects of being in his forties. At 6'4", he was imposingly tall, but the once muscular frame had started to settle around his midsection. Between the rigors of police work, raising three children and dealing with a very demanding wife, he had no time left to take care of himself. He still had a full head of red hair, though, and a healthy, ruddy complexion to match.

The Jefferson County force, which had jurisdictional assignment to the suburban sections of the Louisville metropolitan area, did not encounter a significant number of homicides. The majority of the fifty or sixty murders annually in Jefferson County were committed in the city limits, and therefore, were covered by the City of Louisville police force. Nevertheless, Shutt was well respected in both agencies for his ability to detail and analyze a crime scene, and had a superior track record for solving crimes that took place in the county's jurisdiction.

There was nothing pleasant about a murder, especially a multiple murder. This one was no different. Shutt had learned to anesthetize himself to the grizzly scenes, and work as though there was no human element to the victims. Depending on the victims, that was either easy or very, very difficult. There was generally no gray area in between. His initial reaction to the two younger victims, as he entered the kitchen, was they looked like punks. He foresaw no problems getting emotional over this one.

The paradox was almost comical. There were people everywhere. Dusting everything in site, bagging anything that look suspicious or related to the crime, photographs being snapped from every direction, and three people lying dead, that could easily be mistaken for furniture.

There was no question there was another shooter, thought Shutt. The blood spray patterns on the two young males, the positioning of their bodies, led Shutt to conclude the shots came from where he was standing, on the other side of the kitchen table, just in from the foyer. The blood on one of the punk's hands, along with the proximity of a long stiletto-type knife just off his fingertips, was sure to confirm that the old man was probably killed by the one with the bandage on his face. *Why was that dude all bandaged up?*

Brian Crockett, from the coroner's office belatedly noticed Shutt as he entered the kitchen and began surveying the carnage. "Hey Toby, how goes it?"

"Good Brian and you?"

"No complaints, except I was hoping to play golf this afternoon. Don't think that's gonna happen now."

"Can you fix the time?"

"Earlier this morning, everything's still pretty fresh. I understand the witness outside saw these two arrive around eight. It had to happen shortly after that."

"Did you notice the patterns and entry wounds on those two?" Shutt pointed at Syron and Nieron.

"Yeah. You've got somebody else that did these two. The old man took a knife in the jugular; my guess would be from this poor slob," Crockett nodded his head in the direction of Syron, who still lay crumpled on the floor, a pool of dark, sticky blood surrounding his head. "Can we mark 'em and bag 'em?"

"Have at it," Shutt insisted.

The Language Arts building had only been a ten-minute walk-through campus from the museum, but the silence between the two had made the time pass much slower. By the time Courtney and Ferguson arrived the hallways were filled with students breaking from class.

Ferguson couldn't help but notice the eye contact and turning heads Courtney was receiving from most of the male twentysomething's as they shuffled out of the classrooms and down the halls.

They reached Dr. Karl's office, only to find it locked and no sign of lights or life inside. Without saying a word, Courtney looked diagonally down the hall, and without hesitation made off for the last door on the right in the corner.

"He's not here today, never showed up for class," said a cute little blond female mingling with a group by the water fountain.

"Thanks, did he give any reason?" Ferguson replied, quickly trying to catch up to Courtney.

"No. Nobody's heard from him," as she vanished in a sea of other students.

Courtney had already stepped into the open door, which yielded a small, silver-headed woman in her late-fifties or early-sixties, seated behind a congruence of metal desks and tables, busily typing on a computer while balancing a phone between her left shoulder and ear.

"Hi Ms. Day," Courtney whispered, bending over and offering a short wave with her right hand.

Beth Day let go of the phone with her shoulder and caught it with her left hand, replacing it in the cradle. "Hello Miss Lewis."

"Please Ms. Day, Courtney!"

"Only if you call me Beth!"

"Fair enough," Courtney conceded. "I didn't mean for you to hang up so abruptly."

"Oh, it's okay. I have been trying to raise Dr. Karl for the last several hours and I keep getting his internet answering machine. I already left him a message this morning, so I'm hanging up when it comes on."

"Is he at home?"

"No one knows. He did not show up for classes and he has not called in. I tried his cell phone too, but there's no answer. I'm beginning to get a little worried, he's never done anything like this."

"But you think he might be at home?"

"The line's busy, but I have no way of knowing for sure. I thought I might drive by there when I finish up here, but that will be another couple of hours. I need to wait on his three o'clock class in case he doesn't show up this afternoon."

"Well, I tell ya what," Courtney waved her hand back and forth between herself and Ferguson, "We need to talk to him ASAP, and I've been to his house on several occasions for tutoring, so we'll drive by there right now and report back to you what we find. How's that?"

"I sure would appreciate it Courtney. It's just not like him to miss classes without touching base with me," she scribbled a phone number down on a post-it-note and handed it to Courtney, "You can reach me at this number. Thanks."

"We'll be in touch."

*** 

The Taco Bell across the street from the Language Arts building could not have been a better coincidence for Carlos Garagua. He was beginning to get hungry just as Courtney Lewis and the young man accompanying her exited the museum on foot. The mode of transportation had caught him somewhat off guard, since he had expected her to leave via the parking garage in the sleek little Porsche.

Nevertheless, the diversion of following them on foot had allowed him to dash into the fast feeder for something to eat. He had just paid for his order as he turned to see the two of them exit the large red brick building, and head back the way they had come. He quickly grabbed a handful of hot sauce packets and napkins, rudely pushed through the people waiting in line, and hurried out the door as he tried to keep pace as discreetly as he could.

His surveillance took him back the same way he had come. Lewis and her companion re-entered the museum and Garagua returned to the rental car, parked in the fraternity row parking lot across the street, to relax and dispose of his now cold lunch. A brief conversation with Bolivar had provided directions to his location. He would be there within the next half hour to pick up the equipment and return to Lewis' apartment.

*** 

On the way back to the museum, it was mutually agreed upon, that since Ferguson's house was on the way to Dr. Karl's residence, they would follow each other to Ferguson's, leave his car there and drive on together in Courtney's car to visit Dr. Karl.

Ferguson was not surprised when they returned to the museum's parking garage that Courtney slipped into the well-polished, black

Porsche parked next to his Explorer. The car fit her personality perfectly...fast, sleek, beautiful, and expensive. Courtney knew where Elmwood Lane was, and instead of following Ferguson home, she turned over the 6-cylinder, 300 horsepower German engine, and by backing out before Ferguson could even get his door open, indicated she was going to lead. Ferguson shrugged indifferently, climbed behind the wheel, and managed to stay relatively close behind.

As she exited the garage and made a right turn onto Third Street, he emerged from the same exit and tried to catch up, figuring she knew the best way to I-65 from the museum. As he turned right in pursuit, a white Ford Taurus sedan, sitting across the street, hurriedly turned left in front of him, causing him to brake hard, and mutter a mild expletive at the "jerk" behind the wheel.

It took him until the Zorn Avenue exit, almost eight miles from the museum and only a few miles from his house to pull up behind her. When they reached Elmwood Lane, she pulled over and allowed him to lead them to his home halfway down the first block. Neither one of them noticed the white Taurus pull onto the street behind them and drive on past as Ferguson led Courtney into his driveway.

Securing his car in the garage, Ferguson returned to the Porsche, and the two of them headed for Dr. Karl's. A considerable distance away, Garagua's Taurus had turned around and was headed back to resume the tail. Pulling out behind him was a black, Ford Crown Victoria adding to the procession of cars following one another.

Garagua keyed the one-way phone and spoke. "Julio?"

"I hear you Carlos. What's up?"

"Just checking in. The girl has gone from the museum, to a walk around the campus, back to the museum, to a man's house over on the northeast side of town, and I am now following this man and Miss

Lewis in her car to God knows where. We're headed further east on Brownsboro Road. She's a busy little bitch."

"I don't care where she goes Carlos, keep with her and keep in touch if anything suspicious comes up. I'll relieve you when she comes home."

"I hear you boss. I'll touch base with you later."

***

Dr. Karl's was less than ten minutes away. The horde of police, emergency and crime scene vehicles were still there as Courtney and Ferguson pulled up to the yellow "Police" tape stretched in every direction in front of Dr. Karl's yard, driveway and portions of the street. They both looked at each other simultaneously, and without saying a word, conveyed the concern and confusion that was starting to infect both of them.

They exited the car together and approached the closest officer to them, who was chatting with some of the onlookers that refused to go away.

"Excuse me officer," Courtney interrupted, "What's the problem here? Is Dr. Karl alright?"

"We've got a triple homicide miss, that's the problem. Do you know the owner of the house?" the young officer replied, beginning to feel the exhaustion of the day creeping in.

"Pardon me officer, maybe I can help here," Shutt broke in as he was making his way back to his car and overheard the inquiry. "I'm detective Shutt. Did I understand you knew Mr. Karl?"

"I know a Dr. Karl," responded Courtney.

"I'm sorry Miss...?" Shutt fished for a name.

"Lewis. My name's Courtney Lewis."

"And you're Mr. Lewis?" Shutt glanced at Ferguson.

"No. I'm just a friend of Courtney's," Ferguson held out his hand, "Matt Ferguson."

Shutt shook his hand and then extended it to Courtney who returned the favor. "I'm afraid you knew him. He's deceased."

"What happened?" Courtney persisted.

"We don't have all of the facts Miss Lewis, but we do know that he was murdered. How do you know Mr., excuse me Dr. Karl?"

"I was a student of his. He's a professor at U of L."

"I see. And how did you know where his home is?"

"I'm not a student at U of L. I am an assistant curator at the Speed Art Museum. Dr. Karl was tutoring me in German. Sometimes it was more convenient for him to tutor me after work hours, which often meant I came to his house."

Shutt shook his head in affirmation and turned to Ferguson, "And did you know him?"

"No, I'm just accompanying Courtney. She...we went to see him at his office on campus and he had not shown up. So, she volunteered to drive out to his house to check up on him."

"Volunteered to whom?"

"His secretary," Courtney declared as she was dialing the number from Beth Day on her cell phone. "I'm going to let her know what's happening." As Beth came on the line, Courtney turned and walked away for some privacy as she relayed the horrible news.

Shutt, pulled a pack of Marlboro Lights from inside his coat pocket, tapped one out, and gestured to Ferguson, who declined. By the time he had it lit, Courtney had returned.

"That wasn't very pleasant!"

"No, I'm sure it wasn't. Do you mind if I ask a few more questions?" Shutt persisted.

"I'm not really sure how much more I can tell you about Dr. Karl. I didn't know him that well," Courtney was beginning to get agitated.

"I'll be very brief," Shutt pulled out his notepad and scribbled both Courtney's and Ferguson's names onto a blank page. "Did you know if he had any immediate family, or have you met any of his friends, acquaintances, significant others, girlfriends, boyfriends, you name it?"

Courtney's patience was thinning out rapidly, and Ferguson was feeling very uneasy about the "twenty questions" Shutt was continuing with. They both looked at each other and then back at Shutt.

Courtney took the lead, "Look, Matt has no clue who the guy is, and I told you I don't know the man other than him teaching me the German language. That's it! I don't know anything about his family, friends, his habits, behavior, or even his sex life. I do know that his secretary, who I just spoke to on the phone, probably can tell you volumes about him. You can reach her at this number at U of L" Courtney handed over Beth Day's phone number to Shutt, who flipped closed the notepad and took the folded piece of paper.

Ferguson stepped forward and lied, "I really need to get back to the office, Courtney. Detective Shutt, if you don't mind, we need to be going."

"Certainly, I understand," Shutt retrieved two business cards from inside his coat pocket and handed one each to Courtney and Ferguson. "If there's anything that comes to mind about the good doctor that you think would assist me in my investigation, would you please give me a call."

They both shook their heads politely in unison as they received the cards. Courtney reached out and took Ferguson's arm in her hand, which was just enough of a prompt for Ferguson to turn the two of them around and head back towards the car. They got in and drove away as Shutt glanced back before entering his own car, to watch them disappear down the street.

Courtney was the first to speak, turning on to Herr Lane as they exited Dr. Karl's neighborhood. "This is starting to get a little scary."

Ferguson grunted a "yeah". He was preoccupied with staring into the rear-view mirror; his suspicions confirmed when they came to a stop before making the turn.

As they had left the scene at Karl's house, he had noticed, what appeared to be the same white Taurus and driver that he had nearly run into at the museum. While they negotiated their way out of the neighborhood, he had kept his eyes glued to the mirror, but with no Taurus immediately in sight. However, there he was, just enough distance to keep up, but not clearly noticeable.

"Are you alright?" Courtney glimpsed over her shoulder.

"Pull in the Chevron station up there, let's get some gas."

Courtney looked at her gas gauge. "I don't need any gas."

"Pull in the gas station damn it!"

Courtney dispensed with the blinker and swerved hard left, bouncing hard against the change in pavement and pulled up to the self-serve pumps and slammed on her brakes. "I've about had enough of all this bullshit today. What the hell is so important about getting gas?"

Ferguson looked her hard in the eyes. "I think we're being followed. Ever since we left the museum." Out of the corner of his eye, he subtly followed the Taurus as it drove past the station entrance. While he emerged from the car and walked over to the pump, he noticed it pull in the adjacent parking lot, circling around to the exit of the fruit market next door. *Shit!*

"We definitely have company," Ferguson walked back to Courtney, who was still seated behind the wheel. "Turn it off and I'll put a little gas in it."

Courtney was dumbfounded. She switched off the ignition and stared at Ferguson. "Which one is it?"

"He's in a white Taurus, parked in Paul's Market next door. Don't make it obvious!"

"I won't!" Courtney climbed out of the car and headed into the station's market. She looked casually around in several directions, easily noticing their tail nearby. She returned a few minutes later with a coke and package of Sugar Babies. "Put five dollars of premium in. What do we do when we leave?"

"I don't know. The question is who's he following and why?" Ferguson looked warily at Courtney as she re-entered the car.

"Oh, let me guess, I'm a suspect again. He's my henchman, operating on instructions from me."

"I didn't say that." There was a long pause, "What if he's after you?"

Suddenly, a small alarm went off in Courtney's brain. A dreadful feeling of fear started to creep over her, and the consternation showed on her face as well.

"I didn't mean to frighten you, but with what happened to me, the murder of Dr. Karl, who knows, this whole thing is getting very weird and way out of hand."

Courtney broke down. "Matt, I swear to you...I promise you I've had nothing to do with any of this. Your attack, Dr. Karl's murder, I have no idea what's going on either."

Ferguson got back in the car. "Let's do this. Take me home. You drop me off and head to Azalea's restaurant on Brownsboro Road. It's just down the street from my house. You know the place?" Courtney nodded affirmatively. "Good. "I'll lag behind for a few minutes and follow you up there. Either I'll catch him following you, or he will still be with me. Okay?"

Courtney nodded again, started the car, pulled out towards Brownsboro Road, and both of them watched in their mirrors as the white Taurus again fell in line several cars behind them. The black Ford sedan, two cars behind Garagua, was oblivious to all of them.

***

Mr. Jones had been waiting outside Ferguson's house shortly after he had left the bloodletting at Karl's. He had switched automobiles. The light blue Mercury Marquis he had been driving at the time of the shootings was headed to a local chop shop, where it was destined to lose its identity. The black Crown Victoria was benign in appearance.

Hoping for an opportunity to search Ferguson's home for the missing portion of the letter, he knew he had to catch Ferguson when he returned to complete what the two morons he had hired had not been able to accomplish. However, he had not expected Ferguson to return home as soon as he did, nor to merely drop off his vehicle and leave with the lovely Miss Lewis. His interest piqued, Jones followed Courtney and Ferguson, and was curiously surprised when they went to Karl's.

When they returned to Ferguson's house, he had visions of the two of them entering Ferguson's, giving him a golden opportunity to confront the two of them, discover the whereabouts of the original letter and disposing of both. However, he watched with dismay as Courtney pulled into the driveway and let Ferguson out.

Jones decided he would go for Ferguson now and deal with Courtney later. He pulled beyond Ferguson's house and parked his car in the driveway of a vacant house for sale on Brookfield, which ran parallel to Elmwood, one street over. He stepped out of the car fully dressed in jogging shorts, t-shirt and a well-worn pair of Nike running shoes. Tucking his silenced Walther into the holster beneath his shirt, he took off jogging around the corner of St. Matthews Avenue and down Elmwood.

He was approaching the house when Ferguson came down the driveway in his Explorer, pulled into the street and sped away. *Damn! Well, I'll search the house while he's gone, and deal with him later.*

Jones continued jogging up to the end of the street, circled and came back the same way, darting up Ferguson's driveway, while he scanned for any inquisitive neighbors. He hopped the fence and pulled out a lock pick from inside his sock. He entered the house and shut the door behind him.

*** 

Garagua was beginning to get annoyed at the amount of activity involved in tailing Courtney Lewis. He had envisioned a nice long afternoon at the museum, followed by a return to her condo. In reality, he had covered half of the east end of Louisville and she was not finished yet.

Having just dropped off her male companion for the afternoon, she was headed home, or that's what he thought. A few miles from her last stop, she pulled into a restaurant, parked, and proceeded to go inside. Garagua pulled in past her and parked in the back lot of the restaurant.

He gave her a few minutes and then entered through a rear entrance, sat down at the bar and watched as she ordered a drink five stools down from where he ordered a Margarita on the rocks. He asked for a menu, in case she decided to stay for dinner.

Five minutes later, the same young man from the afternoon showed up and they were delivered to a table on the outdoor brick patio. He shuffled down a few seats at the bar for a better view outside, ordered an appetizer and another drink, and settled down for a couple hours of down time.

***

After being seated and ordering a couple of cocktails, Ferguson responded to Courtney's anguished expression. "He's following you."

"Shit! What in the hell does he want with me? Where is he?"

"I'm not sure, but I think he might be the south-of-the-border dude sitting at the end of the bar, or the blond guy in the camel hair sport coat sitting by himself in the first booth as you go in the door." There was a lengthy silence, "I haven't a clue what they want with you. Are you sure you didn't reveal any of this to someone else, even inadvertently?"

"Not a soul!"

"But your dad and the others knew."

"Yeah, but I told you dad wouldn't say anything. I specifically told him to keep it quiet. When I first called him, I told pretty much everything I knew," Courtney's voice trailed off as she realized what he was thinking. "He might have trusted those details to Allen, Hancock and Keeney, but I'm telling you, no one else. Look, I can call him right now and find out who knows what."

"Well, at this point it doesn't matter how somebody's found out. The problem we have is somebody knows all about it. The letter, the contents, the whole thing."

"But they don't have the map. They don't know where the crash site is. That's why they're after...me...you...both of us."

The waiter interrupted their revelation. He lifted two very chilled glasses from his tray and placed an Absolut Martini with two olives and a Maker's Mark Manhattan with a like number of cherries on the table. They both ordered the pasta special, and Ferguson added a bottle of Blackstone merlot. They decided to split a Caesar salad. They sat in silence for the next few minutes, sipping the straight-up mixtures of pure alcohol, adding to the state of numbness their bodies had contracted as a result of the day's events.

Ferguson knew what he was about to say to Courtney would not help her mental condition. Nevertheless, he realized if she was telling the truth about her innocence, she was probably in as much immediate danger as he was, and unfortunately, as much as Dr. Karl had been.

Someone, or some people, extremely dangerous and very ruthless, had acquired enough information and knowledge to understand the potentially enormous rewards for finding any, or all of this lost treasure. Moreover, their intentions appeared to be to get it, if any of "it" still existed, at all costs.

"Courtney, I know you probably don't want to hear any of this, but I think you might be in some serious danger. Is there anywhere you can go? Someplace you can hide...somewhere nobody, or only a few people might know about?"

"I've been sitting here thinking the same thing. I don't really have any place in particular to go. I guess I could go to a hotel, or out of town. Hell, maybe I should take a vacation somewhere far away."

"I'm talkin' about immediately...tonight!"

"No. But if I rack my brain over dinner, I'm sure I can come up with something."

"Well, I've got an idea. There's a place I know about, I think both of us can probably hide out for the next day or two. That should give you enough time to figure out somewhere to get away to."

"What about you?" Courtney asked.

"I'm headed to Switzerland. I'm going to personally check this thing out to see if there's any validity to this whole mess."

Courtney did not like that answer, but looked away without saying a word. She wasn't keen on the idea of being involved in this thing up to her eyeballs, and being told to get lost while Matt goes off trying to solve this mystery. She could help him resolve this nightmare faster than if he tackled it on his own.

"I want to go with you," she blurted out.

Ferguson froze with his drink at his lips. "Where?"

"Switzerland."

"No way!"

"Yes way!" Courtney leaned over the table and stared him straight in the eye. "I can help you!"

"You're not going with me to Switzerland. That's final!"

"Give me one good reason."

"They're too numerous to mention," chuckled Ferguson.

"That's because you don't have one."

Ferguson was trying to come up with one good reason. He knew if he spoke impulsively, the first thing out of his mouth would be that he did not trust her. However, the better part of reason took over, and he said nothing. He barely knew this girl, albeit that she was incredibly attractive and obviously quite intelligent. Nevertheless, that was not enough to convince him to take her along. Still he could not disagree with her; he really did not have any other concrete reasons. "You're not going." That effectively ended the conversation until dinner arrived.

*** 

Quietly closing the door behind him, Mr. Jones slipped out the back of Ferguson's home, and ran down the driveway and out into the street as if he had been jogging for miles. After thoroughly searching the house, he had found nothing remotely related to the letter, or any other shred of information that might provide some clues to where the letter might be. He concluded it was best to get back to his car and move on before a nosy neighbor thought to inquire about an unfamiliar vehicle that was in the driveway of an unoccupied house.

It was time to visit Courtney Lewis's apartment he thought. Between the two of them they had to have something he could go on, and she might be less inclined to be more cautious at this point. Nothing had happened to her to alert her suspicions. If anything, he could surprise her, or better yet wait for her inside her place without alarming anyone. Additionally, he reasoned, if there was any love interest between the two, she might be just the ticket, with a little coercion, to persuade Ferguson to produce the letter. The complete letter. He felt no regret that he would still have to dispose of the two of them.

***

The pasta, even though heavy on the garlic, was excellent. Ferguson kept the bottle of wine flowing and immediately changed the subject of conversation to an inquiry about Courtney's life history. She had accommodated the change in dialogue quite nicely, and they spent the next thirty minutes in a very pleasant discourse, actually getting to know a lot about each other.

They split a cheesecake with fresh raspberries, and both ordered coffee, with Ferguson spiking his with a shot of Amaretto. Reality returned to the table.

"Do you know the name of the woman I inherited the letter from?" Ferguson asked.

"I haven't the slightest idea who she is or what her name is."

Ferguson was almost certain that he had never mentioned Uncle Max's name to either Karl or Courtney, and the fact that Courtney did not correct the reference to a female, was enough to convince him completely.

"I have an idea where we can go for the next couple of days to help sort out where we go from here," said Ferguson.

"I say, where we go from here, is to Switzerland. The two of us," Courtney responded.

Ferguson was not about to get into that discussion again. "We can discuss that matter further, but first we need to get to someplace safe, where whoever is after us can't find us."

"What about our company up at the bar?" Courtney discreetly shifted her eyes toward the bar to make sure their 'friend' had not vanished. It was obvious now; the only guy who hadn't moved for the last hour was the Hispanic fellow. Unfortunately, he was still there.

"We need to lose him, and I've got another thought on that as well. First, we both need to get a change of clothes, and then we can disappear. I will leave, while you stay and have another drink. I'll run home, throw some clothes together, and come back here. We'll leave from here, go to your house, and get you some things for the next couple of days. In fact, you might want to get enough to cover you for longer."

"You know, you were right. It's the Mexican-looking guy, he's still at the bar. Are we going to let him tag along?"

"Yeah I noticed he hadn't left. Once we leave your place, we'll go in my car. At some point we'll take a four-wheel-drive detour that he can't handle. That should fix him," Ferguson pushed himself away from the table, "Can you pick up dinner?"

"It'll be my pleasure."

"Thank you 'me lady'," Ferguson bowed his head. Do you have a cell phone?"

"Yeah, it's in my purse," Courtney retrieved her purse and rummaged through it for the phone and a business card. "Here's a business card, the number is on it."

"Thanks, keep it on. I'll call you in about twenty minutes when I'm headed back."

"You're coming back, right?" Courtney got the sudden suspicion of an abandonment coming on.

"In the words of General MacArthur, I shall return," Ferguson stood up from the table. "He looked intently into Courtney's beautiful green eyes, "I promise!"

\*\*\*

The young man left the table and then walked out of the restaurant. Garagua saw the check delivered to the table, but Courtney Lewis appeared to be perfectly happy to remain in her seat, and in no hurry to leave. In fact, the waiter returned with more coffee and a cordial glass of liqueur.

His dinner of grilled salmon had been superb, and the Margaritas had left Garagua more than relaxed. He was glad to see she was in no hurry to bolt. At this point of the evening, he figured when she decided to leave, she was headed home. That meant when she got back to her place, he could pass her off to the boss for the evening, and get some shuteye.

He and Bolivar had gotten almost no rest from the time Rocca had summoned them yesterday evening until now. They had hit the ground running ever since the Rocca International Gulfstream #3 had touched down at Louisville International airport early that morning. There was time on the flight to gather and assimilate enough information on Courtney Lewis to get them started on the basic surveillance, which they had managed to accomplish earlier in the day. That had allowed Bolivar time to do more in-depth research on Ms. Lewis, while Garagua had been following her to work and beyond.

That research had netted them credit card numbers, bank and investment account information, club and organization affiliations, and other specific personal data that Bolivar loaded into his laptop and processed through a proprietary database software that created a comprehensive profile of Courtney Lewis and a history of her activities for the last few years.

Garagua knew that program had probably been completed earlier, and that Bolivar had most of the late afternoon and evening to relax and catch up on his own sleep. Soon it would be his turn to trade off, and get enough sleep to tide him over. It did not require much to keep him going, but at this point, his tank was empty.

***

Ferguson had no idea of what to pack for Switzerland in May. He did know, he would undoubtedly be in the mountains, so he prepared his clothing selections accordingly. As he hastily stacked clothes on his bed, he wasn't sure, but something was just not right. He stopped, listened for a few seconds, looked around the room, and then shook his head as if he was certain he was going crazy.

He stuffed everything he laid out into a Rossignol oversize, ski duffle bag, and added what was left on hangers to an L.L. Bean garment travel bag. He froze again, and had an inexplicable feeling he was being watched, or that something was not as it should be. He thought his paranoia was starting to get out of hand. Nevertheless, paranoia or not, it was time for him to get out of this house for a while. He shut down all the lights that weren't on timers, he turned the thermostat to 'off', picked up the two bags, and warily peeked into the garage before scurrying to his car. He was in and out of the house in less than fifteen minutes. He would be back to Courtney in another five.

# Chapter 9

## *May 20, 2001. Louisville, Kentucky*

Toby Shutt was finishing off the last vestiges of black coffee in his University of Kentucky plastic thermos. He made a mental note that he would have to fill it up one more time to keep him going through the paperwork that had consumed him since returning to the station. The reports, write-ups and never-ending documentation that had to be accounted for in any investigation, let alone a triple homicide, never ceased to amaze him. It had been a long day.

Unfortunately, after the paper trail was finished and filed, the real job of detective work began. It was going to be an even longer day.

Detective Shawna Hammer, the newest, and first black female detective in the Homicide Division, stepped into Shutt's cubicle and dropped a large 9 x 12 manila envelope into his *IN* box. "I.D.'s and bio's on the deceased and preliminary crime scene results from Forensics. You can thank Danny for putting it together so fast."

"Thanks for dropping it off."

"My pleasure. If there's anything I can help you with, let me know."

"Thanks Shawna, I will. If you don't mind, can you drop these off with Michelle and tell her to file these, and put these with the evidence boxes?"

Shawna grabbed the two stacks of files from Shutt's outstretched hands, nodded and walked away. She respected Shutt and appreciated how he had treated her with the same respect ever since she had hit the ground running two months ago. However, she was also cognizant of, and resented the impression that many of the other detectives had, that she was merely a product of affirmative action fulfilled. The reality was, she was a damn good cop, and hers was a well-deserved merit promotion.

Shutt moved everything in the middle of his desk off to the side, and proceeded to spill the contents of the envelope in front of him. There were three tabbed file folders, each labeled by last name, then first. Inside each folder was whatever Danny Woods, the JCPD's resident computer wizard, had been able to scrounge up from his amazing electronic investigative skills. He started with the folder marked *Karl, Johann, PhD.*

He scanned over the faxes and reproductions of info from the Department of Motor Vehicles, the U of L Faculty Directory, Social Security Administration, a credit history report, and bank loan and mortgage applications. He settled on a resume with a single page of handwritten notes from Danny paper clipped on top.

Shutt took in the highlights: *Emigrated to U.S. in 1947 from Munich, Germany. Graduated from University of Pennsylvania in 1950. Graduate studies at Ohio State. A PhD in 1956. Teaching assistant while going to school. Came to University of Louisville in 1962 to teach German and European History. Wound up Dean of the College. Impressive service! He's an old fart. No wife, no kids.*

He referred to Danny's observations in the notes of no immediate next of kin, and a concern that his cursory search of some available

German database had turned up no record of a Johann Manfred Karl in Munich, or anywhere else for that matter, that came close to the age of the deceased. He reckoned, that given the timing of the date he left Germany, that it would not have been unusual for a former German soldier or Nazi party member that settled outside of Germany to change their name or identity. He speculated that Karl could have been either, or records of him could have easily been destroyed in the war.

The other two files were rubber banded together, again with a note from Danny.

*These two were easy! Their prints were on file. Both of these clowns are real winners! I'm not sure it means anything, but these two have some history with anti-Semitic and Neo-Nazi groups. You might check out an Aryan race or Nazi connection?*

*Danny*

Again, Shutt perused the rap sheets and history of Jimmy Syron and Jay Nieron. Typical dead-end backgrounds. Neither one finished high school. The obvious drug involvement, followed by a long list of misdemeanors, and finally the prison-time felony. Both did time in Eddyville Penitentiary, were paroled, and began affiliations with a long list of undesirables. *Blah, blah, blah...Losers!*

The forensics and ballistics reports were the last of the paperwork in the file. It simply confirmed what he had deduced from his visual of the crime scene. The slugs pulled from Syron and Nieron did not match either one of the guns they were carrying, and in fact neither of those weapons had been fired. The stiletto was responsible for the neck wound to Karl, which had caused his death. Prints lifted from the handle of the knife belonged to Syron. Shutt tapped his fingers on the open file, drew a deep breath, and while exhaling looked up, staring blankly at the wall in front of him as if drawing some divine inspiration. *For reasons unknown, Syron killed Karl, and then was systematically shot, along with Nieron; by a third party that appeared to know what he was doing when it came to firing a handgun.*

Shawna stuck her head into the cubicle again, interrupting Shutt's train of thought, causing him to unconsciously close up the folders in front of him. "By the way I forgot to tell you before, we cross-matched prints on one of your 'stiffs', Jimmy Syron. His prints were on a knife recovered from a botched robbery attempt in the east end earlier this week; a house off Chenoweth Lane. The description on that blade is similar to the one we found on him at the Karl house. The victim, he actually fought off this Syron character, was a guy by the name of..." she glanced at a sheet of paper she was carrying in her right hand, "Ferguson. That's it, Matt Ferguson," she nodded affirmatively and walked away.

It took a few seconds to register, but the mental image of the young man, in the street in front of Dr. Karl's house, reaching out to shake his hand, materialized clearly in his memory... *"I'm just a friend of Courtney's. Matt Ferguson."*

*Bingo!*

"Shawna!" Shutt yelled out. No answer.

He picked up the phone and dialed an extension. "Hello sergeant, Toby Shutt in Homicide. Yeah, you can help. There was a robbery earlier this week at the home of a Matt Ferguson, somewhere off Chenoweth Lane in the St. Matthews area. Right! Can you have the file forwarded to me as soon as possible? Yep! Toby Shutt. Thank you, sergeant."

\*\*\*

Courtney was enjoying the peace and quiet of being alone for the first time since this morning. She felt perfectly safe in the crowded restaurant, and the alcohol was achieving its desired results. She had already taken care of the bill, tipping the waiter handsomely while asking, and receiving permission, to languish at the table for another ten to fifteen minutes.

The cell phone was barely audible as it rang inside her purse. She answered on the fourth ring. "Matt?"

"Yeah, I'm pulling up in the parking lot right now."

"Alright, meet me at the back entrance. I want to pass right by this joker on the way out."

"Don't do anything stupid Courtney!"

"I'm not. I'll see you out back."

Courtney took one last sip of her coffee, stood up, grabbed her purse, and headed up the patio steps into the main dining room. She walked past the hostess' desk and right at Carlos Garagua who was hurriedly paying his bill with the bartender.

She intentionally appeared to stumble and fell into a well-dressed young man, who, after a murderous day at the office, was enjoying his third beer of the evening with three of his buddies. The majority of that third beer capsized strategically onto Garagua's lap, while Courtney was dramatically apologizing to the young executive, and then in turn to Garagua.

She started to reach into her purse, "I'm so sorry! Please let me pay for everyone's tab."

The young man, obviously infatuated with the beautiful young woman who had fallen in his lap, laughed aloud, and then ignoring the beer-drenched man beside him, politely looked at Courtney, "Are you okay? You didn't hurt yourself?"

"No, I'm fine thanks." She looked at Garagua and without a hint of the intended sarcasm said, "I'm really very sorry!"

Again, the young man deflected the apology. "We're fine. Really we are." He looked at Garagua and winked.

Garagua stood up and was mopping his pants and jacket with a towel offered by the bartender. "Everything's alright Señorita, nothing that can't be cleaned." He was trying not to look at Courtney, going out of his way not to give her a clear shot of his face.

"See, no harm no foul. Put your money away. In fact, what are you drinking?" The young man snapped his fingers at the bartender. "What can we get ya?"

"I'm so embarrassed! I am actually leaving. I'm late for an appointment. Thank you for the offer."

The disappointment was obvious on the face of the young man, as Courtney quickly closed her purse and started for the back door. She stopped abruptly and stepped back to give him a one-armed hug, and then a kiss on the cheek. "Thank you for the offer, but you've done quite enough, thanks!"

She could hear the razzing the young man was taking from his pals as she walked out the back door, up the stairs, and climbed into the car with Ferguson.

\*\*\*

*Shit! The stupid bitch!* Garagua threw the towel back at the bartender and shoved his way through the yuppie happy hour. He reached the back door in time to see the same *Explorer* from this afternoon drive off with Courtney in the passenger seat.

He bolted out the door and headed quickly for his car as he watched the SUV circle the back parking lot and head for the exit onto Brownsboro Road. He pulled out of his parking space and fell in behind them, turning on his headlights to disguise himself in their mirror. *Shit! Shit! Shit! I smell like a fucking brewery.*

Garagua did not get a good look at the driver, but he was convinced it was the same guy she had been with earlier in the day. It certainly was the same car. He followed them west down Brownsboro Road, until they turned north onto Zorn Avenue. A half mile down Zorn they both turned west again and climbed the ramp up to Interstate 71 headed for downtown.

***

"This is gonna be fun!" Ferguson scooted his butt back and forth in his seat, settling himself deep into the leather. "You might want to brace yourself," Ferguson smiled at Courtney, "we're going to do a little lane jumping."

Courtney mimicked the same movement with her derriere and grabbed the armrests with both hands.

Ferguson reached for the dashboard and turned the switch from two-wheel drive to four-wheel drive, waited for the automatic conversion to take place, and scanned the grass median ahead to locate the deepest and steepest slope he could find. He slowed down gradually from about 70 miles per hour to 60 without applying his brakes, found the spot he was looking for and removed his foot from the accelerator. They slowed further, and at the moment the white Taurus was within a few car links, Ferguson braked hard, yanked to the left on the steering wheel, and dove into the grass and down the embankment.

It was a severe depression, but the four wheels powered the Explorer down and then up to the other side of the Interstate with very little difficulty. Ferguson drove along the edge until the oncoming traffic raced by, and then accelerated onto the main road and into the right lane, the grass and mud thumping against the wheel wells as it released from the tires. By the time he returned the switch to two-wheel drive, they had reached the eastbound Zorn Avenue exit, where Ferguson immediately veered off the interstate and down the ramp that led back to Zorn Avenue.

Ferguson and Courtney maintained eye contact with Garagua through the whole process, and once they had safely reached the bottom of the exit ramp, looked at each other and burst out laughing hysterically. They reached her apartment in less than ten minutes.

***

It took Garagua twenty minutes. The next exit off I-71wasn't for another two miles when he reached the downtown Louisville riverfront area, where 71, I-64, and I-65 all converged in a morass of asphalt ramps, exits, bridges and interchanges, locally referred to as "Spaghetti Junction". It was no coincidence he got hopelessly confused and wound up on the streets of the central business district.

During his exploration of the downtown area, he had placed an angry and embarrassed phone call to Bolivar, recounting the latest developments in his bungled surveillance of Miss Lewis. However, before he could finish explaining the details, she and her four-wheel driving companion had just showed up at her apartment, much to the delight of Bolivar, and much to the relief of Garagua.

From the alley across the street from the Willow's garage and main entrances, Bolivar recognized the Ford Explorer from Garagua's description, and watched as it parked in the visitor's parking area and Courtney and Ferguson emerged and entered the tower. He leaned over to examine the electronic gear he had loaded in the front seat and made sure it was operational. He started the small recorder, reclined his seat, put on a pair of padded headphones, leaned back and closed his eyes.

When Garagua arrived, he parked down the same alley, but well out of direct site of the front entrance. He strolled over to the Concorde, tapped lightly on the passenger-side window. Bolivar motioned for him to get in the back seat and electronically unlocked the doors.

"Sorry amigo!" Garagua apologized as he climbed in back, the doors locking behind him.

"No harm, we still have her, but they're in a hurry. I heard them when they first came in. They've guessed correctly, that if you've been tracking her this long, you might know where she lives."

"What are they doing?"

"She's packing. Other than that, I haven't heard anything said between the two of them for a while. They appeared to be arguing earlier. Something about going somewhere, she says 'yes', and he says 'no'."

"Well, if we have to follow them again, we need to take this car. They've seen the other one."

Bolivar adjusted the headphones and pulled his seat back up. "I'll take 'em. You can get some rest. You smell like a frickin' six-pack. I thought I told you to keep the drinking to a minimum when you're working!"

"I only had two margaritas; the beer was compliments of the young lady. She spilled it all over me, the little bitch!" Garagua gestured toward the Willows tower.

They both chuckled in unison. Neither paid any attention to the dark green Lincoln that also pulled into the visitor's lot.

***

Courtney pulled her passport out of the dresser drawer and tossed it on top of the clothes neatly stacked in the suitcase spread open on the bed. She paused briefly, grabbing her chin with her thumb and forefinger, glanced around the room and into her closet, and then nodded in confirmation that she had everything she needed.

She was in a hurry, but she had managed to get two suitcases strategically packed, along with a large, black shoulder bag full of cosmetics, toiletries, and jewelry. She looked every bit the pack mule as she dragged all three items out of her bedroom and into the main living area.

Ferguson had spent the fifteen minutes she had taken to pack to wander around the apartment in amazement at all the art and sculpture scattered throughout the room and on the walls. He was staring at the large bronze nudes when she emerged.

Courtney gave an exaggerated clearing of her throat, "Excuse me, can I get a little help over here?"

"Sorry!" Ferguson turned and walked to her grabbing both suitcases from her hands. "I was admiring all the artwork, it's spectacular!"

"Thanks, but only a few of them really fit that bill. The others are some mid-level works, and the oil over the fireplace is from a relatively unknown artist as a birthday gift."

"That's funny, I rather liked that one the most," Ferguson embarrassingly admitted.

"Me too!" Courtney replied. "It's actually my favorite. Its value is purely sentimental though. I'm still trying to get him on the map."

"Are you ready to go?"

"Yeah, I think I've got enough to hold me. If I get desperate, I'll go shopping."

Ferguson picked up the two suitcases, while Courtney went to an elaborate control panel on the wall. She punched in a variety of commands on the keyboard, while several of the lights around the room dimmed or shut off completely. She turned to see Ferguson at the front door waiting, picked up the shoulder bag and walked to the alarm panel next to the door.

As she opened the door to let him out, she programmed the alarm system and followed him through, locking the door behind them.

***

The security guard, all 5'3" and 135 pounds soaking wet, leaned up from his reclined position behind the reception desk to greet the stranger that had entered the Willow's lobby area. He casually deposited the latest issue of Hustler magazine in the top drawer of the desk and took a quick look at the bank of video monitors, as if to give the appearance that he was in charge and quite important in his position of authority.

"Can I help you?"

"Yes, I'm detective Warren Steele. I'm investigating a homicide, and I need to speak with a Miss Courtney Lewis. Could you please tell me which apartment she's in?" He obligingly removed a leather wallet from the breast pocket of his sport coat and flashed a detective's badge at the guard.

"Miss Lewis' apartment is on the ninth floor, number 901. I'll ring her and let her know you're comin', I just saw her come in about a half hour ago."

"That's not necessary, she's expecting me."

"Well, Mr. Steele, I'm supposed to check with our residents before I let anybody—"

"I said that won't be necessary," he interrupted; snapping shut the wallet, his eyes meeting those of the guard, who got the message loud and clear.

"Yes sir, detective."

Directed to the elevators, he entered the open car and pressed the brass button with the number nine. The elevator smoothly ascended the nine floors and with a subtle ding, opened up to a beautifully appointed anteroom that had two hallways leading off in opposite directions. He took the one to the left that had a brass plate that read '901-903' with an arrow guiding him down the hall. Much to his surprise, Courtney Lewis and Matt Ferguson were at the other end of the same hall headed directly at him.

"Excuse me, Miss Lewis?"

Courtney and Ferguson stopped in the hallway, just down from her door. "Yes. Who's asking?"

"My name's Warren Steele. I'm a detective with J.C.P. homicide." Once again, he displayed the badge, "I need a word with you please."

"I'm headed out of town detective, and I'm already late for my flight," Courtney lied. "Can we not do this in a few days when I return?"

"Now Miss Lewis! Let's step back into your apartment please."

"Detective, are you sure we can't do this at a later date?" Ferguson asked.

"I don't know who you are, but this is none of your business. On second thought, I'd like to speak to you, too. Both of you step inside."

The three of them re-entered Courtney's apartment. After Courtney switched off the alarm and Ferguson deposited the bags by the door, they both turned around to find Mr. Jones staring at them with the barrel of the Walther PPK, silencer enhanced, waving at them in a motion toward the center of the room.

Instinctively Courtney and Ferguson lifted their arms in the air and stepped backward in shock.

"I don't think the gun is necessary detective," Ferguson said. Alarm bells were going off in his head as he noticed the large cylindrical silencer attached to the front of the pistol. *That doesn't look like a standard issue police weapon!*

***

"Did he say gun?" Garagua pulled himself up from the back seat and leaned next to Bolivar.

The two of them had fully expected to find Ferguson and Courtney exiting the Willows shortly, but the commotion of them re-entering her apartment and the voice of a third party had piqued their interest.

"Yeah! Quiet!" Bolivar replaced the headphones over his ears and simultaneously plugged them into the receiver. He listened intently, while Garagua waited anxiously in the back.

"We've got ourselves a problem!" Bolivar finally said.

He jerked the keys out of the ignition and handed them to Garagua. "In the trunk is a Papa John's pizza bag with a couple of pizza boxes inside. There's also a hat and sweatshirt to match. Put them on and grab the pizza bag. Take your gun with you."

"You want me to go in?"

"Yes. Get in there and get the girl out. I don't care what happens to anyone else. You understand? We want the girl...alive and well.

Garagua, dressed the part of pizza deliveryman, ran down the side street, across Locust Lane, and slowed to a walk as he entered the Willow's lobby.

"I've got a delivery for Courtney Lewis. She said it was apartment 901," Garagua addressed the guard, who once again had risen to his feet as if in complete control.

"Go ahead." The guard directed his right hand, thumb extended, toward the elevators. He decided against calling to announce the pizza. *Miss Lewis sure got busy in a hurry. That wasn't the usual pizza guy?*

*Hell, the damn Mexicans are taking over every job there is. The son-of-a-bitches will be after my job soon enough.* He sat down and reached for the top drawer of the desk to retrieve his reading material again.

Mr. Jones had waved Courtney and Ferguson over to the comfort of the overstuffed leather couch, and had positioned himself opposite them in an antique wingback chair. He stared at them in silence, as if evaluating what to do with them. The desired effect was taking its toll on both of them, as they nervously looked at each other and then back at Jones.

Finally, Ferguson had had enough. "What the hell is goin'...."

Jones raised his free hand facing the palm toward the two of them. "Shut up! I'll be asking the questions." He shifted his weight, dropped his hand down, leaned back into the chair, and crossed his legs.

"Mr. Ferguson, you have proven to be very elusive. And Miss Lewis, you seem to be in the wrong place at the wrong time."

Ferguson immediately felt the sweat emitting from every pore in his body. His mouth went dry. He suddenly had a chilling epiphany; this was the man who was responsible for all the problems that had taken place in the last 48 hours. This man was big trouble, and things were about to get worse before they got better.

"I'm afraid I don't understand what's going on here," Courtney replied.

From the expression on his face, Jones was certain that Ferguson knew. "Why don't you explain it to her Matt...you don't mind if I call you Matt do you?" It was more a statement of fact, than a question.

"My guess is this is the gentleman that has been wreaking all the havoc lately. I presume Dr. Karl's murder, along with the attempts on my life, were all his responsibility," Ferguson sighed. "How am I doing so far?"

"Close. I would like to take credit for everything, but I am just a small spoke in the wheel. Nevertheless, you left out the 'why?'"

Courtney's shoulders nearly fell to her waist. She went pale, and grabbed at the cushions for balance.

"Why?" Ferguson asked, as he grabbed for Courtney's right arm to steady her.

Jones snapped forward in his chair and aimed the pistol directly at Ferguson's head. "Don't play games with me. You know why...and where, and most importantly, what. We want the letter! All of it! Not just the list, but the map as well."

Ferguson knew the secret was out. If he denied the letter's existence now, he was liable to get a head full of lead. *I can acknowledge the letter, but I have to make sure he needs me to get it. If I give it away now, we're both dead. We'll never make it out of this apartment. He said 'we'. How many bad guys are there?*

The doorbell and knock on the door startled all of them.

"Miss Lewis, it's the maintenance man," Garagua called through the door. He had decided to drop the pizza disguise; because he knew it was possible, he would never be let inside for just pizza. Therefore, he crafted a better idea on the way up in the elevator.

Jones leapt to his feet and redirected the gun at Courtney, waving it toward the door. "Get rid of him."

"You can't come in right now, I'll have to let you in later," she yelled out.

"Miss, you have a leak in your bathroom pipes, and it's pouring water into the apartment below. Either you let me in right now, or I let myself in."

*Shit!* Jones did not anticipate company. He waved Courtney over to the door, pointed the gun back at Ferguson, and mouthed the words 'don't move' in silence. Courtney and Jones reached the door together.

"When I tell you, let him in, and point him to the bathroom. After he goes in, we are leaving...together. Anything goes wrong, you are all dead. Do you understand?" Jones whispered. Courtney nodded. He sidestepped back toward the chair he was in, and sat down again. He picked up the *Vanity Fair* magazine from the glass coffee table and placed it over the gun, which he pointed again at Ferguson. Settled, he nodded at Courtney to open the door. The door opened, and Garagua stepped in quickly. He was still holding the pizza bag over the Gloch automatic in his right hand, and he scanned the room quickly, honing in on the stranger.

Jones recognized the look of disbelief on Courtney's face, and recognized the bag as a pizza warmer, not the tool bag of a repairman. There wasn't a moment of hesitation. He wheeled around in the chair and clicked off two rounds that struck Garagua in the right thigh and middle of the chest. He wavered briefly, dropped the bag and tried to lift his weapon to aim. Jones stood up, and his third bullet hit him square in the nose as Garagua let off a wild shot that hit the kitchen counter. He pitched forward and fell face first onto the floor.

Courtney screamed and fell to her knees, her hands clutching her chest. Jones hesitated as he looked over at her. It was all the time Ferguson needed. The second the first shots were fired, Ferguson seized the oriental vase seated on the concrete pillar display stand next to the couch, hurtled the coffee table, and took dead aim at the side of Jones' head. It was an added bonus when he stood up for the last shot. Before he could turn back to cover Ferguson, the vase slammed into his left temple, shattering the Oriental heirloom all over the hardwood. Jones dropped to the floor like a rag doll. Ferguson never saw the gun hit the floor and slide under the couch.He searched frantically around the floor, while Jones moaned and Courtney sobbed hysterically.

"Where's the damn gun?" Ferguson met Courtney walking to him and grabbed Courtney by the shoulders, still looking around the floor for Jones' weapon.

He shook her once and then looked her in the eye. "It's over, get hold of yourself! Take a deep breath. If I could find his gun, I'd finish the bastard off right now," he let her go and started to search again.

Jones was starting to regain consciousness. Courtney grabbed Ferguson's arm, "I'll call the police."

Ferguson took one last look, but still could not find the gun. Frustrated, he walked over to Jones and kicked as hard as he could at his exposed ribcage. He heard the crack of bones and a rush of adrenaline swept over him. He lined up on the face, and kicked again as if it was an inanimate ball. The crack of more bones, and a muted grunt from Jones. A wave of anger gushed forth out of Ferguson, anger like he had never experienced before.

Courtney shook him out of it. "Stop it! We'll get the police."

Ferguson looked down at Jones as he wiped the sweat from his forehead with both hands. A series of multiple beeps sounded off. Ferguson looked at Courtney in disbelief. Before he could say anything, an electronic voice crackled from the dead maintenance man.

"Carlos?" Bolivar keyed the one-way phone. "Carlos, is everything okay amigo?" There was the sound of static and then the line went dead.

"Shit!" Ferguson ran to the front door and looked down the hallway. Nothing. He sprinted to the front window, yanked back on the white slatted blinds and peered down the nine floors to the front entry of the tower. His eyes frantically searched the ground for any signs of activity. Under the street lamp across the street from the front entrance was just what he suspected, a single man running directly at the Willows.

"What's wrong?" Courtney asked, panic returning to her voice.

"I was wrong, it's not over!" Ferguson released the blinds and vaulted toward the front door, grabbing Courtney's hand and yanking her along with him. "We've got company!"

"Who?"

"Friends of your repairman."

"He's not the repairman..."

"No kidding," Ferguson interrupted.

"He's the guy from the restaurant, the one that was following us."

"Great! He could be the police, but we're not waiting around to find out," Ferguson scooped up the bags by the door, "Can you trip your alarm?"

"Sure."

"Do it...now!"

Courtney programmed the key pad and the alarm shrieked. "What about those two?"

"One's not going anywhere. The other one the police will get. We'll call the police...that detective we met, from the car. We'll explain it to him."

"We'll have to turn ourselves in," Courtney pulled the locked door closed.

"Maybe, but not right now," Ferguson led them to the emergency stairs. "You heard the one guy, he's a small spoke in a big wheel. He talked in 'we's'. There's a lot more of him where he came from. We've gotta get the hell out of here."

They reached the basement exit and stepped out into the garage entrance. Ferguson looked around for anything that moved. It was quiet. They calmly walked to the front lot and Ferguson's car. Once outside, they inhaled the cool evening air as if it were their last breath on earth. With luck it had not been. They could hear the police sirens approaching as they drove away.

***

Detective Shutt's mobile phone was sitting on the kitchen table next to an empty bag from Jersey Mike's Sub Shop, and the Gloch 38, safely encased in the leather belt holster. His wife Rhonda and all three kids had left town for the weekend, off to visit her sister in Nashville. Once Rhonda had heard the news of the murders, she knew her husband would be out of it for the next few days, and felt it wise to get out of his hair while the gettin' was good. The phone began to ring less than ten minutes since he had discarded it.

"Damnit!" Shutt cried out. "I can't even eat dinner in peace!"

He deposited the last half of his sandwich on the family room coffee table, walked to the kitchen and picked up the phone evaluating the incoming phone number in the display window.

"Hello?" Shutt inquired, not recognizing the caller.

"Detective Shutt?"

"Speaking."

"This is Matt Ferguson, we met earlier this afternoon at Dr. Karl's house."

"I remember. What can I help you with?"

"Well...Miss Lewis, who you also met earlier, and myself, well...we've got a bit of a problem.

"And what would that be?"

"We we're involved in an incident tonight that we believe is tied in with Dr. Karl's death."

"Go on."

"Well, unfortunately, as we speak, the police are responding to an alarm at Miss Lewis' apartment at the Willows Tower. When they get there, they're going to find another dead body, and the shooter unconscious on the floor."

"Mr. Ferguson, please tell me you're pulling my leg." Shutt responded in a calm and controlled voice.

"I wish I was," Ferguson said.

"What the hell is going on?" The calm and control were slipping away. "Either you, or both of you are in some deep shit young man!"

"Yes sir, but we're not responsible for killing anyone. In fact, the man you will find knocked out on the floor of Courtney's apartment is the one responsible for it all. He was going to kill us both until the dead man showed up and got in the way. I was able to knock him out before he could do any more damage."

"Why'd you leave? You should have stayed put, called the police, and waited for them to arrive," Shutt regained his composure.

"There were others," Ferguson continued. "I don't know who they were, but they were on their way up to the apartment and there wasn't any time. I also wasn't interested in getting into some gun battle."

"What do you mean others?"

"Look, detective, there's something that Courtney and I have...certain information that other people might be interested in. Information that could lead to a great deal of money. The interested party, or parties, appears to be much larger than one or two people."

"Then you need to come in and let us get you some police protection," Shutt said. "Then we can sort out everything that's been going on and find out who this so-called 'shooter' is and squeeze him for more information. Maybe he can lead us to the others."

"It's not that easy. We're safe for now. Let us talk over where we go from here and we'll call you back."

"Wait...wait a minute, don't hang up!" Shutt did not want to lose the conversation. "Is Miss Lewis with you?" He needed to keep them on the phone and talk them in.

"Yes, and we'll get back to you soon," Ferguson replied, feeling the need to end the conversation for now.

The line went dead.

"Shit!" Shutt looked down at the phone and immediately punched up the incoming call list from the phone's menu, and dialed Ferguson's cell phone.

Ferguson looked at the incoming caller I.D. and let it ring until the voicemail picked it up. Fifteen minutes of numbed silence later, he turned on his left blinker and exited Brownsboro Road onto Rose Island Road. Four minutes later, he turned into the driveway of Uncle Max's house. He left Courtney in the car while he canvassed the exterior grounds and then disappeared through the front door. He returned to the car shortly, and determining it safe, he escorted her and their bags inside.

He tossed his bags into the master bedroom, stowed Courtney's luggage into one of the empty guest bedrooms, and returned to find Courtney clutching a bottle of Knob Creek Bourbon and dispensing ice from the refrigerator into two glasses.

"I thought you might need one. I know I do!"

"Thanks," Ferguson said, "Most definitely."

They both fell onto the overstuffed leather sofa in the great room, and stared blankly at the large creek stone fireplace that stretched from the floor to the top of the vaulted ceiling. They sat in silence again for some time, the tinkling of the ice cubes the only sound, rolling forward and settling in the glasses with every sip.

Courtney spoke first. "What are we gonna do?"

"I don't know. I *really* don't know," Ferguson sighed wearily, as he closed his eyes.

# Chapter 10

*May 21, 2001. Louisville, Kentucky*

The smell of bacon permeated the morning air as Courtney shuffled down the split timber steps that led to the foyer and into the kitchen. Warm sunshine streamed in from the exhaustive supply of floor to ceiling windows that encompassed the east face of the log home's great room. The woods that surrounded the house broke the light into radiant beams that projected an almost heavenly appearance as they danced around the room.

Ferguson was busy over the island stove punching at the bacon frying in the skillet, and the browning pancakes on the rectangular built-in griddle.

"Good morning," Ferguson looked over his shoulder at Courtney as she entered the wide-open kitchen area. "How'd ya sleep?"

"Very well...considering. Where did all the food come from?"

Courtney was eyeballing the two sacks of groceries spread out on the eating counter that surrounded three sides of the cooking island.

"I biked up to the Five Star on Brownsboro. It was a beautiful morning and I couldn't sleep. It gave me some time to think, especially after I got a chance to check my cell phone mailbox."

"That sounds ominous," Courtney caught a glimpse of herself in the large antique mirror that hung in the breakfast nook. She was still in a large Cleveland Browns t-shirt Ferguson had found for her to sleep in. Her hair was headed in about 15 directions at once, and she quickly ran her fingers through it to give it some semblance of clarity. It had been a while since she had awakened anywhere with a man in close proximity.

Ferguson had not failed to notice her either. She looked incredible in his eyes. Her long legs were beautiful, there were silhouetted hints of her unsupported breasts underneath the cotton shirt, and her hair had a wild sexy look to it. He was trying not to be too obvious as he caught glimpses of her in between his efforts to complete breakfast. He slipped her a cup of coffee across the tile counter and started to load up two plates of pancakes, bacon, and fresh blueberry muffins.

"Would you like any orange juice?"

"Yes, please! Sorry I did not dress up for breakfast, this was a little unexpected. I haven't had a man fix me breakfast in..." Courtney hesitated, "I don't think I've ever had a man fix me breakfast, except my father."

"You gotta have a good breakfast to get the day started right. And God knows we need to get today started right. As for the voicemails, yeah we got some more interesting news from our detective friend."

"Bad news?"

"I wouldn't call it good. I had three messages from him. The first one was insisting that we come in to the station and give him statements on what transpired last night. The third was more of the same, but with a little more vigor and some threats of issuing warrants for our arrest as material witnesses in a capital murder case."

"Do I even want to know about the second?"

That one was a little more disturbing. When they arrived at your apartment, they discovered the dead Latino, but...but our other friend was nowhere to be found."

"You're kidding...right?"

"I obviously didn't hit him hard enough. He must have regained consciousness and found a way out of there. I knew I should have killed him! If only I could have found a gun in time, I would gladly have put a bullet in him."

Courtney was shaking her head. She could not believe that all this was happening. When she woke this morning, she was hoping against all hope that this had all been a dream, a nightmare. Unfortunately, it was a real-life nightmare, and it was getting worse.

Ferguson broke her train of thought. "I had pretty well convinced myself last night that we could turn ourselves in and tell Shutt what had happened. I was hoping to talk about the art, but not give away that we knew where it was. Just tell them we knew of its existence and leave it at that. They had the dead guy and the murderer, and they could track down the origins of both. Who and where they came from, and in the case of our gunman, who he worked for and how many others were involved. His disappearance changes everything now!"

"How's that?" Courtney inquired.

"Well...if we turn ourselves in now, I think we have a pretty good chance of getting out from any significant charges. Shutt knows we didn't kill anybody. We would have to come clean on the art, but, just maybe, we could still get by without telling him we know where it is. But even if we get that far, the charges dropped or minimalized, we still have our killer out there. As soon as we're out on our own again, he, and more likely he and his friends, will come hunting for us. I'm convinced there are definitely more of him from whatever rock he crawled out from under."

"Yeah, but the police could protect us!"

"Yes, they could but for how long...months...years? Look, as long as the questions never get answered, the information that I have, that we both know, puts us in danger. If we keep what we know to ourselves, we would have to stay under protection indefinitely. If they never find them, would we have to go into hiding, change identities, or something crazy like that? I don't know about you, but I do know I'm not ready for that kind of change in lifestyle. On the other hand, we could give up the crash location, wash our hands of the whole thing, and have somebody else get the opportunity to discover the find of a lifetime. The downside to that is there are still no guarantees they may ever catch the people who are after us."

They both interrupted their thoughts and hungrily started in on the plates of food Ferguson had sat before them.

"The only other option I see is this," said Ferguson as laid his fork onto the plate. "We're still in control. We still have the advantage of being the only ones to know where the art is, and if we find it for ourselves and do it quickly, we can reap the rewards and end the whole thing. There will be no need for anybody to pursue us once we have made the discovery and everything's out in the open. It would be over!"

"You keep saying 'we'. Does that mean I'm going with you?" Courtney asked.

"If you want to go. If you want to turn yourself into Shutt, I would certainly understand. Just give me a few days head start and I'll have this thing ended soon."

Courtney stared at Ferguson in silence as they returned to breakfast. She felt a tinge of excitement. What he had said made sense, and the expectation of the adventure that lay ahead was more than she could stand.

"Hell yeah, I'm going with you! When do we leave?"

"You've got about one hour to get ready. We need to get to the bank for some money and my passport. I took the liberty of going through your purse this morning for a credit card number to book you a ticket with me to Switzerland."

"Pretty confident I was willing to go with you?"

"No, only hoping. Besides, I saw you packed your passport in your purse. Pretty confident you were going?" Ferguson chuckled.

"There was never a doubt in my mind," Courtney smiled.

# Chapter 11

*May 21, 2001. Louisville, Kentucky*

The homicide division office at the JCPD was alive and kicking bright and early this morning. Truth be told, it had not stopped humming since late last night. Shutt's phone had been ringing incessantly since he arrived at 6:00 a.m. Four murders, all connected, within 48 hours of each other, undeniably gets the attention of a department that usually sees that many over the course of several months.

Steve Stewart, Toby Shutt's partner, was back on duty, and was in early to join Shutt in beginning the nuts and bolts investigative work and theoretical postulation surrounding the killings. Shutt towered over Stewart's 5'5" thin, but solid frame, as they both stood at the easel-supported bulletin board that Shutt had erected in his office.

Stewart ran his hands through his full head of dark brown curly hair, taking time to scratch the back of his head. This was turning out to be the first multiple homicides case he had been involved with in his second year in homicide, and most certainly the largest.

At 32, recently divorced, and without any children or current love interest, he was ready and eager to tackle this case head on. He was already lamenting the fact he had taken a day off and missed the crime scene from the Karl house.

The photos from those murders, as well as the photos of Courtney Lewis' apartment, were arrayed before them on the large board, held in strategic groupings with pushpins, accompanied by 3 x 5 index cards containing notes that he and Shutt thought pertinent to the investigation. Directly behind the easel was an even larger, solid white, dry marker writing board that consumed nearly one entire wall in the office. It looked like an abstract maze of names, geographic locations, and all forms of miscellaneous subject matter, all connected with a haphazard alignment of arrows stretching to and from the different word groups. It made sense to Shutt and Stewart, but more than likely, to no one else.

Shutt had begun an exercise of pulling connective information from all the murder victims. There was quite an array of open files and paperwork of all kinds laid out on a 4' x 8' portable table erected flush against the back of Shutt's desk. Shutt had Karl's file in his hand and was scribbling with a black marker on the writing board.

Under a heading titled *Karl*, the first connection he was looking for materialized. As he wrote down the word's *language/university professor, bachelor/no family, German heritage, ex-Nazi???*; he stepped back and noticed under the heading *Nieron*, he had written *White Supremacy/Aryan*, and one column over under *Syron*, the same description.

"Do you see what I see?" He looked back over his shoulder at Stewart.

"No. Enlighten me," Stewart replied.

"We've got a combination of Skinheads and a possible Nazi. That bears some further looking into."

Before Shutt could finish writing, Shawna Hammer entered the office with one large and one small manila envelope and two file folders.

"Hot off the presses gentlemen. Here's the Willow's video masters," she tossed the oversize envelope on the table, "with black and whites of your imposter detective. The security geek on duty that night has already been in this morning and verified that that's your man." She added the smaller envelope on top of the larger, "That's what little they found on the person of your dead Latino. And here are files on both," she set down two files next to the envelopes. "As of now, there's nothing coming up on either one of them."

"Thanks Shawna!" Shutt stopped his scribbling, picked up the files and handed the envelopes to Stewart.

Stewart sat in one of the two well-worn wooden chairs accompanying the table, and examined the 8 x 10 black and white photographs reproduced from the Willow's garage and front desk security cameras. Shutt took the files.

With no positive identification on either one of them, the files were sparse. The Latino's file had a few more tidbits than the white John Doe, due to the fact he was physically left behind. An autopsy report, a complete physical description, duplicate photos of the crime scene with him as the star, and a neck up mug shot from the morgue that was currently making its way through police and F.B.I. databases.

John Doe's file was worthless at this point. More duplicates from the security cameras, with one extremely grainy reproduction of a close-up of his face. It had been doctored and retouched, and was as good as it was going to get given what they had to work with. Again, this one was already surfing the electronic databases for any kind of hit.

Stewart had dumped the contents of the smaller envelope on the table and was scattering them about to examine them individually.

"This guy traveled light," Stewart remarked sarcastically. "No wallet, no identification. Let's see...a wad of cash, two peppermints, a single car key with a *Hertz* key chain, and a folded city map with a *Hertz* logo. I'd say we have an out-of-towner."

"Sorry this one just arrived also," Shawna leaned around the doorframe again and handed another file to Stewart as he popped out of the chair.

Stewart opened it up and leafed through a couple of pages.

"You'll like this," Stewart said.

"What do you have?" replied Shutt.

"Ballistics matched up the slugs from Jose here," Stewart lifted a picture of Garagua, "and the two punks from the Karl house."

"So, we've got the same shooter from both scenes." Shutt walked over to the bulletin board, stuck a pin through the close-up of Mr. Jones and added it to the collage. "My guess would be this is our gunman!"

"Looks like it," Stewart walked over to the board.

Shutt scratched the back of his head, "Who the fuck is this guy, and why does he want these three people dead?"

"I'd say the secret lies with Ferguson and the girl."

Shutt somberly stared at the writing board and saw only two names listed as *actors* under both crime scenes...Matt Ferguson and Courtney Lewis. "I'd say you're right on the money."

\*\*\*

The Gulfstream taxied to the private hangar on the west side of Barbados' Bridgetown airport. The jet stopped short of entering the building, long enough to let down the fuselage door and expel Julio Bolivar, before slowly penetrating the large double doors that had just completed retracting open.

Bolivar walked across the open tarmac to an idling Land Rover, taking in the incredible orange, blue and purple pastel sky rising from behind the island's mountain backbone. A large, native black man opened the back door to the vehicle and closed the door behind Bolivar as he eased his tired body into the leather seat next to Guillermo Rocca. The vehicle shifted into gear and slowly pulled away from the airport.

"Good to see you Julio. I'm sorry about Carlos," Rocca said matter-of-factly.

"Good to see you Mr. Rocca. I'm sorry for the screw-up," Bolivar replied, knowing full well the conversation was going to be a subtle ass chewing, with punishment masked as pleasantries.

Rocca crossed his right leg over his left and shifted his body position to face Bolivar. He reached out and touched his shoulder, as if a father would his son. "Tell me what happened."

For the third time, the first face-to-face, Bolivar explained the sequence of events from the time they first got to Louisville, to his aborted attempt at trying to recover Garagua. The story never changed. Bolivar knew that Rocca was testing him, trying to find a crack or inconsistency that would indicate something other than the truth. He was okay with that. He would do the same if a subordinate had screwed up as badly as he and Garagua had.

Rocca listened patiently, and then said, "And you have no idea who the other man in the apartment was?"

"Not a clue Mr. Rocca. We never paid any attention to anyone going in other than Courtney Lewis and her man friend."

"Well, I have to believe he knows what we know, and he is willing to kill for it. A very dangerous development. Have you given any thought to damage control?"

"Yes, I have some ideas, but I'm afraid that we're not going to be able to keep the company out of this mess."

"I didn't think we would," Rocca's voice reflecting some of the anger that was bubbling under the surface. "Let's hear some of your thoughts."

"Well the biggest problem we have is they have Carlos' body. I have his I.D. and other personal stuff he had with him, but I couldn't find the keys to his rental car. I have to assume he had them on him and the police have them now. We made the mistake of using the corporate card to book the cars, so that will undoubtedly allow the authorities to discover Carlos' identity and lead them back to us. That means they will eventually get to Juan, or quite possibly you."

"Go on," Rocca casually nodded his acceptance of the predicament. He had already informed Juan Sanchez, president of Rocca International, of the situation and given him some direction on how to handle any inquiries that might come his way. However, he was still interested in where Bolivar was headed.

"I'll take the blame. I will say that Carlos and I had gone to meet Miss Lewis on your behalf to discuss an exhibition of a part of your collection at her museum. I went to meet her at her apartment, but two men were there. She asked me politely to leave, but there was obviously something wrong about her guests. After discussing it with Carlos, he decided to go back in to see if he could help. I told him to leave it alone, but he was adamant. I will say I think he was infatuated with her. He paid off a local pizza delivery boy for the hat and delivery bag, took a gun and went back up to the apartment. The next thing I knew, the place was crawling with cops. When Carlos did not come back out of the building, I knew something was wrong. I got scared and ran."

Rocca stroked his chin with his right thumb and forefinger, while he shifted his gaze out the window. He said nothing. The Land Rover came to a stop outside two large iron gates that seem to grow out of an enormous outcrop of local vegetation. The gates opened and another native islander, with an AK-47 slung over his shoulder, waved at them as they drove through the gates and down a tunnel of palm trees lining a shell gravel road.

As they emerged from the trees, Rocca's palatial estate came into full view. Perched upon a bluff overlooking the Caribbean from the northern side of the island, Bolivar was privy to a magnificent sunrise out his side window, as the large, orange, hazy ball was radiating an intense streak of light across the placid blue and green sea.

They arrived at the front entrance of the white stucco, Mediterranean style mansion via a circular driveway, and were escorted by three houseboys from the truck, through the large foyer and hallway, to the large semi-circular veranda on the backside of the house. Along the way Rocca ordered champagne and breakfast and then guided the two of them to a round table, shaded by a large market umbrella, at the edge of the railing overlooking the 100-foot tiered drop to a secluded bay below. The white sand beaches and turquoise water were coming to life under the rising sun.

"It's a good story, very plausible," Rocca spoke first.

Bolivar sat at the table but offered no response.

"They're sure to find the bugs in her apartment. How would you suggest we handle that?"

"Carlos and I paid cash for the surveillance equipment. The bugs were all made from domestic, off-the-shelf stuff. They cannot trace that to Carlos or me. I'd say we play dumb on that one, and let them infer they were planted by the shooter," Bolivar replied.

The eggs benedict, toast and jam, sausages, assorted fruits, and champagne arrived accompanied by two servants, and Rocca pulled the bottle of Tattinger from the large silver ice bucket and poured two glasses. Bolivar visibly relaxed, sensing this may not be as big an ass chewing as he thought it was going to be.

"Here's to Carlos!" Rocca said, as he raised his glass right-handed, while handing Bolivar the other glass with his left.

Bolivar received the offering and lifted it to meet Rocca's with a gentle clink of the crystal. "To Carlos!"

They both sipped the sparkling wine simultaneously, and returned the glasses to the table. Rocca looked off at the rising sun just as it crept higher over the watery horizon, and then returned his piercing brown eyes to meet Bolivar's.

"If you fuck up again like that Julio, you'll be eating dust in the mines. You understand me?"

"I understand completely," Bolivar replied somberly.

Rocca stabbed his fork at a plate of sliced fruits that rested between their plates and called out for the servants. "I'll have them set you up on the beach. It's a wonderful place to take a nap. I'm sure you could use one."

"Very much so! *Gracias.*"

*\*\*\**

It had been raining in Munich for hours, with no sign of letting up. Between the wind and the three broken ribs, Mr. Jones was struggling to keep the umbrella up over his head as he walked south down Maximilianstrasse.

The flight over from New York had been easy. A hydrocodone for pain, two Ambien for sleep, three martinis to enhance the effect, and the majority of the first-class flight had been consumed by half sleep, half coma. The bumpy approach and landing had signaled the return of the pain he had been in since he had stumbled out of Courtney Lewis' apartment less than 20 hours earlier, minutes before the police had arrived.

He had settled himself in the Bayersicher Hof Hotel roughly one hour earlier, and as instructed by the message at the front desk, he was strolling along Maximilianpaltz, one of Munich's most splendid boulevards, waiting to be picked up by a passing auto.

Not more than five minutes after embarking on his walk, a large silver Mercedes sedan pulled to the curb just in front of him and stopped. Out popped a chauffeur from the driver's side who promptly opened the rear door and offered an open palmed entrance to the car with his right hand. Mr. Jones limped noticeably to the open door and climbed in.

Seated to his left was a very distinguished, silver haired gentleman, impeccably dressed in a three-piece Armani suit, who gave a brief smile of greeting as the door closed behind him.

"*Guten tag, Gerhard,*" said Erwin Leiter as he waved at his chauffeur to proceed.

"Good to see you Herr Leiter," replied Gerhard Alden.

"Was it as bad as you look?" Leiter inquired.

Alden had removed the sunglasses he was wearing, revealing the multiple bruises on his face. "Just as bad, if not worse!"

"Well, you will have some recuperation time. I've decided we will not pursue the letter."

Alden had an initial look of confusion, but quickly disguised his dismay. "As you wish Herr Leiter."

"Don't be discouraged Gerhard, we are not giving up. Quite the contrary, we have been able to track Mr. Ferguson and Miss Lewis via their credit cards. They are both booked on flights that will take them from the U.S. to Zurich. We will trail them from there, and let them lead us to the crash site. If and when they discover it, we will be there...excuse me...you will be there to clean up this little mess once and for all," Leiter's eyes bore a hole through Alden. "And please, don't screw it up this time, or it will be the last thing you will do in this lifetime. *Verstehen Sie?"*

*"Jawohl* Herr Leiter," Alden sat up rigid, "I understand completely."

Erwin Leiter, at the age of 79, was one of the wealthiest industrialists in all of Europe. He was a principal shareholder in Allianz, Siemens, Volkswagen, UBS, Robert Bosch, BMW, Bayer and AXA. He privately owned, or held controlling interest in another dozen companies located in France, Denmark, Switzerland, Italy and Saudi Arabia. Additionally, his real estate holdings rivaled the largest private holdings in Western Europe. Well respected among his peers, he had endless political and social clout, money, and above all else...charm.

Leiter controlled enormous purse strings. He doled out large sums of money from his wealth to a variety of persons and organizations all over the globe, and in return poured vast sums back into his coffers through his actions and the actions of those he impacted. Without a doubt, he was one of the most influential men on the planet.

Born in Munich, Germany in 1923, to Sophia Leiter, he was the illegitimate son of Heinrich Müller, one of the most notorious and powerful SS officers in the Nazi state terror system.

Sophia Leiter had been widowed in 1922 at the tender age of 22. Relying on her incredible beauty, a product of her northern Italian heritage, and blessed with a wonderful singing voice, she began performing in the burgeoning nightclubs of Munich to make ends meet. It was at the *Club Decanter* she met a young police officer by the name of Heinrich Müller. They had a torrid love affair that lasted almost two months, and consumed all of Müller's attentions. It ended when Müller's immediate boss, Reinhard Heydrich, the Bavarian Police Chief, politely suggested the tryst end or Müller risk the end of his career in the increasingly influential Gestapo wing of the Nazi Party.

It ended abruptly. Later that fall, Sophia gave birth to her one and only child, Erwin Leiter. The following spring, Sophia and Erwin moved to Berlin. It would be ten years before Müller found out about the child. He would eventually provide Sophia with a considerable stipend for her and his young son. He set her up in a comfortable apartment and managed to wield his growing power and import to set up Erwin in the finest schools in Berlin. His impact came to fruition during the war, as he was able to implore his friend from the old Gestapo days, Hermann Goering, to take a young Erwin Leiter into the Luftwaffe as an officer, and assign him to the general staff, well out of the way of the action. Müller went to great pains to keep the existence of his son a secret. No one was remotely aware, or ever discovered the connection between the two.

Ironically in the latter stages of the war, as Hitler's paranoia grew demonstrably, young Leiter was recruited by his father to help spy on Goering and his staff for the SS, and to report of any possible actions that might appear as though Goering intended to remove Hitler from power. For this, he was greatly rewarded both personally and financially. He achieved the rank of Captain at the very young age of 22.

In March of 1945, with the war undeniably headed to a close, Müller met with Leiter and revealed his long-kept secret. One week later Leiter joined a very select group of SS officers at a remote chalet in the Black Forest on the outskirts of Stuttgart. At that meeting were senior members of what remained of the vaunted SS. Realizing the inevitability of the war's outcome, and recognizing the resultant fury civilized man would loose as a result of their actions, a master plan of action was conceived to enable the escape of its members and to afford them the opportunity to integrate back into the world's societies. As a result of that meeting, the *Organisation der ehemaligen SS-Angehorigen* or Organization of Former Members of the SS was created. Commonly referred to as ODESSA, the organization was formed to help facilitate the means by which this master plan could be fulfilled.

Financial instruments were established, providing vast resources to be drawn upon in the future to affect the group's long-range goals. However, initial efforts concentrated on securing the disappearance of many of the murderers to other countries. Many others never left Germany. Operating under new identities, they blended into the populace, and went to work setting up political and financial networks, right under the watchful eye of Allied rule.

Heinrich Müller remained loyal to Adolph Hitler to the very end. All trace of Müller was lost on April 29, 1945, and to this day, his whereabouts could never be confirmed.

Erwin Leiter never left Germany. There was never a shred of evidence that he had any affiliation with the SS. His father had gone to great pains to provide for that. His Luftwaffe record was unremarkable, and even though he served on Goering's staff, his age and the fact that he never officially joined the Nazi party, precluded him from being connected to any responsibility for the atrocities wreaked on the European continent. He was the perfect choice within ODESSA to manage and grow the collective financial wealth the organization had cultivated in the closing months of the war. After serving the required two years in a prisoner of war camp, he was released, and immediately began exploiting the untapped financial resources in a post-war reconstructive Western Europe. He never disappointed, exceeding even the wildest possible scenario for success.

The Mercedes sedan returned to the street corner outside the Bayersicher Hof Hotel. Alden prepared to exit the vehicle as it came to a halt.

"Enjoy your stay Gerhard. Get some rest. We will contact you the minute they arrive in Zurich," said Leiter.

*"Danke Herr Leiter!* I'll be ready."

Alden exited the car with some pain. Before he could reach the front door, Leiter's Mercedes had disappeared.

*** 

The Cincinnati/Northern Kentucky International airport is just under 70 miles from downtown Prospect. Uncle Max's fully restored 1968 Triumph TR250 made it into the long-term parking lot in 66 minutes, 40 minutes ahead of their 11:00 am departure time. For Ferguson and Courtney, the ride up Interstate 71 in the old convertible was exhilarating. The prospect of flying off to Switzerland in search of lost treasure, the lingering effects of the day before, and the crisp spring air rushing over them had fine-tuned their senses.

Earlier that morning, after making substantial withdrawals from their respective bank accounts and retrieving his passport, they had driven out scenic Covered Bridge Road on their way to accessing the Interstate. Stopping at the Crestwood exit to fill up with gas, they placed a phone call to detective Shutt's office from the pay phone in the parking lot. He picked it up on the third ring.

"Detective Shutt speaking."

"Detective...Matt Ferguson here. Before you jump all over me, please let me explain why we have not come in."

"I'm listening," Shutt stood up from his desk chair, covered the mouthpiece, and yelled at Stewart from his cubicle, "Steve, get a trace on this call, hurry!"

"We got your messages. Based on what you said, Courtney and I still feel we cannot come in yet."

"You two better get your asses in here, and quick!" Shutt interrupted, stalling for time.

"Please detective, let me finish." There was silence on the other end of the phone. "As I told you before, we are in possession of knowledge that is potentially worth a lot of money, I mean a lot of money. There is nothing illegal about it, but apparently, there are people out there that have discovered what we know, and feel a need to get the information and the financial return it can offer. Obviously, at any cost. Unfortunately, the only link to who they are, escaped from Courtney's apartment last night, before you were able to get him. We would have been willing to come in if you had gotten him. There is no doubt in my mind that he was responsible for the death of Dr. Karl and the other two killed with him. He definitely was responsible for the murder of the guy in Courtney's place. We have no clue who that fella was, but it appeared as though he was trying to help us before he was shot. If I had the opportunity, if... if I could have found one of the guns last night, I would have killed the bastard that got away."

"You're not telling me anything I pretty much don't already know," Shutt admonished. "Do you have any clue who the gunman was that you knocked unconscious?"

"I haven't the foggiest idea who he was, and therein lies the problem."

"And what would that be?" Shutt asked.

"Without him, we have no way of knowing who he is, or more importantly, how many more of him are there. I can assure you he is not alone."

"The more reason for you two to turn yourselves in so we can protect you," Shutt stood up to face Stewart, who was circling the pointed index finger on his right hand, indicating to keep the conversation going.

"Actually, that's the reason for us not to turn ourselves in right now. Neither one of us wants to be held captive in protective custody, over something we may, or may not know. Particularly if it's going to be for an indefinite period of time that we have no control over. If you can't find out who they are, then they are waiting for us as soon as we're back on the street. In the not-too-distant future, we can prove whether the information we have is worth what we think it is. If it is or is not, we will have the opportunity to make it public knowledge, which will eliminate the need for anyone to harm us in the future. That may not solve your case, I realize, but I'm more concerned about saving Courtney's and my life."

"We have a line on the suspect. We are running information on him as we speak. We'll get him, I'm certain of that," Shutt lied.

"Who is he?" Ferguson asked.

"That's privileged information, I can't tell you. I don't want to jeopardize our investigation," Shutt replied.

"Well, until you can, we are not turning ourselves in." Ferguson called his bluff.

Steve Stewart flashed the thumbs up sign with his right hand.

"Well, let me explain something to you Mr. Ferguson. Right now, you and Miss Lewis are witnesses in a capital murder case. If necessary, I will change that to suspects, and issue warrants for your arrest. I can appreciate your interest in trying to save your bacon, but I think we are probably the best outlet to do that for you. So, get your shit together, and get you and your girlfriend down to the station where we can put you somewhere safe until we find out who's responsible for all the hell that's breaking loose."

"Let me think it over. I'll call you back first thing in the morning," Ferguson waved at Courtney, who was leaning on the hood of the car sipping on a Coke, to get back in the car.

"Make it first thing. After that, we will be coming for the both of you. Understood?" Shutt asked.

"Understood," Ferguson hung up the pay phone receiver and joined Courtney in the car. They exited the gas station parking lot, turned right up the entry ramp to Interstate 71, accelerated into the right lane and settled in for the one-hour drive to the Cincy airport.

***

"It's a pay phone out in Crestwood. A Shell gas station," Steve Stewart said, handing Shutt a small piece of notepaper with the address on it.

"Get a uniform over there ASAP!" Have them check it out, and call me back. If they're still there, arrest them both," Shutt grabbed the back of his neck with his right hand and started to rub the kinks out. "Crestwood? What the hell's in Crestwood?" He yelled at Stewart as he was walking away. "Steve, also start canvassing Crestwood and Pewee Valley for anything that resembles a hotel, motel, bed and breakfast, anyplace they could be hiding out. We also need background checks and bios on both Ferguson and Lewis. Get whatever you can on the two of them. Immediate family, phone records, contacts at work, banking info, credit cards, the works. You and I can sift through it later tonight."

Shawna Hammer waited for Stewart to leave before intruding on Shutt. "I've got some good news and bad news. The bad news is we got a big fat zero on the face from the garage video."

"FBI?" Shutt asked with a look of bewilderment.

"Notta. We ran it through every data bank we have."

Shutt was confused. This person was no doubt a professional. The hits at Karl's house were way too clean. People like that usually always have some kind of history on the radar screen. He plopped down in his chair and stared at his bulletin board. "And the good news?"

"Our dead Latino is Carlos Garagua, Bolivian. He rented a car after flying in two days ago. Get this..." she threw down the file labeled *Garagua*, "he flew in on a private jet. Belongs to an outfit called Rocca International, solely owned by some highfalutin, richer-than-god, businessman playboy from South America," Shawna turned to leave.

"Wait!" Shutt called to Shawna. "Karl was German. Our stiff is from south of the border. This is starting to have an international flavor about it. Did you try Interpol?"

"No! Everything we ran was domestic," Shawna replied.

"Send our shooter again. Try every avenue outside the borders. In fact, make sure we run him through German police agencies; maybe this Nazi connection will bear some fruit. If need be, get the Feds to help you out with the overseas stuff."

"You got it boss," Shawna exited down the same hall as Stewart had five minutes earlier.

***

High pressure dominated the weather pattern in the northeast, so the flight to Newark was pleasant and unremarkable. After making their connection, Ferguson and Courtney boarded the L-1011 for the balance of the 18-hour flight to Zurich.

At the check-in counter in Cincinnati, while Ferguson had disappeared to the bathroom, Courtney had taken the liberty of checking on upgrades for the second leg of the trip from Newark. With several available, she had paid for two of them, and they were now being seated up front in the larger more spacious accommodations of first class, and the flight attendant was already asking for their drink orders.

"Are you responsible for this?" Ferguson cocked an inquisitive eyebrow at Courtney.

"I thought we could stand to travel in style, especially for the long flight. My treat, I didn't think you would mind," Courtney replied.

"A very nice treat. Thank you!" Ferguson turned from Courtney to the waiting flight attendant, "I think we'll have some champagne," he looked back at Courtney, "my treat, is that alright by you?"

"Perfect!" She winked, with a slight grin.

Ferguson could not help but notice how incredibly beautiful she looked. He caught himself staring at her, and realized she was gazing back in return. Just for the moment, they were both aware of the chemistry that was fermenting between them.

After liftoff and three glasses of champagne, they spent the next two hours talking and laughing over a bottle of Trefethen merlot and filet mignon, an excellent meal by airplane food standards. The conversation was more discovery in nature, as they both let down any inhibitions they were holding on to, and began revealing more intimate details of their life's histories. They were in their own little world. It was as if nobody was around them. No mention of the immediate problems at hand. Not a word about the adventure that lay ahead.

Once the movie started, and the alcohol and tiredness had set in, Ferguson found himself reclined and on the verge of sleep, while Courtney had strategically placed her pillow so that it gravitated onto his shoulder, and was already in a deep slumber. He couldn't remember the last time he felt more relaxed. Sleep came easy.

***

"Excuse me Mr. Bolivar," came an inquiry in heavily French- accented English. It was accompanied by a gentle nudge from a tall, lanky and very black servant standing over Bolivar, who was nestled comfortably in a rope hammock strung between two leaning palm trees.

Bolivar struggled with his eyelids as he slowly acknowledged the prodding by the servant.

"Mr. Bolivar," Jean shook his shoulder with a little more force, "Mr. Rocca told me to bring you back up to the house."

Awake, and now fully cognizant again of his whereabouts, Bolivar laughed at the mention of the word *house*. *Castle* maybe, but not a house.

"Do you need any help with anything?" Jean asked politely.

"I'm fine, thank you...Jean is it?"

"Yes sir. I will go tell Mr. Rocca you will join him shortly. He said you will find him on the veranda."

"Thank you, Jean, tell him I'll be there in a few minutes."

As Jean disappeared through the lush tropical growth that covered the steep bluff, Bolivar had rolled over to a sitting position in the hammock, and listened in silence to the slow lapping sound of the crystal-clear water washing up against the sandy inlet beach. It was no wonder he had fallen asleep in no time. He shielded his eyes as he looked up to the sun high over his head. There was no question he had been asleep for several hours.

He lifted himself out of the hammock and followed the same path Jean had taken up the carved stone steps that zigzagged halfway up the cliff, before giving way to a walking path that wound around to the side of the property. The path eventually deposited out on the terrace of a multi-leveled stone swimming pool and hot tub overlooking the same view as the rest of the estate. Up a set of adjacent stairs and Bolivar was on the veranda again with Rocca, who seemingly had never left the table, which had been replenished with oysters on the half shell and boiled shrimp on ice, and a plate full of rare grilled tuna on a bed of shaved ginger. Rocca was eating heartily from it all.

"Join me Julio, you haven't much time," Rocca pulled back an empty chair and gestured to Bolivar to sit. "Please get something to eat."

Bolivar sat immediately and began to add food to the plate that Jean had set in front of him as he scooted himself to the table.

"It seems our Miss Lewis has surfaced again. Thanks to one of my experts on loan from R.I.'s I.T. department, and the use of his extensive computer skills, we have dug deeply into Courtney Lewis' background, including her credit cards and their recent usage. We discovered she is currently flying to Zurich, Switzerland. A little additional work has yielded the name of a young man accompanying her. His name is Matt Ferguson. He is the owner of the SUV Carlos chased around, and very likely the one in the apartment with her when Carlos was killed. It was very foolish of them to be using their plastic. If we can find them, I am sure anybody else can. That tells me that our other interested party, if he's at all capable, shouldn't be far behind."

Bolivar ate in silence, listening intently.

"We are readying the jet now, and I'll need you on it within the hour, Julio," Rocca laid an envelope down on the table. "Inside you'll find the particulars on their flight. Neither one has booked accommodations or a rental car."

Bolivar opened the envelope, scanned the contents and looked at his watch. "I don't think I'll be there in time to meet their plane."

"No, we weren't able to access the information in time to get you there before them. I have made arrangements with a third party we've used in other company and personal matters, and he is there now waiting on them to arrive."

"Is this him?" Bolivar asked, pointing to a name and series of phone numbers on the paper in front of him.

'That's him," Rocca affirmed. "He will keep tabs on them once they arrive, and will turn them over to you when you get there. Terry Sullivan will be joining you on the trip. He will not stand out like a sore thumb. There aren't many Chicanos in central Europe."

"Excellent," Bolivar nodded approvingly. "I forgot to mention it earlier, but I called Miguel as I was leaving Louisville, and had him fly there to wait and keep track of the girl. We need to call him off."

"That's taken care of. He is headed to Chicago. I have something else for him to do," Rocca speared a well-dressed raw oyster off the open shell and slid it into his mouth. "You'll like Switzerland, Julio, it's a beautiful country."

# Chapter 12

*May 22, 2001. Zurich, Switzerland*

Gregory Keitel adjusted his newspaper to let his sad, brown eyes peer over the top of the national news and at the boarding door to gate 22, in the North concourse of the Zurich International airport. His eyes did not reflect the intensity that lay beneath the surface of the capable and ruthless private detective.

Nine years removed from the local city police force, having resigned in a cloud of accusations involving corruption related to a large narcotics investigation, Keitel had escaped the ensuing judicial inquiries. He had quietly moved into the private sector with a sizable bank account, well-hidden and well-funded by the guilty he delivered from arrest and prosecution. His training, and connections to the good and bad sides of the law had proven to be much more lucrative than being a career police officer.

At 5'10", with a full head of sandy hair and blocky facial features, he had a solid, muscular build, honed daily in a popular downtown fitness center. At 300 Swiss francs per hour, plus expenses, he could afford to be well dressed, but not too flashy to attract attention. He managed to blend in well in any situation or occasion, and the crowded airport terminal was no different.

The descriptions of Matt Ferguson and Courtney Lewis, received from the early morning phone call, were flawless. There wasn't any question as to who they were when they emerged from the exiting door, as Continental Airlines flight 78 from Newark debarked.

They headed toward customs, which along with baggage claim, Keitel knew would be a drawn-out process. He rose from his seat in an adjoining gate area, tucked the paper under his arm, worked his way casually through the crowd, and stayed on pace twenty yards behind them.

After clearing customs in a sooner than expected fashion, they all moved on to the baggage claim area. At the large baggage carousel surrounding the brightly lit sign listing the Continental flight number, a seemingly endless stream of nearly identical luggage disgorged from an opening in the raised floor. Each piece dropped onto a moving conveyor and wound aimlessly around in a circle, until one person after another materialized from the crowded hoard surrounding it, stepped forward and laid claim to their possessions.

After nearly half an hour, Ferguson thankfully captured his and Courtney's luggage, and after clearing customs, the two of them moved to the car rental section at the far end of the main concourse level. Keitel followed carefully and advanced closer, joining them in the line at the Hertz counter, two customers back. He was in perfect earshot of Courtney as she stepped to the counter in front of Ferguson addressing the agent in her newly cultivated German.

*"Verstag mir, sprechen sie English ur French?"*

*"Ja,* I speak English," replied the young, and very attractive brunette from behind the computer terminal.

"Beautiful!" Courtney sighed, while Ferguson appreciatively exhaled his relief and stepped closer to the counter.

"We need a one-way mid-size to be dropped off in Lucerne," Ferguson said.

The young agent immediately began typing onto her keyboard, while Ferguson delved into his wallet for an American Express, his Hertz Gold card, and driver's license.

Courtney said nothing, but frowned a perplexed look in the direction of Ferguson.

"I'll explain later," Ferguson said, sensing her confusion. "Here's my card and license", as he handed the Hertz Gold Club card to the agent, who retrieved the cards with one hand while still typing with her right, her eyes never leaving the computer monitor.

"And you would like the rental and insurance on the American Express Mr. Ferguson?" Asked the agent in heavily accented English.

"Please" Ferguson replied, handing the card to her outstretched hand.

Five minutes later the rental was consummated.

"Thank you, Mr. and Mrs. Ferguson", said the agent as she slid the keys, Ferguson's cards, and a folder with contract information and a Swiss map across the counter. "Have a nice stay in our country."

Courtney chuckled silently at the reference to marriage, and glanced down admiringly at her naked left ring finger for effect.

The gesture was not lost on Ferguson, as he thanked the agent, grabbed the material from the counter and stooped down to pick up his bags. "Shall we go Mrs. Ferguson?" He asked mockingly.

"Gladly, Mr. Ferguson, but while we're in Europe, we really must do something about my jewelry. I seem to have misplaced my wedding ring."

"Gladly, Mrs. Ferguson."

Keitel had already disappeared. Once he heard about the one-way destination, he had discreetly exited the line at the counter and headed for the first bank of automatic glass doors that led outside. Once outside the main concourse, near the bus and taxi transfers, he made himself comfortable on a bench and dialed a number into the flip top cell phone he took from his pants pocket. Within five minutes, a large, heavy-set man in his fifties hustled up to meet him.

Keitel's instructions were simple...go to the Hertz rental car staging area, keep an eye out for the man and woman he described, and forward the make, model and license plate number of the car they get into. Keitel and the burly man exchanged a cash handshake and Keitel quickly headed off to the parking garage for his car.

Ferguson and Courtney showed up at the rental car lot fifteen minutes later, having stopped off for two cups of hot coffee. They found the silver Mercury Sable in the designated spot, deposited their luggage in the trunk, and climbed into the front seats. Ferguson was behind the wheel familiarizing himself with the various instruments and controls, while Courtney unfolded the map, studiously examining the city of Zurich on one side, and giving a cursory look to the map of the country on the other side. After proclaiming her navigational confidence, they fired up the engine, pulled out of the garage lot, and with Courtney's help translating the multitude of signs, headed for the airport exit and national expressway A3.

Keitel reached for the chirping phone as it lay in the front seat of the navy-blue BMW 525.

"Yeah? "They're headed out of the garage in a silver Mercury Sable, license number BEZ654. They should be on you in about two or three minutes. Nice doing business with you." The line went dead.

***

Gerhard Alden sped southward on the A4 autobahn toward Zurich, the large black Mercedes sedan cruising flawlessly at 110 miles per hour. His two passengers were both teetering on the edge of sleep.

Two hours earlier Alden had been awakened by the knock at his hotel room door. The two large men responsible for the intrusion smiled at him as they entered his room uninvited and greeted him cordially.

"*Guten morgen, Gerhard,*" declared the smaller of the two, slapping his shoulder with a powerful right hand. Horst Marshall passed by Alden and walked over to the window.

Entering immediately behind him and extending his hand was Paul Knabel. He silently winked at Alden as they shook hands.

"It's a little early to wake up to you two," Alden stretched, grimaced with pain, and rubbed his eyes with his right thumb and forefinger. "You might have called and given me some warning."

"Not enough time, we need to get a move on to Zurich," replied Horst, staring out the third-floor window to the dark street below. He glanced back to Alden, "You look terrible. I heard you got into a bit of a scrape."

"I'll survive, I've been in worse shape. Have they already arrived?" Alden inquired.

"No. We're going to intercept them as they come off the plane," Knabel interjected. "We're only to follow and keep an eye on them."

"Exactly!" Alden limped to the bathroom. "Give me five minutes and I'll be ready to go."

Marshall and Knabel both made themselves comfortable in the two leather armchairs that flanked the French provincial desk in the far corner of the room.

The intrusion, Alden reflected while washing his face was a pleasant one. Leiter could not have delivered him two better comrades to be working with. They were intelligent, physically imposing, and most of all, very reliable. They had also had the opportunity to use each of those traits on several demanding occasions, all very successfully, which added experience to their resumes. A far cry from the two idiots he had mistakenly employed in Kentucky.

Horst Marshall was 34 years old, and a perfect Aryan specimen. At 6′ 2″ 210 pounds, with thinning blond hair, and crystal blue eyes set deep within a pair of high cheekbones, he still sustained an imposing physique he had developed as a paratrooper in the German army. Disavowed by his widowed father for not furthering his education at the university, he drifted aimlessly for six months before a recruiting officer convinced him to enlist in the service at the age of 18. Discharged three years ago, he had made the rank of lieutenant, and would have probably been a career army man had it not been for the unexpected recruitment of him by the Sturtzburn Corporation as a security officer. Sturtzburn was a subsidiary of a Saudi valve manufacturer, which fell under the empire of Irwin Leiter.

A talent watcher for ODESSA had spotted Marshall early in his career, which included combat assignments in the Gulf War and Kosovo. An expert marksman, he was also skilled in demolitions and electronics, but it was his intelligence duties, particularly during the latter conflict, that earned him several commendations and his final bump in rank.

However, the lure of a substantial increase in money, and an opportunity to travel frequently back to the Middle East, an area of the world in which he had become enamored, was enough to spur his exit from the army and embark on a career in the private sector. A personal interest taken by Irwin Leiter, resulting in a private meeting with the billionaire that had portended of even greater personal and financial opportunities in the future, had made the decision that much easier. Paul Knabel was physically the antithesis of Horst Marshall, but equally as capable. He was imposing in size at 6′5″ and well over 300 pounds, but there was nothing chiseled on his round frame. He had long forsaken the crops of brown hair that flanked the hairless top of his head, opting to shave them regularly for a totally bald look. Six years Marshall's junior, he had been handpicked by Marshall two years earlier at a local fitness center frequented by both.

Knabel was there only to rehab a career-ending Achilles tendon injury suffered in the trenches of an NFL Europe game with the Rhein Fire. His bitterness, and lack of any future job prospects, made him easily agreeable to follow Marshall's call, doing whatever necessary to keep cash in his pockets. Ironically, his street smarts, garnered from the various stays in orphanages and foster homes growing up in northern Germany, proved to be of great value in the so-called "security" functions he had been asked to perform in the name of Sturtzburn.

Marshall's coded mobile phone rang twice, before he recovered from his semi-conscious state to catch it on the third ring.

"*Ja?*" Marshall shifted the phone from his left ear to his right, while he listened to the one-way conversation streaming from the other end.

Knabel groggily awoke from his short nap catching his bearings from the road sign that flashed past his front seat, passenger side window.

"*Ja, Ich verstehen,*" Marshall snapped the phone shut.

"That was Rudi. He has picked them up off the plane, and they have rented a car. One-way to Lucerne. He has made our life very easy. With a little help from the rental agent, he managed to get to the car before them and plant a little help on board. He will meet us on the open road to Lucerne and give us the receiver. He says the signal is perfect."

"Is he following just in case?" Alden asked.

"He's within sight. He has the make, model and plate numbers as well."

"Beautiful," Alden smiled and returned his concentration to the road, thinking out loud. "Lucerne. A one-way drop off of a rental.

That would make sense if it's around there. They'll need more than a car if they find what they're looking for."

With Courtney's help, Ferguson moved beyond the maze of the airport and accelerated on to the A3 on the way south of the city. It was going to be a gorgeous day. The low pressure that had blown through the day before had left the turquoise blue sky cloudless, the only obstructions being the incredible snow-capped peaks that poked up out of the mountainous horizon.

Once they moved to the open road, Courtney pulled her mobile phone from her purse and tapped out her father's home number. He picked up on the second ring.

"Sorry to wake you Daddy," Courtney paused briefly, "No, I'm fine." There was another pause, "No, everything's alright. Let me talk, you listen. I'm in Switzerland. I just landed in Zurich."

His daughter did not alleviate Grayson Lewis' concern, and he continued to interrupt, inquiring about her wellbeing.

"Daddy, please shut up for a minute and let me do the talking. Has anyone tried to contact you? The police in particular."

Relieved that he had not been reached by anybody, she was free to summarize her ordeal and bend the truth to allay his apprehension over what she was about to tell him.

"Well, I'm sure the police will probably try to get in touch with you soon. To put it as simply as I can, someone tried to kill me yesterday. I'm fine, and wasn't hurt, thanks to a friend," she looked over at Ferguson, smiled and winked, "but someone else was. A pizza deliveryman was shot and killed in my condo, and the man that was trying to kill me got away. The police are after him, and I thought it best to get out of town for a little vacation until they get him, or they think it's safe to return."

Lewis's angst was not diminished and his suspicions were there was more to the story than she was telling him, and he told her so.

"Dad, please relax and listen to me. The police are investigating and I am perfectly fine. When they contact you, let them know that I called, and that I was taking a little vacation overseas and that I would call you when I reach my ultimate destination, which I will. Once I call back, I'll explain everything to you in more detail. It's all gonna be fine, please trust me!" One last pause, "Thanks Daddy, I love you!"

Courtney clicked off the phone and returned it to her purse.

"That didn't sound like it went all that well," Ferguson said.

"I've never been able to lie to my father very well. He's always had the ability to see through them," she replied.

"How does your phone work overseas?"

"It's a T-Mobile system. It works domestically and internationally."

"Cool! Can I borrow that in a little while to contact Shutt? If he doesn't already know by now, he's gonna hit the roof when he finds out we've skipped the country," Ferguson chuckled aloud.

\*\*\*

"I'll be damned! They've skipped the country!" Detective Shutt had just hung up the phone from Continental reservations, and was staring at Stewart, his tongue boring a hole inside his left cheek.

A little over an hour ago, Shutt had asked Shawna to run a check on Ferguson's and Courtney's credit cards to see if they could pick up any activity that might reveal their whereabouts. If that did not work, he would move on to next of kin. Both of them had fathers out of town that he would have to speak with. Those calls could wait as of now, for ten minutes ago, they scored a hit on one each of their cards. The resultant information that lay on his desk had raised Shutt's blood pressure exponentially.

"I screwed up. We should have gotten into their credit cards sooner," Shutt shook his head in disgust of himself.

"Take it easy on yourself Toby, they didn't kill anybody," Stewart tried to ease the pain.

"No, I realize that, but they're running. Why are they running? They must be telling the truth. They have got something...something big! They said it was information...information that somebody else wants or needs."

"Sounds to me like they're scared, and they're running away from someone."

"It may be more than one. They said there could be more, and I don't think they're running scared. I believe they're trying to solve this thing on their own. They don't think we can, or they know enough about the situation that they think they can deal with it. They're trying to figure this out on their own, and part of the answer lies wherever they're headed."

"Switzerland?" Stewart asked incredulously.

"I think so or somewhere around there. Germany perhaps. Karl was German...very German."

Shutt's phone rang and he picked it up immediately, angrily greeting the inbound caller.

"Excuse me for interrupting Toby, but I've got somebody on the line that I think can shed some light on our John Doe," Shawna Hammer said excitedly.

"Excellent. Who is it?"

"See for yourself, I'm transferring him now."

"Detective Shutt?" The man's voice inquired as the click in the line signaled a change of connection.

"Speaking."

"This is Clark Burkley, I'm with the Justice Department. We had an inquiry that came to our attention that funnels back to your department. You're looking for an I.D. on a scratchy photo your office has been circulating to everyone and anyone?"

"That's correct. Can you help?"

"We can help. What's the interest?"

"He's a prime suspect in three homicides here in Louisville. Why do you need to know?"

"Your John Doe is actually a man by the name of Gerhard Alden. He goes by the aliases Thomas Michaels and Irwin Jones. He generally has been traveling as Jones in the U.S. He owns and operates a so-called 'security company' in Berlin. The company offers expert advice on personal and corporate security matters, including personal protection, computer system security and industrial espionage. He does contract work for a number of reputable and not so reputable firms and individuals, mainly in Germany and the Middle East.

"He managed to generate a criminal record in Germany for being somewhat overzealous in a few of his personal security duties. Nothing major, but enough to have two criminal indictments and one conviction, and to keep the local law enforcement agencies interested. In fact, that interest bore fruit as Alden's activities began to take on an international flavor. Besides Western Europe, he began frequenting the Middle East, predominantly Syria and Egypt, and made some trips stateside. That has also piqued the interest of some of our overseas intelligence communities, as well as the FBI and Justice. The CIA has also made some inquiries pertaining to our friend, Mr. Alden."

Shutt was busy scribbling notes as Burkley rambled on. "Are we going somewhere with this Mr. Burkley?"

"If you'll show a little patience detective, I'm about ready to connect the dots."

Shutt decided that no response to the attempt at admonishment was warranted, and he waited for several seconds in silence for Burkley to start again.

"Thank you, detective," Burkley said sarcastically. "As I was saying, Alden's international endeavors involved on and off contact with some very nefarious individuals, many of whom have direct and indirect links with some nasty terrorist organizations. We believe he may be operating as an intelligence intermediary or a financial courier for international supporters of Islamic fundamentalist terrorist groups in the Middle East, and white supremacy organizations operating in the U.S.

"It's no secret that there are still factions within Germany, many with roots back to the old Nazi regime from World War II, that have the financial resources to back organizations still bent on destroying Israel, and the Jewish population in general. These factions run the gamut from lowlifes, to some of the most important and influential people in Europe, and across the globe. Moreover, they are a very well organized and financed group. There was a particular organization known as ODESSA., which was created at the end of the war, solely for the purpose of aiding and abetting a large number of Nazi leaders, helping them to blend back into mainstream life or flee the country, all with new identities. ODESSA., and subsequent splinter groups, we believe are still viable organizations today, albeit much smaller. Lots of their constituents or members are deceased. However, we also believe they have been actively recruiting for decades, so we assume that there is fresh blood. We also have no other reason to believe that they have not grown financially over the years and have some significant resources to bear. Their missions have changed. They no longer need to protect their own, but instead have focused on renewing the extermination of Jews and the Jewish state.

"We're also of the belief that instead of openly using their own organization to further the cause against the Jews, they are utilizing the other terrorist operations out there that are more than willing to do the front-line dirty work for large sums of cold, hard cash in return. Are you still with me detective?"

"I'm lining up the dots as we go," Shutt fired back.

"Excellent, because that's all I have."

"So, you know the whereabouts of Alden?"

"Of that, I'm sorry, we don't. As you can probably surmise, we have never had enough solid evidence against him here in the states to pick him up, and he does a very good job of losing himself once he enters the U.S. We do know he entered the states two weeks ago and we're trying to confirm if he has departed the country."

"Well, let me help. I would say he is long gone from this neck of the woods. He managed to pop off three people here, so I doubt he had plans on stickin' around."

"Well, we'll do whatever we can to try and help locate him, and get him back for you, if possible," Burkley replied sincerely.

"I appreciate any help the Feds can provide. I do have one last question, however. Why is the Justice Department keeping tabs on a guy like Alden?"

"We're responsible for tracking down, prosecuting or deporting any suspected Nazi criminals residing in the U.S. We work closely with other international and domestic agencies connected to hunting down and ultimately punishing those Nazis responsible for crimes against humanity. We also like to keep apprised of the Aryan, skinhead and white supremacy movements domestically. As you might expect, many civil rights issues come into play there. Alden has managed to associate himself with quite a lot of riffraff that covers that realm of interest. Does that help answer your question?"

"Indeed. So, if I have anybody that we come across that we might suspect as being a Nazi, particularly from World War II, or a white racist you can help?" Shutt inquired, immediately making the mental connection of Dr. Karl, Syron and Nieron with what he had just heard.

"It's possible," replied Burkley, "but it can be very difficult in these days and times to prove anything as it relates to the World War II vintage Nazis. Names have changed, identities buried, and very few witnesses are left to help positively identify individuals responsible for atrocities over 50 years ago, but we never say never. You can always try some of the other organizations out there, particularly the Wiesenthal Center in Los Angeles. As for the newer breeds of white supremacy groups, we have some considerable resources to bring to the table there. Is there someone you need help with currently?"

"Thanks! No!" Shutt lied. "I appreciate the info. You will be the first contact if we come across any animals like that. Please let me know if you have any luck tracking Mr. Alden down."

"Our pleasure, and we will."

The line went dead and Shutt hung up from his end.

As if on cue, Steve Stewart entered Shutt's cubicle.

"Steve, I need you to do me a favor," Shutt had stood up from his desk and met Stewart at the door.

"You got it. What do you need?"

"I'm gonna go talk to the captain and plead my case for a little overseas journey. I need you to find me a contact in the Swiss law enforcement community that can provide me some help in Zurich, and probably around the country. It can be local or federal, I don't care."

"You can't fool me; this sounds like a little vacation compliments of the department."

"Damn you're good. That must be why you made detective."

"I didn't know you spoke their language in Switzerland, whatever they speak."

"I don't. I think they speak a little bit of everything, French, Italian...German. Whoever you find, make damn sure they speak English. Also, requisition me another cell phone, one of those T-Mobile units that work overseas. I need to have the option of being in immediate contact with you back here," Shutt turned left and headed down the hallway to the corner office.

Stewart obligingly returned to his desk, and after an unsuccessful cursory look in the blue pages of the phone book, he keyed in a search on his computer for the U. S. State Department. A few minutes of research later, he pulled up the contact information for the U. S. Embassy in Bern, Switzerland. Forty-five minutes later, with help from the Consul's office, he had a contact in the Federal Criminal Police Division of the Federal Office of Police.

Jean-Luc Daniel, thankfully spoke fluent and very intelligible English. He assured Stewart that he would coordinate with the local authorities in Zurich to assist the Americans with their investigation. Fortunately, his caseload was light at the current time, and he would be able to accompany them to Zurich, and any of the other cantons in the country they needed to visit. Unfortunately, for Stewart, *them* probably meant only Shutt. He doubted the department had the financial resources to send both of them to Switzerland. In fact, he doubted Shutt would even raise the possibility with the captain of both of them going.

As it turned out, he was right and wrong. The captain reluctantly agreed to let Shutt go alone. Shutt had asked if he could take Stewart along, but was vehemently denied, and in the process, received the obligatory budget constraints diatribe from the captain, and warnings about keeping his expenditures in check.

Ironically, and unbeknownst to Shutt, he was booked on the same flight out of Cincinnati to Zurich, that twenty-four hours earlier had carried Courtney and Ferguson to the same destination.

# Chapter 13

*May 22, 2001. Lucerne, Switzerland*

The trip to Lucerne had been both beautiful and quick. Much to Ferguson's surprise, Switzerland was actually a very small landmass, and the 65-kilometer trip from Zurich by car was just under an hour. Very little conversation transpired between the two, as the relaxing beauty of the countryside consumed them both. As they headed south, staying on the National Highways, there was a spectacular mix of rolling green hills that quickly gave way to mountainous foothills, backstopped by the snow-covered Alps rising majestically into the azure sky. Small, lazy villages with pristine, old world architecture, magnificently preserved through centuries of blissful political neutrality, passed by the windows peacefully.

When Ferguson reached the outskirts of Lucerne, he pulled over to the side of the road, reached into the back seat, and retrieved the black leather carry-on bag that had never left his sight from the time they departed Cincinnati. Milling around inside with his right hand he finally produced a manila file folder labeled "Swiss Travel" in handwritten block print.

He shuffled through several papers before finally settling on three sheets stapled together that he handed to Courtney, tossing the rest of the papers back in the folder and sliding it down between the seat and center console.

Courtney accepted them with a look of suspicion. After a quick preview of the top one, she visibly relaxed, casually licked the thumb and forefinger of her right hand and leafed through the remaining two pages, separating them between her remaining fingers.

"These look pretty nice!" Courtney returned to the first page that described in detail the *Grand Hotel National*.

"They should! They are the top hotels in the city. Hell, they're some of the top hotels in Switzerland! I figure we might as well splurge at the rate we're going."

"I had a photographer friend that used to stay and do work for the Palace," Courtney thumbed to the next page and folded over the sheets to reveal information on the *Palace Luzern*, "he always said it was beautiful."

Well, pick one out, and get me to it. If I recall correctly, from looking at them earlier, the top two are both on the same street. If you look in the folder, there's a map of the city."

"I say the Palace. In case I ever run into Mark again, I can say I've stayed there." Courtney picked up the folder and pulled out a map of the city of Lucerne, as Ferguson glanced over his shoulder for any oncoming traffic, and seeing none, guided the car off the shoulder and back on to the road into the city.

Just in sight up ahead was the mighty stone Musegg Wall. Erected between 1350 and 1408, the almost perfectly restored fortification, over 800 yards in length, formed the northern half of the ring wall, that led to a series of tower bridges over the Reuss river to the southern half of the wall. The landmark allowed Courtney to catch her bearings on the map. Having found Haldenstrasse, the street where the *Palace* was located, she backtracked to two of the most famous tower bridges, the Chapel Bridge and Spreuer Bridge. They were in view to their left, running parallel to A2 over the river, and she began the mental navigation of the maze of streets between the two points.

"You need to exit onto Baselstrasse. We'll go through downtown and back over the river. It's a piece of cake."

Ferguson sarcastically nodded in agreement. "Uh, Huh."

\*\*\*

Bolivar cleared customs under a Mexican passport bearing the name Alex Garcia, while Terry Sullivan passed into Switzerland as Kevin Sandler, a resident of Montreal, Canada. Both documented their occupations as geological engineers in the employ of DKG, Incorporated, on a visit to scout sites for a metallurgic factory destined for construction somewhere in central Europe. All of it was total fiction, but very well received by the local Swiss officials.

For Terry Sullivan, a French-Canadian cover was ideal. Born and raised in Jacksonville, Florida, he had decided to forgo college immediately after graduating high school, and opted for a summer of biking in the French, Swiss and Italian Alps. The youngest of three children, his graduation and departure from home was the final act that allowed the inevitable separation and divorce of his parents. It happened with such rapidity, that he was notified less than two months into his trek. He never went home.

Bouncing around for several years from odd job to even odder jobs, he developed a strong understanding of the languages and cultures of central Europe, particularly French, and a keen knowledge of the Alpine countryside.

By the age of twenty-five, he had completed three years of steady employment at a Burgundy region winery, complementing that experience as a sommelier at a white tablecloth bistro in Lyon, France.

He was an incredibly handsome young man. At 6′ 3″, he boasted a full head of wavy, blond hair on top of a long angular face. He maintained a well-tanned complexion, and a wiry but very strong physique, honed over the years from riding bicycles both recreationally and competitively through the mountains and flatlands of the regions.

By happenstance, the young wine steward had so impressed one of the restaurant's patrons one evening that he was summoned to the patron's hotel suite the following evening. Guillermo Rocca made Sullivan an offer he could not refuse. As a personal sommelier for Rocca International, he would be charged with creating, building and managing a wine collection for all of Rocca International's professional affiliates, the multitude of Rocca's personal residences, and the several restaurants that he held private investments in, or owned outright. Add to that, the incredible boost in income and the unlimited travel opportunities, and Sullivan accepted on the spot.

Seven years later, and his duties had expanded to include operational oversight of an Australian winery purchased by Rocca in 2000, and a distribution company in New York handling the Australian label, and several others. Detective work was not a part of his resume. Aliases and assumed identities were also new and confusing, but he was smart enough to have figured out over the years that not everything that went on in the Rocca Empire was above board. So, he was happy to oblige when asked to accompany Bolivar to Switzerland to offer his assistance in any way that he might be needed. He was told to listen to Bolivar, keep quiet and anonymous, and not ask a whole lot of questions. Once again, he knew he didn't need to be told twice.

They had walked in silence to the transportation area where Sullivan was busy negotiating in fluent French for a taxi to take them both to the STS Main Station. They had both agreed on the inbound flight that they would take the train to Lucerne and determine their transportation from there.

Bolivar picked up his black hanging bag and leather duffle and began walking to a quiet alcove that recessed into the wall of the main terminal, just off to the side of the one of many porticos that sheltered the automatic entrance and exit doors. He punched in the pre-loaded cell phone number of Gregory Keitel, who answered on the second ring.

"Herr Keitel, this is Julio Bolivar. Mr. Rocca suggested I get in touch with you. I understand that you are babysitting an important package for us."

"*Ja*, I have been for the last several hours. Your package has actually just been delivered to the *Palace Hotel* in Lucerne. Are you familiar with it?"

"No, but my traveling companion is very familiar with Switzerland, so I'm going to assume he knows where to go."

"Where are you now?" Keitel asked, slight frustration in his voice.

"We have just arrived in Zurich and we are headed to the train station."

"Call me when you get to Lucerne, and I'll arrange a meeting point," Keitel responded, realizing the "companion" must know enough about Switzerland to have chosen the trains. The Swiss Travel System was one of the finest in the world, and an excellent way to travel the country. "Enjoy the ride, it's a beautiful day."

"Thank you. We'll call...you when we arrive." The last sentence never made it through, as Keitel had already hung up on the other end.

Bolivar snapped the flip phone shut as he watched Sullivan pick up his bags and head for the taxi waiting on the curb in front of him.

"Does he still have them?" Sullivan queried as he handed the remaining bags to the driver.

"Yeah. They're in Lucerne, checked into the *Palace Hotel*," Bolivar offered a hushed reply, out of earshot of the driver.

"Ah, I know it well. I have spent some time on the Lake over the years, and the restoration on the Palace was excellent. It's one of the better hotels in Switzerland... right on the lakefront. It's quite nice!"

"Then you shouldn't have any problems getting us there?"

"None whatsoever."

They entered the backseat of the cab from both sides simultaneously. The vehicle pulled away from the curb before the sound of the closing doors had subsided.

\*\*\*

The stocky, young Latino walked through the front door of the Chicago Fairmont Hotel at 11:28 in the morning and was immediately met by Jason Allen. They introduced themselves, having had no contact whatsoever until now. The description of Allen, given to the young man by Rocca 20 hours earlier, had been dead on. "Forty-ish, boring looking little shit, with nothing remarkably distinguishable about him."

Actually, Allen was the first to exchange communication, given that a well-dressed Latino had just entered the hotel at the exact time indicated on the phone message Allen had received yesterday evening.

"Mr. Enstrada?" Allen asked hopefully, as he converged on the front desk at the same time as the stranger and extended his hand.

After an affirmative nod and recognition that the man's hands were occupied with a folded leather travel bag and matching briefcase, Allen quickly dropped his hand and continued. "My name's Jason Allen. It's a pleasure to meet you."

"My pleasure. If you please, you may call me Miguel. If you don't mind, give me a few minutes while I check in, and then we can go somewhere for lunch."

"Sure, no problem. I'll be down there when you're ready." Allen thumbed over his shoulder to a recessed, open lobby area encircled by a dozen large Greek columns. He stepped down onto the marble tile floor, sat at an empty cocktail size table, and gazed up appraisingly at the young man as he went through the formality of registering for his room.

Miguel Enstrada was 28 years old, short and stocky, with a full head of black, curly hair that helped narrow his round face. The Tommy Bahama khaki linen slacks emphasized his dark, South American skin color, and taupe, tan and cream flowered silk sport shirt. The stockiness was actually nothing more than serious muscle mass resulting from a stout training regimen that had begun while becoming an all-state tennis player in high school, and continued with two years of service on the University of Texas tennis squad. He had never relinquished his love of the sweat equity involved in fitness training.

The one important aspect of the young Ecuadorian that Allen had not been made aware of was Miguel Enstrada was the nephew of Guillermo Rocca. Rocca International had employed him since graduating from U. T. with a Finance degree almost six years ago. His mother, Lolita, Rocca's youngest sister, had given birth to Miguel out of wedlock at the tender young age of 17. After the father had refused to marry the expectant Lolita, Rocca had personally beaten him to near death, before giving him the choice of a one-way ticket out of the country, or letting the two henchmen that held the sobbing and bloodied man castrate him on the spot. The former offer was quickly accepted, and he was never heard from again.

Rocca had seen to it that Lola and her baby boy never wanted for anything, even after she later married. He remained active in the young boy's upbringing, which included providing for a high school and college education in the United States, and similar educations for his other three nieces and nephews.

Enstrada, however, had been the smartest and most ambitious of the lot, and that had earned him not only an entry-level position with the corporate office right out of college, but a warm spot in the heart of the boss. His entry-level status was short lived, however, and he moved upward through the organization quickly, proving his merit by masterminding two rather ugly and ruthless acquisitions that had proved to be extremely complementary to the mining side of the business, and extraordinarily profitable.

He was quiet, charming and unassuming, but underneath the demure exterior lay a hard and merciless young man. He had won the faith and trust of his uncle both in the boardroom and out, and was the one person everyone in the Rocca organization felt was the successor to the old man. Ironically, he also held a similar fanatical passion for the arts and the opposite sex.

Enstrada completed the process of checking in and tipped the bellhop with a twenty-dollar bill to forward his luggage to the room.

He turned to find Allen, who had jumped to his feet and was up the stairs to greet him again.

Enstrada reached out his hand this time, "Sorry Mr. Allen, Miguel Enstrada. Please excuse my shortness back there," he nodded over his shoulder to the front desk, "It was a long flight, and as usual the taxi drivers in the United States speak less English than they do in Ecuador."

Allen took his hand, "Nice to meet you. If I had known when and where your flight arrived, I would've been more than happy to have picked you up."

"That's quite alright Mr. Allen, I wasn't—"

"Please, call me Jason," Allen interrupted.

"Thank you, Jason. As I was saying, I wasn't sure what flight I was going to make until last night."

"I'm double-parked right outside, if you would care to join me, we can head for some lunch and you can fill me in on why you need my assistance," Allen directed the two of them out the revolving door and to the waiting BMW 540i that was being carefully guarded by the doorman, who was still sporting the ten-dollar bill Allen had given him 20 minutes earlier.

"Any preference on food?" Allen asked as they pulled out from the hotel entrance onto the East Lake street service level that led down to Michigan Avenue.

"Italian sounds nice."

"We have plenty of those," Allen laughed sarcastically. "One of my favorite spots is Luciano's over on Rush Street."

"I'll look forward to it," said Enstrada enthusiastically, hiding his fear of the quality of restaurant that this little pussy would classify as "one of his favorites".

As it turned out, Enstrada's concern over the restaurant was unwarranted. Cafe Luciano was excellent. They had been seated at a two top in the front dining room, adjacent to the open-air front window that provided a very attractive view of the Triangle Park across Rush Street and bordered by Chestnut and Wabash. It also allowed Enstrada to light up the Cuban cigar he had been entertaining in his shirt pocket since taking off from the Dallas/Fort Worth airport earlier that morning.

The food had been superb, and far superior to the casual, but weary conversation, dominated by Allen's attempt at making his persona larger than it truly was. To ease the boredom, Enstrada had excused himself to the restroom once, and stepped away to the bar to answer a phone call and place two others.

Enstrada grew weary of Allen's collective portrayal of himself as a talented starving artist turned master art critic, with an insatiable desire for wine, women and money, of which he claimed to have no problems fulfilling at any time. Enstrada recognized his feeble attempt at self-importance, hoping to command respect from one of Rocca's employees. If only he knew. Actually, it was time he knew.

"Let's get to the point of my visit Jason. I need your assistance on a very important matter for my Uncle."

Allen slumped back in his chair and tried to disguise his shock and embarrassment. His sales job on himself had probably fallen on deaf ears.

"Please, no one gave me any particulars on the message I received about your visit." Allen replied in a confident manner, trying his best to recover.

"You provided some important information that has actually progressed to the point of potentially coming to fruition."

"They found the works?"

"Let me finish, please," Enstrada said admonishingly.

A brief, uncomfortable silence ensued.

"Once again, as I was saying, you have been of some enormous help, and you will be rewarded for your loyalty and discretion, but the outcome is still in doubt. We need another favor from you. And it will certainly up the ante on the monetary return as far as you're concerned."

Allen's pulse quickened, sensing a larger payday than he had imagined. He wondered to himself if he should start a bargaining process to determine the exact amount of compensation, but he was cognizant of Rocca's reputation for ruthlessness, and he quickly extinguished that thought, particularly given the bowling ball of muscle that sat across the table from him.

"You will need to consider me an emissary of my Uncle, representing his interests, specifically his art collection. We may have an interest in placing his collection in exhibit, and because of his fondness for Chicago, we are seriously considering the Art Institute as one, or possibly the only location."

Allen's curiosity engaged. He instinctively was having doubts about the overture. Rocca's collection was well known, but as many experts suspected, was reputed to have a number of illegal works. Consequently, he had never expressed an interest in exhibiting his collection. Even if he exhibited his legitimate works, the exposure was sure to touch off a firestorm of accusations and negative publicity that might raise questions and inquiries that Rocca would have no interest in dealing with.

"Would that be of interest to you and Mr. Lewis?"

"I'm sure Grayson would love to have some discussion regarding Mr. Rocca's collection," Allen replied without hesitation or a hint of the apprehension that was setting in.

"Fabulous, can you make those discussions a reality? Can you put me in front of Mr. Lewis?"

"Sure. I think that part would be easy."

"And you think what would be difficult?"

"Nothing...actually, just putting the whole thing together," Allen stuttered in reply. He unwittingly had just divulged his concerns in his confirmation of arranging a meeting with Grayson Lewis. He was struggling mightily with the whole direction of the request. Something else was happening here, but he was not sure what.

Enstrada recognized the insecurity in Allen's voice and realized that he was probably surprised by the idea advanced for exhibiting Rocca's collection, and why he was involved in setting up a meeting with Grayson Lewis. Nevertheless, he could care less about the imaginations of one Jason Allen. He was certain that Allen would never figure out what was about to transpire.

"Can you speak with Mr. Lewis and get back to me in the next 24 hours?"

"Sure, I'll see him this afternoon and can call you at your hotel this evening. Is there a time you had in mind?"

"I would be happy to meet with him tomorrow or the next day, whichever is convenient. Lunch...dinner, either one, my treat."

"I'll let you know."

"Excellent." Enstrada took a long last puff on the Cuban and extinguished it into the glass ashtray. "I'll wait to hear from you."

With that, Enstrada stood, signaled to Allen to remain seated, pulled a money clip from his pocket, peeled off a one-hundred-dollar bill, and placed it on the table.

"Can I give you a lift back to the hotel?"

"Thank you, but that won't be necessary."

As if on cue, a black Mercedes limousine pulled to the curb outside the front entrance on Rush Street. Enstrada, exited the dining room, walked out onto the sidewalk as the black suited chauffeur opened the back door to let out a long-legged blond in a peach colored tube dress that appeared painted on the more than ample figure. She emerged just in time to give Enstrada a hug and kiss a returning soldier would be proud of. They crawled into the back seat still entangled. The door closed...and they were gone.

Allen laughed to himself. *Samantha? No, that's not it. Serena? No, it was Sabrina. That's right, Sabrina, obviously per Uncle Guillermo's recommendation.* The recollection could not help but conjure up memories of Ginger, who had been nothing short of spectacular.

***

The black Mercedes sedan pulled over to the curb a good one hundred kilometers down Haldenstrasse from the Palace Hotel. The driver and two passengers waited patiently as a fourth man stood up from a wood bench located in the public green space adjacent to the Palace's Le Maritime restaurant, and walked down the tree lined sidewalk to the rear passenger door.

Rudi Koch climbed into the back seat next to Paul Knabel who was holding a Leica SLR camera to his eye, busily adjusting the focus on the long telephoto lens.

"Gentlemen!" Rudi exclaimed with enthusiasm in German. "A pleasure to see you all!"

"The same!" replied Alden in English, as Marshall and Knabel greeted Koch in unison seconds later. "My German is weaker than anybody, can we please keep it to English?"

"No problem," replied Koch. "They're actually on the terrace restaurant, around the corner facing the lake. They were just seated. They have checked in and their car is in the garage below. The signal is pretty poor through the concrete, but it is strong enough to know if they are here or not. Here are two receivers, in case one craps out on you," he handed them both to Alden over the headrest of the front passenger seat.

"Which room?" Alden inquired.

"Suite 203. They got comped a suite for regular room deal. The place is pretty full."

"Damn. We'll need to get Horst and Paul a room. I'll go somewhere else. They are sure to recognize me if I get within eyesight. Do both of you have enough currency to make sure the desk clerk comes up with a room?" Alden directed his gaze at Marshall behind the wheel.

"Plenty. The boss fattened me up pretty good before we came for you," Marshall spoke for the two of them.

"Excellent," Alden reached into his pocket for an envelope and handed it back over the seat to Koch, who eagerly accepted it. "Thanks for your help Rudi. Nice work."

"My pleasure! Do you need me for anything else?"

"Not right now. Are you going to be around the area?"

"I'm working on an infidelity case, and I'll be down in the south of France for the next few days taking pictures. Koch gestured to the camera Knabel was still perusing. "It's a nasty one. It will cost the guy millions when my client gets her greedy little hands on the stuff this guy's into. She will bust his chops good when she hits him with a divorce decree. His little forays make the hardest porno movies look tame."

"Excellent, I'll call you on your mobile if we need you for anything else."

With that, Koch tucked the envelope into the pocket of his field jacket and exited the car walking the opposite direction from the hotel.

"Capable man?" Knabel finally spoke.

"Very. He is one of the best detectives in Munich, and very busy. He does quite well financially," Alden said.

"And I'll bet we just fattened his account a little more," Marshall laughed.

"Substantially, but he's worth it. He has a steel trap for a mouth," Alden stared at the Palace Hotel. "Enough of Rudi, we need to get you two into the hotel and find you a room. Horst, I will leave that up to you. I'll drop you and your luggage at the front and take Paul with me down the street to the National. He can walk down later. He'll know the phone number and my room."

"You want me to try to bug their room? I have some basic stuff with me," Marshall turned over the engine and pulled away from the curb and onto the street, heading for the front door of the Palace.

"No, let's just keep an eye on them for the time being. I am going to assume they'll be headed into the backcountry sometime tomorrow or the next day. Maybe one of us can stay behind and rig up their room then," Alden slouched down in his front seat and replaced his sunglasses as they reached the hotel entrance.

Marshall put the car in park and left it running as he hopped out of the driver seat and retrieved two sets of luggage from the open trunk. Knabel emerged from the back seat, closed the trunk, and replaced Marshall in the driver's seat. They gently pulled away from the temporary parking area as Marshall dropped the luggage onto a cart, and began negotiating with the bellhop who was eagerly assisting him as the Mercedes sped away.

***

An hour earlier the same bellhop had also been most accommodating in handling Courtney's and Ferguson's luggage, while the valet driver ticketed the rental car and keys, and removed it to the parking garage beneath the six story, "Art Nouveau", century old structure.

They entered the hotel on the western end of the building, highlighted by marble statues and a shaded glass portico that protected the entrance, up a flight of marble stairs, and into a large open-air, luxurious lobby. Courtney and Ferguson made their way over to the traditional wood and brass reservation desk, with Courtney again preparing to test her German on the young man that visually greeted them as they drew near.

*"Guten tag mein herren, sprechen sie English?"*

"Pretty well, but I could always improve," said the young reservation clerk with a pleasant smile, and a French accent.

Relieved once again, Ferguson started to initiate the request for rooms, but this time Courtney beat him to the punch.

"*Ausgetsichtnet!* My German, I am sure, is worse than your English, and my French is even worse. We need a room please. Two beds," Courtney looked at Ferguson. "How many nights?"

"I'm not real sure...let's make it for two nights at least." Ferguson shrugged his shoulders.

The clerk interjected, "We are very full. The only room we have available, with sleeping accommodations for two, this evening is a Corner Suite."

"Ouch," Ferguson muttered softly, envisioning the price tag. "Can you give us any suggestions on other hotels close by?"

The clerk was quick to continue, recognizing an opportunity for an open-ended stay. "Yes, but however, please let me inquire with management to see if we can provide at our deluxe room price, if that's of interest," He didn't wait for a reply and was already dialing the desk phone and turning his back away from them as he spoke softly and nodded his head profusely to the mystery manager on the other end.

"What prompted that?" Ferguson asked Courtney, who was gazing admiringly around the lobby.

"Beats me, maybe he's taking pity on us. I haven't had a shower in sometime, and I look like the cat just drug me in."

Ferguson laughed obligingly, "Speak for yourself, I feel, and I'm certain, I look like a million bucks." He could not help but think how incredibly beautiful she looked regardless of her assessment. "Figment of your imagination," Courtney responded with a hint of sarcasm.

The clerk turned back to the two of them and winked as he began to peck at the computer keyboard in front of him. "We can give you the Suite at our Deluxe room rate of 345 francs per evening. We can book you for two nights, and you may renew indefinitely for each day thereafter."

"The exchange rate at the airport was .75 francs to the dollar," Courtney added.

"Sold," Ferguson pointed his finger at the clerk.

"Excuse me?" Questioned the startled clerk.

"He means we'll take it," Courtney said.

"Very good. And the name?"

Ferguson handed him an American Express card.

The clerk began typing. "Mr. and Mrs. Matthew Ferguson. And your address?"

Courtney looked at Ferguson as the two of them burst out in laughter.

"If we plan on cohabitating in the same room, I might as well have the respect of being your wife."

"It'll be my pleasure," Ferguson turned to the clerk and proceeded to answer all of the questions posed to him in registering the Fergusons in the Palace Hotel.


Le Maritime restaurant, an outdoor cafe on the lakefront side of the hotel, was crowded for lunch. It was understandable given the incredible spring day in the Swiss Alps. The sun was shining brightly in a virtually cloudless sky, and the temperature had risen to 18 degrees Celsius by early afternoon.

Courtney had finally been able to utilize her newly developed skill in languages. The waitress was fluent in French, and spoke a respectable amount of German, but her English left a lot to be desired. They settled on German.

Over a plate of cheese, fruit and homemade French bread for Courtney, and Ferguson's corned beef sandwich on identical bread, they shared a bottle of St. Veran Caves des Grand Blanc white wine.

"When we finish lunch, I need you to go shopping...sightseeing," Ferguson announced, acting as if evaluating the wine as he swirled his third glass directly in front of his face.

"Okay. I can do that. Am I looking for something in particular?"

"No, but I want you to use your credit cards. Nice choice on the wine, this is really good."

"Thanks. What's with the credit cards?"

Ferguson held up his hand and paused to finish chewing the last bite of his sandwich. "Everything we've done to get here has been on credit cards. Airline tickets, rental car, hotel room, everything is traceable. I have no doubt that the police have traced our credit cards and know exactly where we are. Maybe not the hotel yet, but as soon as the transaction goes through for the room, they'll clue in.

"The same goes for the bad guys, whoever it is that's still after us. They may not be as close as the police, but I'm going to assume that they have the ways or means to track us down, and if I were in their shoes I'd start with personal history, which includes credit cards."

"So why did we do that...the credit cards I mean? You could have warned me."

"Well," he finished off his glass, "because by tomorrow we won't be here. And where we're headed, hopefully, no one will know for a while."

"Let me guess," Courtney sighed and pushed herself back from her plate, "We're not even close. At the very least we're headed in the wrong direction."

"Let's just say we're in the right country, and leave it at that."

"So, you're not going to tell me where we're going?"

"Not for now," Ferguson poured out the balance of the bottle of wine, moving from glass to glass measuring out even amounts in both.

"Oh ye of little faith."

"Oh ye of scared to death, particularly if the bad guys find out where we are. My feeling is the less you know the better and safer for you," Ferguson spoke the truth, but with not enough conviction.

"Bullshit. You don't trust me."

"Not true. You'll know soon enough."

"Yeah, as long as you take me along and don't leave me behind, especially if you had planned on using me as some decoy."

"Damnit Courtney, I'm not going to use you and I'm certainly not going to leave you behind. You're in this with me to the bitter end, unless you want out on your own." The anger in Ferguson's voice was more convincing.

"I'm not going anywhere," Courtney suddenly felt badly for the spontaneous doubt that had overcome her sensibilities. "You're stuck with me. And I'm sorry, I didn't mean to upset you."

"Forget it," Ferguson fought the urge to tell her that he actually was beginning to feel more than a sense of camaraderie. His feelings were starting to run deeper, but he knew now was not the time to go there.

"I'll be happy to go out and spend some credit somewhere. That's one of the things I do best," Courtney attempted to lighten the mood.

"Good. It sounds to me like we are stuck with each other. This whole affair may not be pretty, and it may not be all that fun, but I'll guarantee that there will be no lack of excitement."

"Let me be the judge on the *fun* part," Courtney saluted him with a raise of her wine glass and polished off the remainder of her wine in one large gulp. She continued to stare at Ferguson as he looked off at a placid Lake Lucerne. There was something about this man that she already found exciting.

# Chapter 14

*May 22, 2001. Zurich, Switzerland*

Detective Toby Shutt was escorted into a plush conference room on the second floor of the *Kantonpolizei Zurich* building in Zurich Switzerland. His trip over the Atlantic had been surprisingly comfortable, but it should have been, compared to the last time Shutt had been overseas. That was 17 years ago when he had shipped out in a miserably uncomfortable C-130 as a very young lance corporal in the United States Army, on his way to a six-month tour in Stuttgart, Germany.

Jean-Luc Daniel had met him at the airport, and with an outstanding command of the English language, had made the trek from the airport to a downtown coffee shop a lively and informative one. After a light breakfast and three cups of coffee that Shutt was convinced may have been the best coffee he had ever had, Daniel provided a short tour of downtown Zurich and the lakefront before they arrived at the local police office. Shutt had learned more in three hours about the Swiss law enforcement establishment, than he could have in days or weeks back home. He also had found about thirty minutes to brief Daniel on the two material witnesses he was searching for in Switzerland.

Daniel was middle-aged, tall and thin with a refined air about him. He was handsome, and very polished in a tailored navy wool suit, a starched, white, French cuffed shirt and silk regimental stripe tie. His full head of blond hair was slicked and combed back. He was soft-spoken, but very affable, with a demeanor that exuded professionalism. There was no doubt in Shutt's mind that Jean-Luc Daniel, was someone of importance in the hierarchy of the Swiss Federal Police, or at the very least possessing the intelligence and political savvy to help with a representative of the United States' law enforcement community. In reality, he was right on both counts.

Daniel was head of the Coordination Division of the Federal Criminal Police Division, which manages all inter-cantonal and international investigations and the police liaison offices abroad. The CD also functions as a center for the exchange of information with Interpol offices outside the country. At his age, he was on the fast track to the head of the FCP, and Shutt should have been flattered to have Daniel personally overseeing his visit, if he only knew of his stature.

They had spent the last hour going through the pleasantries of meeting with the officers of the local canton office before being guided to the unoccupied second floor conference room. Daniel excused himself from the room to locate something to drink, leaving Shutt alone to use the new mobile phone that had been requisitioned to him. He glanced at his watch, which he had yet to reset to the correct local time, and read the time at home as 9:37am. He dialed up Steve Stewart's office phone, which was promptly answered before the second ring.

"Steve, it's Toby. Can you hear me?"

"Loud and clear boss. Are you on the T-Mobile?"

"I am. I am also in Zurich at the local canton police office. By the way, thanks for coming up with Jean-Luc, the guy's a godsend."

"Glad to hear it, he sounded pretty professional over the phone."

"Very much so. Have you had any luck while I was buzzin' the Atlantic?"

"Actually, we have," Stewart grabbed his notepad from in front of his computer, and swiveled his seat around to kick his feet up on the edge of his desk. "They're headed to Lucerne, which is south of Zurich. Not too far away, according to the map I have up on the computer. They booked a rental car for a one-way drop-off in Lucerne."

"Very good. Hold on just a second," Shutt reacted to Daniel returning with two cold bottled waters. "Thanks Jean-Luc. Hang on just a minute, I'm talking to my office back in Louisville, and I may need your input." Daniel removed his coat, tossed it over the back of one of the ten cushioned armchairs surrounding the long mahogany conference table, and selected a second chair to sit in.

"Sorry Steve, go ahead." Shutt returned his conversation to the mobile phone.

"That's all we know at this point. We are getting a list of all the hotels in Lucerne, and Shawna and I will get started on calling those to look for any Ferguson or Lewis that might have registered. If the names don't come up, we'll go with descriptions, and if it's anything close, we will fax pictures. We pulled photos from DMV. Both of their credit cards are being monitored, but nothing has hit the screen. We did find out Courtney Lewis' cell phone is also a T-Mobile, and she had a very recent conversation with a Chicago number that we're tracking down now."

"You've been busy."

"Somebody better be. It seems you're on vacation."

"Amusing," Shutt deadpanned. As soon as I finish with my sauna and swim, I'll call you from the massage table to get an update. Better yet, if you get a hit on any hotels call me back ASAP and I'll get the locals to help me here. Jean-Luc seems to think we should be able to get any help we want to bring them in for questioning. In the meantime, give me Miss Lewis' mobile number again, and I'll give her a little jingle to see if she's around."

Stewart read off the number as Shutt scribbled it down in his leather-bound notepad, passed on his farewell, and hung up.

Shutt turned his attention back to Daniel. "It appears my friends are in Lucerne. Is that close?"

"Quite. Just south of here on A4, no more than an hour by car."

"We're trying all the hotels. We don't know if they've gone underground or traveling under their own I.D."

"What can we do here to assist you detective?"

"Please, I've already told you, call me Toby," Shutt reminded him of an earlier request. As for the help, nothing significant right now. As I mentioned earlier, I do not believe these two are dangerous. They are basically running scared from some bad folks. If you don't mind, I could use you, and your ability to call for some backup if we run into a situation that calls for surrounding them. I really don't anticipate it coming to that."

"As I said before, I'm at your disposal. I can call the Lucerne office to let them know we'll be headed their way and to be ready to provide us assistance if requested," Daniel couched it as much as a question as a statement.

"That would be perfect, thank you very much," Shutt responded in his most politically correct tone.

Daniel glanced at the large round clock on the wall above the door, pursed his lips and touched them lightly with the barrel of his right forefinger as he wandered briefly into thought. In immediate recognition, Shutt cocked his head and raised his eyebrows, looking directly at Daniel waiting for an inevitable proclamation of something important.

It came quickly. "It's almost five o'clock. Since we are unaware of the whereabouts of your runaways, why don't we get checked into a hotel here in Zurich. That will give you time to catch your breath from your flight, and we can arrange to have a nice meal. If anything comes up from your research back home, and they are fortunate enough to locate them, I will have the local office attach some officers to keep an eye on their location until we get there. We can be in Lucerne first thing in the morning, and you will be able to catch up on some sleep."

"I had always heard the Swiss were loaded with hospitality, but if you keep this up, I'm going to have to agree with my partner back home."

"And what would you be agreeing to?"

"He's accused me of being on vacation."

"No one ever said you couldn't mix work with pleasure. This evening we will work on the pleasure."

"I'm at your disposal," Shutt mocked, extending his right arm to the opened door.

***

It was late and the Le Artistes restaurant had extinguished most of its guests. Nevertheless, there was still a hand full of tables of die-hard diners unwilling to relinquish the night. The beautifully lit Belle-Epoque architecture of the dining room, the breathtaking view of Lake Lucerne at night eclipsing the entire south wall of exterior facing windows, and the outstanding Mediterranean cuisine made their decision to leave a difficult one. The cocktails and wine had only served to enhance the exceptional white tablecloth experience for those still relishing the evening.

Courtney and Ferguson were still enthusiastically ensconced at a table for two by the same windows overlooking the torch lights and large canvas umbrellas of the Le Maritime restaurant outside. Adjacent was the tree-lined sidewalk bordering the Lake, where the small ornamental lights strung in the branches reflected off the black water as if mirroring the stars in the dark sky above. It had been a delightful evening for both of them. The faint aroma of garlic and curry still lingered from their shrimp and chicken pasta entrees, battling for olfactory supremacy over the scent left by the apricot flambé that neither claimed they had room to finish, but had left nary a crumb on the plate.

"Picasso could have painted this scene to perfection," Courtney observed. "Or Degas. Any of the impressionists for that matter would have loved the mix of light, color and reflection to blend into a nebulous replica."

"It sounds to me you've been artistically inspired by your trek today. Either that or it's the second bottle of wine talking," Ferguson mirrored her stare out the window.

Courtney had taken Ferguson's advice earlier in the day and had walked by foot along the lakeside quays, across several of Lucerne's old squares, and through the streets of old town. She had shopped successfully along Kapellgasse and visited Altes Rathaus, an impressive masonry Renaissance building and tower from 1602, which served as the old town hall. Just left of the town hall on Furrengasse is the A-Rhyn-Haus, a 17th-century building housing a small but choice collection of the works of Pablo Picasso. Courtney was familiar with its existence, and was mindful to make that her top priority while sightseeing the city.

The collection had been a gift from Siegfried and Angela Rosengart, who presented the city of Lucerne on its 800th anniversary with eight masterpieces by the famous artist, one for each century. The outstanding works include *Woman and Dog Playing* (1953), *Woman Dressing Her Hair* (1954), *The Studio* (1955), *Rembrandtesque Figure and Cupid* (1969), and a sculpture, *Woman with a Hat* (1961). There were additional paintings and sculptures, as well as drawings, original prints and ceramics from the last 20 years of the artist's life displayed on three levels of the museum.

"I'd say it's a little of both," Courtney cocked her head and stared at Ferguson. "Add to that an incredibly delicious evening, and lastly, the quality of the company."

*I can't believe I just said that. But it's true.*

"I couldn't have said it better myself," Ferguson extended his wine glass toward her and received the slight touch of the glass as Courtney reciprocated the movement.

"It actually has been an awesome day. I had heard some wonderful things about the Rosengart collection, and I wasn't disappointed...and the city is gorgeous. I can't believe I never took the time to get over here when I was working in Europe. What in the world did you do this afternoon, besides take a nap?"

"I needed to rest, get my thoughts together. Organize some sort of strategy on what we do next. Everything we've done to date has been somewhat by the seat of our pants. Now comes the fun part to see if we can find what we came for."

"And were you successful?"

"I think I might've come up with a plan or two."

"Why don't you tell me all about 'em while you escort this lady on a walk by the lakefront. It's a wonderful night outside, and I'm dying for a moonlit stroll."

"I would be honored," Ferguson signaled the waiter, who had been patiently waiting out their table and a boisterous group of six, for a check.

Courtney was right about the evening outdoors. The temperature had cooled to a brisk six degrees Celsius, but still warm for May. They huddled against each other as they strolled through the maze of trees and lights, up to the wrought iron fence guarding the edge of the lake and the small pier and series of individual boat docks that lined the adjacent waterfront area of the hotel.

The three-quarter moon reflected against the water, along with the unobstructed stars and the city lights of the medieval, but still modern little fishing village. There was just enough light in the sky to pick up the blackened and imposing outline of the Alps to the south. They walked in silence for nearly ten minutes up and back Haldenstrasse, until the cold started to set in.

"It's beautiful," Courtney wrapped her arms tighter around Ferguson for warmth.

"Not quite as beautiful as you," Ferguson heard himself say in disbelief.

It was all Courtney needed to stop and pull herself around to face him. "Really?"

That was all that both of them needed. They embraced, kissed each other briefly and then continued kissing each other, oblivious of the cold surrounding them, for another five minutes.

"I think it may be time to go in," Courtney finally interrupted.

The statement was not lost on either of them. They walked quickly arm in arm up the large stone staircase that entered on the lake side of the hotel, and through the large brass doors that deposited them into the warmth of the restaurant and lobby level. After a brief conversation with the concierge, they helped themselves to an empty elevator, and reached the hotel room, again in silence, both comfortably wrapped to one another.

"You're not going to like me very much, after you hear what I'm about to say," Ferguson fumbled for the room key.

"What do you mean?" Courtney replied as they entered the room together. She immediately noticed his luggage stacked inside by the door and turned to face him with a look that in Ferguson's mind actually raised fear for his safety.

Earlier in the afternoon, Ferguson had been busy. Once Courtney had left to tour the town, he had taken the stairs to the lower level garage, found their car, and promptly disabled it. He then returned to the room and called the local Hertz office. After several minutes of an interesting conversation that neither he, nor the agent on the other end, had any clue of what the other said, he was able to speak to someone that knew enough English to understand that the car they currently had rented was not working and that he needed a replacement auto, no later than this evening. It could be delivered to the hotel and the keys given to the concierge, who would have the keys to the other vehicle that was not starting.

The next call was to the front desk. He spoke to the same man that had so kindly booked them the suite, and unfortunately informed him that due to an emergency back in the states they would be leaving early the next morning to return to the Zurich airport. He was willing to pay the full price for the room, but the man at the front desk would not hear of it, and was sorry to hear about their misfortune and politely invited them to stay with the hotel again if they should ever return to Lucerne. Ferguson thanked him profusely, and indicated that the Palace would be their destination as soon as they could return to the area. Deep down he sincerely meant it.

After the phone calls, he rode the elevator to the lobby, and met with the concierge, who thankfully spoke fluent English. After determining that he would be on duty through the late evening hours, Ferguson handed the young man a $100 bill and instructed him as to his role in obtaining a new rental car to be delivered later that evening. If the car did not show up by 7:00 pm, he was to track him down immediately. If it arrived, Ferguson asked that it be taken to the garage and have it available to leave anytime after 11:00. He would call to have their luggage transferred from the room to the car. He handed over the keys to the Mercury Sable that was no longer operational, and left a description of the problem he had encountered with the car, and asked that the same information be passed on to the service people that Hertz indicated would be at the hotel in the morning.

Finally, he returned to his room, took a long hot shower, made himself comfortable in bed with a glass of wine from the bar and picked up the new Jack Higgins book he had started on the flight over. The combination of jet lag, the shower, alcohol, and the book eventually worked their magic. He had nodded off an hour later and slept for three, awakening in plenty of time to meet Courtney as she returned for a shower and dinner. He was grateful for the nap; he knew he would need it.

The concierge received the new rental car early that evening, and therefore never had a need to contact Ferguson. However, as Courtney and Ferguson waltzed through the lobby on the way back to their room from their incredible evening, Ferguson noticed the young man as he went out of his way to signal affirmatively with a circled thumb and forefinger as they approached the elevators.

"Give me just a second," Ferguson said to Courtney, as they released each other, and she watched as he walked over to the concierge.

Ferguson reached into his pocket and retrieved several Swiss Francs, which immediately were transferred to the open palm of the concierge. Along with the compensation, Ferguson proceeded to tell him that the young lady he was with, motioning to Courtney who waved back at the two of them, was a famous model who was about to be inundated with paparazzi in the morning, when they discovered her whereabouts.

Unfortunately, they would need to leave the hotel this evening, and thus the secrecy with the car. He would need their luggage to be transferred from their room to the new rental car within the next thirty minutes, but to be very secretive about doing so. He also instructed him that once loaded with luggage to have the car brought to the interior door of the parking garage, and to ring their room when it was ready.

"Any questions?" Ferguson asked the concierge.

"No," he replied shaking his head. "I'll have you ready to go in thirty minutes. Is your luggage ready?"

"Mine is, hers is not. Give us about twenty minutes, and you can come on up."

"Yes sir," he said smiling, winking his understanding of Ferguson's desire.

Ferguson turned and walked back to Courtney, who was holding an open elevator for them. *I only wish. I'll be lucky if she doesn't kill me.*

Once inside the room, and the door closed, Ferguson recognized the rage, and reading her mind he quickly interjected. "We're leaving tonight, and I do mean 'we'. Both of us. I need you to pack, they'll be here to get our luggage soon. I'll explain in the car."

"Excuse my French, but what in the fuck is going on?" Courtney said, going from a subtle tone to loud anger by the end of the sentence.

"I told ya, you weren't going to like me very much."

"You're damn right! A minute ago, I thought I might be developing some rather strong feelings for you, and God forbid I even had conjugal thoughts in mind, but now I want to punch you in the mouth. Why are we leaving now? You just ruined one of the better evenings I have ever had. You might want to explain before we get to the car. That's if I go to the car with you!"

"Fair enough," Ferguson knew he would not get her calmed down enough to get her downstairs without some sort of explanation.

He opened the door slightly, peeked into the hallway to find it clear, and closed the door again behind them.

"Please listen to me for just a minute," he continued. "I've got a hunch, or call it a bad feeling, that we're already being watched. I did the math on the time we have been here, and how long it would take either the police, or anybody else with the capabilities to locate us in Zurich, to reach us from the U.S. or closer. They could be here by now, easily. Hell, I don't know if they are. I haven't noticed anybody, but I doubt anyone is advertising themselves either. But if my plan to throw them off for a while, by leading them here and then disappearing without a trace, has a chance to succeed, we had better not do it in broad daylight. As far as I can tell, if anybody has been watching us tonight, my guess is they don't think we're going anywhere but back to our room for..."

"A conjugal visit?" Courtney loudly interrupted.

"Exactly. If we can sneak out of here in the next hour, without being seen, we have a good chance of getting lost for a good while."

Courtney was silent. She still could not mask her anger, but she was at least succumbing to the logic. "So, tonight was all an act!" She said emphatically, storming off to the bathroom and slamming the door behind her.

Ferguson walked to the door and thought about opening it, but decided talking through it was the better choice. "Yes and no," he said.

"Yes, I wanted to put on a display that would appear as if we were staying comfortably put for a while. No, I didn't plan on having such a good time in the process. That was probably the nicest evening I have ever had with a woman in my life, and the comments I made about you were from the heart, honest. I have a hard-enough time speaking like a normal human being around women, much less one as beautiful and as smart as you are. Believe me, my feelings for you run deeper than you damn well know."

Silence.

As Ferguson turned to walk away, the door to the bathroom cracked open, and Courtney stuck her nose and mouth out and spoke quietly. "Give me five minutes. I'll be packed and ready in five minutes."

"Take your time, I'm going to call the concierge and he's going to run our luggage in shifts. You have at least 20 or 30 minutes," Ferguson replied calmly, overcoming the urge to go back to the open door and take her back into his arms.

# Chapter 15

*May 23, 2001. Lucerne, Switzerland*

Julio Bolivar was blowing the steam away from his recently refilled cup of coffee, and surveying the breakfast menu at the Le Maritime restaurant when Terry Sullivan approached and sat down opposite him.

Sullivan was clean shaven and looked refreshed, which was a significant improvement compared to Bolivar, and Keitel who was around the front of the Palace Hotel still seated in his BMW. The two of them had been alternating shifts in the vehicle throughout the evening, one napping while the other held vigil on the hotel lobby and garage. The lucky one of the three, which in this case turned out to be Sullivan, mainly for the obvious reason that he was as green as grass when it came to surveillance and detective work, got to bed down in the National Hotel for the evening.

Keitel and Bolivar had dropped Sullivan off at the hotel early the previous evening after Keitel had decided to meet the train they had taken in from Zurich. He had Bolivar's cell number on his cell phone from the incoming call Bolivar had placed from the airport. It had been easy to talk them out of the train station and to his waiting car on *Bahnhofplatz*.

They could see the Palace and National Hotels from across the lake and made it over to both in less than ten minutes. With Keitel already having determined the lack of vacancy at the Palace, he had promptly secured a room at the National down the street. Sullivan was deposited at the National, while Keitel and Bolivar visited the Palace Bar, confirmed the registration of the Fergusons, and grew more acquainted with each other over dinner in Jaspers and another eleven hours of partnered vigilance.

"Morning Julio," Sullivan said cheerfully. "Have you ordered yet?"

"Good morning. Not yet, I'm still trying to wake up. I trust you slept well."

"Very well. Thanks for giving me the night off."

*We didn't have a choice you dumbshit.* "You're welcome," replied Bolivar. "You're back at work as of now, however. We are going to put you in the lobby for a while. Hopefully, some rooms will become available this morning and we will book a room that all of us can share. If they're still booked up, either Greg or myself will go back to the National and clean up. Have you eaten?"

"No, I came straight here after you called."

"Well, let's get an order in, and go check with the front desk for a room."

Bolivar signaled at the attractive blond server two tables over that was in the process of delivering a tray of food to Horst Marshall and Paul Knabel.

Marshall removed his elbows from the table as the plate of blintzes with fresh strawberries was laid in front of him, his right hand still holding the cellular phone to his right ear.

"Where are you now?" Alden's voice asked from the other end of the connection.

"We're getting breakfast in the hotel."

Knabel was eagerly wading into his plate of French toast and bacon.

"Any sign of our lovebirds?"

"Haven't seen them this morning. You saw 'em last night. Judging by their behavior out in the waterfront park, I'm guessing they may have been up late satisfying their carnal lust." Marshall looked at his Seiko diver's watch, which read 8:36. "I wouldn't expect to see them for a couple more hours."

"Maybe," Alden's voice sounded some caution. "They're here for something more than a sexual rendezvous. I would hope the lust for lost art would override their lust for each other. If you don't see them in an hour, let me know. I'll plan to bring the car over around ten."

Bolivar waited impatiently at the front desk for the clerk to return his American Express card. Thankfully, a room with two double beds was available later this morning. He phoned Keitel in the car and told him he could come in for a shower and some R&R in a few hours, and in the meantime, he or Terry would run some more coffee and Danish out to him right after they finished breakfast. Keitel shrugged it off as fine with him. They could even take their time; he was in no hurry. Bolivar was certain that Keitel was an iron man, and that all-night surveillance work was nothing new to him.

"Thank you, Mr. Garcia," said the desk clerk as he returned the card. "Your room will be available by 11:30. Can we take care of your luggage for you now?"

"No. I'll bring it in after we finish breakfast. We're in the Maritime restaurant."

"Very good. Enjoy your meal!"

Bolivar turned from the front desk and nearly bumped into Toby Shutt as he and Jean-Luc Daniel approached the front desk.

The drive to Lucerne had been as easy as Daniel had said it would be. Shutt enjoyed the opportunity to be a passenger and soak in the incredible Swiss countryside. They had gotten on the road early, after Shutt received the late-night phone call from Shawna Hammer confirming a registration for two under the name of Matthew Ferguson at the Palace Hotel in Lucerne. Shutt dutifully copied the address on the Hotel Tiefenau stationery next to his bed, and promptly woke Daniel and asked that they get on the road by seven o'clock the next morning. Wake-up calls were issued, and Shutt mercifully caught up on some badly needed sleep.

They had pulled up to the Palace Hotel front entrance at half past eight. Daniel had called ahead and asked for two uniformed officers to meet him at the hotel at 8:00, but to remain out of sight until he arrived. They had been patiently waiting for him in their patrol car, parked across the street and down one block from the hotel as instructed.

Daniel drove the black, four door Audi sedan parallel to the *Stadtpolizei* car and held up his Federal Police I.D. through the open driver's side window, then waved at the two officers to follow him while he continued forward down Haldenstrasse.

At the hotel, Shutt was introduced to the two officers in English, and then listened with no understanding whatsoever as Daniel instructed the policemen in Swiss German to remain out front with the two vehicles, while they entered the building. They were told that they were looking for two American citizens that were needed for questioning as material witnesses in a U.S. crime, and that neither was of any danger. If they needed backup, either he or Shutt would return for help.

Daniel and Shutt waited in line behind the middle-aged Latino at the front desk, and then avoided him as he hurriedly turned around to leave the desk.

Daniel removed his Federal Police I.D. from his coat pocket and spoke first, again in perfect Swiss German. "Excuse me, I'm Officer Jean-Luc Daniel with the Federal Police and you have two Americans that have registered with your hotel, and we need to speak to them please."

"Their names, please," the desk clerk replied as he slid in front of a computer keyboard and screen.

"Ferguson, Matt," said Shutt, as he stepped forward in response to Daniel's gesture to join the conversation. "F-e-r-g-u-s-o-n."

The clerk typed in the letters and hit the enter key.

"We need the room number, please, and we'll take it from there," Daniel requested as the computer processed the information.

The clerk responded with a pained expression. "I'm afraid the Fergusons checked out this morning," he replied, in excellent English.

"Shit. This is becoming a habit," Shutt sighed.

"Can you tell us when they checked out, or if they have left?" Daniel asked.

"Not by the information I have here. But I would guess if you asked the concierge, he might be able to tell you when their luggage was removed from their room."

"Thank you. We'll need you to also check with your garage to see if their car is still here, and your doormen to see if any of them saw if or when they may have left this morning."

"Brian, the concierge this morning, is upstairs with room 312, but should be down shortly, and the doormen have all been here since 6:00 am."

"Very good, please have them all gathered together for us in fifteen minutes, and you can give us the information on the Fergusons' car at the same time," said Daniel emphatically.

"Yes sir, fifteen minutes," replied the clerk, who was already dialing the garage attendant.

Daniel turned to Shutt. "It appears they have, as you Americans might say, flown the coop."

"Yeah. Like I said before, they have been one step ahead of me for quite some time. It is starting to get a little irritating. I would have asked you to come down last night, but I really didn't think they would be bugging out this quick. Something or somebody has them on the move again. For their sake, I hope we can get to them soon."

\*\*\*

Ferguson had spent the better part of the last four and a half hours taking their new rental car on a nighttime exploration of northern and northeastern Switzerland, more than twice the time Ferguson had anticipated.

After leaving the hotel a little after midnight, he had barely retraced their incoming route back to the northern edge of town, before Courtney was out like a light. Her anger had visibly subsided after the first five minutes inside the hotel room, and had given way to denial in the bathroom as she gathered her composure. After another ten minutes of repacking her luggage and getting into some loose cut Gap jeans, a white Polo turtleneck, and an oversize University of Illinois sweatshirt, she progressed into acceptance, and felt relaxed and comfortable enough to climb back into the car for another drive to *who knows where?* Nevertheless, not a word exited her mouth from the time she emerged from the bathroom until she had fallen asleep in the car, and not even a glance or smile in his direction.

Ferguson had recognized the non-verbal behavior, otherwise known as the 'cold shoulder'. Nothing malicious, but he was familiar with this 'silent running' form of emotional response from a female when upset, and he knew better than to try and instigate any conversation for fear of triggering any of the other, more unattractive forms.

Once on the open road back to Zurich, Ferguson had again retained the travel folder he had kept hotel information in, and removed from it a Map Quest map of Switzerland and driving instructions that were to take them from Lucerne to Wildhaus in a simple 1 hour, 44 minutes. Unfortunately, the detailed instructions were not as simple, with a list of 22 maneuvers involving turns, mergers, exits, one road becoming another, etc. Without the services of the sound asleep and unwilling-to-communicate navigator in the passenger seat, the inevitable occurred...Ferguson got lost.

He was doing an admirable job of reading the instructions under the driver-side map light while negotiating the vehicle, pulling over to the side of the road when he thought absolutely necessary, but at instruction number 15 he missed exit number 42 that would have taken him off A3 to A53. As a result, he drove another 40 minutes east in the wrong direction, got lost turning around in Flums, and proceeded to miss the same exit coming back. The slur of expletives on the second miss, stirred Courtney, but did not wake her.

The sign to Stein read 5 km, and the gravel crescent to the side of the road was a perfect place to pull over to watch the unfolding marvel.

Ferguson switched off the engine and headlights, and looked over at Courtney, who was still sleeping quietly in the reclined passenger seat, her head tucked into the folded brown leather flight jacket crammed in between the seat and door. *Wow, what could have been?*

He was acutely aware that he had probably sacrificed an excellent opportunity for an incredible evening with one of the most beautiful and intelligent women he had ever met, much less laid eyes on. He kept assuring himself that it was the right thing to do. The prize was out there somewhere in the mountains, not riding next to him in the car. Even so, he was having a hard time believing it, and the thought kept creeping into his mind that maybe the opposite was true.

As quietly as possible, he opened the door and stepped out of the Volkswagen Passatt, gently closing the door enough to extinguish the dome light inside. The mountain air was cold and damp, his breath billowing small clouds as he walked to the front of the car and sat down on the hood.

He warmed his sweatered arms with opposite hands, rubbing them up and down, as he watched the landscape unfold before his eyes. Rich, horizontal bands of graded blues and purples, encouraged by a layer of orange beneath, pushed skyward into a star-filled black sky. The mountains seemed to grow as the sky lightened with each passing minute. He nearly jumped out of his skin as Courtney threw his aviator jacket over his shoulders.

"Sorry to scare you. I thought you might need this," Courtney whispered, so as not to spoil the serenity of the event.

"Thanks," he looked to see that she had wrapped her own Patagonia mountain coat around her shoulders. "Sorry, I didn't mean to wake you."

"I'm upset you didn't try. It's gorgeous!"

"Wow, at the rate I'm going, you may never speak to me again."

"You were not on my good list a few hours ago. Frankly, you were being relegated to the junk heap. However, you're gaining ground with efforts like this."

Courtney slid her left hand and arm under Ferguson's right arm and pulled herself close, as they stood in silence, huddled against the cold, as the sun peeked up over the snow-capped Churfirsten mountain range.

The small cafe in the middle of Unterwasser was a welcome respite. Ferguson was into his third cup of extraordinary coffee, trying to knock the sleep that was steadily creeping into his brain. He was recounting the previous night's driving adventures to Courtney, and was pointing out on the maps he had printed before he left Louisville, their current position and their destination, which was just a few minutes down the road.

"You don't suppose we can stay in one place for a while, do you?" Courtney asked sarcastically.

"I believe we'll be hanging out here for a while. We are very close to the place Uncle Max went down. It's around here somewhere, but we'll need help finding it."

"What kind of help?"

"Once we get settled into the hotel, we'll need to find a guide. Someone who knows the area...the mountains and lakes. Maybe even somebody who's been around these parts for the last sixty years."

"You seem to be mister travel guide, with your folder of maps, hotels, driving instructions. You got a place for us to stay, in...where was it?"

"Wildhaus. We're headed to Wildhaus," Ferguson pointed to the small town on the map. "Right there."

\*\*\*

With a room secured for the three of them to share, Bolivar had been contemplating going up for a shower and shave, and maybe even a short nap. However, it was approaching noon and he was beginning to feel a little uneasy that neither of their quarry had emerged from their evening of passion.

He folded the *USA Today* newspaper he had retained from yesterday's flight, which he had read from front to back more than once, and with a touch of annoyance stood up from the wingback lobby chair to stretch his legs. He walked over to the bank of phones to the right of the front desk, picked up one of the house phones and dialed Sullivan, who was in their newly acquired room two flights up preparing to replace Keitel outside.

"Hello?" Sullivan answered on the first ring.

"Ah good, Terry you're still there. It's Julio, before you go to relieve Keitel, I need you to go upstairs to the sixth floor and casually take a walk by our lovebirds' room. It's suite 603, and should be on the corner. I still haven't seen either one of them yet, and it's getting pretty late. Whatever you do, don't look conspicuous, do you hear me?"

"I hear you Julio," Sullivan answered slightly annoyed.

Sullivan was beginning to think this cloak and dagger stuff was getting to be a little ridiculous, and he wasn't very thrilled being talked to like some little kid. Nevertheless, he realized that he had been handpicked by the boss, who was emphatic that what they were doing was extremely important, so he was committed to try and live with it as long as could. He took the vacant elevator from the second to the sixth floor and exited to his left, taking another left at the brass plate signaling rooms 601-615 with an arrow in the appropriate direction. As the numbers descended and grew closer to the corner suite, the sound of the vacuum cleaner grew louder. Reaching the end of the hallway, he stepped into the recessed entrance area for the door that had the brass numbers "603" on the front, eluded the maid's cleaning cart, and entered the room.

"*Veiderholen sie, bitte,*" Sullivan yelled at the back of the short, stout, silver haired housekeeper over the noise of the sweeper.

The maid literally jumped several inches in the air and nearly fell over, as she turned around and feigned a heart attack while recovering her composure.

"Forgive me, I didn't mean to frighten you," Sullivan continued in German.

"It's okay," she answered in Swiss German, visibly shaken.

"The young man and lady that were in this room last night, are they still here?"

"They've gone. I believe they checked out early this morning."

"You're sure. Absolutely certain," pressed Sullivan.

"Quite," with a touch of indignation in her voice.

Sullivan quickly exited the room, bumping into the cart on the way out the door, knocking a box of miniature soaps and shampoos to the floor. When he didn't stop to pick them up, he could hear the maid cursing him as he turned down the hallway, nearly colliding with Paul Knabel, who was busy pretending to open the door to room 604 with an imaginary key.

It was another three minutes before Sullivan reached the lobby and found Bolivar back in the same chair he had left him in earlier just after breakfast. Bolivar saw him coming over the *Der Spiegel* magazine he had found to replace the worn-out *USA Today*, and noticed the concern registered on Sullivan's face.

Sullivan inhaled to catch his breath. "We've got a problem."

"I can see that," replied Bolivar having risen from the same chair again.

"They're gone."

"They're what?" Bolivar yelled in response. Immediately realizing the intensity of his vocal outburst, he visually surveyed the lobby to see whose attention he had attracted. He casually grabbed Sullivan by the arm and escorted him toward the men's bathroom opposite the bank of phones he had just visited. Once in the bathroom, Bolivar searched the stalls to make sure they were alone.

"How do you know they're gone?" Bolivar asked.

"Their room was empty."

"What do you mean empty? How did you get into their room?

"I walked in, it was open, and it's fucking empty! I ran into the maid cleaning the room, she said they had left earlier this morning!"

"Shit!" Bolivar ignored Sullivan's resentment, pulled out his cell phone, and stormed out of the bathroom with Sullivan reluctantly trailing him out several seconds later.

Bolivar pecked at the number pad on his phone and placed it next to his left ear as he headed for the front desk.

"Yeah?" Keitel answered his chirping cell phone, recognizing the number as Bolivar.

"You haven't seen their car leave the garage this morning?" Bolivar asked.

"No, I haven't seen them," replied Keitel.

"Come on inside, they're gone. We'll be in the lobby," said Bolivar.

Before Keitel could ask questions, the phone line went dead.

Bolivar approached the desk, Sullivan languishing several paces behind him, and inquired as to the couple in room 603, mentioning them by name as if to corroborate his assertion that they were friends of his. The response was of no help, and only served to anger him further. They had checked out early this morning and left no forwarding information.

Keitel met them as they retreated from the front desk. "What's up?"

"They apparently left this morning, no trace of where they're going," replied Bolivar.

"I didn't see their car leave the garage," Keitel said defensively.

Bolivar nodded to the elevators. "Let's go down to the garage. Maybe they just left the hotel and they're coming back for their car."

They reached the garage level and spread out in opposite directions, looking for the car as described again by Keitel on the trip down in the elevator. A minute later, a loud whistle signaled twice, attracted Bolivar and Sullivan to a waiting Keitel, who was staring at a Hertz service van parked in front of a silver Mercury Sable with a raised hood.

Keitel stepped forward and spoke to a service man that was head first in the engine compartment. After a few minutes of animated discussion, Keitel returned to Sullivan and Bolivar who were standing off to the side of the van.

"They're definitely gone. They had a new car delivered very early this morning," Keitel said, thumbing toward the mechanic. "This guy says one of the distributor lines was loose. He thought that was a little strange, but it's possible it could have worked its way free. My guess is this was set up. They drove this car here, knowing someone might be following, and they did a little tampering with this one and pulled a bait and switch. The good news is we can find out what their new rental car is, but the bad news is we have no idea where they have gone."

"Shit," Bolivar and Sullivan said in unison.

***

Knabel entered Suite 603 right after nearly being run down by the young man that had bolted the room in a hurry. A quick conversation with the same maid, confirmed the departure of Courtney and Ferguson that morning, and it revealed the same inquiry from the person who just urgently left.

He stepped into the hallway, and quickly hit the redial button on his cell phone.

"Marshall," Horst Marshall answered the phone on the first ring. He adjusted his seat at the bar, so he could maintain his view of the hotel lobby past the couple that just sat in the open seats to his left.

"Horst, we've got problems," said Knabel.

"Go ahead."

"The girl and her boyfriend are gone. They've checked out...sometime this morning."

"Damnit," replied Marshall.

"That's not all. We have another party that looks to be following the same two we are. He is probably headed your way. He's over six feet, thirty-ish, blond, he has an oatmeal colored turtleneck with a brown sweater vest. I think he had a pair of jeans on, but I'm not—"

"I see him now," Marshall interrupted as he saw Sullivan emerge from the elevators. "Get down here as soon as you can."

Marshall closed his phone, got to his feet, threw several francs onto the bar, and walked his drink into the lobby area. He watched as the man Horst described met with another man, older with a dark complexion. As they spoke, the older one nearly screamed something, then caught himself and looked around the lobby in concern. Marshall followed discreetly as they marched off to the men's room.

Several minutes later, after they had exited the bathroom and approached the front desk, he watched as a third man joined the other two. All three went to the elevators, and entered the first available headed down.

Knabel stepped out of an adjoining elevator, as the doors closed to the one manned by Bolivar, Sullivan and Keitel. Marshall met him as he reached the lobby.

"There's more than just the one you saw," said Marshall.

"Where are they? How many?"

"Three so far. They just went down to the garage."

"You think they're looking for their car?"

"Could be. They might be headed for their own," Marshall reached into his black leather jacket and retrieved one of the receivers that were tracking the car. He looked at the repeating red lights, which indicated a strong signal, meaning the car was still in the immediate proximity.

"It's still here?" Knabel asked incredulously.

"Yeah, it's still here. Let's go have a look ourselves, but be discreet, I don't want them catching on to us. I'll take the elevator, you take the stairs," Marshall pointed at the door at the end of the elevator hall with the plaque that read "Autowerkstatt".

Once they reached the garage, they were able to observe from a safe distance, equidistant from the three strangers in conversation over Ferguson's car and a Hertz service truck. They waited until the three were finished in the garage and headed back upstairs via the elevators, before they rejoined each other. Marshall sent Knabel back up the stairs to keep tabs on their new friends, while he had a conversation with the same mechanic, who was decidedly curious as to why so many people were asking him questions...the same questions. Nevertheless, he gave the same answers.

"I think they're in the hotel," said Knabel.

"You're sure?" Marshall inquired again for the second time.

"Look, I got upstairs no more than one or two minutes from the time they got on the elevators in the garage. I covered the lobby and every entrance almost immediately when I couldn't find them. None of the staff saw them either, and I think I asked about everybody that's working right now," Knabel waved at the hotel lobby from the same seat at the bar Marshall had been in thirty minutes earlier.

Marshall was putting off the inevitable. He opened his phone and punched in Alden's number.

Alden was lying in bed reading *Stern* magazine, when his phone nearly vibrated off the nightstand. "*Ja,*" he answered.

"Gerhard, it's Horst. We've got a problem."

"What kind of problem?"

Horst Marshall told him the whole story. There was silence on the other end of the line.

"Gerhard, are you still there?" Marshall asked.

"So, who are these other people? Any clues?" Alden asked.

"No, not right now. We're going to hang around here to see if they surface. Paul's convinced they are in the hotel somewhere, maybe booked in a room or rooms. We'll check on that next. It would help if you can put the word out on Ferguson's new car. I know Hertz delivered a new one to them early this morning."

"I'll get on that, but you need to find out anything you can about where our two friends are headed, and who our new friends are. Check with everybody in the hotel, money is no object. It would help if you can track down who these three new monkeys are. They may have some clues. If you do find them again, try not to lose them. *You dumbfucks!* They may be our only link to finding Ferguson and Lewis again."

Before Marshall could say anything, the line went dead.

Marshall looked at Knabel, "He didn't take it as bad as I thought he would." They both swallowed their remaining beers. "Let's get started."

Alden sat on the edge of the bed rubbing his hands through his hair. *Who the hell are these two amateurs? I'm personally going to cut the heads off of both of you, if you don't cause my death in the meantime. Where, oh where could you be going?*

He looked at the cell phone still resting in his now sweaty palm, and contemplated updating Herr Leiter. He shook off the thought and set the cell phone down. He opened his wallet, took out his Hertz Gold card, and lifted the hotel phone. As he dialed the international number listed on the card, he retrieved his Daytimer from the same nightstand and looked up the number for a numeral 15 listed under the "P's". He wrote the number down on a notepad and began a mental decoding of the number by writing a different number under each of the original numbers.

He had hoped not to dip into the law enforcement portion of the organization, but this was starting to reach the status of an emergency...in fact his life depended on it. Hopefully, Leiter would understand.

\*\*\*

The Pratt & Whitney PW207D engines on the Bell 427 helicopter were nearly maxed out as the Rocca International helicopter roared over the Cordillera Occidental range of the Andes Mountains, on its way from the La Paz-El Alto International airport to Ulloma, Bolivia. Guillermo Rocca sat comfortably, as he and the two pilots cruised at a speed of 130 mph, with dawn forcing its way over the mountaintops to the east. They were only minutes from one of the company's most productive silver mines south of the small Bolivian town.

It was noisy, but he managed to hear the chirping of his cell phone as it lay on the vacant leather seat next to him.

"Hello?" Rocca spoke loudly into the lower portion of the flip phone.

"Mr. Rocca, it's Julio. I'm sorry to bother you sir, but we have a bit of a problem here in Lucerne," Bolivar spoke equally as loud on the other end of the connection.

"Julio, you know I don't like problems. What is it?"

"We've lost Lewis and Ferguson. They disappeared late last night, early this morning, we're not sure."

"Right out from under your noses?" Rocca asked sarcastically.

"We watched them right into their room sometime after midnight. It appears now, they were either aware of us, or guessed that someone was watching them. From what we found out so far, they went to great length to have a new car brought to them in the middle of the night, and they snuck out of their room sometime early this morning, without passing through the lobby. We were vigilant outside, but we weren't looking for them leaving in a different car."

"And do we know what car they left in?"

"Keitel is headed for the Hertz office now. We do know it came from them."

"No idea of where they were headed?"

"Not right now, but we're starting to go through everyone on the hotel staff they were in contact with last night. Most of them are off right now and won't be back on the clock until this afternoon."

"Fine," said Rocca dispassionately. "Keep investigating. I have an alternative option that may bear fruit. Be ready to move when you hear from me."

"We're sorry Mr. Rocca. I cannot believe they know we are here. We have been very careful and Keitel is very professional. I don't think any of us have compromised our situation."

"Save it Julio. All is not lost. I'm pretty certain we'll have Miss Lewis' attention soon, and when we do, she should be more than forthcoming with her whereabouts," Rocca ended their conversation without waiting for a reply.

The engines slowed and the helicopter began its descent to the elevated concrete helo pad, cut out of the top of a hill next to the two-story mining office.

"Your plane is fueled and waiting for us back at the airport Mr. Rocca," the co-pilot's voice chattered through the speakers in the main cabin. "We have priority clearance back to the hangar, whenever we decide to return. I will need to file a plan if we plan on flying out by this evening. Will we be returning today?"

Rocca waved and nodded affirmatively, as the co-pilot looked back over his left shoulder for some acknowledgement. He then opened the cell phone again and hit a recall button, followed by the call key. He waited patiently until Enstrada answered on the fifth ring.

# Chapter 16

*May 23, 2001. Northeastern Switzerland*

Hauptstrasse runs horizontally through the Toggenburg region of Switzerland, stretching along a natural valley through the Alps over to the border with Lichtenstein. Heading east on 16, following their brief respite just outside of Stein to watch the sunrise over the mountains, Ferguson and Courtney passed through Starkenbach, Alt Sankt Johann, and Unterwasser, finally arriving at Wildhaus.

In the exact center of town, on the south side of Hauptstrasse, where the road bends abruptly south and then west out of town, stands the Hotel Hirschen. The five-story, white stucco, Chalet style hotel, consisting of 70 rooms, is typical of the Swiss mountain architecture. Charming and comfortable, it was exactly what Ferguson had been hoping for when he had researched it on-line.

The view to the south of the hotel was incredible. The lush green tentacles of the ski slopes carved amongst the evergreens and rocks, accompanied by a spider web network of lifts, were clearly visible up to the snowcapped Gamesrugg and Chaserugg peaks. The balconies of all the rooms with the southern vista, were all adorned with large baskets of lavender flowers, while the sun that had so beautifully climbed the mountains that morning, was washing a blanket of spring warmth over the entire town.

Ferguson pulled into the lower level parking area and turned off the engine. "Here we are."

"This is where we're staying? For at least twenty-four hours, please?" Courtney cajoled.

"Hopefully, a little longer than that," Ferguson deadpanned.

"Excellent. It looks awesome. Can we go in?"

"Absolutely. Leave the bags; I'll come get 'em when we get checked in."

They climbed from the car and stretched their legs, walked through the nearly empty adjoining street cafe, and entered the hotel through an arched entrance directly off Hauptstrasse.

The check-in went smoothly and quickly, aided by the reservation Ferguson had made the previous afternoon. Anticipating the agitation that he was going to cause by the stealthy, unilateral move from Lucerne, he had booked them into the finest suite in the hotel. Given the degree of dissatisfaction he had caused, he was having second thoughts of not having made reservations for two rooms instead of the one.

Keeping the quality of their accommodations secret, he dispatched Courtney upstairs to size up the room, while he returned to the car to park it in the first-floor garage and retrieve their luggage.

Five minutes later Ferguson knocked on the heavy wood door to the Churfirsten Suite, identified by an engraved brass plate attached to the wall just left of the cut glass door handle. Courtney answered immediately, opened the door with a broad smile and stepped aside to let him and the luggage inside the entryway.

The suite was indeed very nice. It was not the posh quality of a five-star hotel, or even as nice as the suite they had had at the Palace, but it was excellent for a mountain chalet hotel. A large entry hall gave way to an arched entrance into a small, but very cozy living area of upholstered couches and chairs, a stone fireplace, and a glass double door exit onto the balcony with the identical majestic view of the southern mountain range. The bathroom was one big block of marble tiles, with a large whirlpool tub adjacent to a window offering the same panorama as the living area. The bedroom featured a king size bed buried under an oversize, pillowed comforter.

"First the sunrise, now this. Slowly but surely, you're working your way back into my good graces," Courtney nodded to the interior of the room as she reached for her suitcase and bag.

"Thanks. I know it's an uphill battle," replied Ferguson with a raise of his eyebrows.

"Can I unpack my things without fear of having to repack in the near future?"

"You're safe for the time being."

"And that time being what?"

"We'll be here for a few days at the least. Again, I don't think we should stay in one place very long, but I can tell you we'll be here long enough to get comfortable. We shouldn't have to stray too far from the hotel for what we're looking for."

"Here, meaning this is close to the site?"

"As close as we're gonna get. Like I said earlier, it's in the mountains around here. Our next step is to locate a guide, and somebody that has been around this area for a while. Someone who has a memory dating back to 1945."

"Okay. Do I have time to get a shower and unpacked?" beseeched Courtney.

"Absolutely. I need a shower as much as anyone. You first, and I'll go downstairs and see if I can come up with a name of someone in town who can serve as a guide. They're bound to have some shops in this town that cater to hiking and camping, or an outfitter of some kind."

"Are you sure you don't need my help before I clean up?"

"No, I'm just going down to the front desk. The desk clerk had a reasonable grasp of English, so I should be able to communicate well enough with him to get some feedback on what we're looking for."

***

The shower and whirlpool had been therapeutic for both of them. Courtney had spent nearly 45 minutes sampling both, and the effects on her disposition were dramatic. She was energized, and the more she contemplated the nearness of their goal, the more excited she became.

Ferguson's enthusiasm was subdued from a lack of sleep. It was all he could do to keep from nodding off in the whirlpool after Courtney's persuasive recommendation.

While she had been bathing, Ferguson had spent almost an hour downstairs discovering all he needed to know about the best guide in town from the desk clerk, and from the very attractive blond waitress serving him another cup of coffee in the cafe. Both had suggested he go to only one shop, *Der Bergsteiger*, and talk to the owner, Rolf Batemann.

He purchased a map of the town and surrounding area at the front desk, had the clerk indicate on the map with a red 'X' the recommended shop's location, and reviewed it intently over the steaming cup of java. The shop was on the eastern end of town on Diesstrasse. As for the surrounding bodies of water, there were a number of lakes located on the map; however, if his attempted interpretation of the metric key was correct, he was guessing there were only three that had the capability of handling a landing aircraft.

It was obvious there was only one that was significantly larger than any others in the area.

He closed his eyes, imagining himself behind the wheel of a distressed World War II vintage aircraft. Remembering Uncle Max's voice, he allowed himself to create a panoramic view of snow-covered mountains and valleys, as he was flying between them frantically searching for a place to land.

He opened his eyes quickly, startled by the waitress who was asking him in a broken mix of English, Swiss German and mime if he wanted a refill. He waved her off, left more money than necessary on the table and headed back to the room.

***

They had decided to walk to *Der Bergsteiger*. The day was gorgeous, with puffy white clouds gliding amongst the mountains through an azure sky. On their way out of the lobby, the same clerk had warned them to head back before late afternoon, because they were expecting rain for the evening.

Downtown Wildhaus was picturesque and steeped in history. Every bit the old-world mountain town, oozing an aura of rich tradition complemented by modern culture. Courtney and Ferguson wandered aimlessly west, back toward Unterwasser, in the opposite direction of *Der Bergsteiger*, stepping in and out of retail shops that lined Haupstrasse and some of the adjoining side streets. Jewelry stores, leather goods, watch and clock makers, numerous restaurants and cafes, sporting goods and ski shops, even shingles for lawyers and insurance agencies...all blended seamlessly into contiguous façades and architectural relics that had stood for centuries.

After enjoying their walk west, they turned back east and returned to the middle of town, stopping for a leisurely lunch of omelets and champagne at the Haxa Stubbe restaurant in the Hotel Sonne. After an incredibly relaxing meal, and Ferguson nearing the point of dozing off, they pressed on several more blocks east, and then turned south onto Lochmuhlestrasse. Halfway down the street on the left is where they found *Der Bergsteiger*, marked by a hand carved wood sign of a caricatured mountain climber over the door, with the store name painted brightly in red letters arched over the carving.

Ferguson opened the door and held it open as Courtney entered before him. A small bell rigged with a string signaled to the inhabitants their entry. Ironically, it went unanswered as the two of them looked at each other with mutual shrugs and began to browse the store in silence. After several minutes, Ferguson was about to announce the two of them verbally, when a young man, in his mid-twenties, entered from an open door in the back and walked behind the glass and wood counter that surrounded all but the front wall of the shop.

"*Darf ich Sie helfen*?" The young man queried.

Courtney acknowledged her understanding to Ferguson, and stepped forward and spoke in a stuttered, unsure German. "Yes, you can help us. We're looking for the owner, Rolf Batemann."

"You're speaking with him," Batemann replied again in German.

"*Guten tag.* You wouldn't speak English by any chance?"

"Just enough to be dangerous, and probably better than your German. I spent four and half years in the United States at Georgetown University," Batemann shuffled some papers into a lockbox and leaned his left elbow on the counter top. "I'm sorry I didn't greet you sooner, but I was on the phone in the back office."

"That's quite alright, we were enjoying looking through your store," said Courtney, walking to the back of the store and extending her hand over the counter. "My name is Courtney Lewis, and this is

Matt Ferguson," she pointed to Ferguson walking down one of the polished hardwood aisles from the front of the shop.

"It's a pleasure to meet you both," Batemann took turns shaking both of their hands. His grip was powerful and reflected his stout and muscular build, honed from years of rigorously delightful outdoor activities. He was dressed as if headed to the mountains, in a black turtleneck sweater, a pair of olive wool trousers that matched his eyes, and Patagonia hiking boots. The locks of black curly hair flowed freely to his shoulders.

"How may I help you?" Batemann continued.

Ferguson spoke first this time. "We need some help locating a lake around this area."

"We've got several of those. Any one in particular?"

"We'll, therein lies the problem," continued Ferguson. "We don't exactly know which one."

Batemann's face contorted with a puzzled look, as he directed his attention first to Ferguson, then to Courtney, and back to Ferguson.

Ferguson held up the palms of both hands. "Let me explain. We're trying to find a body of water, that is..." he hesitated, not sure of how much information to divulge, "well, something big enough to handle a twin engine aircraft, say if it wanted to make a landing," Ferguson was gambling that this young man wouldn't have the slightest idea of what he was talking about unless he offered some more significant pieces of the puzzle, of which the truthful portions he was not willing to tender at this time.

Batemann's eyebrows raised and his look of bewilderment faded quickly to one of curiosity. "I'm not really qualified to know what type of runway length a twin engine airplane might need to land, but if I were to make a guess, there's only one lake within 25 kilometers of here that would probably fit the bill. Voralpsee. It's probably long enough to handle a landing, but it would have to be in the dead of winter or early spring, when it would have frozen over. If you don't mind me asking, why an airplane, unless it was an emergency?"

Ferguson had already formulated a reply. "Courtney and I are doing some freelance investigative research for a magazine on drug smuggling in Europe. We have reason to believe that Middle Eastern drug operations may have utilized aircraft, landing on the frozen lakes in and around this area. We also believe it's been going on for decades.

"In fact, I was hoping to find someone who may have lived in this area for the last 50 to 60 years, anyone who might have heard rumors over the years, or actually may have seen something that might get us jump started in our investigation."

Batemann smiled. "I've certainly never heard of anything like that in this area, but it's certainly plausible. I know someone that fits the bill perfectly," he paused for effect. "My father. He lives in Walenstadt now, which is less than an hour south of here, but he spent most of his adult life in Unterwasser. This is actually his store…was. We came to a father son agreement two years ago on this store and another one in Stein, not long after I returned from America. We have a third location in Walenstadt that he minds. It keeps him busy and allows him to remain active in the business."

"So, he knows a thing or two about this area?" Courtney asked.

"Like the back of his hand. Not only that, but he was a pilot. Technically, I guess he still is, but he hasn't flown in several years. He owned a pontoon plane for years, and ran fishing trips in and out of the mountains as part of the business. He sold it two or three years ago, and hasn't been up since. But he would definitely know if Voralpsee, or maybe something smaller would be able to withstand twin engine landings."

"How can we contact your father?" Ferguson asked excitedly.

"Don't need to, he'll be here later this afternoon. We had planned to have dinner tonight and go fishing in the morning. I'll speak with him when he arrives and maybe we can get together later tonight, or tomorrow afternoon. Where can we reach you?"

"We're staying at the Hotel Hirschen," chimed Courtney, "under the name of Ferguson. We would be happy to treat you and your father to dinner, if you would care to join us this evening. We're also prepared to pay both of you for any assistance you can offer in helping us locate the area we're looking for."

"Thank you for the offer. I'll talk with him and see if he's up for it," Batemann came from around the counter and walked to the front of the store where he flipped a sign in one of the bay windows that projected the word *CLOSED* out to the sidewalk. He looked at his watch. "He should be here in the next couple of hours. As soon as he arrives, I'll talk to him and call you shortly afterward."

Ferguson and Courtney understood the clue that their conversation with Rolf Batemann was over.

"Thanks for your help Mr. Batemann," said Ferguson as he held the front door open for Courtney and shook Batemann's extended right hand. "We'll look forward to hearing from you."

"Yes, thank you for your help!" Courtney said, as she led them both out of the shop and onto the sidewalk.

"Please call me Rolf," Batemann stood in the doorway. "And I'll be in touch shortly."

The sound of the ringing bell signaled the end of their dialogue. Ferguson and Courtney walked north up the street, and then turned west onto Haupstrasse and headed back to the hotel. The sky was darkening, the white puffy cotton balls having given way to burgeoning gray storm clouds that had engulfed the warm sunshine from that morning. The desk clerk had been correct, a storm was blowing in.

\*\*\*

The phone rang just as the two of them were headed out of the room in search of dinner. It was just after 8:00, and they had given up hope of hearing from Batemann and his father this evening. Courtney ran back into the room first, and cradling the receiver to her ear, answered on the fourth ring.

"Ms. Lewis? It's Rolf Batemann; I hope I'm not calling too late."

"No not at all," Courtney nodded affirmatively at Ferguson still standing at the door and waved at him to come back into the room. "Matt and I were just heading out to find some dinner."

"Oh, very good. My father was delayed getting here, and just arrived. We were also looking to go out for some dinner. Would you care to join us? My father would be pleased to talk with you and said he would be happy to help in any way he can."

"We would love to have dinner with you and your dad. Please tell us when and where and we'll be there."

"Well actually, the restaurant in your hotel, the *Diesfurger* is excellent, and we haven't had a meal there in weeks. Would that be acceptable to you and Mr. Ferguson?"

"That would be perfect, but please call me Courtney, and I know Matt would appreciate his first name as well."

"Would 8:30 be okay with you?"

"8:30 would be perfect. We'll head down in a few minutes, so you might look for us in the bar."

"We'll see you and Matt shortly. Thanks, and my apologies again for the short notice."

The line went dead before Courtney could respond any further.

"Dinner here in a half hour," said Courtney standing up from sitting on the arm of the couch.

"Perfect. Did I hear you say we'll be in the bar?" Ferguson asked.

"Yep. You heard correctly. They'll find us there."

Ferguson returned to the door and held it open for Courtney as they exited the suite and headed downstairs. "After you madam."

Courtney curtsied, "*Danke shoen.*"

***

The young, dark haired waiter, who wore a nametag that identified himself as 'Tim', and had needed no introduction to the Batemann's, was busy clearing away the dinner entree dishes while inquiring about dessert.

Rudi Batemann quickly interjected and authoritatively spoke for everyone. "Tim, please tell Chef Andreas we would like to have four of his famous chocolate soufflés."

"Yes sir, Mr. Batemann. When I told him you were here, he predicted there would be at least one soufflé for the evening," Tim dutifully scraped away some crumbs from the white tablecloth, and disappeared in the direction of the kitchen.

The elder Batemann looked at the two American guests. "Andreas is an excellent chef, but his soufflé is out of this world."

There was no disagreement between Ferguson and Courtney, their dinner had been wonderful, and Rolf Batemann was nodding his head in agreement with his father.

Two hours earlier Ferguson and Courtney had reached the bar prior to the Batemanns' arrival, they spent a few minutes choosing a glass of wine for themselves, and then noticing a crowd developing in the dining room, decided to claim a table. After the Batemanns arrived, and formal introductions were made by Rolf, Rudi Batemann changed up the table so Tim could wait on the four of them. It was quickly revealed that Tim was a local ski instructor, who had worked for the

Batemanns as a teenager, and continued to direct quite a bit of tourist business to the three *Der Bergsteiger* shops. The Toggenburg region, as Courtney and Ferguson were beginning to understand, was a small world.

Rudi Batemann had been delightful. At 79, he was remarkably well preserved. His tanned complexion was considerably weathered and accentuated by a full head of combed back silver hair. Physically, he looked twenty years younger. His six-foot frame was well conditioned and he was dressed impeccably in a pair of loose-fitting corduroy trousers, a tight-fitting silk turtleneck and a plaid fleece pullover.

Most of the evening's conversation had funneled through him, which had been perfectly fine for the other three diners. He was charming, witty, and his knowledge of the area, and local history had been fascinating for Courtney and Ferguson.

As Tim placed the four desserts around the table, Chef Andreas walked up with a bottle of Gaston De Lagrange brandy and four snifters.

"Ah, here is the creator of these masterpieces," said Rudi Batemann, as he stood to greet all six feet and 330 pounds of Andreas Kline.

After several hugs and warm handshakes all around, followed by an excessive number of compliments regarding the food, Chef Andreas poured four generous servings of brandy on the house, thanked everyone at the table, and retreated to the kitchen with Tim and the bottle in tow.

"Andreas has been a chef around here for almost twenty years. He's a fixture in Wildhaus," said Rolf Batemann.

His father sipped at the brandy. "I've been a fan of his food for as long as he's been here. We've spent many a long evening partaking in his passion and mine, French cognac and brandy."

After a brief silence, as everyone sampled their respective spirits, Ferguson resumed the discussion that had developed during dinner, in which the senior Batemann had taken a keen interest.

"So, Mr. Batemann, you're convinced that the Voralpsee lake is the only lake capable of handling an airplane landing?"

"A twin engine like you're suggesting...yes. I don't think there is any margin for error on some of the other choices, but, as I said earlier, I've been around this area for the better part of 60 years, and I have never heard of anybody landing a plane on the Voralpsee when it was frozen over. Intentionally.

"I also have never heard of any rumors or stories of drug smuggling going on in this region either. There's no doubt that our banking industry has probably been very kind to the drug smugglers, and the cartels that operate that industry; however, Switzerland as a whole does not approve of illicit drugs and smuggling in our country and does not have an excessive drug abuse problem.

"Why is it you keep referring to a twin engine? Do you know something more specific about the type of aircraft that you believe has landed in this area?"

Ferguson didn't flinch externally, but his heart nearly skipped a beat internally. The old man had just caught a mistake. He had given up too much information. "No, not really. The information I had regarding the amount of smuggling, total quantity or weight, would require a dual engine versus a single." *When confronted with a hard question, always respond with a question.* "Why, would it make a big difference?"

"Absolutely, it might be the difference in a few hundred feet of landing length," said the father.

"Which could open up a few other bodies of water around here," interjected the son.

Courtney sensed the need to squelch any further interest of the details. "Well, I think we should start with the...Voralpsee? Is that how you pronounce it? It sounds like the best candidate for now."

"I agree," Ferguson concurred quickly.

"Yes, your pronunciation is correct. Moreover, the Voralpsee is very close. Rolf and I can drive you up in the morning and show you around. It's part of a natural preserve and is owned by the state."

"I'll need to be back by 3:00 Dad, I've got two climbers coming in to the shop for outfitting. We'll also be climbing the next day, so if we don't fish in the morning, it'll be next week before we can go again."

"We don't want to interrupt your fishing trip," said Ferguson apologetically. "How about if we follow you to the lake, you give us a quick lay of the land, and then you can go on fishing. If we have any questions, we can come by the shop later in the afternoon."

The Batemanns looked at each other and shrugged their shoulders in agreement.

Courtney signaled Tim as he approached the table with the bill in hand and proffered her American Express card. It took him less than five minutes to return with the processed card and check copies, where Courtney added an exorbitant tip, signed and returned the merchant copy to him as he tended to an adjoining table of diners.

During the wait, it was determined that the Batemanns would arrive at the hotel in the morning at 8:00. From there, Ferguson and Courtney would follow them into the mountains, assured that they were within a half hour drive to the lake. They were also forewarned that there would be some walking necessary to get to certain areas of the waterfront, if that was their intention.

Everyone thanked Courtney for her generosity in paying for dinner, another round of handshakes was realized, and the Batemanns left Courtney and Ferguson in the lobby area of the hotel.

"A nightcap?" Courtney asked a yawning Ferguson.

"Absolutely, but keep nudging me if I try to nod off." The lack of sleep over the last 36 hours, coupled with the wine and brandy at dinner, was turning Ferguson into a walking zombie.

Ferguson ordered a port, and Courtney doubled it, as they commandeered two stools at the nearly deserted bar. The fresh logs in the nearby fireplace popped and hissed while a Frank Sinatra ballad played softly in the background.

"I can't wait for tomorrow," said Courtney. "Do you have a clue what you're looking for?"

"I've got a general idea. There was a little more information that Uncle Max had left that you and Karl didn't get an opportunity to digest. Given that, and what I heard Uncle Max ramble about for years, I'm pretty certain I can draw some conclusions. I won't know for sure until I look around. We'll see tomorrow."

"Thanks again for letting me be a part of it. I know if you had your druthers, I wouldn't be here today."

"Probably, but the way it's worked out has been better than the alternative. I've enjoyed the company, and if we're lucky it'll be fun to share the experience, particularly with you."

"Thank you, my sentiments exactly."

*** 

Courtney emerged from the bathroom, refreshed from a short stint in the whirlpool again. The fire in the fireplace was struggling, but still emitted enough flame to produce dancing shadows in the darkened room. Ferguson was stretched out on the couch.

She checked the lock on the door again and took a few steps into the living area, a large white bathrobe the only article of clothing covering her soft, warm body. The conjugal thoughts she had harbored in Lucerne had returned as she sat in the watery massage, and she felt the urge to test the sexual waters with the handsome young man in the next room.

"Is there any room on that couch for me?" She asked softly.

There was no response from Ferguson.

She loosened the tie on the robe slightly, enough to expose a sufficient amount of cleavage. She shook her hair and ran her fingers through it as she approached the couch.

"Have you got any room for me?"

Ferguson didn't move, and as she leaned over to his face, she realized he was sound asleep.

*I'll be damned.*

She debated waking him up, but realized his exhaustion. She kissed him lightly on the cheek, pulled a fleece throw from a wicker basket next to the couch and laid it gently over him as she retreated to the bedroom.

Slipping a large Chicago Bulls T-shirt on, she was pulling back the covers to the bed when she heard the muted ring of her cell phone. Tracing the rings to her purse on the floor in the closet, she pulled out the phone and looked at the caller I.D… 'Dad-Work'.

She decided this is one call she could answer. "Hi, Daddy".

# Chapter 17

*May 24, 2001. Chicago, Illinois*

Miguel Enstrada had no difficulty tracking down Jason Allen. The phone call from his Uncle earlier that morning had interrupted what little sleep he had managed after an evening of carnal lust with Sabrina, and the excessive consumption of alcohol and a half a gram of nearly pure Bolivian powder.

His head was a train wreck and he was in no mood for uncooperativeness. After Allen's initial balk at his request to meet with Grayson Lewis that afternoon, Enstrada made very clear the consequences of not complying with his request. Not only would it be significantly distressing to Mr. Rocca, it conceivably could jeopardize Mr. Allen's physical wellbeing.

The call back took less than twenty minutes, and Mr. Lewis had agreed to a thirty-minute block of time that afternoon. He was speaking at a fundraiser luncheon and was due back at the office at 2:00, and was scheduled to be at the mayor's office at 3:00, so he would have to leave no later than 2:30.

Enstrada assured Allen the half hour would be sufficient and he was emphatic that the meeting be private, between Lewis and himself.

However, he wanted Allen to stick around until after they had discussed Mr. Rocca's offer.

In reality, the meeting only covered about fifteen minutes of Grayson Lewis' busy day. He was ten minutes late returning from the speaking engagement, and the limo sent by the mayor arrived at 2:25. Nevertheless, Lewis was ecstatic at the proposal of a Rocca exhibit, but was expectedly skeptical as to why Chicago and why now? What was Rocca's motivation for taking his collection public? Regardless, another meeting was scheduled for June 15, where he and Mr. Estrada could flesh out some details, and maybe uncover the true stimulus for such a proposition.

Enstrada shook hands with Grayson Lewis as they exited his office and stood in the narrow hallway.

"Thank you again for seeing me on such short notice Mr. Lewis. My schedule was so hectic I was afraid I wouldn't be able to get back to Chicago for several weeks."

"It was my pleasure Mr. Enstrada. Your Uncle's collection, as I mentioned, is a source of much speculation and conjecture, and would generate an incredible amount of interest. As you well know, the secrecy surrounding it only fuels the buzz. The Institute would love to be a part of such an impressive exhibition. Thanks again for thinking of us! And please extend my thanks and appreciation to your Uncle!"

Jason Allen walked down the hallway, having heard the conversation move out of the office.

"Jason, can you please see to Mr. Enstrada. I'm afraid the mayor's office has a car waiting for me downstairs and I need to be going."

"Certainly Grayson."

As Lewis turned and walked away, Enstrada interrupted. "Mr. Lewis, I need to make a private phone call, would you mind very much if I could use your office for a few minutes?"

Lewis never stopped walking, but turned his head to face the two men in the hallway. "Absolutely. Jason, anything he needs, please feel free to help."

"Thank you again," shouted Enstrada as Grayson Lewis disappeared from their sight.

"Well, did you get what you so desperately needed?" Allen asked.

"Yes, thank you for your help. Give me a few minutes on the phone and I'll be right with you."

"Dial 9 to get an outside line. I'll be out in the reception area. Take your time."

Enstrada entered Lewis' office, closed the door and sat behind the large hand tooled leather and wood antique desk and picked up the phone. He removed his palm pilot from his sport coat pocket and punched up the number he had loaded in this morning. Courtney Lewis answered on the fifth ring.

"Hi Daddy."

There was a slight pause. "No Miss Lewis, you can call me Michael. I'm sitting in your father's office meeting with him on some rather delicate matters regarding art, which segues nicely into a similar predicament that involves you and your boyfriend."

Enstrada could sense the fragility of the connection. "Please don't hang up on me Miss Lewis, or you risk putting your father's life in jeopardy. Are you alone?"

Courtney's throat had grown incredibly dry, and she was afraid she wouldn't be able to speak.

"Miss Lewis are you still there? I'm not a very patient man."

"Yes, I'm here. And yes, I am alone. What do you want?"

"I'm getting to that. You see, we have been following you. You and your companion are on the trail of a potentially incredible art discovery, one which we have a great interest in, and you and Mr. Ferguson have been very uncooperative in allowing us to tag along.

"In fact, you have done a remarkable job of giving us the slip in Lucerne. My want...is to know where you are now, and if you fail to tell me, I will personally see that your father encounters an unexpected, but tragically fatal accident. Do you understand what I'm telling you Miss Lewis?"

Courtney responded in a parched and nearly inaudible voice. "Yes, I understand."

"I'm sorry, I couldn't hear your answer."

With more anger this time, she answered again. "I understand!"

"Excellent." There were several seconds of silence, "I'm waiting Miss Lewis. Where are you?"

The few seconds had allowed her to gather her thoughts and she recovered quickly. "I haven't the slightest idea. Matt's the only one who knows where we're going, and he doesn't trust me enough to tell me. I was asleep in the car when you called. We're parked in front of a small roadside restaurant. Matt went in to get some coffee and a bite to eat. I was tired so I stayed in the car to sleep."

"What is the name of the restaurant? What road are you on?"

Courtney had the presence of mind to go way back in time. To a photo shoot she had done in St. Moritz almost a decade ago. There was an all-night diner that had been around for years that the whole crew had frequented on more than one occasion. She only hoped it was still standing and open. "The sign says the *Olympischen Hutte*. I don't know what road we've been on, but I do know we're somewhere near St. Moritz."

"I do hope you're telling me the truth Courtney Lewis, for your father's sake."

"I don't have any reason to lie to you." *So why am I lying? What in the hell am I doing?*

"I'm going to call you back tomorrow. At exactly 6:00 pm your time. Be prepared Miss Lewis to answer the phone...alone. By that time, I fully expect you to have all the answers. Where you are going. Where you are staying. Where are you at that time. Do I make myself clear?"

"Very! My father has no idea what's going on here. Please, do not hurt him."

"Do as you're told Miss Lewis and no one will get hurt. Your father is a very nice gentleman. I would regret anything happening to him. Six o'clock tomorrow. Don't forget."

The line went dead and Courtney's heart was about to bust out of her chest. She ran to the dresser and grabbed a water bottle from the welcome basket. She fell back onto the bed in a state of shock. She had to think...clearly, if it was at all possible.

After several minutes of agonizing over the phone call, she turned her attention to analyzing the situation, and what she had just done. She could not believe she had just put her father's life in danger over somebody else's problem, a problem that she didn't have enough sense to walk away from at the outset.

*Matt was right from the very beginning. I should have never gotten involved. God bless him, he tried to tell me stay out of it. This whole affair was turning back into the nightmare it had been at home.*

*It should have never gotten this far. We should have gone to the police. For what selfish reasons do I not tell, whoever it is that just called, the truth, and then get the hell away from this mess? What is it about a discovery of this magnitude that is worth risking anybody's life? What about Matt? What if I get out now, what about him?*

Courtney's head swirled with a multitude of questions and what ifs. She lay still and concentrated on nothing. She successfully blocked out everything in her mind for a few valuable seconds. Slowly she began to calculate a solution. She thought about Matt, and his comment at the *Palace* hotel. 'You're not going to like me very much'. That would have to be her answer to Matt when everything was said and done. For everyone concerned, this would resolve it once and for all. She reached again into her purse and retrieved her wallet. Inside one of the pockets, she pulled out a thin stack of papers and cards, and leafing through them, found the business card of Detective Toby Shutt. She dialed the number on the card into her cell phone and waited patiently as the plan formulating in her mind began to make perfect sense.

\*\*\*

The T-Mobile cell phone simultaneously rang and vibrated in the breast pocket of Toby Shutt's tweed blazer, as it lay draped over the stool in the *Kaufleuten* bar, one of Zurich's more popular and trendy nightspots. Jean-Luc Daniel had decided they both could use a nice meal and a couple of cold drinks to wash away the complete disaster the day had brought.

After their failure at the *Palace* hotel, and subsequent interviews with the staff, they decided to return to Zurich and try to manage the investigation and search for the new rental car from there. Alerts had been issued to the other cantons for the make, model and number of the Volkswagen, and photographs and descriptions of Matt Ferguson and Courtney Lewis. Explicit instructions were given not to apprehend if sighted, but to contact the Federal Police, specifically Daniel, and keep the two Americans under surveillance until further notice. Shutt had been highly impressed with the assistance Daniel and his office were providing, and the resources they were making available.

Shutt was fortunate to have his rib cage leaning against the jacket, where the vibration caught his attention, because the noise of the crowded bar drowned out the muffled ring.

He looked at the number of the incoming call and frowned as he failed to recognize the number or the caller. He thought about not answering it, but he was cognizant that there were a number of people involved in the search for Ferguson and Lewis, and it could be any one of them trying to reach him.

He punched the send button as he covered the opposite ear with his free hand to block out the racket of conversation and music. "Hello, Detective Shutt."

"Detective Shutt, it's Courtney Lewis. You're a hard man to get a hold of, but I managed to convince your office to give this number."

Shutt looked up wide-eyed at Daniel and didn't say a word.

"Please try to hear me out before you interrupt me or attempt to rip me a new one," she paused to see if he would go ahead anyway, but the other end of the line remained silent. It actually gave Shutt time to run from the bar to the quiet of the evening sidewalk on *Pelikanstrasse.*

"I'm ready to tell you everything that is going on, and I'm ready to tell you where we are and why we're here. But you have to promise that you will give me something in return."

Shutt pushed his way out through the crowd at the front door, hesitating until he knew she was waiting for a reply. "Do I have a choice? What do you want?"

"I need your assistance in protecting my father, and your word that you'll not interfere with what we're doing until I give you the okay. It's important that we complete what we came here to do, and in the process, I think we'll uncover your murderer, or at the very least, the people associated with him. Can you agree to that?"

"I can probably live with that."

"No probably's, I need a firm yes!"

"Yes, damnit!"

"Good. Here's the deal," Courtney took a deep breath knowing full well she was about to compromise Matt and his whole endeavor, but she had worked it out several times in her mind, and she was convinced that it would work out for him in the long run. Most importantly, it would keep her father safe, and bring this whole quagmire to an end.

"We're both in Switzerland. We've been here for a couple of days. We're in a small town called Wildhaus, in the eastern part of the country. We're here because Matt has information that was passed on to him from a recently deceased uncle who was a German aviator in World War II.

"His uncle was responsible for transporting looted artwork out of the country at the end of the war and crashed into the mountains in this area. He survived the crash, and always maintained that the plane and the artwork survived as well. Whether it has survived almost sixty years in conditions where it crashed is another matter. We do know that the plane crashed into a cave at the time, and we're hoping that it remained in the cave and entombed itself. If the artwork was crated or had some sort of shipping over wrap of any kind, and the environmental conditions of the cave were reasonable and maintained over the years, it's entirely possible the pieces are still in repairable condition.

"If that's the case, the works that we have since discovered were on that plane, are worth millions. Major millions!"

"You're serious," queried Shutt.

"Very, and apparently there is somebody, or what we believe are somebodies, that have found out about our little lost treasure and are adamant about making sure they get their hands on it first. Which leads me to my father. I received a phone call from some lowlife about a half hour ago; threatening to make sure my father meets an untimely death unless I tell him where we are. You see, Matt had a feeling that we would be followed and he arranged for us to disappear yesterday after leaving enough of a trail to another city here in Switzerland. Obviously, it worked, and it pissed them off, whoever they are.

"Regardless, I need you to arrange for my father's protection in Chicago. I can tell you how to reach him, but whatever you do, it cannot be obvious. We need to maintain the illusion that everything is going along fine and the police are not involved. I'm stalling the shithead that called, but I am going to have to tell him where we are within the next 24 hours.

"Once I do, I'm going to bargain with him to let us finish the discovery...good or bad. I think he will be agreeable to that, since they still have no idea where the plane is. We do all the work, and then he can come in and take it from us...the artwork for my father. He should be agreeable to that. If you can get over here and get the local authorities involved, you can keep an eye on us from a distance, and pick up the bad guys when they decide to take what we find."

Shutt was chuckling to himself on the other end, but was having a hard time disputing the logic of her plan. "You know they're likely to kill you when they take the art."

"I figured that, but I was counting on you being close enough to keep that from even being a remote possibility."

Daniel had found Shutt outside pacing back and forth with the phone still ensconced to his ear. He remained quiet while Shutt continued his conversation, managing to mouth the words 'Courtney Lewis' as he pointed to the phone.

"I'm still not real comfortable with you playing amateur undercover detective. There has to be another way we can approach this without putting you and Ferguson in danger."

"You gave me your word detective. I expect you to honor it!"

"Yes, I did. So are you planning to call me back?"

"You call me when you get to Switzerland. You have my number now."

"Courtney, I'm in Switzerland. The curveball you threw the bad guys in Lucerne at the *Palace*, struck us out too. We just missed you."

Courtney laughed. "Matt had pretty good instincts. Where are you now?"

"Zurich, and I have the Federal and local police involved. I'll take care of your father immediately, but I'll need that information on how to reach him before you hang up. I want you to call me tomorrow...twice. At noon and six o'clock. Keep me updated. Where are you staying in Wildhaus?" He emphasized the city as he looked at Daniel, who acknowledged his familiarity with a nod.

"We're staying at the *Hirschen*. It's right in the middle of town. Please, do not blow it detective. I want Matt to have the opportunity to finish what he came here to do. I want him to have his day. This is a very big deal for him. Hell, it's a big deal for me. It could conceivably be one of the biggest art discoveries ever. I will personally make your life a living hell if you don't uphold your end of the bargain," Courtney recited off her father's name, home address and phone number, and his office location and phone number. "I'll call you tomorrow, but it will be at 6. I'll be treasure hunting in the afternoon and I'm not sure I'll be able to steal away to call you then."

The line went dead. "I'll be damned," muttered Shutt. "The Hirschen hotel in Wildhaus, did you get that?" He looked at Daniel who nodded and was already speaking into his mobile phone. "You are not going to believe this."

They walked back into the bar and Shutt proceeded to tell him the whole story.

\*\*\*

Gerhard Alden sat on the wooden bench in the dark of the early morning, just outside the *Palace* hotel. He stared at the rolling water of Lake Lucerne. The storm from the previous afternoon and evening had churned up the lake, but the calm had returned with the cessation of the bad weather, and the tranquility of the surface was returning with the absence of any measurable wind.

Unfortunately, the tranquility did not extend to his present state of affairs. He had just hung up from a most unpleasant phone conversation with Erwin Leiter, where the magnitude of his assignment was once again confirmed, and the repercussions of his failure were gravely implied. He was convinced that an unsuccessful resolution of the current situation in front of him, would result in his death. He was of the belief that the circumstances were that critical.

Horst Marshall approached him from behind. "Any news on the car?"

"Nothing," Alden replied. "I just got off the phone with Leiter. I am a walking dead man if we do not find these two within the next forty-eight hours. I'm not sure we'll have any luck tracking the vehicle in that time."

Marshall knew that if Alden felt the way he did, that his and Knabel's existence may be on feeble ground as well. He decided that Paul did not need to know the fragile nature of their predicament. He wasn't certain how he might react.

"Did you have any luck with any of the other staff," Alden continued.

"No. But we did confirm that we definitely have company in our same predicament. The problem is that some of that company is the police."

"The police? I thought you told me that it was three guys you flushed out yesterday. The ones staying in the hotel."

"They're still part of the equation. In fact, Paul is back in the hotel keeping an eye on them as we speak. However, I had a conversation with the concierge just a few minutes ago. He had some visitors yesterday, above and beyond the three stooges we know about. That is part of the reason we could not find him yesterday. A Federal police investigator, and get this, an American police officer, had questions for him that involved Matt Ferguson and Courtney Lewis. They were looking for them as well."

"Well, well, well. This party is starting to heat up. Do we know where the Feds are now?"

"Paul and I haven't seen them, and according to the concierge, he thought they mentioned that they were headed back to Zurich. Maybe if we tell Mr. Leiter that the police are involved, he'll give us a little more leeway in terms of time."

"No. I don't want to involve Mr. Leiter any more, not until we have some good news. The police involvement, I think, would only complicate matters worse."

"You're right, sorry for mentioning it," Marshall knew he was grasping for help, when there wouldn't be any. It was their problem. They needed to fix it...fast.

Alden's cell phone rang again in his hand and he answered it immediately. He hung up after a few seconds.

"That was Paul. Our three other friends are checking out," he tossed Marshall the car keys. "The car is just down the street on the left. No more than fifty meters. Meet us at the hotel entrance. I'm going up to meet Paul. Keep an eye out for any of our friends that are driving. Here, keep this as well. We'll call from Paul's," Alden handed the cell phone over, turned quickly and jogged up the granite steps to the lake entrance of the hotel.

It was a piece of cake tracking Bolivar, Keitel and Sullivan. They were completely unsuspecting of Alden, Marshall and Knabel. Pretending as if there was a mix up in luggage, Marshall actually had time to paste a tracking bug in the open trunk of Keitel's BMW, as the bellhop loaded their bags. Alden and Knabel were able to hop into the Mercedes, with Marshall back behind the wheel, less than 15 seconds after Keitel pulled away from the curb.

"Here," Marshall handed the receiver to Alden, as the blinking red light shone brightly on the small monitor that displayed a street map. "The wonders of GPS."

Alden and Knabel laughed in unison.

"How did you manage that?" Knabel asked.

"It was easy," replied Marshall.

"Well, the good news is Paul here is one step ahead of you," said Alden. "He overheard them at the front desk. They're headed to St. Moritz."

Marshall smiled. "Excellent, I've skied the mountain several times, I know the area well."

"Good, but let's let our friends show us the way, shall we," Alden said.

They all nestled back in the plush leather seats, and settled in behind the navy blue BMW as it sped away west from the city of Lucerne.

# Chapter 18

*May 25, 2001. Wildhaus, Switzerland*

Ferguson had awakened before the sun was up, his internal clock still not having adjusted to the transcontinental change. He had checked on Courtney and found she was sound asleep in the bedroom. Again, he could not believe how beautiful she was as he quietly pulled the door to and exited the room for the lobby. On the bathroom sink, he left behind a short note revealing his intentions to eat breakfast downstairs. He would return when he had finished.

He spent the last remaining forty-five minutes of the fading darkness in the *Dorfstube* restaurant with another incredible cup of coffee and fresh baked Danish. He held Uncle Max's papers in his hand, flipping them over, back and forth, studying the contents. He stared at the map and the drawing, looking again at the paper clipped sheet of notes he had added when he had dissected the global coordinates of longitude and latitude that Uncle Max had included on the scribbled sketch.

They were definitely in the right place. He was convinced the Voralpsee Lake was the spot. The question was, would he recognize the spot? Would it still be the same after nearly sixty years? Would the cliffs be there? Would the cave still be there, and if so, will the plane still be intact? Questions buzzed through his head, as the coffee and the adrenaline jump-started his metabolism.

He was starting to ponder how they would lose the Batemanns once they found the lake, when Rudi Batemann showed up in the lobby. Ferguson, stood up folded the papers away in his flight jacket, and waved at him as the same young, blond waitress from the previous day pointed Batemann in Ferguson's direction.

*"Guten morgen, Herr Ferguson."*

"Good morning to you Herr Batemann," Ferguson looked at his watch, which he had reset to the local time. "You're a tad bit early. Where's your son?"

"He'll be along shortly. I had him go to the shop before he meets us. I hope you don't mind, but I'm having him bring some hiking boots, jackets and some other gear that might come in handy on your little excursion. I also wanted him to bring his jeep along, so you could have a vehicle to navigate around the area, when we leave to go fishing."

"That's extremely nice of you." *Very damn presumptuous, but nice.* "Thank you! We'll be more than happy to pay Rolf some sort of rental, obviously."

"We figured that. He's rented it out on numerous occasions to his repeat customers. By the way, the boots and other gear are strictly up to you, but it sounded last night like you traveled light, and as you can probably surmise, I'm a sneaky salesman. Anything to make a buck."

"No need to apologize. You're exactly right; we don't have any of the gear we're going to need. I appreciate your thinking of us."

At that moment, the increasingly attractive waitress appeared with another cup of coffee and more Danish, and placed it in front of Batemann.

*"Danke Greta. Du ist lieblich wie gewohnlich."*

She blushed, winked at him and then walked away.

Batemann laughed. "She hates it when I flirt with her."

A half hour later, Rolf Batemann arrived at the table at the same time Courtney stepped off the elevator. After renewing acquaintances, and allowing for some breakfast for Courtney and the younger Batemann, they all proceeded to Rolf's jeep to select from a dozen different sizes and choices of hiking boots for Ferguson and Courtney.

After deciding on their new shoes and accompanying wool socks, Ferguson succumbed to the Batemanns' subtle salesmanship by adding a navy Patagonia shell with fleece lining and Courtney submitted to a similar style woman's jacket in yellow. The Batemanns threw in two backpacks, at no charge.

They had arranged at breakfast to rent Rolf's jeep for the next three days. Hence, they split up in the vehicles, Ferguson joining Rolf Bateman in his future rental, while Courtney combined with his father in the elder Batemann's Land Rover. They left Wildhaus at 8:15 and headed east on 16.

Just three kilometers down the road, they turned south and worked their way southwest up the steep *Grabserberg Road*. The fifteen kilometers into the mountain range took almost thirty minutes as they weaved their way up the grade. The landscape was rugged, with sporadic congregations of hardwoods and pines. There were several smaller lanes that exited off the main road, and Batemann's Land Rover chose the second one on the left about half way up. The narrow route headed due south and gradually dissolved from asphalt into gravel, then gravel to dirt. Eventually it terminated in a dead end composed of a large crescent shaped rocky façade

Rudi Batemann circled in front of a craggy outcropping, parking the Land Rover so that it faced back to the remnants of the road. His son pulled the jeep up parallel to them and killed the engine.

Ferguson could hardly breathe, the adrenaline rush had been simmering ever since they headed into the mountainous terrain, and it was peaking as he exited the vehicle. Courtney was in a similar state of anticipation, but they both managed to suppress it visibly.

"We'll walk you up from here, but once we reach the lake, you're on your own," said Rudi Batemann. "All you have to do is get back on the road down and it will take you right to 16, that's the main road that runs into town. Are you ready?"

"Ready," Ferguson and Courtney replied in unison.

They headed up a small, stony path that widened quickly into a panoramic view of a multitude of contiguous sharp peaks. At the crest of the path, the magnificent view of Voralpsee Lake opened up below.

"Wow. This is gorgeous," Ferguson exclaimed.

"That it is," added Rolf Batemann. "Actually, there's very little activity on the lake, no commercial entities. Quite a bit of fishing, rock climbing on the cliffs, some water sports if you're up to it, but that's it."

They wandered down the slope closer to the water's edge.

"There are a number of entrances into the lake area, but the way we came in is the easiest," Rolf continued. He pointed back to the path and then to a small ramp and elevated boat dock about 50 meters down the shoreline. "You can't miss the entrance to the path, because it's just this side of that small dock. There's also a drivable entrance where you can offload a boat. It's just around the rocks where we parked the cars."

Ferguson looked north down the lake past the dock and surveyed the images on the lake's horizon. One sharp triangular peak after another, small ravines and narrow valleys squeezed between them. His eyes systematically worked their way around the shoreline to the west, then south. As he turned around over his left shoulder to face the eastern slope, he froze and nearly lost his balance. In front of him, was a large cliff that looked as if it nearly rose out of the water. He stared at the curvature of the jagged face comprised of a mixture of rock and native grasses. The two inverted triangular gaps along the top ridge gave it the unmistakable image of a 'W'.

"The locals like to climb there. They call it the 'Wall'," said Rudi.

His father and Courtney noticed Ferguson's trance.

"Local folklore says there are things hidden behind those walls," said the elder Batemann.

"There don't appear to be any doors," Courtney laughed as she walked up to Ferguson and put her arm around his waist.

The display of affection was not lost on the Batemanns.

"Well Dad, I think the fish are waiting for us at the Wildhusur."

The *Wilhusur Thur* was a large stream west of Wildhaus that provided the locals and tourists an excellent trout fishing experience. It had been a favorite of the Batemanns for years.

"I'm ready when you are," Rudi Batemann waved at Ferguson and Courtney. "We'll see you two back in Wildhaus. Please call us if you need anything else. We'll check back with you in a couple of days if we don't hear from you sooner."

"Thanks," replied Courtney. Ferguson had hardly heard a word as he continued to be mesmerized by the 'Wall'.

The sun was rising over the peaks by the time the Batemanns were half way back to town, and Ferguson and Courtney had negotiated the relatively flat ground that wound around the eastern edge of the lake where they had started, to the southeastern edge and the enclave that was the start of the 'Wall'. The uneven bank between the base of the cliffs and the water was restricted to only a few meters in some spots, with the widest no more than ten meters.

The face stretched approximately 100 meters in length with about a fifteen-degree angle right in the middle. The height was more or less even across the top, except for the two natural indentations, and was roughly 75 meters at the tallest point.

Ferguson stood in front of what appeared to be the center point, at the apex of the angle. He stared at the wall, then turned around to face the lake and recreated a mental image of a plane touching down on the water in front of him. He imagined the landing path in his mind. A twin-engine Junkers aircraft, just the way Max had described it, boring in straight at him. Why hadn't he listened more closely to his Uncle, instead of dismissing his recollections and conversations as delirium.

Courtney stood off to the side watching him. She knew not to say a word. He was obviously studying and composing something mentally, and she was not about to disturb him until he was ready.

He turned back and forth, alternating staring at the cliffs and then back at the water. He closed his eyes briefly, and opened them again as he held his hands at arm's length in front of his face. Placing both index fingers and thumbs together he created a frame, and through the opening a focal box. He directed it out on the lake and then slowly walked back and forth along the bank.

"It came in here. It had to. But in order to miss that little finger of land that sticks out," he pointed to a small grass and rocky stub of land down the left side of the lake from where they stood, "it would have to stay on this line and come in here," he turned and pointed at the left side of the cliffs.

"So, you're saying that according to your uncle, somewhere behind these cliffs is a plane loaded down with millions of dollars' worth of art. It went straight into the wall," Courtney finally interrupted his train of thought.

"According to what I can remember him talking about, now that I know he wasn't crazy, and considering the letter with the drawings and descriptions, this is it. If it's still here, it's in there," Ferguson nodded at the cragged edifice.

"Like I said before, I'm not seeing a door anywhere. Where the hell could it have entered?"

"It has to be in one of the spots where the grass is. Either that, or where there's loose rock."

There were a number of spots along the face that had some sort of grass or ground cover, and they both instinctively advanced on the cliff face picking out the areas within reach that were covered with anything but stone. Neither had any idea what they were looking for, but they spent the next half hour unsuccessfully clawing and digging with bare hands at any spot that had a semblance of green to it.

Ferguson was the first to stop and realize that the opening that was made had to be large enough to accept the fuselage of an airplane. Certainly, a hole that size could have closed up over the years, but it seemed prudent to look for the biggest spots and start with those and work down.

He explained his theory to Courtney and they divvied up the remaining terrain. One futile hour later they sat down and rested. Courtney walked down to the water's edge and washed the dirt and mud off her hands. She stood and shook her hands in a feeble effort to dry them. She glanced at the right end of the wall, closer to the point where the cliffs tapered off slightly and blended seamlessly into a mountainside that retreated from the lake.

Still staring ahead, she theorized aloud. "What if they crashed into the cliff because they didn't have enough room to come to a stop?" She looked out onto the lake and the narrow, little bulge of rocky ground 25 meters in front of her. "Or they hit something, like a finger of land that stuck out into the lake and caromed into the wall?"

Ferguson heard her and watched as she began walking to the other side of the cliff where her eyes were fixed on a large vertical seam of grass that stood out dramatically toward the end of the face. He hopped up and began trotting over to her as they reached the spot together.

"It sure looks big enough," said Courtney.

Ferguson had picked up a sizable branch that was lying nearby and was busily breaking off the smaller branches under his foot. He fashioned a single, sturdy stick much more capable of digging than their hands. He ascended the slight incline of rocky soil in front of the base and attacked the area with vengeance. He quickly tired after ten minutes of producing nothing but a large hole about a half-meter deep. Courtney took up the fight and deepened the hole slightly, but also tired, gave in, and sat down next to Ferguson.

It was getting close to noon, and it was increasingly self-evident that they were both growing discouraged. Ferguson had suggested they head back to town, get some lunch, and find a hardware store where they could purchase a pick and shovel and return and continue their excavation. They rose and he rammed the stick into the center of their dig in frustration. It hit the dirt with a clang.

They looked at each other, then lunged forward and started to dig deeper around the protruding stick with their hands. It took only a matter of minutes and they unearthed a two-foot-high rusted skeleton of steel that seemingly grew out of the dirt several inches. There was obviously more of it in there, but they stopped and stood back to admire their discovery.

From the curved shape, Ferguson knew immediately what it was. "If I were a betting man, I'd say that looks like a tail rudder."

It had taken nearly two hours for Courtney and Ferguson to reach Wildhaus, find a hardware store, carry out some lunch, and return to the lake. They both hauled a pick, two shovels, a sledgehammer, several flashlights and four eight-foot lead pipes. The food was devoured on the way back up the mountain.

Ferguson placed one of the pipes about a meter to the left side of their discovery. He pounded away with the sledgehammer as it stubbornly entered the 'Wall'. With no more than a foot and a half showing, he struck the head of the pipe and it shot into the ground and disappeared. Ferguson looked again at Courtney and their eyes lit up together.

She handed him the pick. "What the hell are you waiting for? Get busy," she grabbed a shovel and started in next to Ferguson who had already wielded the pick and was driving it into the dark soil and rock.

They broke through in about 45 minutes. Having dug at least two meters into the surface, Ferguson nearly lost the pick as it vanished into a sizable hole that gave way as he drove the point into the softening dirt.

From the dirt and rock they had been stripping away, they had created a small mound in front of the newfound entrance, and Ferguson slid down the natural slope and grabbed a flashlight from Courtney who had pulled several out of one of the backpacks they had filled from the hardware store.

He crawled up to the edge of the hole, which was approximately one meter in diameter, stuck his head and shoulders through and shined the beam from the flashlight into the pitch black. The ray of light went well into the blackness before reflecting off what appeared to be another rock wall.

"Can you see anything?" Courtney asked.

"Nothing. Except there looks like plenty of room in there. Give me the lantern flashlights and I'll go on in. Leave 'em in the backpack."

Courtney complied with his request and hoisted the pack up to him. "Please be careful."

"If I'm buried alive, you promise to come get me?"

"Stop it. Just be careful."

He decided to go feet first, and kicked away at the edges around the hole to widen it. He easily slid through and with the flashlight in his right hand gingerly reached out with his feet to feel for solid ground. He stumbled briefly, but caught himself and stood upright inside with ease.

He concentrated the light in front of him and was amazed at the size of the cavern in front of him. The light hit an opposite wall more than 15 meters away. He turned the light to the left and the opposing rock wall was closer, but still several paces off. He turned it skyward and the light diffused before it hit anything. He turned the flashlight to the right and it fell upon on the fuselage of a Junkers Ju-52.

***

Under explicit orders from Ferguson, Courtney remained outside the cave in case there was any kind of collapse. She would have to be free and clear to mount a rescue. Her curiosity, however, was agonizing, and she repeatedly asked to switch places so she could take it all in. She never got an answer.

The cave was cool, but had no signs of any lingering moisture or water. Ferguson had set up three of the lantern lights on the floor of the cave while he walked around, and crawled over the mangled shell of the plane. *How in the world did this thing get in here?*

He immediately noticed the absence of wings. *They must be at the bottom of the lake.* He examined the smashed cockpit area, realizing that what was once probably an engine, was now a tangled archeological heap on the top of the fuselage. *How in the world did Uncle Max ever survive this mess?* Despite everything, the fuselage was substantially intact from behind the cockpit to the tail, which eerily dissolved into the cave's inner wall.

He eventually found the rear door and tried to open it. It wouldn't budge. He tugged on it harder, but feared any excessive force might cause the completely fatigued mess to give way. He held his breath, put his right foot up against the decaying steel, and gave one final pull. The door popped open and he went sprawling backward onto his butt, slamming the back of his head against the hard floor.

"Shit!"

Courtney heard him scream and yelled into the hole. "Are you alright?"

"I'm fine, just lost my footing."

He picked up the flashlight and flooded the inside compartment. "Holy Shit."

He struggled to climb up and over the loose assortment of wood boxes and crates. He got far enough to the front of the fuselage to shine the light on a severely damaged crate that was split in half. The decaying contents were still easily recognizable.

"I'll be damned," he muttered under his breath.

Two minutes later, he nearly gave Courtney a heart attack as he emerged from the cave without warning.

"Damnit... let me know when you're coming out of there next time."

"Sorry."

She noticed the astonished look on his face. "So...what did you find?"

He caught his breath. "We found the mother lode."


Charles Pernod was escorted into the conference room at 2:15, and introduced by a sharp looking, young female officer with the Zurich state office. Shutt and Daniel rose from their chairs and greeted him in English, as Daniel had determined his fluency hours earlier in the phone conversation that prompted this meeting. They all thanked the officer, and watched her admiringly through the full glass windows as she exited the room and disappeared down the hall.

"It's a pleasure to meet you Jean-Luc. I've heard some very good things about you from Georges Leumerre."

"Thank you, Charles, please tell him hello when you see him again. Detective Shutt and I are very appreciative of your joining us in the investigation."

"Yes, thank you very much," Shutt added.

"My pleasure. It sounds as if you might have something very significant here, so I'm looking forward to offering any help I can."

Pernod was an investigative officer in the Specialized Crimes Department of the Police Services Division of Interpol. He had been assigned to the Works of Art Task Force nearly ten years ago, and was considered one of the most knowledgeable minds in the world when it came to stolen and lost art.

At 41 years old, he had spent a lifetime in the research of art. A struggling artist before earning his degree, he spent twelve years as an assistant and professor of art history at the Universite Lumiere Lyon, until he was recruited by a friend into Interpol, specifically for his expertise in 18th and 19th century paintings, the centerpieces of the looted art from World War II. At 5'9", with a round body fashioned by years of classroom and deskwork, and amplified by age, he possessed a balding head of salt and pepper hair and pale complexion. His blue blazer and gray wool slacks were modest and unassuming, a mirror of his personality. However, his intelligence and attention to detail were well known and appreciated, and his reputation of being direct and to the point quickly became obvious.

"If you'll both take a seat, I'll give you some brief history and we can discuss how you plan to approach your interesting discovery."

They all sat, as Pernod removed three folders from his briefcase and slid two over the table to Shutt and Daniel.

"This is a synopsis of what I'm about to discuss, with certainly more detail than I'll bore you with.

"Forgive me Jean-Luc, I may repeat myself from our conversation this morning, but for Mr. Shutt's benefit I'll cover it again. Please, again, no offense to your country is intended."

Daniel held up his hands, palms up, in a gesture of approval and concession, and then waved him on.

"It's no secret that during World War II, Germany and Switzerland had widespread economic and trade links, and were virtually allies in disguise. Swiss Banks, and the banking laws that govern them, were conduits for large sums of questionable money, art, jewelry and other valuables that were deposited, laundered, or hidden away for perpetuity.

"The Nazi party, particularly the chosen few in Hitler's immediate hierarchy benefited mightily from the looting of cash, jewelry, precious metals, art, and various other antiquities. Some of the thugs in the party fancied themselves as collectors, and were actively engaged in targeting particular individuals and their collections, with specific items in mind. Hermann Goering, in particular, was an avid art collector and amassed a priceless collection of fine art, which he robbed from all over occupied Europe. He had a personal affection for the religious masterpieces, but was reputed to have a sizable collection of impressionists work he was not as fond of, but has never been recovered.

"If the person or persons that you are investigating believe they may have access to a potentially large cache of stolen art, or know where it might exist, it is very possible they are correct. It is made more probable, given as it appears; they believe it resides within the borders of Switzerland. There still remains an enormous amount of unaccountable financial wealth in Swiss banks, which cannot be traced or recovered. I would hate to guess how much of that wealth was gained illicitly and illegally.

"Since the mid-nineties, the Swiss government has been working with the international community and Jewish organizations in the recovery of Holocaust victims' assets. The results culminated in a large settlement with the Swiss commercial banks in 1998, and the release of a critical report from the Volcker Commission, that had conducted an investigative audit of dormant accounts believed to be held by Nazi victims. Even though The Commission had the blessing of the Swiss Bankers Association, according to the report the banks showed a 'general lack of diligence'--even active resistance--in response to private and official inquiries. They continue to this day to be the world's best at harboring ill-gotten gains.

"In your folder is the Volcker report and a listing of known artwork in existence in Europe as of the start of World War II, that cannot be accounted for today. There is no question, some of the listed pieces reside in private collections that will never be made known publicly. However, there are a significant number of pieces that are surely lost, misplaced, or even possibly belong to individuals who have no concept of what they have in their possession.

"My only issue is the manner in which Jean-Luc described the possible location of the art as described by your suspect. It's plausible, but the condition of the goods would be at great risk if they were not adequately protected from the elements...especially moisture. But as I said anything is possible, and I've certainly seen stranger things in my life when it comes to the world of art."

Pernod finally came up for air and leaned back in his chair to wait for any feedback.

Shutt spoke first. "Very informative Mr. Pernod, thank you. At this point I have no way of knowing the condition of the potential treasure trove, but I'm hoping in the next 24 hours we'll get a good fix on it."

Daniel stood up, signaling the end of the meeting. "Very well, then. We all need to be on our way to Wildhaus. It will take us a couple hours from here. However, the hotel has been under surveillance since early this morning, and our two suspects have been gone since breakfast. We have confirmed they checked in yesterday, and as of right now Toby, they're still registered."

"Hallelujah," Toby looked at his watch, which read almost 3:00.

Ferguson and Courtney had spent the balance of the late afternoon returning to the hardware store, and with the help of the owner, sourced an open bed utility trailer from his brother-in-law down the street. Fortunately, he also had a hitch mount that fit Batemann's Jeep, and he was more than happy to pick up 1,000 Swiss Francs cash for a 24 hours rental. They were back at the hotel before dark.

The desk clerk in the lobby tried to keep his eyes focused on the paperwork in front of him, but he stole several glances at Ferguson and Courtney as they struggled to carry another large, narrow, wood crate over to the elevator for the second time in the last ten minutes. They returned to the lobby a third time, went out to the garage, and came back in again with each carrying smaller versions of the previous cases.

Thirty minutes after they had disappeared upstairs, Courtney returned to the lobby alone, and walked into the lounge and ordered a glass of Bordeaux. She pulled out the cell phone from the front pocket of her blue jeans and set it on the table she commandeered by the fire. She checked her watch again, waiting for the phone to ring, and the show to begin. At 6:01, she was not disappointed.

She answered it on the second ring. "Hello."

Julio Bolivar leaned on the wooden fence post just outside the front door of the *Olympischen Hutte*. Fate had been good to Courtney. The local diner had been a fixture for years in St. Moritz, and showed no signs of going away any time soon. Bolivar, Sullivan and Keitel had spent the better part of the last 14 hours testing the breakfast, lunch and dinner menus in the eclectic eatery. They were still unaware of the three pairs of eyes several hundred meters up the hill that had been monitoring them for an equal number of uneventful hours.

"Miss Lewis, my name is John. Michael is unavailable, but sends his regards. He said he felt it more important that he remain in Chicago and that you would understand. He is also waiting to hear from me shortly of your whereabouts. You do have some information for me, don't you Miss Lewis?"

"Yes. I have some information...John," she said coldly. We're in Walenstadt right now, but are headed back to a small-town tomorrow morning called Stein. We found what you want, but we'll know for certain tomorrow afternoon what can be salvaged. We're going to recover what's left and try to store it in Stein.

"And where would that storage location be Miss Lewis?"

"I haven't the foggiest. Matt was there today with somebody he knows who lives in Walenstadt, and they thought they would have to find out how much they can save. Mr. Batemann, Rudi Batemann is the friend of Matt's, did mention something about storing it in a shop he owns in Stein. I don't know the name of it. Mr. Batemann left for there about an hour ago, and we're meeting him at the recovery site in the morning.

"And where is that site?"

"I don't know that either. We were way up in the mountains, part of the way on foot. We were somewhere on the south side of Stein. Frankly, even if I knew I wouldn't tell you. As much as Matt does not trust me, I still want him to be able to find and recover the art. It's his deal and I am not going to take that away from him. Wherever he stores it, you can come steal it from him. Isn't that what you all are...common thieves?"

"Very noble Miss Lewis, and also very insulting. But alas, you have half of it correct. Thieves...yes, common thieves...no, far from it. You don't appear to be very knowledgeable about anything when it comes to your geography. Therefore, I fully expect to see you in person tomorrow Miss Lewis, so we can put all of these 'I don't knows' to bed.

"You will take impeccable notes on directions to the recovery area. I will phone you again tomorrow from Unterwasser at noon, and I'll look forward to not having anymore wild goose chases like our trek through St. Moritz. If I don't feel you're being truthful with me, I won't hesitate to tell Michael. I'm certain he was very explicit as to the consequences of any lies and deception. Do you understand?"

"Yes, and I'm not lying to you. And I won't be ready to take your call at noon. I'll try to be ready for your call at 5:00, but I will not reveal the whereabouts of the art, until it has been recovered, stored away, and I hear from my father. Do you understand?"

"You're in no position to be dictating conditions Miss Lewis," replied Bolivar angrily.

"Oh, I believe I am. I value my father's life, but I'm betting you value the location of millions of dollars in artwork more than you're willing to kill an innocent man. If he dies, I'll make certain you never find anything, even if I have to destroy it myself. Now, do you understand?"

"I understand. 5:00 tomorrow Miss Lewis. We'll be waiting in Stein."

*Perfect. You be waiting right there.* "I'll be waiting for your call."

"No sooner than she ended the call from Bolivar, she had recalled Shutt's number and hit the 'send' key.

"Hello Courtney."

"Detective."

"It appears you've been busy today."

"Let's just say we had a very successful venture into the mountains. We brought out a couple of items we're going to look at tonight to see how damaged they are. We got into one and it is in remarkably good shape…a Gauguin, from his Polynesian work, probably worth several million after some minor restoration. It looks as though there are quite a few more where that came from. We'll hopefully have them out of there tomorrow."

"And your friends?"

"Just spoke with them. How's my father?"

"He's fine. I just got off the phone with detectives in Chicago. They have the interest of the FBI and Justice Department, who have him under constant watch from a number of folks. By the way, he knows, and he is cooperating fully. What did your friends say?"

"I didn't really want him to know what's going on, but if that helps, so be it. Make sure he knows I'm okay."

"I already have."

"Thanks. My stalkers are going to let us find it and store it. After that, we've agreed that I will give them the location and they can come get it. It may very well happen tomorrow night, but I'm going to try to hold them off as long as I can. I will call you tomorrow afternoon if I can get service at the crash site. It's way up in the mountains. If not, I will get a hold of you when we are back in town. I'll make sure we speak by…let's say 3:00. My thieving friends are calling back at 5:00, and I'll set them up for you late tomorrow afternoon or evening. Be ready!"

"We'll follow you up into the mountains?"

"No. You'd be pretty obvious. We're not going to run away this time, and nobody else knows where we are yet, so don't screw things up by showing up on the lake. We'll be back down as soon as we can load up what's salvageable. You know where we're staying. Wait for us to get everything down to the hotel."

"We'll be here. By the way, what do Rudi and Rolf Batemann have to do with this?"

"Nothing. We went to them and asked for their help in locating and guiding us to the lake. They drove us up there and rented us the jeep. They don't have a clue. Just stay close and I'll speak with you tomorrow."

"I'll be waiting."

Courtney finished her wine, purchased a bottle of champagne, and confiscated two glasses. She stopped by the front desk on her way back to the room and arranged to rent an additional room for tomorrow morning, specifically requesting one on the first floor with an outside entrance. The only thing available that met that criterion was a banquet room that had an inside entrance, but included a small, adjacent storage room that had a connecting door into the garage. She approved immediately, and the clerk reserved the space indefinitely and told her it would be ready by 9:00 a.m. He gave her a key in advance.

She caught the elevator, and on the way up, she was overcome by a sudden case of the guilts. It was as if she was Judas, and was selling Matt out...taking it all away from him. She managed to reconcile her actions with the belief that he would understand once he knew her father's life was in danger. He would lose the art, but he would be a hero for finding it. There had to be some substantial reward, and probably a sizable insurance settlement. Publicity galore. He would come out of it very well financially. She would make certain of that. However, she knew she owed him more than that, and honestly, she was afraid that he may never speak to her again.

Once inside the room she could hear the water running in the bathroom, so she tiptoed into the closet and hastily removed her clothes.

Courtney entered the bathroom and caught Ferguson by surprise as he was preparing to enter the whirlpool. He was clad only in a white towel wrapped around the waist.

She had reprised her outfit from the previous evening, the white bathrobe with nothing underneath but her naked body, a more aggressive display of the hollow between her bosoms. She produced the bottle of Perrier Jouet champagne and two glasses.

"I thought you could use some company."

Ferguson was momentarily speechless. As she gave a look of disappointment, he recovered quickly. "Uh, this kind of company I can always use."

She took a few steps forward and leaned up to kiss him lightly on the lips. He slipped his right hand behind the back of her neck and returned the kiss, with significantly more passion. He reached out with his left hand and took the bottle and glasses from her hands. She responded by untying the belt to her robe, slipping it off her shoulders and letting it fall to the floor.

They kissed again, as she loosened the towel around his waist and removed it, with some difficulty, as it caught briefly on his enlarging groin area.

"Sorry," Courtney giggled, as their lips remained pressed against each other.

"As you can probably tell, the rest of me appreciates the company as well."

The kissing grew more lustful and Ferguson grabbed her by the waist and pulled her to him as he backed up to the side of the whirlpool tub, bubbling steam rising from the water. He sat back on the marble and pulled her closer, exploring with his tongue from her chin to her belly button. She moaned very lightly as he moved back up her rib cage, spending several minutes negotiating both breasts and nipples and caressing her back and buttocks with his hands.

She grabbed the back of his head with both hands and stepped over the edge of the tub one leg at a time into the pulsating liquid. Straddling him, she slowly eased herself down and gently took him inside of her.

Ten minutes later they sat on opposite ends of the tub, legs entwined like pretzels. Ferguson poured more champagne, spilling several ounces into the water, as they laughed in unison.

"I apologize for my lack of endurance; it's been a little while since I have had my sexual fantasy fulfilled by the most beautiful woman in the world. I'm hoping for a second chance to prove my worth."

"There's nothing for you to apologize about. Your worth was fantastic. I enjoyed it thoroughly. As for second chances, yours begins about thirty seconds after we get out of here."

Ferguson fumbled his glass and dropped it into the water. They both laughed again, as he made sure to feel everything below the surface before he discovered the missing glass.

# Chapter 19

*May 25, 2001. Voralpsee Lake, Switzerland*

After nearly ten minutes, since reaching the dead end of the road, Ferguson finally found the access through to the boat ramp and navigated the jeep down the gravely path to the lake. He stopped, engaged the four-wheel drive, and continued along the shoreline within 10 meters of the cave entrance. It was still dark, and the headlights bounced up and down over the rough terrain, in sharp contrast with the still reflection of the moon off the lake, which intermittently peeked through the patchy mist that drifted lightly over the water.

The air was cold this far up the mountain, and at 5:30 in the morning the sunshine wouldn't be out for another two hours to alleviate the chill and the fog that fought a losing battle for survival as it reached out at the earthy edges. The jackets purchased from the Batemanns were proving to be a welcome addition.

Yesterday's weather had been most cooperative and today's forecast again sounded superb...thin clouds, mostly sunny, and mild temperatures. Ferguson and Courtney felt that without any unforeseen problems or intrusions, they could extract the balance of the crates by the end of the day, and then face the inevitable decision of what to do with the whole ensemble.

Ferguson angled the front of the jeep toward the face of the cliff and set the high beams so they concentrated directly on the hole into the crash site. He killed the lights, but left the motor running as he and Courtney relaxed inside and sipped from the remainder of the large coffees they had brought with them from the hotel.

They were both exhausted from the lack of sleep, but the renewed adrenaline rush from their return to the treasure hunt, had reemerged.

"So, you think we can get all of it?" Courtney asked.

"Yeah, I'm going to try to pull away some of the fuselage around the door, if it doesn't make anything unstable. That should make it easier to get the bulk of it out. We'll start this morning with the smaller pieces, so we can fill up the jeep and you can take a load down by yourself. While you're gone, I will bring out as much as I can. Do you think you can unload the smaller stuff by yourself?"

"I would think so. Let me see how small the smaller stuff is?"

They both sipped at their coffees, as Ferguson rubbed on the fogged window to peek outside into the dark.

"What in the hell are we going to do with this stuff?" Ferguson muttered aloud with a tinge of uncertainty. He looked directly at Courtney huddled in the passenger seat next to him. "This is about as far as my hair brained scheme took me. Frankly, I didn't think we would find this shit, much less find it in the condition we did. I thought by the time we concluded our little treasure hunt, and then surfaced in the open again, the bad guys and the police would find us. We could tell them the whole story, and they could either be satisfied with what we told them, or go look for themselves...that the whole thing never survived 60 years of Alpine weather. Now we've got a bona fide, frickin' stop-the-presses discovery worth a gazillion dollars. You're the damn art expert. How are we gonna' handle this?"

Courtney laughed out loud and shook her head back and forth. "This is more than I dreamed we'd ever be dealing with. I agree with you, it sounded possible, but I was almost certain we would never find anything that amounted to squat. What we have now is one of the greatest discoveries of art in the last 50 years.

"The only thing I can tell you is that most of what we have, belonged to somebody else at some point in time. Whether the different pieces can ever be traced back to their rightful heirs is another matter. There is certain to be some financial reward, probably from a number of different sources, if you turn it in. The question is...do you want to keep what we've found? All of it, some of it, or none of it?"

"The art doesn't belong to me...I know that. If the heirs of the rightful owners cannot be found, I'll keep it. Still, I think we ought to make sure somebody, or some organization gets an opportunity to make the effort to track down the original owners, or by now a deserving relative. Having said all that, I would like to maintain some control on how it's handled, and it sure would be nice to be rewarded for my efforts. Hell, I'm leaving you out of the equation. You're as much the discoverer as I am. Do you want it?"

Courtney was beginning to feel huge pangs of guilt, knowing full well that this discussion was moot, and in a few short hours, the decision would be out of their hands. However, she saw this as a golden opportunity to subconsciously plant the seed of redemption in Matt's mind, and justify what was surely going to be the result of her giving them up, and their discovery, too.

"Noooo! I have no intentions or interest in anything that does not rightfully belong to me. There are organizations out there that go to great pains to reunite lost or stolen art and antiquities with their proper owners, and I am totally in favor of turning over everything we find to them. Nevertheless, I'm a curator of art, and I would love to see what we found shared with the world. I'm not sure you can comprehend the significance of what we have. It's incredible stuff. It's very exciting to be responsible for discovering something of this magnitude. It's an unbelievable story!"

"Okay, we're in agreement that we find someone to handle this stuff, with us definitely running the show, but who? And we need to make sure the information on the discovery gets out to the right media outlets, quickly, so we can get the lunatics that are chasing us off our backs."

"I'd say we start with the International Council of Museums. They have an agency or department created explicitly for provenance research, and I'm sure they cooperate with other organizations across the world doing the same thing."

"What's that? Provenance?"

"Provenance is ownership, or the history of ownership. They investigate ownership of art works, and explore and attempt to arbitrate claims and questions of history. They will also have some historical perspective of museums during World War II and the Holocaust. The ICOM is an international organization made up of museums and museum professionals and they're also independent of any governments, which should make them easier to deal with."

"Excellent. They sound perfect." Ferguson gulped down the last of his coffee. "That's a relief. I really wasn't sure how my conscience was going to resolve the moral issue of all this. I'm sure I can reconcile the loss of the monetary value better when I understand that all of this stuff really and truly belongs to someone else."

"I think you're doing right thing." *God, I hope he believes what he's saying. He's gonna give it up to another authority at some point in time. Maybe he won't hate my guts as much when he realizes I sold him out. Maybe he'll understand when he realizes my father's life was at stake.*

"Well, now that that's settled, let's go get the rest of the greatest art discovery in the last half century."

***

Gregory Keitel nibbled on the remaining scraps of a poppy seed bagel and glanced up from the *Cosmopolis* newspaper, casually surveying the small coffee shop through the throng of loyal patrons. Discreetly focusing on the *Rosca* coffee logo'd mirror on the wall in front of him, he could visually monitor the large black Mercedes sedan parked down the street facing his back.

Bolivar and Sullivan joined him at the corner table by the window and sat down with their trays of pastries, doughnuts and coffee. They both dove into their respective plates in silence.

"Keep eating and don't look around in alarm, but I think we've got some company," said Keitel said as he leaned back in his chair, crossed his legs, and refolded the paper.

Bolivar looked at him from across the table and dabbed a napkin to his mouth. "Where?"

"You're looking right at them. Down the street, a large black Mercedes four door."

Bolivar kept his head focused on Keitel, but rolled his eyes slightly to the left, finishing with the napkin and replacing it in his lap. "I see it. Two occupants."

"Three. The other disappeared down the street about ten minutes ago. I think he went into the gas station about a block behind you."

Sullivan listened, but an attempt to look over Bolivar onto the street would have been too obvious. Since he felt as if he was beginning to catch on to this detective business, he did as he was told and kept on eating and listening as if nothing was going on.

"So what makes you think they're tailing us?" Bolivar mumbled through a mouth full of powdered doughnut.

"The car looks like the same one that I noticed a couple of times in the mirror on our excursion across eastern Switzerland. Not to mention, the guy I saw walking down the street a few minutes ago, looks like the same chap I saw in the outdoor restaurant at the Palace. As I recall, he had another fellow with him then."

"Coincidence?" Sullivan asked. "There are a lot of black Mercedes sedans around these parts."

"I don't believe in coincidences Mr. Sullivan. My profession doesn't allow that luxury." The reply was accompanied by a cold stare.

Sullivan recognized the admonishment and decided not to speak again until spoken to. Bolivar admired the hardened response and the keen eye of a seasoned investigator, and was certain that if Keitel thought they were being followed, that they were definitely being followed. "Police?"

"I don't know. That was my first thought, but three in the same vehicle...that doesn't sound right."

"Well, we'll know soon enough. Let's finish up breakfast and we'll head over to Stein and wait to speak with Miss Lewis. Bolivar pulled out the crumpled road map from his hip pocket and found Stein. "It's only about ten minutes down the road. We could have probably made it there."

"My fuel gauge said otherwise," replied Keitel. "Besides, we'll fill up at that station up the street, and maybe I can get another look at the fellow who wandered down that way. He certainly hasn't returned yet."

All three stood, kept their coffees, and walked out the front door of the *Cafe Knaus* onto *Hauptstrasse*. They climbed into Keitel's BMW, that was parked on the street right in front of them, and drove up the block to the *POCO* service station.

While Sullivan pumped gas, Keitel made an intentional trip into the station for a water bottle and a Milky Way candy bar. He caught Knabel by surprise, seated in a booth in an adjacent glass enclosed dining area, the remnants of his own breakfast lying in front of him. Knabel quickly jerked up the newspaper he had been reading and opened it up in front of his face. It was too late. Keitel had seen enough to confirm his suspicions.

Alden and Marshall were already driving up the street in pursuit of Keitel's BMW. Having called Knabel's cell phone to alert him that their quarry was on the move and they were on their way to pick him up, they hung up before they could warn him that their three friends had decided to pull into the service station for gas.

At 9:46 in the morning, the navy-blue BMW and the black Mercedes both exited the service station within thirty seconds of each other, headed west out of Wildhaus to Stein. Only two minutes later, Courtney Lewis pulled into the same station to fill up the Batemanns' jeep.

*** 

The two-way radio in Jean-Luc Daniel's hand briefly crackled with static before officer Peter Kirsch's voice broke clear. "The transmitter is in place and operational. We're picking up the suspect loud and clear."

Daniel acknowledged and turned to Shutt, who was busy focusing a pair of binoculars on the dark green jeep, 75 meters away, taking on a much-needed tank of gas.

Daniel slowly pulled the Audi away from the curb. "Hang on, we're headed that way. I don't know if you understood that, but they said the transmitter on her car is working fine. It was nice of her to leave it unoccupied at the hotel."

The two of them, along with Pernod who was crammed into the back seat, drove up the street and into the open parking area of the service station and double-parked on the edge of the lot. Shutt hopped out before the engine died and approached Courtney from behind as she watched the pump's display of rapidly changing numbers.

"Fancy meeting you here."

Turning around very slowly, Courtney found Shutt leaning on a neighboring pump. "You couldn't wait for me to call you?"

"I thought we'd let you know that we're here, and keeping an eye on your backside."

"We?"

"I think we have the entire Wildhaus police force-all three cars anyway-half the canton police, a few federal officers, and a little help from Interpol. Oh, and me!" Shutt smiled broadly.

"I'm feeling safe already. But I wish you would stay clear until I tell you."

"Well, your track record makes me nervous. I thought I'd let you know that we're not going anywhere without you, so please nothing bizarre or unusual."

Courtney looked over his shoulder at Daniel and Pernod, who maintained their distance just outside the car. "How's my father?"

"Checked on him again about an hour ago. Sound asleep, but under careful surveillance. We've scoured his home, auto and office, and he appears to be quite safe."

"Thank you."

"You're welcome."

Courtney topped off the tank, replaced the nozzle, and tore off the receipt from her American Express auto payment as it printed out. "We're not finished, but we will be by this afternoon. I just brought down a load of eight pieces, smaller ones that I could handle myself. Matt is loading the trailer and I'm headed back up now. We should be able to get it all down by this afternoon. I'll be hearing from the other lowlifes this afternoon and letting them know where we are. I'm sure they will want to join us at the hotel as soon as possible. We have a meeting room there on the first floor where we're stashing the art as we bring it down. That is where I will need you to come in and get the sons-of-bitches, but let me get them there first. Agreed?"

"Agreed. We'll be watching, from across the street. How are you going to let me know when they're there?"

"They're going to call me around 5:00," she looked down at her watch. "That should give us enough time to get everything we can recover back down to the hotel. I'll give them the hotel location, call you, and warn you they're coming. They will be coming from Unterwasser, so it won't be more than five or ten minutes before they arrive. Be ready."

"We'll be ready. Make sure you stick to the plan. These people are very dangerous, and I'm still not thrilled with you putting yourselves in a position to get hurt. If you stick to the plan, we can make this thing work."

"I'll make it work."

Courtney climbed into the Jeep and pulled away headed east and back up to the crash site.

Shutt returned to Daniel and Pernod and they followed in the same direction, but a half mile down they pulled into the parking lot opposite the *Hotel Hirschen*, eventually settling into the second-floor law office that faced *Hauptstrasse* and the front door to the hotel. Jean-Luc Daniel kindly asked Mr. Thomas Weber, attorney at law, that the local and Federal authorities would be most appreciative if he took the day off. He was more than happy to cooperate with law enforcement.

They escorted him, and his equally happy secretary, out of the building, accepted a set of keys as they locked the doors to the vacant office, and headed north for two blocks to the *Alpstein* restaurant. Shutt, Daniel and Pernod would be expecting to hear shortly from the air surveillance on the location of Courtney's Jeep, once she reached her destination. They figured there was time to get a quick bite to eat, before having to travel into the mountains to ascertain the site of Courtney Lewis and Matt Ferguson's treasure. Besides, the two officers from the police ski patrol would have been discreetly dropped from the helicopter by that time, and have them under surveillance by the time the chopper returned for the three of them.

\*\*\*

The call to Alden's cell phone came just as they entered Unterwasser. They were several minutes behind the navy BMW, whose signal was still registering on the receiver in Knabel's hands, but clearly showed that it had come to a stop just ahead of them. Knabel confirmed their position with Marshall and Alden in the front seat, and Alden gestured to Marshall to pull off the main road. The Mercedes pulled into the vacant lot of a local ski shop and circled around to face the street, 100 meters west of Keitel's parked car, and out of view of its occupants.

The man on the other end of the line was calling from a pay phone just outside the Federal Office of Justice and Police in Bern. Considering his prominent position in the Federal Police's Main Division, Service for Analysis and Prevention, the call needed anonymity, privacy, and would certainly be brief.

After an exclusive, coded introduction confirming his identity, Alden provided a reciprocal cryptic acknowledgement and then listened intently to the disguised voice on the other end. It described an inconspicuous activity between the Federal Police and the local St. Gallen Canton Police, in conjunction with a United States law enforcement representative. The operation seemed to be directed at locating two U. S. citizens, a male and female traveling together, with explicit instructions that when found they were to be observed and not arrested. They were registered in a hotel in Wildhaus, the *Hotel Hirschen*. The voice was unable to confirm both of the names for fear of arousing too much suspicion, but he had determined that the name of Ferguson was used as the registered name at the hotel.

Alden thanked the caller, gave a mystic salutation and the connection ended abruptly. He leaned back in the soft leather passenger seat and sighed, as a smile of satisfaction emerged while he stared briefly out the window back in the direction from where they just came.

"Good news?" Marshall asked, inferring the question from the look on Alden's face.

"Excellent news. Never underestimate the brotherhood Horst, and how deep and devoted it remains. Our two little fugitives have been found. They are back in Wildhaus in the Hotel Hirschen. They were right under our noses thirty minutes ago."

"Should we turn around, and head back?"

"Absolutely. I don't know about the idiots we've been following. It appears they are close, but they haven't figured out where just yet. We need to be very careful when we get to the hotel. It's under surveillance by the police."

"Do you know where it is in Wildhaus?"

"I don't, but let's head through town and if we don't see it, we'll stop to find out."

They pulled out of the lot and headed back west on *Staatsstrasse*, while Bolivar, Keitel and Sullivan watched in bewilderment from their table at the small alfresco cafe up the street.

"Where do you think they're headed?" Sullivan asked.

Before the stupid question received a stupid answer, Bolivar interceded. "I'm smelling the police. I've got my concerns that our lady friend may have gone to the authorities, and they're just one of many that are keeping an eye on us."

"They don't look like police to me. I wouldn't jump to that conclusion just yet. However, it's something we need to be concerned about when we find the girl and her boyfriend," said Keitel.

"Agreed. We'll need to be alert to anyone that looks suspicious, particularly anybody that resembles the police. By for now, let's relax, have a beer and some lunch," Bolivar looked at his watch, "and kill the next six hours. By this evening, we should have most of the answers to our questions." He raised his hand and waved at the apron-clad waitress who was standing at the open-air bar making conversation with the young and very handsome bartender.

***

The sun was high overhead and the air warming, when Courtney returned to the recovery site. Ferguson had just sat down on the back of the trailer to take a break, and was busy wiping the sweat from his face with the back of his right hand, as she emerged from the Jeep and walked up to admire the work he had put in since she left.

"Wow, you've been busy!"

"It's not as difficult as I thought. I was able to peel away some of the plane's fuselage and open a pretty good hole on the side."

"It looks like you were able to widen the cave entrance as well."

"That was by accident," he stood up and turned around to reveal his entire backside covered with drying mud and dirt." I had a bit of a tumble through the hole."

Courtney chuckled, "It didn't appear to slow you down any." She walked up to the trailer that was now holding over a dozen crates.

"There are seven more left, and another one that's torn up pretty good. The picture inside was broken also, and it's pretty well decayed, but I picked up what I could and laid the remnants right there," Ferguson pointed to the twisted carnage of an ornate gold frame and oil canvas to the side of the hitch, all of it having taken on a blackish, moldy skin. "I'm going to need your help with the others. I could have probably got them out, but I'm afraid if I manhandle them too much, or drop one of them, I'll damage the contents."

"I'm at your service."

"It seems I might have heard those same words last night."

"I'm multi-talented," Courtney turned and walked toward the cave entrance.

"I'll say," Ferguson mumbled just loud enough for Courtney to hear the response. He stood and followed behind her. Neither of them paid any attention to the faint sound of helicopter rotors overhead.

"So, we're going to go in together?" Courtney asked.

"If you're okay with that?"

"Yeah, I'm betting if you stumble footed into it and it didn't come down on you, it's safe.

"Thanks, I appreciate your concern," Ferguson said sarcastically. "Anyway, I've taken some tools, flashlights and water inside already in case we have some problems. I also laid several of the pipes through the hole that might give us some airlines if it caves in. Hell, we'll be fine. We won't be in there any longer than a few minutes at a time, and we should be out of here in another hour."

"Let's go. The sooner we get it out, the sooner we can get it back down to town. The banquet room will work out great. There's a garage door on the backside of the hotel that leads into the garage area. We can park the trailer there. Just inside that door is a set of double doors that leads into a storage closet that's connected to the banquet room by another set of double doors. It's perfect, we can unload without being noticed. Once we get it all in, we can lock up and figure out how we let the world know what WE found!" Courtney's voice gradually escalated into a shout as she ran over, jumped into Ferguson's arms, and planted a big kiss on his parched lips.

Fifty minutes later, they placed the last of the crates onto the trailer, and Ferguson began pushing all of them together and as far forward as they could go. He tied rope down on one corner and haphazardly started lashing back and forth across the irregular assortment of crates, until he was satisfied he had enough containment from the nylon spider web he had created. Courtney had gathered up the tools and was busy carefully trying to load the splintered and torn masterpiece into the back of the Jeep.

Ferguson climbed back into the cave and into the plane's fuselage one last time. He walked forward and hoisted himself into what was left of the destroyed cockpit, shining a flashlight around to look for anything else worth saving. Everything was covered in dust and mold, or combinations of both. After a few minutes, he gave up and stepped back into the body of the aircraft, which was still lit up from the two lantern flashlights they had hung on opposite walls during their excavation. He gazed around the vacant shell. There was the rotting container of a parachute he had stumbled on earlier, with a torn portion of the canopy hanging out the side. He decided to pick it up and bring it along, just in case it might have some historical value to a museum somewhere. It nearly felt apart when he lifted it up, and discarding it, he determined that in the condition it was in it was of probably no use to anyone.

He stepped across the decaying remnants of cargo netting that had obviously accomplished its purpose in saving almost the entire load of precious cargo, and saw nothing else. Removing the two hanging lanterns, he descended from the wreck through the gaping hole he had managed to produce earlier. He turned and held up the lanterns to face the remains of the old Ju52 one last time, snickered, and shook his head in disbelief at the notion of what had transpired nearly sixty years ago.

As he exited the cave for the last time, Courtney greeted him with a metal briefcase she had found next to the damaged artwork. "What's this?"

"I'm guessing it's a German officer's briefcase," he took the gray metal case from Courtney and pointed to the Nazi Swastika embossed on the side. "I found it inside the plane, in the back with the crates. It might be my Uncle's for all I know. We can open it up later tonight. Right now, we need to hitch the trailer up and get out of here." He tossed it into the backseat of the Jeep, climbed into the driver's seat, and started the engine. Maneuvering back and forth, with Courtney's guidance, he positioned the hitch under the trailer's coupler, hopped out of the car, and lifted the stand away as the trailer fell into place on the hitch ball. He locked it in place and connected the chains. He hadn't been able to marry up the electrical connections that morning, so he didn't even bother this time around.

They both looked at each other and smiled, then silently took a long last look at the face of the cliff and the surrounding lake. Without saying a word, they climbed into the idling vehicle and drove away.

From their perch over a half kilometer away, one of the two local police officers who had been ferried in by helicopter, lowered his binoculars and spoke to the other officer holding the portable radio.

"Tell Daniel they're on the move. Let them know, they appear to be finished here, but we'll stay in place as long as they need us to. I've mapped the coordinates of the suspect site."

He raised his binoculars again, as the radio crackled with static. He chuckled to himself, realizing that he had personally climbed 'The Wall' on many occasions, and never fathomed the existence of a cave.

# Chapter 20

*May 25, 2001. Wildhaus, Switzerland*

The garage to the hotel was quiet and occupied by only a handful of cars. The last one to enter was a large, black Mercedes driven by Horst Marshall, and it was parked five spaces away from an inside entrance into the *Hotel Hirschen*.

Ten minutes earlier, Alden, Knabel and Marshall had easily found the hotel on a cursory drive through the middle of downtown Wildhaus. Having returned to the garage, Knabel had gone inside and met with the desk clerk, explaining that his sister and boyfriend were staying at the hotel and he would be very appreciative if he could find out which room they were in.

Since the inquiring gentleman knew them by name, and he had shown his appreciation with fifty Swiss francs, the clerk was remarkably helpful. He went so far as to tell Knabel that in addition to the *Churfirsten Suite*, they had also rented the *Wildhussersaal Nord* banquet room, located around the west corner of the lobby at the far end of the hall.

After thanking the clerk, Knabel headed toward the garage, which was in the same direction as the aforementioned banquet room. The clerk's final effort in offering the extraordinary service the hotel was noted for, told Knabel that his sister and Mr. Ferguson had been gone for most of the day, but he expected they would be back for dinner, since his sister had requested some suggestions on the finest restaurants in town. Knabel waved and disappeared around the corner.

He climbed back into the rear seat of the Mercedes. "Good news. They are here all right. The stupid fag at the front desk was most helpful. They have been out since this morning. They have a suite that they're staying in, and they've rented a banquet room just inside that door." Knabel pointed at the same door he had entered and returned from.

"That's where they're stashing the artwork," said Marshall.

"That would be my guess," replied Knabel.

"Any word on when they're due back?" Alden asked.

"No, but the clerk thought they would be home at least by dinner, because the girl was asking about restaurants...the finest ones in town."

"Good. Is there enough privacy to get into either room without being seen?"

"I didn't go upstairs to the suite, but the banquet room is in a secluded hall, and I think we can probably get in there if someone keeps an eye on that door and the lobby entrance." Knabel again pointed to the garage door entrance to the hotel.

"Alright. We're going to go into the banquet room first. Paul, you watch the lobby, I'll watch this door, and Horst will pick his way in. Once he's in, we'll join him. Keep the lights off and keep your voices to a whisper. Once in, we'll have a look around. Maybe we'll get lucky and it will be there, but if not, we'll send Horst upstairs to check the suite and we'll wait here for the two lovebirds to return. Any questions?"

Knabel and Marshall shook their heads no. Alden lifted a briefcase from the floorboard, opened it, and proceeded to dole out a

Beretta compact, AWC silencer and three spare clips to everyone in the car. Marshall patted over the breast pocket of his coat to confirm that his lock pick set was where it was supposed to be.

"Let's go."

***

The lunch had been very good, but the *Appenzeller bier* on tap had been outstanding. Bolivar had paid the check and they were still relaxing in the open-air sunshine, sipping on their third round, when his cell phone rang.

He answered immediately, and was quiet and listening intently for the next few minutes. He acknowledged the receipt of information, assured Guillermo Rocca they were acting on it immediately, and thanked him profusely as he flipped the phone closed.

Bolivar took a large gulp from the pilsner glass and smiled. "We got 'em."

Before either Keitel or Sullivan could inquire, Bolivar explained further. "That was Mr. Rocca. It seems our little miss know-it-all and her boyfriend made a mistake. I spoke to Mr. Rocca last night after I had my conversation with Miss Lewis. It was a long shot, but after she mentioned Unterwasser and Walenstadt, we agreed to apply some resources to checking hotel registrations in those two towns, bordering towns, and everything in between. Less than an hour ago, they discovered a registration for Ferguson, in Wildhaus, at a *Hotel Hirschen*. Upon further investigation, they found that an American couple is sharing a room under that name. Finish your beers gentlemen...quickly. We are headed back to Wildhaus."

Without another word being said, they all three downed their beers, walked quickly to Keitel's BMW, and departed.

***

Daniel, Shutt and Pernod hurriedly crossed the street to the front door of Weber's office, unlocked the door and entered. They had been thoroughly surprised at the speed in which Ferguson and Lewis had extracted the artwork and were headed back down the mountain, and were now having to speed up their plans. On the way up the narrow office stairs, Daniel was on the radio immediately asking for undercover surveillance to be initiated on the hotel, and all uniformed officers to assemble across the street in the *Hotel Bellvue* as back up.

Four plain-clothes canton officers, in two unmarked Audi sedans, had been biding their time in the parking lot of the *Hotel Sonne* for the better part of seven hours, waiting for the order to go. One officer from each vehicle exited the passenger side and walked to their prearranged locations inside the hotel, in the lobby and the *Dorfstube* restaurant. The two drivers drove their cars to designated spots inside the hotel garage and in an adjacent retail parking lot on the backside of the hotel.

A police car passed by on the street below and turned right into the *Bellvue* parking lot. That was followed by another 30 seconds later. They had both been parked nearby the *Hirschen* since early that morning to keep visual contact on the hotel. All four officers waited in their cars, out of sight.

The shades were drawn and the blinds cracked slightly in the second-floor law office, and Daniel, Shutt and Pernod intermittently scanned the hotel with binoculars, while Daniel translated to Shutt in English everything that was transpiring or being said.

Daniel's radio crackled with activity. "Ground from Air One Five, Ground from Air One Five, your suspects have turned west on to *Hauptstrasse* and are 500 meters from you."

"I copy Air 1, thanks."

"They'll be here any second, Toby."

\*\*\*

The Jeep with trailer in tow slowed and pulled into the open-air parking lot on the west side of the hotel. Courtney directed him behind the hotel and up to a freshly painted garage door that led into the hotel's enclosed parking garage. He backed the trailer up to the door, killed the engine, and removed the keys.

Courtney went into the garage through a pedestrian doorway, and the garage door began to rise slowly. Ferguson waited until the door reached just over his head and he stepped in and gestured to Courtney to stop. She pressed the red button on the electric panel and it stopped immediately.

Courtney opened a set of double doors just inside the garage and flipped a light switch that illuminated an overhead bare bulb, "Let's go inside and I'll show you the room." She inserted a key into another set of double doors and walked into a darkened banquet room. Light from a series of windows on one wall sneaked through the closed blinds, enough to allow Courtney to see a bank of switches on the wall just in front of her. She stepped forward, with Ferguson following behind her, and reached out to the wall plate.

The door behind them closed and a man's voice froze both of them in their tracks. "Welcome you two."

Gerhard Alden stepped forward from the opposite end of the room. "A little light Horst, if you would please."

Marshall gradually opened two window blinds until there was enough light in the room to distinguish the surprised faces of Ferguson and Courtney, as they recognized the face of Mr. Jones. It didn't take long for them to realize he had two other behemoths with him, all of them brandishing silenced pistols.

Alden walked over to Ferguson and closed his face to within six inches of Ferguson's, "I'm still a little sore from the beating you administered." He took the butt of his gun and rammed it into Ferguson's abdomen, sending him to his knees. He followed that with a knee to the jaw that hurled him back against the wall.

"Leave him alone!" Courtney screamed, as she turned and leaned down to help him up.

"Leave him alone," said Alden menacingly.

She slowly got to her feet and backed up into the corner of the room.

Alden looked at Ferguson who was coughing for breath and wiping the blood away from the split in his cheek, and then at Courtney, who for the first time realized her plan had just backfired and that they were in real jeopardy of losing their lives. "We want what you have found. We want it now!" Alden rubbed his chin with his left forefinger and thumb. "It's not here," he gestured around the room. "Where is it?"

Neither of them spoke.

"WHERE IS IT?" Alden screamed.

Marshall and Knabel both cringed at the volume of Alden's voice, and stepped toward both doors as if to increase their vigil against visitors. Alden got the message.

"Go fuck yourself," muttered Ferguson.

Alden stepped forward and cocked the hammer on the Beretta 9mm handgun and placed the barrel of the silencer on the middle of Ferguson's forehead.

Courtney felt weak in the knees and thought she was going to pass out. "I'll tell you. I know where it all is. I can lead you to it, but you'll have to put the gun away first, or shoot both of us," she was right on the edge of hopelessness, because if they knew the goods were right outside that door, they were both surely dead. Her only hope was to make themselves visible, and hope that Shutt was outside somewhere watching the hotel.

"Is that so?" Alden pulled the gun away and lowered the hammer.

Ferguson breathed an internal sigh of relief, not sure what possessed him to say what he just said. He remained quiet and let Courtney go where she wanted to go.

"We just brought down a handful of crates from the crash site. We can take you to the location, and you can have everything. We just want to get out alive," continued Courtney.

Alden shook his head up and down, and looked around the room indiscriminately, as if mulling over the offer. Before he could answer, Marshall hushed them all with a forefinger to the lips as the sound of voices could be heard coming from the double doors leading from the garage. Alden waved his pistol at Ferguson and Courtney and replicated Marshall's request for silence. He quietly walked over to the windows and closed the blinds again, thrusting the room into semi-darkness.

There was a very soft knock on the door, which went unanswered.

"They may have gone up to their room," Bolivar suggested to Keitel in a whisper.

Keitel turned the doorknob, which still had the key in it. He pushed open the door very slowly. He led Bolivar into the room and waited for their eyes to adjust.Once again, Marshall slammed the door behind them at the same time Alden pulled open a shutter.

Keitel raised a Walther handgun and aimed it at Alden. He was too late. Two dull thuds migrated from the vicinity of Alden, and Keitel dropped like a rag doll. Marshall placed his gun to the backside of Bolivar's head and asked him to drop his weapon. An identical Walther fell to the floor right in front of Ferguson. Alden reached down and picked it up, smiling at Ferguson and shaking his head back and forth. Unable to control her flimsy legs, Courtney slid down the wall on her back until she hit the floor.

"Who are you?" Alden asked Bolivar.

"Who are you?" Bolivar asked Alden.

Alden aimed the Beretta at the floor and popped off another round right through the top of Bolivar's left foot, who fell to the floor grimacing in pain. "I'm asking the questions."

"Who are you?"

"My name's Julio Bolivar. I'm employed by someone who is interested in what these two people have discovered," he looked up at Alden and waved his hand back and forth between Ferguson and Courtney.

"I see," Alden had a look of curiosity. "We were following you for a while, how did you get to here?"

"We were in Stein, where you followed us and then took off. We knew you had been tailing us since Lucerne. Not long after you left us at Stein, we found out these two were staying here. We arrived about a half hour ago and were parked in the garage, when they showed up with a trailer of stuff they were going to unload. I assume you know what's on that trailer?"

"Yeah, I know," Alden scratched his forehead and then started to point his finger at Bolivar. "Wait a minute. The other Latino, the one at her apartment, the pizza delivery guy...you two peas are out of the same pod."

Bolivar also put two and two together and realized that the man standing in front of him was Carlos' killer.

"Where's the other guy that was with you? The younger guy, there were three of you."

"We left him in Stein."

Alden raised his gun again and aimed it Bolivar's other foot.

Bolivar held up his hands in front of his face. "He's in the garage in a blue BMW."

Alden nodded to Marshall who slipped out the back doors into the garage. It took him ten seconds to locate the BMW. Slipping up behind an unsuspecting Sullivan, he tapped on the window with the Beretta, instantaneously extracting a frightened Sullivan from the car. With an additional wave of the gun, Sullivan wasted no time walking in front of Marshall back to the party in the banquet room.

\*\*\*

It was half past three o'clock, and Shutt was beginning to get a little anxious that he had not heard from Courtney Lewis.

Daniel's radio crackled again and startled the three occupants of the law office.

"Control, this is Kirsch in the garage. I've got a problem. I just had a large, white male come pull another white male out of a car at gunpoint, and disappear into the hotel."

"Lobby one, this is control, did you have anybody that fits that description come through your area."

"Negative control. The lobby is empty and has been for the last fifteen minutes. There are some meeting rooms around the corner, they could be back there."

"What's going on?" Shutt asked.

"We got problems," answered Daniel, as he translated the conversations.

"We need to go," said Shutt. "They're probably trying to store the stuff in one of those meeting rooms. They must have company, and we never saw them get in."

Daniel started to put the radio to his mouth to order everybody into the hotel, but Shutt put his hand up to stop. "Wait, let me try something to make sure," he pulled out his cell phone and hit the redial on Courtney's cell phone number.

The ring came through muffled, but loud enough to hear on the phone in Courtney's pants pocket.

"Is that you?" Alden looked at Courtney.

She pulled the phone out, as the ring grew louder. "Yeah.' She looked down at the number, "It's my father."

She answered it before Alden could say anything. "Hello Daddy."

Shutt spoke quickly. "If you're in trouble, say 'I'm fine'."

"I'm fine," Courtney responded.

Alden pointed the gun at her. "Hang it up. Tell him you'll call back later."

"Get them into the garage, by the trailer, anywhere out in the open," pleaded Shutt.

Alden took a step towards Courtney. "Off...NOW!"

"Thanks, but I have to go Daddy. I'll call you back later," she ended the call, turned the phone off, and put it back in her jacket pocket.

Shutt turned to Daniel, "Let's go. We need to cover the garage and all the hotel exits. Let's hope she can get them into the open where we can make something happen. Otherwise we'll wind up with a hostage situation, and I'm not real confident of the stability of the guys we're dealing with."

Daniel spoke into the radio and barked orders to everyone on the team. Shutt had already headed down the steps with Pernod in tow. Daniel caught up with them as they hit the front door of the hotel. The three of them joined the two officers inside the hotel that had sealed off the end of the hallway leading back to the banquet rooms area. Officer Kirsch manned the garage side entrances, and the fourth plainclothes officer covered the back of the hotel by the open garage door. Uniformed help was on its way over from across the street to back up both of them.

Knabel was getting antsy about all of the commotion that occurred in the last ten minutes. "Boss, we might want to move him out of here," he pointed his free hand at Keitel's slumped body, which was beginning to spread blood onto the carpeted floor, "find what we came for, and get the hell out of here ourselves."

"I've gotta agree," Marshall added.

Alden looked first at Ferguson, then to Courtney. "So, you found some things from this crash site, and you have it outside in the garage?"

"That's right. Some of it, but not all," Courtney lied. She was betting that he wanted all of it, and he would keep them alive until he found out where the rest of it was.

"I'm looking for one thing in particular," Alden grabbed the collar of Keitel's shirt, drug him over to the back doors, and handed him off to Marshall. "Horst, put him in the storage closet for now."

Courtney's curiosity got the better of her. "What are you looking for in particular?"

"I'm looking for a metal briefcase, silver with a Nazi inscription."

"I found one," Ferguson mumbled, as he finally lifted himself from the floor, still rubbing at his gut.

"Yeah, I saw it too," said Courtney. I'm not sure if we brought it down or it's still up there."

Ferguson was certain she knew where the briefcase was, realized she was up to something, and played along. "I'm not sure, but I know I got it out of the plane and the cave, and put it in the pile."

The tension in the room was suffocating and the temperature seemed to have grown incredibly warm. Beads of sweat were prevalent on everyone's face, and Alden wiped at his forehead with a flick of his thumb. "Where's your car and trailer now?"

"Just outside the doors. It's a Jeep, backed up to an open garage door," said Courtney

Alden rubbed hard at his forehead, and then looked at Courtney. "Is there room for us to pull a car up behind you?"

"I think so. Yes, definitely."

"Paul, you get the car and bring it up to this door. We'll load these two in our car," Alden kicked at Bolivar on the floor and thumbed at Sullivan standing next to Marshall, "and you and Horst go with them. I'll ride with the other two. We'll dump the dead one in the back of their Jeep. We'll exit from here and drive west until I call you on the cell phone. Don't lose sight of me. You, pick him up and get him outside," he gestured at Sullivan to help Bolivar off the floor.

Knabel had already gone for the car, while the others congregated in the storage area. Alden instructed Ferguson to help Marshall pick up Keitel and drag him out to the Jeep. The Mercedes pulled up behind the trailer as Marshall watched Ferguson struggle to load the lifeless body of Keitel into the rear cargo area of the Jeep.

"Well I'll be damned," Marshall stepped forward; keeping his gun trained on Ferguson, and grabbed the metal briefcase that was lying in the open on top of a stack of tools. "Look what we have here."

Alden came out into the garage with Courtney next to him, while Sullivan was busy helping Bolivar, who was cussing incessantly under his breath, into the front seat of the Mercedes.

"Would this resemble something you might be looking for?" Marshall held up the briefcase in front of Alden.

Before Alden could reply, a police car skidded to a halt in front of the Jeep, and a voice called out from inside the garage.

"This is the police, please drop your weapons, and lay down on the ground face first spread eagle."

Marshall responded immediately by dropping the briefcase to the floor, wheeling around and firing off three rounds at the police car, then crouching forward while letting go two more rounds in the general direction of the voice. Knabel had no line of sight towards the police car outside the garage, but he took aim and fired at a silver Audi about twenty meters away that had an armed man hiding behind an open driver's side door. The windshield and door window exploded and the dull thud of several rounds crunched into automobile steel.

The briefcase skidded toward Alden, who snatched it up under his arm, spun to his right and aimed his pistol at Courtney who was on her knees hiding against the concrete wall. His shot went wide right just over her head as Ferguson came crashing into him shoulder first, the two of them and the gun skidding across the pavement. By the time Alden had recovered his pistol, Ferguson had grabbed Courtney's arm and dragged her back into the storage room.

He pushed her through the other open door into the banquet room tumbling onto the floor.

"Don't move." Shutt lowered his Sig Sauer P220 pistol. He peeked around the right corner of the door just in time to see Alden step in from the garage, notice his face, and loose off three shots that splintered the doorframe and sailed wildly into the banquet room.

"Shit!" Shutt pulled back and wiped away blood dripping from his forehead. Without hesitating, he moved the gun from his right hand to his left, stuck it out in the open door and triggered five rounds wildly into the closet. Daniel crawled up behind him while another officer dove across the open doorway to the other side and leaned forward against the wall.

Alden retreated into the garage, retrieved the briefcase, crawled on hands and knees behind the Mercedes, and then between two cars parked together five meters away. He thought about shouting to Marshall and Knabel, but soon realized he had not been seen.

Knabel crawled into the driver's seat of the Mercedes and called to Marshall who squatted down in front of the car to reload his weapon, "Get in here. It's time to get out of this mess." He looked over at Bolivar, planted two bullets into his left cheek, and kicked him out of the car with his right foot. He aimed at Sullivan who was squatting outside the open passenger door, but before he could fire, Marshall yanked him away by the shirt collar and threw him back against the wall.

The uniformed police officer outside by the Jeep had just about had enough of being fired upon by Marshall. While his partner had continued to return fire, he secured a Sig 551 SWAT rifle from the trunk of their bullet riddled cruiser, and rolled on the ground until he came up on the left side of the crate-filled trailer. He established a perfect firing lane between two crates and opened up on the Mercedes as Marshall was climbing into the front seat.

The entire front windshield disintegrated and the radiator spewed coolant, as the semi-automatic rifle sprayed 15 rounds of .223 ammunition across the front of the big German sedan.

"Get in the damn car!" Knabel raised his head off the console after ducking down to avoid the gunfire. He looked up just in time to see Marshall stumble backward, the large hole in his chest pumping blood out onto the white turtleneck. He regained his balance, stared blankly at Knabel and crumpled to the pavement.

Another staccato of fire rained down on the Mercedes, one round creasing Knabel's chin, another slamming into his left shoulder, and a third removing a large portion of his left ear. He had enough. He tossed his gun out what was left of the front window and screamed out a surrender. He remained hunkered down, as it got eerily quiet. He never heard the 9mm slug from Marshall's gun penetrate the top of his skull. Sullivan dropped the weapon and yelled another plea of surrender.

\*\*\*

Alden walked briskly west down *Haupstrasse* away from the hotel as if he was just heading home from another day at work. The stairwell from the garage was 50 meters behind him. He looked across the street, then in both directions, and crossed over into a deserted side street on his way to *Ahornstrasse.* His senses were still on high alert and he listened for any footsteps behind him. He started to whistle to relax his nerves.

A dog barked as a young woman opened a side door to a beauty salon and placed a handful of letters in the wall mailbox. An elderly man appeared out of nowhere, stepping through a wrought iron fence that guarded a flight of stairs to a tavern located below street level. He nodded and smiled at Alden as he walked past in the opposite direction. Alden reciprocated and continued straight ahead, but before he could resume his whistling, the muzzle of a gun pressed into his back, and he was forced several meters forward and then into a narrow alley between buildings.

"Easy old man."

"Shut up Gerhard. Drop the briefcase."

Alden did as he was told. "I'm sorry, you have me at a disadvantage, I don't know your name."

"You don't need to. Lie down and put your arms behind you." The older man pulled a large plastic cable tie out of his pocket, knelt down with one knee in Alden's back, and pulled his wrists together laying one over top of the other. Unfortunately, he compromised his control of the gun he had been training on Alden's back, and Alden seized the moment.

He spun quickly, lifting the old man off his back, while his right leg swung around and whipped the man forward into the wall. Alden rolled up on his knees, pulled out the Beretta from the crook of his back, and leveled it on the old man's head.

"I guess you have the advantage now," said the old man, rubbing at the developing lump on the top of his head. He eyed his Walther pistol lying on the ground in front of him.

"I wouldn't consider it," said Alden. He reached out and pulled the weapon over to him while concentrating his eyesight and gun on the woozy old man. "Now, since you know my name, won't you be so kind as to give me yours."

"Can't do that."

"Well that's a shame, I usually know the names of men I kill."

"Directly, yes. Indirectly, no."

The response drew a complete look of puzzlement on Alden's face. He could hear the escalating shrill of police sirens in the distance. "I don't have time for games old man. You just butted in to something you had no business getting involved with," he raised his gun to target the old man's forehead and heard the muted pop of a silenced pistol discharging a single round. He lost all feeling and motor function, dropped the gun, and was already dead as he fell face forward into the briefcase lying on the ground.

"Jesus, what took you so long," said the old man.

The stranger at the end of the alley lowered his silenced Walther and stepped forward to help his father to his feet. "Sorry, once you got out of the car, I had a hard time locating you."

***

It was organized chaos back at the hotel. Law enforcement officials from every conceivable branch were involved, forensic and crime scene teams were being dispatched from Zurich, and would soon be descending on the small town of Wildhaus. Television crews and reporters were already arriving at the site of the dramatic shootout.

Ferguson and Courtney sat in shock on a sofa in the lobby of the hotel, sipping on coffee and trying to re-establish their heartbeats. Shutt sat in an armchair across from them, while a medical technician put the finishing touches on a bandage to his forehead. They had yet to speak a word to each other.

Daniel stood by the front desk in his sweat stained shirtsleeves, radios and phones interchangeably attached to his ears, barking orders at everyone in sight. He was indisputably in charge of the whole mess, and he had an effective hold on everything, save for the whereabouts of Gerhard Alden. He had every available man fanning out across the town looking for anyone that came close to resembling the man Ferguson and Courtney had just vividly described. Roadblocks had been set up on 16 from Stein to Granz.

Pernod had secured the trailer of precious antiquities. He had it moved into a far corner of the garage and covered with a canvas tarpaulin to conceal the entire cargo. He nearly had a heart attack, when his curiosity got the best of him and he busted into one of the smaller crates, only to discover a Pissarro village landscape in nearly pristine condition. He hadn't been off the phone since.

Rising from his seat, Shutt walked over to the sofa and squatted in front of Ferguson and Courtney. "You two all right?"

They both nodded in unison without saying a word, Ferguson's curiosity at Shutt's presence still nagging at him, while Courtney was working up the nerve to unload her prepared confession.

"I'd say everyone is pretty lucky, given your little plan didn't quite work out as you thought it would," Shutt looked at Courtney.

Ferguson slowly turned his head to face her, an acerbic look in his stare.

"I think I owe you an explanation," said Courtney, a lump the size of a golf ball forming in her throat.

Before she could get out another word out, Daniel stepped over and interrupted the three of them. "Excuse me Toby, but I need to have a word with you and Mr. Ferguson. Over here if you wouldn't mind," he shook his head toward a table just inside the lounge, where Rudi Batemann was seated.

Courtney could feel the disappointment and anger stabbing at her from Ferguson's glare, as he rose with Shutt and walked over to the table. Batemann nodded and smiled at Ferguson as they approached the table.

"Detective Toby Shutt, this is Rudi Batemann," said Daniel making the introduction. "And Mr. Ferguson, you obviously know if he's with you."

Ferguson was already clouded with enough confusion, but was now totally bewildered to find out he 'was with' Rudi Batemann. Shutt and Batemann shook hands.

Daniel gestured with his right hand toward Batemann. "The floor is yours Mr. Batemann."

"Thank you. First of all, let me clarify my position here," he held out a small billfold that he opened to reveal his Central Intelligence Agency credentials. Ferguson went from confused to shock. The other two realized things were about to get a lot more complicated.

"Mr. Daniel, you can call off your manhunt for the gentleman that got away. You will find him behind the hotel, in the parking lot, under a blanket by the dumpster. Unfortunately, and regrettably, he met an untimely end. Since it was him or me, I'm happy it was the former. We would like to have had a chance to interrogate him, as I'm sure you two would have also, but that's not going to happen."

"We?" Shutt and Daniel asked simultaneously.

"I have another agent working directly with me locally, as well as Mr. Ferguson here, who has been cooperating with the CIA for some time," Shutt looked at Ferguson quizzically, who manufactured a slight raise of the eyebrows in return. "Needless to say, this entire investigation has been open for some time. We cannot thank you enough Detective Shutt, and you Mr. Daniel, for helping us bring this to a conclusion after years of dead ends."

Shutt and Daniel had been in law enforcement long enough, and dealt with a number of Federal security and police agencies over the years, to know what was about to come next.

"I know you have a lot of questions, but for the immediate time being, we need to debrief Mr. Ferguson on the operation. We will both be available tomorrow, or the next day if you need us, however, it's highly likely you can get everything you will need from Miss Lewis and the other suspect you apprehended, and the CIA would appreciate being left out of this entire proceeding."

"Let me guess, you were never here," Shutt said caustically.

"Something like that. Ironically, you know as much as we know," Batemann smiled.

"For him that may be true, Mr. Batemann, but as for the Swiss Federal Police we have a large mess here, and I'm certain I will need your cooperation. His, too," Daniel pointed to Ferguson.

"I would suggest you contact your office Mr. Daniel, as I think you'll find the United States, particularly the State and Justice Departments and the CIA, are already providing an enormous amount of cooperation, and I'm going to bet we are finished here. However, if you find any loose ends and need more information, here's where you can reach us," Batemann handed over a business card.

There was silence. Daniel looked at Shutt who shrugged his shoulders in a sign of capitulation.

"If that's all gentlemen, Matt and I will take our leave," Batemann put his arm around Ferguson and guided him toward the front door and out to the street, where Rolf Batemann sat behind the wheel of an idling Land Rover.

"Wait a minute!" Ferguson slipped out from under Batemann's arm. "Why am I leaving all these police to join you and your son? No offense, but I'm not totally certain of who you are, or if you're with the CIA as you claim. In fact, you may very easily be one of the same SOB'S that just tried to snuff me out." He began to back away toward the door and the familiarity of Toby Shutt.

"I'm a friend of your Uncle Max."

Ferguson stopped, and eyeballed him suspiciously, without speaking a word.

"My name IS Rudi Batemann, and I've been with the CIA since it was created over 50 years ago."

"How did you know my Uncle?"

"If you'll get in the car, I'll tell you on the way."

"No! You tell me now, or I walk back through that door."

Batemann hesitated and stared into Ferguson's eyes. "I was the other pilot on that plane you just found."

Ferguson stood motionless, and then looked away as if seeking some divine intervention for the emotional roller coaster ride that seemingly has no end. He turned back toward the street, quietly walked over to the vehicle, and climbed into the back seat. Batemann joined him and they drove away.

# Chapter 21

*May 26, 2001. Zurich, Switzerland*

The boarding call for first class passengers on Swiss Air Flight 18 came over the intercom in English. Courtney picked up her luggage and made her way over to the doorway. The ticket attendant checked her ticket and then checked to see if Miss Courtney Lewis was okay. Her puffy eyes and weary appearance gave her away. It had been a long twenty-four hours.

Not long after Ferguson had been ushered from the scene by the Batemanns, Courtney had been subjected to three intensive hours of interviews with Daniel, Shutt and a stealthy representative from the local canton police that never bothered to introduce himself. She assumed his grasp of English was limited, because Daniel had been forced to translate the more important parts to him upon request.

She had done a remarkable job of summarizing the whole story, from the day she met Matt Ferguson at the University of Louisville, up through the shooting at the hotel that afternoon. She had been very cooperative.

Terry Sullivan was singing like the proverbial canary. He had pencil and paper in hand and was doing an excellent job with his own synopsis of the events. Pernod had immediately alerted his office, and the wheels were already in motion for international cooperation on a full investigation into Rocca International, and Mr. Guillermo Rocca specifically.

By the end of the evening, Daniel was beginning to believe Batemann was correct. They had enough information to put most of the pieces together, except the hierarchal links to Gerhard Alden, Horst Marshall and Paul Knabel. Their identities had been confirmed, but any substantive connection to anyone or anything else was vague at best. Daniel and Shutt were both suspicious that they were not acting alone and believed that in all probability they reported to a higher authority. Who or what that was, would be left up to further investigation. Daniel felt like he might speak to Batemann and Ferguson after all, if for no other reason than to cause them the same irritation they had inflicted on him and Shutt.

They had allowed Courtney to stay in her suite that evening and planned to escort her back to Zurich the following morning, with the recovered art in tow. The masterpieces had been transferred into a panel truck with environmental and temperature controls.

It was agreed she would be off limits to the media, until the investigation reached a satisfactory conclusion. The press had already determined enough to report on the shootout, and dug deep enough to summarize that the cause was the result of two Americans who were involved in the discovery of a cache of World War II era stolen art, probably worth millions. Reporters from every medium, local and international, had been hounding everyone involved for more information and details.

Daniel, Pernod and Shutt assured her that she would get full credit for the discovery, with some restrictions. Per Batemann's instructions it was agreed by all, and reluctantly by Courtney, that Ferguson was to remain nameless.

Courtney had expected Ferguson to return that evening, or at the very least the following morning. She had desperately wanted to explain the circumstances for involving Shutt, and was devastated when he didn't show up. She tried to convince herself it was the media circus around the hotel, but she kept concluding that he probably hated her guts at this point.

Early the next morning, she arranged with the concierge to deliver two pieces of his luggage to Batemann's *Der Bergsteiger* store. Uncertain about the exact street, her concerns were laid to rest when he knew exactly where it was located, and he would deliver them to Rolf Batemann personally. She tagged them with hotel luggage tags and put Matt Ferguson in c/o Rolf Batemann on both. She also called the front desk and instructed the clerk to keep the suite reserved on her credit card until Ferguson returned.

At the suite's mahogany desk, on hotel stationery, she hand wrote a long letter of explanation to Ferguson from her perspective, and expressed a hope that he would understand and one day could find it in his heart to forgive her. She signed it "much love, Courtney". She pinned it to his clothes still hanging in the closet, packed the rest of her things, and left the room.

Two hours later, she arrived in Zurich. Shutt made arrangements for both of them to return to Louisville on flights that afternoon, but Courtney decided she wasn't ready to go home and wanted some time away. Rest and relaxation were in order before the whole world found out the magnitude of their discovery, and the publicity extravaganza that was sure to follow.

She called her father and then her travel agent. She was booked on a 4:05 departure that afternoon to New York, and then on to Barbados. A week in the sun at Treasure Beach would help.

She nestled into the first-class cabin seat and ordered a martini. When it arrived, she extracted an Ambien from her purse, washed it down with two gulps of the cocktail, and ordered another one as the Airbus Industrie Jet taxied for the runway.

***

For Ferguson, the ride from the *Hotel Hirschen* with Rudi and Rolf Batemann spelled the beginning of the end of the roller coaster ride. He had sat in silence for nearly thirty minutes, his mind trying in vain to assimilate and control the range of emotions he had experienced over the last week…grief, curiosity, intrigue, angst, excitement, love, elation, awe, fear, anger, and betrayal.

He wound up returning to curiosity. "So why did you hustle me out of the hotel?"

Rudi Batemann stared straight ahead at the front seat. "Because I felt like I owed your uncle. I wasn't sure how deep you were involved in everything that was going on, in particular if you had done anything illegal. Word from Langley, was you were involved in some way with a murder in Kentucky, and were being pursued by local authorities. In a nutshell, we were trying to save your skin."

"What do you mean you owed Uncle Max one?"

"He saved my life. We crashed landed on that lake and that was the last thing I remember. They told me later that the other pilot had pulled me from the wreckage of the plane, dragged me to safety in a small boathouse, and patched me up just enough to keep me from bleeding to death. I was just this side of dirt when they got to me."

"Who are they?"

"Some local farmer and his sons were out looking for some lost livestock, when they saw our plane go down. They found us. Your uncle was treated and eventually left the local hospital. I was out of it for a long time. In fact, I was in a coma for over a week and was transferred to Lucerne. By the time I recovered, your uncle was long gone. I never saw him again."

"So how did you get involved with the CIA.?"

"I was already in. Well actually, in those days it was known as the OSS or Office of Strategic Services. We were an espionage organization created by Bill Donovan during the war. Eventually we became what you know today as the Central Intelligence Agency. I was recruited in the United States for overseas duty in Europe."

Ferguson cocked his head in surprise. "You're an American?"

"Born and raised in New York City, at least as a youngster. My father was in the wine distribution business and traveled all over Europe. I went with him a lot. I eventually came over to a boarding school in my early teens. I learned the language, the customs, and how to fly. When the war broke out, I went home, but was too young to join the services. In 1944, I joined the Marines with an eye on flying. The OSS. found me immediately.

"They trained me for only one operation. In early 1945, the victory in Europe was a forgone conclusion. However, the Allies needed eyes and ears in the German armed services. They wanted to keep track of the whereabouts of the Nazi upper brass. There was legitimate concern that they would disappear and some of the bastards responsible for the unbelievable atrocities that had occurred would slip away, never to be found. My job was to keep track of the Luftwaffe, in particular Hermann Goering.

"They infiltrated me into a Luftwaffe transport wing in March of '45. With a little money in the hands of the right officers, I landed the co-pilot's seat opposite your uncle," Batemann breathed deeply and exhaled. "He was a very nice man. Let me assure you he was no Nazi, but he was a helluva fighter pilot fighting for his country and not the regime. In the eyes of this soldier there's nothing disrespectful or evil about that."

"Well, I appreciate your concern, but your rescue of me is misguided. The police were tracking Courtney and me because we were witnesses to a murder. We were not involved, and there is no hard evidence to support that we were. It was a misunderstanding, and somewhere along the line, Courtney decided otherwise. It would seem she was working with them the whole time. So really, we're finished here. I would appreciate you returning me to the hotel so I can get my name cleared, grab my bags and get the hell back to Louisville."

"In due time young man. There is more to the story than just your colossal discovery of stolen artwork, and let me emphasize, it is stolen art. It does not belong to you and in due time it will find its way back to the rightful heirs. Having said that, I think you'll want to see what we've been waiting and hoping to find in that discovery for over fifty years."

For the next twenty minutes, Batemann chronicled the history of ODESSA. It was very much identical to the recitation Clark Burkley had given Shutt, but with a more spirited elaboration of the tentacles that organization and affiliated groups had in the international terrorist networks.

"They are especially influential in the underground fascist movements inside Germany, and the Islamic fundamentalist terror groups operating in the Middle East. The seething hatred of the Jews, and in the Jewish state of Israel, makes them strange bedfellows with some of the worst terrorists on the face of the planet," Batemann continued.

"Their reputed association with one in particular, a Saudi outcast by the name of Osama Bin Laden, is very troublesome. His network, which goes by the name of Al-Qaeda, is internationally entrenched, well organized and funded, and is of considerable concern to the United States. Their recent efforts against the capitalized world are well documented, and his followers are fanatical and have already caused substantial problems."

Rolf Batemann slowed the Land Rover perceptibly and turned onto a single lane driveway that curved up a steep hillside with no apparent destination.

Ferguson peered out the window as they reached the apex of a hill. On the other side straight in front of them was a beautiful A-frame chalet built into a bluff overlooking an enormous lake and small town below.

"Where are we?"

"This is my home," Batemann leaned across the seat to point out the window on Ferguson's side. "The town below is Walenstadt. The body of water is Walensee Lake."

Rolf Batemann switched off the vehicle.

"So, what's the connection? What have you been waiting to find all these years?" Ferguson was growing impatient with the mystery and the history lesson.

Batemann reached forward into the front seat, where his son handed him the metal briefcase that Ferguson had found in the plane's wreckage. "Does this look familiar?"

\*\*\*

On the second floor of Rudi Batemann's home was a wonderful stone, stucco and wood beamed great room. Set up on two portable tables, that faced out an entire wall of windows onto the magnificent view of the lake and valley, sat two personal computers all connected by an array of conspicuous cables and electrical cords. Ferguson was introduced to the man behind the computers, first name only.

"Are you ready Stephen?" Rudi Batemann inquired.

"We're good to go," replied Stephen Sutter. Sutter was one of the brightest electronics intelligence experts Langley had ever produced.

"Our friend Stephen here is what you might call a computer genius. More like a wizard. There is nothing in the world, given some time, that he cannot find out the who, what, when, where, why and how of anybody or anything," said Batemann, as his son was busy opening the latches on the metal briefcase laid on the coffee table in front of them.

"You're way too kind Rudi," Sutter said, "but there are plenty where I come from."

"You're way too modest my friend," Batemann stared at Ferguson as Rolf handed him a thin stack of papers, "this is why we're here," as he shook the stack flimsily and handed them to Sutter. "The rest of the briefcase is yours Matt. I think you'll find that the remaining contents will more than compensate you for all of your troubles."

Rolf handed him the open case. Ferguson looked at a blank case except for four metal cylinders, all approximately eight inches in length, lying on their sides. He picked one of them up and a slight gravely noise came from inside. He massaged the exterior until he discovered the screw off top. He looked up at the other three men in the room before he opened it, but they were oblivious to his activity. They were all encircled around the bank of computers, leafing through the paperwork. Ferguson unscrewed the top and poured the contents into the briefcase. A multitude of glistening cut diamonds tumbled into the tray. Ferguson's jaw dropped.

"Do you have a favorite charity Matt?" Rudi asked. He had to repeat the question to get Ferguson's attention.

"A charity? Uhhhh, no not really," he was having a hard time concentrating on the question. "Wait, yeah. My mother...she died of cancer. How about the American Cancer Society?"

"Good choice," mumbled Sutter as he scribbled the letters A.C.S. onto a scrap piece of paper.

"Come over here and let me show you what we're doing, since what you are about to witness today can never be revealed. EVER!" His eyes bored into Ferguson's. "Do you understand me? If this ever gets out, we'll know by whom, and let me assure you your life will not be worth living."

Ferguson nodded affirmatively, while he felt the nerves in his body shiver. "I understand."

"By the way, artwork ownership can be traced. Stolen gemstones don't have that luxury. I very seriously doubt you would ever find the original owners of those stones. It's really not worth the effort, probably the spoils of the Wehrmacht's blitzkrieg through Belgium. I'd guess you have several million dollars' worth in there."

While Sutter had been swiftly typing on alternating keyboards, Batemann put his arm around Ferguson's shoulder and gradually pulled him closer to watch the adjacent monitors. "The paper work and identification in that briefcase essentially confirms suspicions we've had for years. There is a man by the name of Irwin Leiter, who is one of the richest and most influential men in Europe, and the world. No one is really certain of his wealth, because the majority of his interests are privately held. That is his briefcase and the contents do a wonderful job of indicting him in the past, present and future of the Nazi party and their ideals, and the modern-day terrorists who do their bidding.

"We have suspected for some time that he may be one of the power brokers in ODESSA. In fact, we now believe that he may be one of the major players, if not the only player, in control of the purse strings. Purse strings established from large sums of stolen wealth at the end of World War II, and undoubtedly exponentially larger today."

"Bingo. This was way too easy," Sutter chuckled. I don't think anybody thought the two accounts needed any additional protection, one each in two small banks in Zurich. Definitely not household names, but perfect for flying under the radar. You say the word," he looked up at Batemann while extracting a typewritten list from a folder next to him.

"Have at it."

Sutter typed in a command and followed up with a series of additional keystrokes. He waited. Twenty seconds later, he watched as the data on the screen updated. He smiled and looked up at Rudi. "Bingo. The Simon Wiesenthal Center just had an anonymous donation of $2,000,000."

"Holy shit," Ferguson muttered under his breath.

"I agree," said Batemann.

"Why don't you turn it over to the authorities and let them deal with it? Don't you have enough here to put this Leiter guy and his folks away forever?"

"Maybe...possibly, but too much red tape...way too many opportunities for lawyers, and international and political roadblocks. On top of that, what would they do with the money? Swiss banks are notoriously uncooperative with the outside world, and are maniacal about secrecy. We could have some serious trouble getting help and access to these accounts. This way is much cleaner. Wouldn't you agree?" Batemann smiled and patted his shoulder.

Sutter slid in front of himself a typed list of over fifty charitable organizations all across the world with corresponding bank account information. He rubbed his hands together eagerly and began tapping at the keyboard with a wide philanthropic grin running from ear to ear.

Batemann continued. "We have the account numbers and access information to one of the largest underground and terrorist funding sources in the world, and we're about to donate all of it...every last nickel."

"Outstanding," Ferguson mumbled aloud.

"Yes, it is," acknowledged Batemann. "My only concern is the reaction we're about to elicit, the fuse we're about to light."

"I'm not sure what you mean?" Matt cocked his head slightly.

"This will significantly shake up the terrorist community financially. Make no mistake, they will not take kindly to it, and will be forced to respond publicly to maintain their efforts to legitimize themselves and their need for financial support to continue the fight against the Jews and the American infidels. I am afraid the response will be big and it will be ugly. Groups like the P.L.O., Islamic Jihad, and Hezbollah, we know what they're capable of, and have eyes in their organizations. However, it's people like Osama bin Laden and the Al-Qaedas of the world...they scare me," Batemann replied with an ominous tone to his voice.

# Chapter 22

*May 27, 2001. Treasure Beach Resort, Barbados*

The crystal-clear Caribbean water lapped gently at the white sand surrounding Courtney's lounge chair. Simpson, the young beach attendant who was a native of the island, stood over her with his back to the sun, effectively blocking the rays from her face as she placed an order for her second piña colada.

She had been down on the water's edge for almost two hours, and was about ready for some shade. The morning sun had risen to straight overhead and she was beginning to realize that it would be time to get out from under the direct rays soon. It would be difficult to give up the tranquility of the beach, but her lack of breakfast this morning was convincing her that lunch at the pool bar might be a good time to take a break.

"I believe this is your order," said the man with a drink in his hand.

Again, he was silhouetted with his back against the sun, but she recognized that this server was different from the other, taller, and without the accent. She leaned up from her lounge and lowered her sunglasses. Matt Ferguson leaned forward with her piña colada in his right hand. It was all she could do to keep from screaming.

"This is yours isn't it? It cost me extra to wrestle it away from Simpson."

"Yep, that belongs to me. I'll be happy to repay you for your efforts. I think it's the least I could do considering I probably ruined the most important thing that's ever happened in your life."

"Well, that's why I'm here. I think you may be over exaggerating the events. There's more to the whole story than you know and unfortunately you'll never know."

"The only thing I want to know is why you're here. Before you answer that though, I just want an opportunity to apologize to you in person."

"There's no need to apologize to me. I got your letter," he retrieved the letter from the hotel out of his pocket, "and I also had a long conversation with a very nice detective from Louisville, Kentucky. He told me everything that happened, in much more detail than you were willing to take credit for."

The tears from Courtney's eyes were trailing down her cheeks. Ferguson knelt down beside her in the sand, reached up with his left forefinger, and gently wiped them away.

"I'm sooo sorry."

"Please, stop. I would have done the same thing in your shoes. Hell, it's a good thing you did what you did, or we probably would both be dead by now. Not to mention, our little discovery wouldn't be a discovery. So, stop beating yourself up, please, you have nothing to be sorry about."

"But you won't get recognized for any of it, or at least that's what they told me."

"That's right, I need to remain anonymous. You can't mention me by name. They know I exist, but I can't get involved."

"And let me guess, because it has something to do with the CIA, and you can't tell me either."

"No, but I can tell you that the ultimate person responsible for trying to kill us," he dropped a copy of the Wall Street Journal down in her lap, "isn't a threat anymore." She picked up the paper, folded over to reveal a story outlining the suicide death of international financier Irwin Leiter. There were very few details.

"Do I know him? Should I know him?"

"No. And I wouldn't worry about him or anybody else now that it's over."

"It's over for you, but I'm about to be bombarded with attention."

"Yeah, but that'll be fun. This is your business. It's what you do, and you're about to become a star in the eyes of the world. I can't think of anybody more deserving, better suited and more beautiful to carry it off."

"Well, I don't know what to say, except you're the one that deserves it, and I wish you could join me in all the fun. I can assure you, that whatever financial rewards come my way, they belong to you. I don't want them. I want you..."

Ferguson interrupted her by placing his forefinger on her lips. "Listen up. I am fine. I have been well taken care of. Don't worry about me."

The bellhop walked up behind the two of them. "I'm sorry to interrupt Mr. Ferguson, but you said you wanted this out here," he sat down a large black leather portfolio.

"This is yours, I believe," Ferguson unzipped the case to reveal the Gauguin Polynesian that remained hidden and undiscovered in their suite in Wildhaus. "And I left the other three where you had them sent...with Rolf Batemann at his store. He said to call him with an address and he'll forward them to you right away."

"Those were supposed to be yours. I thought it would be compensation for everything that went wrong."

"Thank you, but they're better off with someone who can appreciate them more than I. Maybe you can let me visit them from time to time."

The bellhop cleared his throat and interrupted again. "I'm sorry Mr. Ferguson, but what would you like me to do with the rest of your bags?"

Courtney spoke up quickly. "Please put them in my room," she looked at Ferguson, "if that's okay with you?"

The bellhop flashed a sheepish grin.

"I was hoping you'd say that," Ferguson cracked a smile and offered up a twenty-dollar tip.

"Thank you very much," said the bellhop. "If there's anything else I can..." he didn't bother to finish. They were both preoccupied; Courtney Lewis had leaned forward and planted a large kiss on Matt Ferguson's lips.

Her whisper into his ear was just audible to the bellhop as he turned and walked away.

"They have a whirlpool tub in our room."

# Acknowledgements

*Ghosts of the Past* was truly a labor of love, and fulfills a promise made to someone who was always my biggest cheerleader. I am quite certain she will read it in her own time and heavenly dimension. Hopefully, this is one of many more to come.

Many thanks to my incredible wife Ann who puts up with and allows my disappearing forays into word mangling.

I want to also acknowledge and thank a long list of friends whose names are recorded for posterity in the first and last names of the characters in the book. For the two main characters, I want to thank my father for allowing me to borrow from him, and many thanks to my dear departed friend, Grady, for allowing me to lift his name for another.

Lastly, thank you to John Clark at Old Stone Press, and his support staff for taking on the assignment of *Ghosts of the Past*. It never surprises me how effective it is to get out of the way of the professionals that know what they're doing, and let them do what they do best. I appreciate everything you do to make my work as successful as it can be.

# About the Author

Blessed…and cursed with the creative gene, Mark Downer has always found writing to come naturally, a trait inherited from his father, who he touts as a truly remarkable wordsmith. Having always felt the urge to write and attempt to produce commercially successful prose, the dictates of another career path and raising a family of three children derailed any thoughts of his noble ambition.

Children grown and ownership of a successful and self-sustaining business make that predilection a reality today. With a life full of study and interest in history, particularly the military variety, and a reading library full of some of fictions greatest novelists, it only made sense that he pursue his passion drawing upon those inherent experiences, attended by a personal conviction that good always triumphs over evil.

*Ghosts of the Past* is his first endeavor, created over several years of being drawn back into his creative awakening. It has been the catalyst for his second novel, *Setareh Doctrine*, which is the first book in the Themis Cooperative thriller series due to be released in early summer of 2021. Look for *Caracas Connection* to follow shortly thereafter.